More Advance Praise for *The Devil and Daniel Silverman*

"Social critic Roszak treats himself and us to a deliciously . . . ebullient lampoon, whose targets include writers' frail egos and crowded psyches, the publishing industry's deranged priorities, and the nuts and bolts (especially the nuts) of religious fundamentalism."
—*Kirkus Reviews*

"'Oh no!' cried I when *The Devil and Daniel Silverman* blew into my house as if propelled on the fierce gusts of a mirthful blizzard: 'Not another book to blurb!' To be polite, however, I read the hilarious first couple of pages, which was like eating of the Evil Apple, and I was hooked. Thank you, Eve! I fell right into the infidel trap of this bawdy novel and couldn't stop myself from charging headlong through the wild, delightful, learned, and passionate romp that followed. This book is My Favorite Mortal Sin of the Year, right up there with the best and most outrageous works of Philip Roth and Thomas Berger. It's whacky and wise and very relevant to all the issues of the day: *The Scarlet Letter* meets *Sabbath's Theater*, with echoes of *Little Big Man*. Or would you believe Portnoy meets Theron Ware? Hey, that may sound like a stretch, but this book is a wonderful stretch by a writer galloping all out at the top of his form. How do I know? The Bible tells me so."
—John Nichols, Author of *The Milagro Beanfield War*

"Damn! Here is a novel about America's culture wars that is disguised as nothing but fun. There is much gaiety in Theodore Roszak's *The Devil and Daniel Silverman*—but even more wit."
—Richard Rodriguez, Essayist for PBS News Hour & Author of *Brown: The Last Discovery of America*

"*The Devil and Daniel Silverman* is not only a profound exploration of the political and spiritual schism in contemporary American culture, it is hilarious and one of the best laughs I've had in years."
—Mary Mackey, Author of *The Year the Horses Came*

The Devil and Daniel Silverman

THE DEVIL
and DANIEL SILVERMAN

THEODORE ROSZAK

Leapfrog Press
Wellfleet, MA

Published in 2003 in the United States by
The Leapfrog Press
P.O. Box 1495
95 Commercial Street
Wellfleet, MA 02667-1495, USA
www.leapfrogpress.com

Printed in Canada

Distributed in the United States by
Consortium Book Sales and Distribution
St. Paul, Minnesota 55114

First Edition

Library of Congress Cataloging-in-Publication Data

Roszak, Theodore
    The Devil and Daniel Silverman : a novel / by Theodore Roszak.-- 1st ed.
        p. cm.
    ISBN 0-9679520-7-7
    1. Church colleges--Fiction. 2. Culture conflict--Fiction. 3. Jewish
authors--Fiction. 4. Minnesota--Fiction. 5. Novelists--Fiction. 6. Gay men--
Fiction. 7. Storms--Fiction. I. Title.
    PS3568.O8495 D48 2002
    813'.54--dc21
                                                          2002007887

The belief that there is only one truth and that oneself is in possession of it seems to me the deepest root of all evil that is in the world.

—Max Born

Contents

1

12K Net to You

"Danny, what're you, crazy? We can't turn down money like this."

"But, Jesus, Hanna, look where this place is."

"Hell and gone. It's in hell and gone. Hell and gone is where they pay $12,000 for speakers like you. At Harvard, you pay them to lecture. And Harvard isn't asking."

"Thanks a lot."

"Don't give me hurt feelings. I'm not your mother. I don't do therapy. I do money. Be realistic. Did you ever get offered half that much any place else? One-third even?"

"No."

"Right. So what is it, suddenly you don't need money? You won the lottery?"

"Of course I need the money."

"So?"

"So, what is this place again? A religious school?"

He could hear his lecture agent getting more aggravated by the minute. When she got tense on the phone, Hanna's asthma acted up and she began to wheeze down the line like a trapped gopher. He understood her impatience. This was their third New York to San Francisco call this weekend. He had put her off twice, once with "I'll think about it," the second time with "I'll *really* think about it." So now what? Was he going to tell her he would *really, really* think about it?

"It calls itself a small, liberal arts school dedicated to the highest standards of excellence." She was reading from a brochure. "What's wrong with that?"

"But Faith College. . . . Sounds religious to me."

"All right, so it has a church affiliation. Lots of schools do."

"What church?"

"Reformed something."

"Reformed what?"

She began to wheeze harder. "Come on, Danny, what d'you know from churches any which way? Free Reformed, it says. Free Reformed Evangelical Brethren in Christ."

"Jesus!"

"No, just Christ, it says. No Jesus."

"What is that exactly?"

"How the hell should I know? Theology is not my strong suit. Nor is it yours. Let's think of it as Protestant something-or-other, which, we both know, means for some reason—who cares?—not Catholic. Then some of these Brethren of Christ, they decided to become also Evangelical. So okay. Then a couple of the Evangelical Brethren wanted—who knows why?—to get Reformed. Then some of the Reformed Evangelical Brethren went across the street and became Free. That's how it goes among the godly folk, right? Bicker, bicker, bicker."

"But why do they want *me* to speak? I mean *me*? Why? And for so much?"

"I should do what, tell them you're not good enough? I should tell them you want less?"

"No, but for a religious school—"

"Forget the religion. The dean here, Swenson his name is, he says the school is 'developing an experimental Religious Humanism Program.' That sounds nice, doesn't it?"

"What does it mean?"

"Questions like that we refer to the great god Whoda?"

"Whoda?"

"Whoda fuck cares, Danny? You arrive, you give the chosen Free Reformed people here forty-five minutes of whatever you have around, you eat the rubber chicken, you make small talk about religious humanism or human religiousism or what the hell, you keep a big smile on your puss, you glance at your watch—oops, sorry! time to go, you leave."

"I can lecture on whatever?"

"Whatever."

"Anything at all?"

"Sure. No dirty words."

"Oh-ho! No dirty words. You see?"

"It's a church school, for God's sake. I didn't know you used dirty words in your lectures."

"Well, I don't, but—"

"Well, okay, what's the issue? And no sex, I should think."

"No sex?"

"Come on, Danny. Give them that long, boring thing on the Jewish writers, all the big names, blah-blah-blah. That's religious."

"You think that would be okay?"

"Sure. Of course. Only you know—"

"Only what?"

She took a breath, she wheezed, she coughed. "Make it maybe a little not so much Jewish."

"Ah! This is an anti-Semit place."

"Not at all. Just make it not so Jewish it couldn't be, you know, semi-Christian."

"Or maybe not Jewish at all, is that it?"

"No, no, no, no. A little Jewish is okay. That's why Swenson says he wants you, because you are a 'leading Jewish humanist voice.' Which even I didn't know—so congratulations. He thinks that's what they need up there in Minnesota in these troubled times."

"Jewish humanist? Me?"

"Look, go and lecture on whatever you want. It's in and out."

"In and out?"

"In and out."

"You're sure?"

"Scout's honor."

"No extras?"

"No extras. Forty-five minutes, twelve thousand bucks. Hey, presto! Gone."

"Twelve thousand net? To me?"

"12K net to you."

"Plus expenses?"

"Plus expenses, of course. Airfare. You stay at the school. The

Founder's Suite. Sounds elegant, no?"

"Why not a first class hotel?"

"In North Fork, Minnesota? Be reasonable. The place must be all barns and silos."

"And you get? . . ."

"I get the usual twenty percent. In your case, the unusual twenty percent."

"So let's see, altogether they're paying? . . ."

"If it makes any difference, I'd say about 15-16 thou just to get you in and out, an author whose last book sold, need I remind you, 3,216 copies? Did I get that right? No, I'm sorry, it says here 3,217."

Stooping to sales figures was hitting below the belt, but he let it pass. "And you're sure they've got this kind of money?"

"Schools like this have to have the money. How else do they get even some *putz* to go to northern Minnesota in January? They're depositing fifty percent."

"You think I'm just some *putz?*"

"You? No! You are a very important *putz,* in the opinion of yours truly, your loving *kuzineh.* But think how you'll feel when I tell the next person who calls 'Mr. Silverman's last fee was $12,000?' That gives us some leverage, eh, kiddo?"

"And it definitely has to be January?"

"What else? It's a New Year's millennial thing. 'Welcome to a New Century,' it says. 'We are proud to present the First Annual New Year's Day Lecture on Religious Humanism in America.' Doesn't sound like it could be in April."

"I don't know, Hanna. I should talk to Marty. Marty won't like it. Can I bring Marty along?"

"Danny, it's a religious school, for God's sake."

"Meaning?"

"What if Marty decides to wear his sequin chemise to dinner?"

"Come on! He wouldn't."

"He did in Rio."

"That was Rio."

"And that was the end of the United States Information Agency for you, sweety pie. A steady 2500 smackers a year—gone. If you want me to book for you, no Marty."

"Rio was fun and games. Marty's an actor. He was acting like an actor. It was Carnival, for God's sake."

"And this is Minnesota and there's no carnival in sight. Perhaps you see the difference?"

"So I can bring Marty if—"

"This we have discussed, Danny."

"I can bring Marty— "

"No."

"But—"

"Danny. No."

"Marty won't like it. I'd have to be away New Year's Eve. We always spend New Year's Eve together."

"Marty will like the 12K. That makes up for lots of togetherness. He can buy a whole new wardrobe next time he wants to play the Queen of Sheba."

"New Year's Eve we always kiss at midnight."

"Spare me."

"Well, it matters."

"It matters worth twelve grand to kiss Marty? Give me a break. Kiss him twice before you leave."

"It keeps us together for the next year."

"12 Gs will do more to keep you together. How many Madeleines would Marty have to bake to make that much?"

"Well. . . ."

"Suppose I get them to spring for first class airfare?"

"I assumed they were paying first class."

"Oh, please! When did anybody ever pay first class for you?"

"Well. . . ."

"I'll get first class."

"Well, if you get first class—"

"I'll get first class. Danny, this Swenson, he really wants you. Doesn't that mean something?"

He knew already he wouldn't be able to say no, even if he had to fly economy with his feet in his pockets. Hanna was, after all—distantly, remotely, but still intimidatingly—family: his father's sister-in-law's cousin. The way the Silvermans counted kin, this was almost a blood relative. A feisty divorcée left high and dry by her beast of a husband, Hanna had set up late in life as a small-change lecture agent. That was shortly before Silverman's first novel got reviewed in *The New York Times*. "Please let me represent you," Hanna pleaded when the review appeared, and as a favor to his father, Silverman agreed. Hanna proved to be surprisingly good. She had that kind of persistence that women regard as flattering and men regard as flirtatious. Of course, in those days Hanna's cousin-much-removed was highly representable. It wasn't her fault that the market for Daniel Silverman had since gone through the floor. Six non-sellers in a row had somewhat diminished the effective demand. Nevertheless, though she was now earning well from other clients, she was a good, loyal woman who had stuck by him through thin and thinner, often skipping her own fee when the earnings shrank to microscopic. "What we have on the plate here," she had said after his last $250 outing, "is a crumb so small, I can't cut a piece off. So keep the whole thing, dear. Buy yourself a nice lunch. Someday you win the Pulitzer Prize, you'll pay me back." She meant well, but she had him in a position where she could guilt-trip him with the greatest of ease. This was the first gig she had found for him in eight months, the first that paid decent money in over three years. After so much nickel-and-dime lecturing, what choice did he have?

Two days later Hanna called to report she had gotten first class. "Plus which," she added with more professional pride than she could contain, "so you shouldn't lose any sleep over it, they're fronting the whole twelve thousand. I told them 'Mr. Silverman does not do business on any other basis.' So they agreed. Which proves this is the boonies, right? That's money in the bank, *boychik*. All you gotta do is say yes."

He said yes.

Hanna had other news. "You're not the first."

"First what?"

"First in the big Minnesota humanist lecture series here. I've been asking around. Gore Vidal, he was first."

"Gore Vidal spoke at Faith College?"

"No, he was supposed to speak last New Year's. So you see what kind of league I've got you in here. Some caliber, wouldn't you say?"

"But Vidal didn't speak?"

"No."

"Why not?"

"No idea. It was canceled."

"He canceled? Why?"

"Actually, they canceled."

"Why did they cancel?"

"I talked to his lecture agent. She says they were never told. But get this. They paid him the whole $20,000, no questions asked."

"$20,000? He got twenty grand? How come I only get twelve?"

"Because, *bubeleh*, your name ain't spelled g-o-r-e-v-i-d-a-l. For you I shouldn't even be getting half as much."

"Thanks a lot."

"We have to deal in cold cash realities here, Danny. You're getting three-fifths of Gore Vidal's fee. Do you sell three-fifths what he sells print on the page?"

"But you don't know why they canceled?"

"Nope. They canceled and paid the fee. Now that's class."

"Well, look, can you get them to cancel me and pay?"

"Sorry, love. I think that is also the privilege of best-sellers."

2

Number One Bestseller

Ah, but he had once been a best-seller—if only by the skin of his teeth. In the early eighties, the twenty-one year old Daniel Silverman, second in his graduating class at Brandeis and full of beans, published a first novel that registered on the literary landscape like a flea on the Richter scale: one week at number ten on *The New York Times* best-seller list. It scrambled onto the list two days before Ronald Reagan was sworn into the presidency, an event that meant nothing to Silverman who, as a smug young aesthete, took pride in rising above politics. There were those who talked about a "big chill," but for Silverman these were cheery, warm times. "It's morning again in America," had been that year's winning campaign slogan. Well, it was surely a great good morning for Daniel Silverman. By the arcane statistical protocols of the publishing industry, the momentary merchandising blip that had boosted him onto the lower rung of "the list" qualified his book to be labelled in all further printings as "Number One Bestseller." At lunch one day with his editor and agent, Silverman had been naive enough to observe this anomaly. "You know," he said, "my book isn't actually, really *the* number one best-seller. It's number ten."

There was laughter. His editor then informed him: "There's no such phrase in the publishing industry as Number Ten Best-seller. Who would buy such a book?"

"Well, I think it's pretty good simply making the list," Silverman confessed.

His agent corrected his enthusiasm. "The thing of it is, there's a psychology about lists, Danny. Being tenth on a list of ten reads 'last' to the public."

"Right. Like 'number two' means second best," his editor added. "Once you've got a list, you've got to be at the top or forget it. It's actually better to be off the list than to be number two even. That way people think maybe you're too good for this list, maybe you're on some other list."

"But even so," Silverman insisted, "it isn't exactly true to say that I'm the Number One Best-seller, is it?"

To which his agent, sighing as if he had been asked to explain why one came before two, replied, "You're misreading. See the big numeral one on the cover? That means you are *one* of the books on the best-seller list. From now on, that designation will always be part of your literary identity."

This was true. Even when sales of his novels descended into the low four figures, Silverman continued to be introduced at conferences and lectures as Daniel Silverman, Number One Best-selling Novelist. He soon learned that his hosts liked to see things that way. They liked to talk superlatives, and superlatives take on a momentum that overwhelms critical judgment. After all, who wants to introduce their guest as "Daniel Silverman, a writer of minor importance whom you probably never heard of?" Or "the author whose books go out of print before they reach print." There was, in fact, a certain psychological advantage to introducing an author as "A Really Major Writer You Better Not Say You Never Heard Of." That usually forced those in attendance to behave as if *of course* they knew this world-famous author's books. At first, in response to these exaggerated introductions, a still-confident Silverman would offer a smiling disclaimer, something like "Slight correction: not *yet* number one." That soon became, "Actually not quite number one." And then, "Well, *almost* number one." And finally, as of four years ago, total silence. For, oh, how he had come to cling to that distant distinction! In these leaner days, he wished it had been branded on his forehead.

The novel in question, his lone literary triumph, was titled *Analyzing Anna*. The title was deliberately ambiguous, Anna being both the subject and object of the analytical episodes that made up the story. The conceit of the work was that Anna spends most of the book analyzing her analyst rather than being analyzed by him.

The subtitle made that clear: *The Strange Case of Sigmund F.* The novel was the story of the world's first psychoanalysis as told from the viewpoint of the patient, the dark lady whom Freud referred to in his papers as Anna O. There actually was an Anna O. She was a Viennese social worker named Bertha Pappenheim who suffered through occasional bouts of hysteria, but finally settled down to a productive career. In the annals of psychiatry, Anna O. was famous as the great man's ur-neurotic. Most of Freud's theories were worked up on the basis of her case, especially his most shocking sexual hypotheses. Freud found Anna witty, attentive, flirtatious, and more than normally willing to let off lots of repressed steam. He liked her, but when she left his care she was as batty as ever, the basis for much of her resentment in Silverman's novel.

A quasi-glowing review on page three of *The New York Times* compared the novel's young author to J. D. Salinger. Well, what the critic actually said was, "a style distantly reminiscent of Salinger." Silverman had been aiming more at Evelyn Waugh, but, listen, to be mentioned alongside Salinger, even distantly. . . . That gained the book a movie option. There were plans to star Marlon Brando as Freud with possibly Barbra Streisand as Anna. Once the book got associated with stars of that magnitude, its sales—in the paperback edition—took off skyward. Later that year, he was a Book of the Month selection, well, an alternate added only after the movie deal was announced—but even so. Over the next five years, negotiations on the option spiraled around and down and finally, as is the wont of film deals, out of sight into the great black hole of literary expectations. All that really came of the option were a couple of expensive dinners in Hollywood where the author met, first, a drunken screenwriter, and, second, a very much drunker screenwriter. The first screenwriter, who never wrote a page, spent the whole dinner rehearsing his professional woes and finished by warning Silverman, "the way the directors screw my scripts over is the way you can bet I'm gonna screw your fuckin' book over, buddy."

The second screenwriter, who actually wrote seventy-six pages of a script before he died of congestive heart failure, had a very special take on *Analyzing Anna*. "I'll tell you what's wrong with this thing of yours," he informed Silverman during a 2 a.m. phone call, "It's this Anna character. Do you realize that the whole thing's presented from her point of view, for God's sake? Who cares about her point of view, a psychotic, ugly female? Freud, that's the viewpoint. Freud." This approach to the story resulted in half a script that bore no likeness whatever to the book. Silverman was secretly glad to see the option fizzle. But *Analyzing Anna* remained the work he was best remembered for; it had been his literary meal ticket ever since.

The book also established the literary weight and style that marked the rest of his writing: solid middle-brow exercises in mordant but good-humored social satire. In this case, the story was written in the form of Anna's diary. The opening pages were still warmly received at readings. Silverman knew them by heart. "All right, I admit it," Anna declares. "I have a few problems. Who hasn't? You should see some of my lady friends. They can't even get out of bed. Me, at least I'm getting along. I earn a living. I am invited to parties. I go to the theater. I am courted, I am courted by highly eligible gentlemen of good reputation. If I am not married, that is by choice, for I could be, yes, I could. Meanwhile, I have a vocation. And isn't that the real problem, dear doctor? That I am not the helpless little hysterical mouse you are so used to? True, now and then I lose control, I giggle, I blush a little. Is that a disaster? There are men who think this is cute. Not dear Dr. Freud, of course. But listen, if anybody has problems, it's poor Sigmund. That cigar, for instance. Who does he think he's fooling? Here I am, gagging on the smoke, I complain I'm dying of asphyxiation, but all he has to say is, 'And what does it remind you of, my cigar?' I tell him, 'it reminds me of a turd and it smells even worse.' He thinks I don't know what he's writing down? Not turd, but penis. This man, he can't see past his dong. The cigar is a penis substitute, he thinks. So what am I to make of the fact that you're the one smoking it, dear doctor?"

Pause. Applause. And for sure when he finished, women would gather around to say "How true!" and tell him about their shrink.

Silverman now looked back wistfully on the period that followed his first novel. Those were "the Anna Years," a time of bright reputation and good (if not great) money. Brashly ambitious and willing to travel to every literary occasion in the land, he was mentioned by critics as a worthy successor to various combinations of literary names that included Bellow, Malamud, Heller, Mailer, Gold, Salinger, Roth. Wonderful. But why were the names on these varied lists almost always Jewish, he wondered. That was odd. There were after all some Gentile novelists—a few decent second-raters. Was this in some sense condescending? Was he being ghettoized? How absurd. Why, he rarely thought of himself as Jewish. In fact, that was a bone of contention. Some critics claimed to detect elements of anti-Semitism in his derisive treatment of Freud, whom Anna snidely referred to as "the rabbi." The novel, they said, fastened on the slings and arrows of prejudice poor Freud had suffered during his career and played his plight for laughs. This was true. It was a funny book. It turned Freud's theories about sexuality into reflections of various Jewish child-rearing hang-ups. (Silverman still believed he had done a better job of exposing the patriarchal elements in psychoanalysis than any feminist assistant professors he had ever read—but let that go.) In any case, Anna really did call Freud her "rabbi." He hadn't made that up. And besides, if Philip Roth could get away with poking a bit of fun at his ancestry, why not Daniel Silverman?

The Anna Years now seemed hopelessly lost and beyond recovery, buried beneath a landslide of neglect. In the course of the last ten years, he had seen his career go from gentle subsidence to rapid decline to free-fall descent. On his last so-called, multi-city book tour (eight towns in northern California, southern Oregon, and western Nevada) he found himself being booked on after-midnight campus radio stations or on commute-hour talk shows where he was constantly in danger of being dropped to extend the traffic report. He knew better than to expect that the bored and ill-prepared interlocutors whom authors met along the literary trail of tears had read the book or even the dust cover, but they might at least get his name right. He was now being introduced so often by various combinations of Stein, Silver, Berg, Man, and Gold, that, when one interviewer apologized on the air for calling him "David Silverstein" for the third time, he mordantly responded,

"Not to worry. Anything Jewish will do." Despite the buffets, in his more pensive moments Silverman now saw that his years of success had brought him something more important than transient fame and a bit of fortune. With them had come a feeling of superb existential comfort, a *rightness* he found in simply being a writer. When *Analyzing Anna* scored high and thousands applauded his work, he knew he was where he wanted to be in life. He was at home in Bookville.

Bookville was a secret, the fantasy place that had filled his childhood with intellectual adventure. It started as his mother's idea. One evening, after she had finished reading *Winnie the Pooh* to him, his mother asked him to think of the house where Winnie and all his friends might live. And four year old Daniel did. He thought it up and drew a picture of it. His mother told him that was so smart, so imaginative. Then she said, "Why don't we think of a village where all the people in all the stories have houses as nice as that?" And after he had drawn the village, she said, "I know what. Let's call it Bookville." And that became the home where all the literary folk he met in books still lived, Long John Silver and Natty Bumppo, Jo and the little women, and later Holden Caulfield, Augie March, and Portnoy of the Complaint. Eventually, all Silverman's own characters moved into town, living along streets in chronological order as they rose into existence. He had never mentioned this ongoing exercise in childish make-believe to anyone, not even to Marty. But Bookville and its inhabitants were still there whenever he came walking down the street, all the way back to Winnie and Eeyore.

The quasi-success of his first book made it possible to find an agent for the next, in fact a stunningly commercial agent: Tommy Sutton, who liked to refer to himself as the Willie Sutton of the publishing world. A young man of roguish good looks who delighted in a well-publicized, fast-lane lifestyle, Sutton made no bones about intending to become more famous than any of his writers. "Why not?" he explained. "Then you let the celebrity rub off on your clients. It's part of what they pay for." Though Silverman was a year older than his agent, Sutton insisted on treating him like a kid brother who needed to learn the facts of life. "After all," as he liked to remind Silverman, "you're from out of town." Sutton had promised Silverman the moon and the stars, and he did come through with a terrific second contract, followed by three more that were at least decent enough to let Silverman stay home and write, which was the financial yardstick by which he privately measured success. And even when the contracts diminished, there were lectures, conferences, writers' retreats to buoy up his spirits. If only this could go on forever.

But it didn't. After three novels bombed in a row, Tommy Sutton gave him clear warning that he was in trouble. But not to worry, Silverman told himself. He was sure his next book would turn things around. That book was *Deep Eye,* the perfect concept: *Moby Dick* retold from the whale's point of view. An animal story, a classic, brimming with action, the thrill of the chase, manly men. . . . God! it was even ecological. This was hot, this was so hot, it was burning a hole in his brain. Psyching himself up to maniacal self-confidence like a daredevil motorcyclist out to leap the Mississippi River in a single bound, he flew back to New York to pitch the book.

"Oh, let's not go to one of those greasy places with all the heavy food," Sutton insisted, meaning anything better than an economy class restaurant. "I've been taking on too much cholesterol lately." Silverman would have preferred to avoid having lunch anywhere. In his world, one's lunching power with editors and agents was a leading economic indicator. He could never forget he had once— back in the Anna Years—been worth dinner at the Four Seasons. Alas! The last time he was in New York, his editor had taken him to the Starbuck's in the lobby of his building. Sutton proposed that they meet "someplace where we can eat healthy." This turned out to be, well, not quite a restaurant at all, but a "four-star Vegan cafeteria." The place, located two doors over from Sutton's office, was little more than a glorified juice bar, but so what? This was a working lunch, wasn't it? Point was to get down to business. Right. So, moving rapidly along the serving line, Silverman wound up at the cash register several impatient people ahead of Sutton, who was carefully composing a build-it-yourself tofu, whole-grain and fruit salad. What to do? He paid his own tab. "Sorry. You should have let me get that," Sutton apologized as they moved to a table in a not too quiet corner. "How about I bring us some wine? I think they have some of that non-alcoholic stuff." Silverman, in a crisp tone that said *let's get down to some practical talk here*, told him to forget the wine.

But he wasn't even three minutes into his well rehearsed presentation when he heard a muffled beeping. Quick as a wink, Sutton whipped out a cell phone. It was an impressive move: twenty-first century quick-on-the-draw, the fastest phone in the east. "Give me a second here, Danny," he said, turning away from the table. "It's probably somebody bothering me about money. You know how that is." Silverman couldn't hear a word of the conversation, but he could tell it was indeed about money, much money. There was a fierce, hungry light that came into Sutton's eyes when big bucks were in play. It was actually a beautiful sight to see: a man so intensely alive, so eagerly focused on the ultimate realities. It brought to mind Bernini's ecstatic Santa Teresa speared through the heart by divine love. Silverman had not seen a twinkle of such elation during any conversation involving his books for, how long now? He couldn't remember.

When he was finished, Sutton made a small production of pushing the off-switch on his phone. "See? There. Off—till we're finished, okay? I only have ears for you." But even with the phone lying dormant in his pocket, Sutton couldn't hide his near terminal boredom. Still Silverman persevered. *Deep Eye*. The story that had everything. In his mind Silverman was running his list. *Animal story, classic work, loads of action, thrill of the chase, manly men. . . . Oh boy!*

"The whale," Sutton interrupted. "Moby Dick there—he's doing the talking?"

"Yes, but we don't call him Moby Dick. We call him Shirook Han Omura. That's his name in Whalish, see?"

"Whalish?"

"The natural language of the whales. He speaks in Whalish."

"The whale is speaking Whalish? Which means like what? The book is written in . . . not English?"

"Of course it's in English," Silverman snapped, letting his impatience show. *Christ! Wasn't the man listening? Just because I'm a minor client, he can't rent me ten minutes of attention?* "As I said, there's an author's note that explains the book is translated from the Whalish."

"Not good," Sutton said woefully.

"What—not good?"

"Author's note. That's a killer. It tells you right up front this is a hard read. I never buy books with notes from the author."

"Well, maybe we can do without that. The readers will catch on. The important thing is the footnotes about the semiotics of the animal mind, see?"

"Oh." Sutton had an *oh* like a rabbit punch. It knocked the wind out of you.

"What 'oh'?" Silverman asked, tense now with frustration.

"Footnotes."

"Yes, footnotes."

"A novel with footnotes. That's worse than an author's note."

Silverman had expected trouble about the footnotes, but he had his retort ready, a clever pedantic maneuver designed to outflank his semi-literate agent. "Salinger put footnotes in his novels. Lots of them. There's one about Kierkegaard even."

Sutton wasn't impressed. "Yeah, well, Salinger. That was back then."

"I've been compared to Salinger. Once. Once I was compared to Salinger."

"Because of your footnotes?"

"Well, no."

"Look, I'll tell you the truth, Danny. I never read Kierke-who'sits. I never read Salinger, not past the cover copy, which is what sells the book. Now you tell me he's got footnotes, for sure I'm not gonna read him. Okay? Footnotes—that's a killer."

"In this case, it's a highly original literary device to explore an alien consciousness, which is. . . ."

Silverman stopped in mid-sentence, allowing a pause to develop between Sutton and himself. The pause welled up like water rising below decks in a sinking ship. Into this pause there flowed a moment of suspense that felt like a scene straight out of a romance novel. The loyal wife—in this case Silverman—waiting to be told about the other woman. "Danny, I'm gonna be candid with you," Sutton finally said. "I won't be handling any more of your work. I can't do you any good any more. The best advice I can give you is: fire me, please fire me. Find a better man. You need somebody who's more literary. You know me, I'm a mercenary slob. Definitely you need another agent who is worthy of your footnotes."

Silverman coughed his way into one, two, three sentences beginning with "but," discarding each in turn as too hurt, too angry, too resentful. Then he fell silent. He had no idea how to continue. He realized that a vein had been cut; he was bleeding to death. Sutton picked up the beat. "Please believe me when I say this is about nothing but money, lousy old money. I like you, man. I like your work. Hey, we've been through some great books together. I'm sure you'll bounce back. Look, it's not you, it's me. I'm on to something really big. That's the way I am, you know. Not an idealistic bone in my body. So hate me."

Silverman didn't want to hate him, he wanted to leap across the table and grasp him so he couldn't get away. Instead, as coolly as he could, he dutifully asked the *Is-she-beautiful?* question. What was this really big thing that now threatened to leave him abandoned?

Sutton suddenly warmed to the subject like a hungry man who had been waiting through the small talk at a tedious banquet. Finally dinner was being served; he actually smacked his lips. "This is such a kick," he said with a mock-embarrassed laugh. "You know I've been working with Bobby Wilcox?"

No, Silverman didn't know. "Who's Bobby Wilcox?"

"Where've you been, man, under a rock? You ever go on-line?"

"Well, no, not that much. I use a few university card catalogs."

Sutton blew out an impatient puff. "Come on, Danny, cross the bridge into the twenty-first century. Wilcox is the literary genius of our age. This's the guy who invented the input array frame when he was only fourteen years old—one of these inspired hacker kids. Don't ask me what it is. Me, I'm the worst computer illiterate you'll ever meet. All I know is Intel bought the patent for seven figures. Works sort of like a spreadsheet, only with personal data. That's where the literature comes in, see? These frames, what they are is a bunch of standard storylines sampled from writers like

Danielle Steel, Tom Clancy, John Grisham, biggies like that. Bobby's got their style down pat, you'd be amazed. We're franchising all of them as CEAs."

"CEAs?"

"Chief Executive Authors. You know, titles like Danielle Steel's *Passion Master*, Tom Clancy's *Strategic Imperative*," Sutton answered, hissing on the final s. "That's a couple of our latest. The program writes ninety-five percent of the book. You always need a little adjusting here and there; we hire part-time college kids for that. All the CEAs are in for is that final comma-S."

"That's called an apostrophe," Silverman said caustically. "You mean apostrophe-s."

"Yeah? What d'you know? We've all been calling it a comma. I wonder why Danielle never picked up on that? So what happens is customers log onto Authors@Large.com—you've heard of that? No? Hey, wake up and smell the coffee. That's our web site, four million hits per month. Customers log on and decide what kind of story they want to be in: Romance, action, gothic, legal procedural, all like that. Then they fill in a personal profile: name, age, gender, job, education, where they were born, etc., etc. Plus a whole lot of likes/dislikes. Food, movie stars, car, clothes, baseball team, and so on. Also there's x-rated stuff on sexual preferences, erogenous zones, fetishes, fantasies. Incidentally, all the demographics become our property; worth their weight in gold for on-line marketing. Finally we dump the profile into one of Bobby's frames and zip! like magic, you become a character in the story—sort of like sidekick to the hero. For thirty bucks a copy (we call that the co-author's discount) the whole thing gets printed out like a real book, with your picture on the cover along with Clancy or whoever as 'author's creative consultant.' You see the appeal. All these poor jerks all over the world can chase spies, shoot up bad guys, screw the movie star of their choice. It's been a thing of beauty, watching the dot-com go va-voom. We've already got, let's see, there's the Steele's, the Clancy's, and, oh yeah, there's a Ludlum's—*The Venezuelan Infraction*—three books on the best-seller list."

"Really? I never saw those titles on the *Times* list," Silverman observed suspiciously. Was Sutton making this up?

"No, not *that* list. That's the snob list. Nobody at the *Times*
wants to admit what people are really reading. Their *Book Review*
is a joke; completely out of touch with the non-reading public.
Novelty books, porn, inspirational stuff, how to talk to your gold-
fish. Non-books for non-readers, that's where the large green is.
Wacko medicine, there's a winner. You know: how to be happy
with your hemorrhoids, that sort of stuff. The *Times?* Won't give a
nod. So who cares? What we've got cooking here is more than
books. This is an industry. That call I got? The one I cut off so I
could give you my undivided attention? The dot-coms are having a
feeding frenzy. Barnes & Noble's offering 40 million to take us
over. This is the NHT, Danny. It's really all I've got time for."

For the life of him, Silverman couldn't understand what Sutton
was talking about. Something about computers—computers that
wrote books. What did that mean? In Bookville, Silverman's private point of reference for all things literary, nobody used computers. Most of the residents of his imaginary writers' colony used
quills and pens and wrote by candlelight. Since childhood, that
had been Silverman's sentimental vision of great writers at work.
Shakespeare scratching away with a dripping duck's feather in
some dark corner of the Mermaid Tavern, Balzac scribbling with a
stubby pencil in a noisy Paris bistro, Jack London toiling away on
the back of an envelope in a crowded saloon or a bustling train station. What more did genius need? True, there were a couple
Bookvillians who preferred to use typewriters, second-hand Underwood portables with that open top that revealed the greasy
strike-bars, rattle-traps that pounded out nearly illegible sheets of
paper from a bone-dry ribbon. That was how he saw Hemingway
at work, a hard-drinking professional hammering away at the clat-
tering keyboard, scattering typo after typo across the page while
he dropped cigar ashes down his shirt front. That was as much
technology as Hemingway required, or Dreiser, or Steinbeck. Real
literature arrived in the world splotched and messy, elegant but
only semi-legible prose that others, dedicated editors, would have
to struggle to read. And they would struggle, loving what they read
all the more for the effort. True, Silverman himself now used a
word processor, but as a matter of principle there was only one

font he would commit to paper. Courier, that was all real writers needed. Courier plain old ten-point-nothing. Could anybody even imagine Dostoyevsky or Zola writing in Bernhard Fashion?

"But this . . . this isn't even remotely literature," Silverman protested with as much controlled indignity as he could manage. Could he, perhaps, in what was clearly shaping up to be their last conversation, wring at least a muted note of remorse out of his ebullient agent? No, he couldn't.

Sutton gave a melancholy sigh. "I've been hearing that from every writer I talk to. What can I say? Some people catch the wave and some don't. The truth is, Danny, publishing's become a whole different universe since your time. On-line is where it's at. You could see that coming years off. I mean once they invented the spell-checker, who needed editors any more? Now that we got the Web, who needs publishers?"

In his mind, Silverman, trapped between resentment and desperation, was scrambling madly to put his life back together before lunch was over. "I don't get it," he confessed to Sutton. "When did all this happen? How could so much have changed since my last book?"

An expression of authentic compassion came over Sutton's face. "I know, I know, you're a literary author. It's hard to break the habit. And who knows? You could get lucky. There'll always be some quality that slips through the controls. But that's a crap shoot, my friend. I wouldn't bet on it. Believe me, the future is wall-to-wall digital."

Silverman wanted to protest, but it was as if Sutton was talking a foreign language. "But I can't just. . . ."

His agent took pity. "Look, I'll do what I can for old time's sake, okay? There are probably a couple agents around town who still handle print, some of the older guys. When I get back to the office, I'll look up some names. But, listen, take my advice. Whatever you're working on, try to turn it into some kind of computerized crap."

Sutton did pay for the dessert. Mango sorbet. Two scoops.

After his agent left, Silverman sat stunned and brooding at the table. He found himself struggling to hold off a sense of vertigo as a long, downwardly-spiraling, lightless tunnel stretched out before his imagination. At last he shook himself awake. What was this bottomless abyss he was staring into? Oh, yes, it was his future. As he rose to leave, he caught a reflection of himself in the polished surface of the napkin holder. But it wasn't his face. It was a dinosaur looking back.

In the nine years since the event he remembered as The Last Lunch, Silverman hadn't been able to find another agent. A few of those he approached remembered that *Analyzing Anna* had been much praised, but not in a way that helped. "Oh yes, great book," they were likely to observe in a hurried phone call. "Very literary. Let's see, that was what? Nearly twenty years ago. Well, it's been a long time between books, hasn't it? . . . Oh, you *have?* . . . . *Seven* books since then. . . . Well, you have been productive. I guess I sort of lost track of you." The word of doom. When, in desperate self-defense, Silverman discreetly mentioned that he had been a number one best-seller, potential agents had the uncanny knack of recollecting as clearly as if they were reciting yesterday's baseball scores, that he had not been *the* number one best-seller, not really, not actually. "Actually, you were about five or six on the list, right? For how long? A month or so, as I recall."

"Yes, something like that."

Three books back, ever-helpful cousin-in-law Hanna offered to take a stab at agenting, but she had no talent for it. She was even less literary than Tommy Sutton had been. "Why couldn't you write a cookbook?" was the level of her advice. Besides, she lost her temper too easily and then she started talking dirty. Once, at a luncheon, she got so incensed with an editor from Viking she had told him he could go fuck himself if that was the best offer he could make for a number one best-seller. That was the end of the luncheon and the deal.

So now Silverman was his own agent—the world's worst, next to Hanna. That was because he acted from desperation and accepted humiliating terms.

And still Silverman loved being a writer, loved every vibrant, self-absorbed minute of it. He liked being inside his own head, working out angles and variations on stories. Fine-tuning a plot had for him the sensual reward of craftsmanship, the admiring hand on leather or wood. He joyed in writing even when he knew he was at work on a lost cause of a book, a great, lopsided literary disaster that would hit the water and capsize like a badly engineered battleship. It was still *his* story, a piece of his life. He even relished the long spells of writer's block he frequently suffered because he knew, somehow, he would break through and break free, and the words would come spilling out, a release much like orgasm long delayed. It was his love of writing that made him so vulnerably desperate. Because he knew in the marrow of his bone that he couldn't give up this addictive pleasure—even if he had to go begging in the streets to support his habit.

There had been small compensations along the way as he wound his way down and down. Last year he came across a story reporting that Tommy Sutton's Authors@Large.com had gone bust. It was listed among the ten dot-com companies that had tanked most disastrously in the general Internet debacle; it ranked after recently defunct enterprises named Goldfish.com and Funerals.com. At the time, Silverman wondered if Sutton might be willing to take him on again as a client. But when he placed a call to New York, he got a recorded voice telling him to "check our web site and send us an e-mail." He went no further.

Now, with bankruptcy hounding him, Silverman could get by only by offering courses at the university extension. His reputation was still visible enough to get him a creative writing class. Which meant he spent several hours a week correcting punctuation, doing what he could to save the semicolon from extinction. But he still wouldn't choose to be anything but a writer free to roam the fields of his mind. And he knew he was *good*, even if reviewers and editors begrudged him the recognition. He was especially good at one thing that had frankly surprised him, but had stuck with him all along. He could sure write a convincing woman. On that score, even female reviewers had been impressed by how deftly he, speaking throughout *Analyzing Anna* in the first person, had handled the subtleties of a woman's sex life. He had been struck by that, too, all the more so as he launched into a second novel (*I, Emma*), telling the story of Emma Bovary from Emma's viewpoint.

The seductive passivity of these nineteenth-century, middle-class women, their practiced coquettishness, their obsession with fashion and cosmetics, their nagging insecurities about body image (the hips, the waist, the bust, again the hips)—all this came so naturally to him.

"I wonder why that is," he asked himself. "How come I find it so easy to get inside the female mind?"

On a book tour for *I, Emma*, he passed through San Francisco and met Marty.

Then he knew.

3

The Whole World Isn't San Francisco

Silverman stood in the front hall and sniffed. He sniffed hard. The scent on the air, lingering from early that morning, was luscious, a tantalizing blend of vanilla, brandy, and home-baked pastry. The finest ingredients lovingly combined. Marvelous. But it was the wrong smell.

Three times a week, Marty filled the apartment with the lovely fragrance of Maurice's *A Votre Santé* Madeleines. Baking under the name of Maurice—the pseudonym offered just that hint of the Gallic so dear to San Franciscans—was his day job, or rather his break-of-day job as he liked to put it, his major means of earning during the increasingly long spells between casting calls. He was now up to seventy dozen Madeleines a week. Even if he started in at two in the morning, he was pushing the limit of what their tiny kitchen could handle. A couple dozen more and he would, as he put it, "have to turn seriously commercial." He had been threatening to make the leap for the past three years—from the time his recipe for Madeleines, a skillful adaptation that eliminated the egg yolks and substituted a secret fat-free shortening, had won an award from the city's leading health-food magazine. There were few gourmets who could tell the difference between *A Votre Santé* and its high-cholesterol rivals. Ordinarily, Silverman found it a privilege to enter the home where the healthiest Madeleines on the market were made. But pastry wasn't what he expected today. This was ribs night. What he wanted to smell was the dark side of Marty's culinary talent, his utterly unwholesome barbecued ribs. By this time in the day, the aroma of spiced and charring pig should have crowded out the last fragile vapors of that morning's baking. He sniffed again. Not a trace. Four in the afternoon and no ribs cooking. That could mean only one thing. Trouble.

Silverman had been away for the day, fully expecting that when he returned the scent of ribs would greet him on the front stairs even before he opened the door. The very expectation had kept his mouth watering since high noon. He had skipped lunch to keep his appetite at full strength. That was his custom on ribs night: starve in preparation for the barbeque of the gods.

Cautiously, he made his way toward the kitchen. Clearly no action there. The room was cold and empty. No hard-working cook in sight. Then: "North Fork? Where in God's holy name is North Fork?" Marty's voice, freighted with displeasure floated in from the dining room.

"A little bit west and a little bit north of Minneapolis," Silverman answered as casually as possible. "Sort of west northwest, I'd say."

"And since when are we heading west northwest of Minneapolis to welcome in the New Year?"

"Well, not we. Just me."

"So I see."

"I was going to tell you about it."

Silverman and Marty had been opening one another's mail for years. Unfortunately, Marty had gotten to the mail first that day. A letter bearing the name of Faith College lay on the dining room table and under it a road map. Clearly Marty had found a better use for the table than covering it with magnificent grub. Bending over the map, he was slowly moving a magnifying glass up, up, up, ever more northerly, left, left, left ever more westerly.

"North Fork. Got it. Judging by the size of the type, I'd say it's about one degree up from a cow crossing. Sweet Jesus, look where this is. That's no 'little bit north.' That's to Canada practically. Canadians, Danny. That far north you could be dealing with Canadians. You know what that means." Silverman's last two books had been roughly reviewed in Canada.

Silverman affected total unconcern. "You're being very provincial. I've been to Minnesota. I know the place."

"When were you in Minnesota?"

"I did a reading in Minneapolis. My first book tour. Of course I was only passing through. But I met lovely, literate people. They took me to a great French restaurant."

"A couple hours in Minneapolis twenty years ago? Come on, honey. Cities are cities, and boonies are boonies, and never the twain. Our world ends this side of Modesto and it doesn't begin again until you reach the Hudson River."

"Can we be just a wee-bit more global here?" Silverman asked. "This is two hours by limo from the airport. When's dinner?" he added doing his best imitation of a non-starving man.

Dumb question. He knew full well that dinner was going to be more than a little late tonight. Marty was bringing the Jones-tone into play. The Jones-tone was his utterly marvelous impression of James Earl Jones, the voice that could knock down a wall. He was so good at it. Marty was good at mimicry in general. In the middle of a conversation he could turn on a dime and ambush you with Clint Eastwood, Woody Allen, Judy Garland. But James Earl Jones was his best. In fact it was too good. After Marty had done a couple of voice-over commercials in Jones-tone, he was threatened with legal action if he didn't stop trespassing on the great actor's vocal property. There was probably no way Jones could claim ownership of a voice, but no sponsor wanted to fight the case. In any event, Marty was willing to lay off as a gesture of professional respect. But he was still earning from the Jones-tone. For a stretch of three seasons, Marty had been the star of a television police procedural called *Chopper Patrol*. He found a chance on every episode to invoke his full vocal authority, usually with lines like "Freeze," "Drop it," "On the floor," "Come clean!" That led to earnings that outlived the show. Every year for the past five, he taught a command-voice workshop at SFPD. As one rookie cop told him, "a voice like that could stop a bullet in mid-air." Which left Marty wondering why he so seldom got his way with Silverman around the house when the two of them fell to arguing.

"Two hours?" Marty growled as he measured off the distance with thumb and finger on the map. "That's no two hours. I'll eat my hat if that's two hours. You are way into Viking territory here. I bet they meet you at the airport with a dog-sled. No way you're gonna be in and out in one day."

"Well, actually, Hanna says it works out to be two overnights."

"Oh, so now it's *two* overnights."

"That's how the planes fly."

"December 31, January 1, January 2. Three days. You know I loathe this."

"Think twelve-thousand dollars."

"For three days, not enough."

"Come on! My last lecture gig was $250, if you don't count all the freebies I've been doing to keep my name alive. Be reasonable, Marty. You have dental bills, we've got a car that's limping, last month we barely made the rent, and the credit card is tapped out at twenty percent interest. We're sky-diving here with a 'chute full of holes. How much closer to insolvency do you want to come?"

"So why are these cold-ass Christian Brethren paying you 12K?" Marty was edging the Jones-tone perceptibly closer to Darth Vader. High-level intimidation. Actually, Silverman enjoyed the effect, but he tried not to let that show.

"The dean says they're reading my books in this program. The dean thinks I'm major."

"Why?"

At last a chance for Silverman to play hurt. "And you *don't?*"

"Of course I do. In my minor opinion, you are major. But, Danny, you don't have any books left in print."

"They found copies, I guess."

"Which books?"

"*Deep Eye*, I think."

Deep Eye was his last remotely notable book, written on a shoestring advance he had managed to negotiate for himself after Tommy Sutton bailed on him. At least it had gone into paperback, despite a negative review in the *Times*. No, not negative. Worse. Silverman was convinced there was a category at the *Times* called "cruel." And another called "savage." *Deep Eye* had been assigned to "savage." There were reviewers who were kept in reserve for such hatchet jobs, wounded novelists who had seen a book of their own torn to shreds. These vicious characters were kept penned up and ready to kill, like the hungry hounds that took off after escaped convicts. You could see "savage" coming a mile off. From the first sentence there was a tone of hostile suspicion that said, "Okay, what's this guy trying to get away with?" Reviewers like that could make the best in the business sound like an egregious hack. "Oh, come now, Mr. Fitzgerald, *West Egg*! . . . Really, Count Tolstoy! Not another encomium to the virtuous peasant." Silverman's pit-bull reviewer had actually nominated *Deep Eye* for a new critical category: "novel containing the worst single line of the year," that line being: "If it weren't for all this blubber. . . ."

Well, of course it sounded ludicrous taken out of context. Take any line of Faulkner or Hemingway out of context and what would they sound like? Go ahead, try it! Trouble was, every time he undertook this exercise, all of Faulkner's and Hemingway's lines still sounded pretty good, damn it. But what was the point of rational debate? They knew what they were doing at the *Times*. Savage was all he could expect, and sometimes not even that. Just nothing. Silence. Like when the torturer passes a body whipped into stupor. Not worth the effort of another stroke. Why such sadistic neglect? It was because he had left New York, the lousy weather, the traffic, the pressure. People stuck with these discomforts considered those who departed to be soft and treacherous. Secretly, they were envious.

"These Refried Brothers of Christ are interested in whales?" Marty asked incredulously. "I'll bet it's because they're all Eskimos up there. Eskimos eat people, you know, when they run out of blubber. Bring food. Throw them bones."

"I don't think you're supposed to call them Eskimos any more."

"Don't try to pc your way out of this. You are taking your life in your hands, baby. Don't you dare breathe a word about your sexual orientation. Affect macho. Wear a baseball cap. Lose your deodorant. I shouldn't have to remind you of Thing One in the official gay survival handbook. The whole world *isn't* San Francisco."

"You can't imagine I'm doing this because I enjoy it," Silverman explained. "It really is the money. If I turn this down, Hanna is going to fire me."

Marty did some fast calculating. "Look, we have other possibilities. If I get this commercial I'm up for, and if I bump up the Madeleines by, say, forty dozen—"

"Forty dozen!"

"Forty dozen a week, we can make up for the 12 thou by this time next year."

"Good. Do that. Because we need your 12 thou as well as my 12 thou. We need all the 12 thous we can get."

While he waited for dinner, Silverman read his letter from Faith College.

Daniel Silverman
122-A Fillmore Street
San Francisco, CA

Dear Mr. Silverman:

Your lecture agent Miss Hurwitz informs me that you would like to know more about our school in anticipation of your eagerly awaited visit to North Fork next month.

You may remember me, though I imagine not. Our paths once crossed in the mail. About nine years ago, when I was completing my graduate studies at Redemption Seminary, I was in touch with you about my thesis, which was based on one of your books. You were kind enough to comment on my interpretation of your novel *The Idiot's Sonata*, which I still regard as your finest work. I cannot tell you how moved I was by your ingenious retelling of King Lear from the Fool's point of view. I felt it was a vindication of religious faith *in extremis*.

But more to the point. When I was appointed Dean of Religious Studies at Faith College last year, I undertook to develop a new Humanities program that brings together the finest of religious and humanistic thought. Our motto is "Excellence in All its Diverse Glory." The program gets under way next year. I could think of no better choice for our millennial New Year's speaker than you. I will be frank to say that I believe our student body will be challenged by your remarks. Many have been raised in a strong sectarian tradition, but others are developing a broader worldview, thanks to our extensive on-line capacities. See our Web site: www.byfaithalone.edu.

Until twelve years ago, we were an all-male campus. Women now make up nearly 30 percent of our mainly residential student body of 1237. Only one in four of our students comes from outside the immediate Minnesota-Dakota area; most are the children of Faith alumni. As dean, I have taken it as my highest priority to open new horizons for our community. While Religious Studies remains the mainstay of our school (we are the main training seminary for the Free Reformed Evangelical Brethren in Christ Synod of North America), we also have a well-developed business and marketing curriculum and plan to add a multimedia laboratory in the near future. The lecture series that you will be initiating was endowed by Mrs. Helena Bloore, president of the Snow Ghost Snowmobile Company, the largest employer in northwestern Minnesota. I know that Mrs. Bloore and other members of our faculty greatly look forward to a bracing encounter with you at the faculty luncheon preceding your lecture.

Of special importance to me is the opportunity you will have to socialize informally with our Religious Humanism Committee that evening. All of us on the committee are great fans of your books and eagerly anticipate some good, stimulating one-on-one discourse regarding the place of humanistic values in our faith.

May I also mention that you are invited to attend our first annual Holiday-at-Home Family Barn Dance, a bit of a lark that will allow the students to kick up their heels on New Year's Eve. If your plane arrives on time, you may be able to catch the last dance. The event is sure to run well past midnight—weather permitting, of course.

It is an honor to have you as our guest and mentor.
Sincerely Yours,
Richard Swenson, Dean of Religious Studies

Marty, coming and going between the kitchen and dining room
while Silverman read, offered a line-by-line razzing. He had apparently memorized the entire letter at first reading. Actors!
"Now, what could be a jollier way to spend New Year's?" he asked.
"Being with dull old Marty in dull old San Francisco could hardly
compare to kicking up your heels at the North Fork family barn
dance, weather permitting, of course. Which means if the whole
state isn't under ice."

"I have no intention of attending any barn dance."

"And how about that bracing encounter with Mrs. Snow
Blower?"

"Whatever it is, it won't last long, that much I can tell you. I eat
the rubber chicken and I'm out of there."

Dinner, when it came—two hours late—was more than a small
gesture of protest on Marty's part. It was diet-for-a-small-planet
sadism. Beans and nuts and mountains of boiled kale, nature's
toughest broom. Silverman sighed and despaired. It wasn't only
the food, but the righteous cruelty that he knew would be served
up if he showed the least lack of enthusiasm. He could hear it
coming. "Fava beans are good for you." During their first few years
together he and Marty had argued about diet more than anything
else. "Who are you to police my diet?" Silverman used to ask. "The
man who loves you," Marty answered. Well, that was a pretty good
answer. And it became even more compelling after Silverman was
diagnosed with sky-high blood pressure.

But tonight! Tonight was supposed to be ribs night. Once a
month, Marty—reluctantly but as an act of loving indulgence—
served ribs, the best in town. His recipe, so he claimed, traced back
to the colonial Carolinas through eight generations of family. God,
how Silverman loved those ribs! And that sauce, so fiendishly hot,
it numbed you to the toes and lingered with an aftertaste like liquid
fire until the next morning. "You could open a franchise." Silverman had said it so often Marty could pick up on the first syllable

and echo the phrase. But the compliment fell flat. Since long before they met, Marty was a health-food fanatic with a gorgeous
physique to show for it. Invariably he reminded Silverman,
"*Hozzerai*, man, you know that. You want me to inflict pig food on
the arteries of my fellow man? Bad enough, my best beloved, that I
gotta sit here and watch you committing digestive suicide."

And that was all Marty would do. After dutifully cooking the
ribs—a senselessly tiny portion for Silverman—he would sit and
watch with a disapproving eye while Silverman gorged. Or worse,
he would sit across the table lip-smacking his way through a plate-
ful of pecan rissole or seaweed salad, doing his best to shame Silverman. That never worked, not when ribs were on the table. Ribs
were to die for. "Maybe my mama was a princess of the lost tribe,"
Marty mused as Silverman picked every rib on his plate clean and
licked the bones. "Maybe that's how come I'm more kosher than
you, dollink."

Three days before Danny was scheduled to leave, Marty was
still working on him.

"Do you know what the temperature is in Minneapolis this very
minute? Dead, bloody zero-point-nothing. This is definitely the
Canadian Winter Hell zone. Oh my God! In Duluth, it's minus
four. That's *minus*, you understand? Less than zero. Off the end of
the thermometer. Beyond Duluth they don't even bother to give
the weather. The next stop is the North Pole. Who lives in such
places?"

"You're being an alarmist. The weather will be clear. Hanna has
been watching out. Cold but clear. She says I might actually see
the northern lights."

"That'll be a comfort when you're freezing your *tush*. 'I see
them! I'm frozen solid, but I see them!' You can bet none of these
Viking he-men are going to warm you back to life."

"I'll put the lining back in my raincoat."

"Danny, your raincoat is for a windy day in Sausalito. This is in-
dustrial strength Arctic deep freeze. Less than zero."

"Mostly I'll be indoors."

"With all the jolly Christian Brethren singing hymns. 'Rock of
Ages, cleft for me.' You are very, very brave."

"It's in and out."

But Marty wouldn't give up. He had found the Automobile Club touring guide to midwestern America. In bed, the night before Silverman was to leave, he insisted on reading. "Oh say, here's something you don't want to miss. In St. Agnes, which is only an hour's drive due west of North Fork, there's the largest gypsum deposit in North America. It's called Gypsum Hump. Two-hundred and forty feet high. A hump of solid gypsum. Imagine!"

"Stop! You know we need the money."

"But you will bring me back a souvenir, won't you, honey? I'll bet there's a nifty gifty shoppe that sells these charming little mementos of Gypsum Hump."

"Cut it out! I'm going."

On the day Silverman was scheduled to leave, Marty finally relented and agreed to drive him to the airport. As they kissed at the curb outside Northwest departures, Marty thrust a package under his arm. "This is a special dispensation. Just for this trip, okay? After Saul Bellow and the hockey puck, the next best thing to come out of Canada. My advice is to get sloshed on the plane, stay sloshed while you're there, come home sloshed. You'll feel no pain."

Silverman waited until he was in the VIP lounge to unwrap the gift. It was a liter of Canadian Club.

4

Our Glass Nose

"Seems things are still backed up in Minneapolis after the last snow. They're asking us to hold here at SFO until they get Paul Bunyan to clear a couple of runways. Otherwise, weather in the Twin Cities looks great. Nippy but nice. So settle back, folks, while our cheerful cabin crew looks after your every little need. We'll be pushing back soon."

It was the fourth announcement of delayed departure since Silverman had tightened his seat belt. This time he was sure he heard the captain fighting back a yawn. Must be part of their training, he mused—the way pilots always sound so laid-back when they talk to the passengers. That was probably meant to inspire confidence. Ordinarily, that wouldn't have worked for the sort of skittish air traveler Silverman had always been. Sitting on the ground this long—an hour so far—would have left him explosively tense. Instead he was warmly euphoric. That was because, for the first time in his life, he was flying first class. Of course leg room like this was wasted on a five-sixer like him. Doing his best to stretch, he was still a clear foot short of the luxurious space allotted. Well, he would make up for that with booze. No telling how the peasants back in air steerage were coping, but in first class, delay meant drink—and then more drink, followed by a little more drink.

By the time Northwest flight 432 was in the air, Silverman was working on his third highball, wondering whether he would ever be able to endure less airborne comfort in the future. Luxury like this was corrupting. Especially the liquor, for which he had a disgraceful weakness. Marty had been working on the problem for as long as they had been together. He had succeeded in getting Silverman down to a glass of wine at meals and a couple of New Year's Eve toasts to love and good health. Well, but Marty himself had given him the Canadian Club, plus the special indulgence to make liberal use of it. So who was Silverman to turn down the Welcome Aboard Champagne, followed by the double vodka tonic with refills, followed by a selection of aperitifs that all sounded so good? "Oh, try one of each," Raoul, the flight attendant, recommended. Such a persuasive guy, and very good-looking, a broad grin and piercing black eyes. So Silverman did as told: one of each, followed by wine with whatever the meal had been—oh yes, boeuf bourgignon sliced rare at the side of his seat—followed by brandy, followed by. . . . He remembered his trip to Minneapolis as a journey down the royal river of booze.

By the time he was over Boise he was too woozy to follow the on-board movie, an animated sequel to an animated original based on *The Hunchback of Notre Dame*. A Disney job filled with those Disney-pretty cartoon girls that have no noses. The movie utterly depressed him. All movies depressed him. They made him wonder why none of his novels had been optioned after *Analyzing Anna* a hundred years ago. But in this case he was left especially morose. After all, had he not himself taken a shot at reworking Hugo's *Hunchback*? One of his more serious efforts, a vast historical panorama dealing with great existential issues of life and death and . . . well, life and death, wasn't that enough? *His* Esmerelda had been a veritable force of nature, a hot-blooded Gypsy lass whose explosive female passions no writer of our time could better capture on paper than the remarkable Daniel Silverman, famous non-woman writer of women. Imagine! Hugo had not even mentioned Esmerelda's breasts, which were of course magnificent. What a feast for the eye the Silverman version would have been on the silver screen, or even perhaps put to music on the stage. Mobs, spectacles, riots, carnivals. Yes, a bit on the order of *Les Misérables*, but totally, completely original and deeper, far deeper. *Parliament of Monsters*, it was called—such an excellent title—the story as narrated by a brooding, eternal gargoyle atop the cathedral. Why hadn't Disney used that? Too adult. Too philosophically demanding. No noseless females. Quality was dead. Literature had gone into hibernation. We are living in the eclipse of intellect. His thoughts grew gloomy, and the gloom became a blur, and the blur became. . . .

"We're deplaning, Mr. Silverman." Raoul was shaking his shoulder gently. "Sorry for the delay."

Silverman glanced at his watch. Nine-fifteen. "Weren't we supposed to get in at seven-fifty?"

"We were in a little after eight. But we've been waiting for an open gate."

"This long?"

"They haven't cleared away from the last snow. That's always a problem in Minneapolis. I'm afraid we'll be disembarking the old-fashioned way: with roll-away stairs."

Silverman peered into the blackness beyond the window. "But it's not snowing now."

"Lucky us, we slipped in between."

"In between?"

"There's a doozy coming up."

"Oh? When?"

"Tomorrow night."

"That wasn't in the forecast. Nippy but nice, that's what the pilot said."

"We always say things like that." Raoul was on his hands and knees searching for Silverman's shoes under the seat. What an excellent fellow he was. Attentive, nurturing, broad in the shoulders, narrow in the waist. "Cheers the passengers up. Of course, the locals up here are real hearty types, oh God are they! They never lie about the weather. I'm told they regard it as punishment for their sins. Anyway, forecasting for Minnesota this time of year is pretty hit and miss. Last April we had a storm that shut down everything for four days. Imagine! In April. Your best bet is to expect rotten weather from December straight through to May. You might be delightfully surprised, but you won't be disappointed. Myself, I can't wait to get back to the islands."

While Silverman stood in the aisle creeping toward the exit, the jolly flight attendants used the intercom to try raising tired spirits. "For any of you who are new to the Minneapolis area, the airport's offering shivering lessons." Passengers chuckled, but not Silverman. Twenty people back in line, he could already feel the cold probing its way between buttons and through zippers. Stepping out of the plane onto the open staircase, he felt the heat drain from him instantaneously, sucked out of him the way people suck a sautéed snail out of its shell with one slurp. With the other passengers huddling around him, he rushed across the tarmac toward the terminal. His feet were numb before he was halfway there. There was no wind, only still, frigid air. It was as if he had been teleported into a solid block of ice.

He made his way into the terminal on rubbery legs, the liquor still looping through his metabolism. Inside the first class arrival lounge, his escorts spotted him before he spotted them. Two young people, man and woman, and, it seemed, a baby wrapped in the woman's arms. "Professor Silverman, let me take that," the man said, stripping Silverman's suitcase from him immediately. "I'm Dick Swenson." He pumped Silverman's hand in a warm welcome.

Silverman couldn't help it. What he registered first were the teeth. Big buck teeth. Swenson and the woman at his side, both of them, big people attached to big teeth. Silverman had a shameful prejudice about buckteeth. He associated them with imbecility. Probably some distantly remembered connection with Mortimer Snerd. His only way to see around buckteeth was to call up a mental picture of Eleanor Roosevelt, long-revered in the Silverman household. He promptly did so. "Yes, hello," he answered putting out a hand. "We were delayed."

"We know. We could see you out there on the runway. I hope they kept the plane warm. Last week there was a flight that sat on the tarmac so long the passengers nearly turned blue. This is Sylvia, my wife. And Jessica, our daughter. Our babysitter never showed up. Probably snowbound. So here we are, the whole Swenson clan."

Swenson, buck-toothed though he might be, had a certain craggy, Nordic handsomeness. He must have stood six-foot-five and was making no effort to stoop to Silverman's stature. Worse, his wife was equally enormous, a lanky woman with a baked-on smile and a large, flushed face. In even minor high heels she might have been as tall as her husband. Silverman secretly hated people who made him aware of his five-six smallness, especially big women. His strategy with tall females had once been to slump so that they felt even more embarrassingly Amazonian, but that ploy had stopped working a decade ago. Women were getting larger and seemed to have no regrets. Probably because there were so many taller men. With the booze making him steadily more morose, Silverman began to bemoan his anatomical fate. Everybody was getting taller except him. He had never been tall. He was convinced there was a runaway basketball gene loose in the world that was producing ever loftier people. As he trudged along with a towering Swenson on either side, he felt as if he were walking in a ditch. It was so unfair. There ought to be a government program. Everybody above six-four has to share an eighth of an inch with the shorties; they'd never miss it.

"We did plan to send a limo," Swenson explained as they made their way across an Arctic-cold parking lot ringed by heaps of snow. "The company said it didn't want to commit to a trip north just now. But not to worry. The good old Saab never fails." Silverman had jammed his gabardine rain hat down over his ears and brow as far as it would reach. It did no good; his head was a lump of ice. But trudging along beside him, Swenson and his Mrs. were cheerfully hatless. "This weather is great for the circulation," Swenson assured him. *Oh sure,* Silverman groused. As far as he could tell, his circulation had retreated into the depths of his organism, leaving his extremities to go numb. The Swensons' battered van was parked an agonizingly frigid hike away. "Couldn't get in any closer," Swenson apologized as he unlocked the door. Silverman had hoped he could snooze in the back seat on the way to the school, but Swenson insisted he sit up front so he could be "clued in" about what to expect. Silverman hated being "clued in." That always meant agreements and arrangements and understandings that assumed you wanted to be where you were, which was so rarely the case. What he wanted was in-and-out, no deals, no promises. Ah, but there had been a change in plans. Since the plane had been so late, Swenson intended to take Silverman home with him to spend his first night.

"I'd like to be on hand tomorrow morning to make introductions," he explained, "and, well, frankly, to smooth the way."

Smooth the way. Was that necessary, Silverman wondered.

"As I think I mentioned, you're here as part of a pretty significant turning point for our school. I'd say this is a historical moment, wouldn't you, Syl?"

"Historical," said Syl from the back seat of the van.

"We've been thinking of you as our glass nose," Swenson added, "if you follow my meaning."

"Your glass nose?"

Behind his shoulder, Silverman heard Syl say, "Oh, stop!"

Swenson chuckled. "Glass nose, that's what Syl thought it was. You know, *Glasnost?* like in the Soviet Union there, our opening to the world."

Silverman tried to imagine himself as the Gorbachev of northern Minnesota. Nothing came to mind. Blank. He was too weary either to giggle or protest. Instead, he began nodding as soon as the engine started. But Swenson was carrying on nonstop.

"You see, our church is . . . well, I don't imagine you know all that much about confessional Evangelicalism."

Right you are, Silverman answered inside his head. *Zip, zero, nada.* "Rather little," he said aloud.

"But I think, and Syl thinks, we both think—and we're not alone in this—that our church, well, possibly all the evangelicals, may be on the brink of a new era. We were both raised in the faith. We want to stay loyal to it in our own way. We see ourselves as a new generation of Free Evangelicals. If we're going to reach out toward a much wider public, we need to lighten the heavy hand of our Augustinian legacy. Isn't that right, Syl?"

"Right," said Syl. She was doing her best to comfort what seemed like a very colicky baby.

"Most of the Free Reformed Evangelical churches," Swenson went on as if from a prepared script, "have been resigned to going their separatist ways. The city on a hill principle, you know. Which, Lord knows, has always had its honorable place in Christian history. I mean where would we be without it? But I frankly believe," his voice became a taut whisper barely audible over the laboring engine of the Saab, "that day is past. I have high hopes for a true ecumenism."

What the hell is this man talking about? Silverman wondered as a flood of weariness poured through his skull. *Is he going to mouth off like this all the way there?* "How long is the trip?" he asked aloud, more to get Swenson on to some other track.

"Well, *normally*, we'd be there in under two hours."

"*Normally?*"

"There's been a big pile-up on the interstate. That was this morning. Eighty cars and trucks. Four people killed. And then it all froze over. Welcome to Minnesota highways. So we'll have to cut around that. Which should add about, oh, at most not more than half an hour, don't you think, Syl?"

From the back seat Syl answered. "If we're lucky." She didn't sound as if she expected them to be lucky.

Silverman turned to ask what that meant. He was surprised to discover Mother Swenson nursing her young. She smiled at him over her open blouse. That struck the most encouraging note so far. A nice liberal atmosphere—like any public park in San Francisco. Silverman turned back to Swenson. "You don't mind if I relax a bit along the way?"

"Not at all. I'll prattle on to keep us all awake for the trip. Because, you know, on roads like this. . . ."

In less than a minute Silverman, his forehead vibrating against the side window, was sleeping the sleep of the dead.

He awoke, his cheek still pressed against the glass, his misty eyes staring into the passing darkness. He heard a baby sneeze and then cry. Ah, yes, the infant Swenson in the back seat. Peering into the night, he glimpsed something on the right brightly lit by the floodlights of a closed-down filling station. The image might have stepped out of a dream. It was an enormous goggle-eyed cow as big as a truck. "What the hell's that?" Silverman asked as the figure glided by in the night.

"Babe the blue ox," Swenson answered. "You've heard of Paul Bunyan? There are a couple more along the way."

"And every one is the original," Syl added.

Silverman squinted at the dashboard clock. 12:47! "We're not there yet?" he asked, turning to Swenson.

"Some of the back roads were blocked by the last snowfall. I expect all the equipment in the area is out on the interstate. But we'll be there within the next hour. I thought we might be able to get to the barn dance before it broke up. I think we'll be a bit late for that."

Why did this guy think he cared about anything called a barn dance? "I'm not much for jigs and reels actually."

"Oh, I didn't imagine . . . we simply wanted you to look in. I'm sure our Holiday-at-Home would seem pretty cloistered to you. But you see, most of our students—74.8 percent to be exact—come from right around here in northwest Minnesota and the Dakotas, so their families try to give them as much as they can over the holidays. Otherwise the kids might start looking elsewhere for a good time. As you can imagine, we're very strong for family. In that respect, the barn dance is quite a breakthrough."

"It was Richard's idea," Syl volunteered with a distinct note of pride. "It's dancing."

"Isn't it in the nature of a barn dance for there to be dancing?" Silverman asked.

"Oh yes," Syl answered. "But at our school . . . dancing."

"That's special?" Silverman asked.

"You betcha," Swenson answered.

"They touch, the girls and boys," Syl added.

"Well, barely," Swenson said. "They touch at the waist, the boys, you know, hold the girls—around the waist. With one hand. Right there, at the waist. Above the hip. We had a lot of discussion with the parents about that."

"That's considered daring?" Silverman asked.

"Oh yes. Our school is committed to a policy of parent-sanctioned courtship."

"Really? Even over the age of eighteen?"

"The official Free Reformed Brethren teaching is that a true disciple is never old enough to sin," Swenson explained in a tone that implied no necessary approval on Silverman's part. "Most parents around here still regard twenty-one as the age of adulthood, no matter what worldly law might say. But we're hoping next year we can move on to 'swing your partner.' I know that may not seem like much to you, being from San Francisco."

"That's true. We've been swinging our partners for quite a while out there."

"Of course, we know that one way or another, lots of the kids get together for the kind of dancing our church once thought of as a temptation of the devil. We aren't naive about that. There's a bowling alley in Thief River where they play rock music, which is why some parents have put bowling off limits for their kids. It's a struggle to protect our little universe from the outside world. Some of us think there's no point in trying anymore. Syl and me, for example—we're sure it's time to stop being a holy huddle, and to start finding ways to fulfill our gospel aims as part of a greater fellowship."

Mercifully, with his eyes concentrated on the dark, icy road ahead, Swenson stopped talking for the next few miles. Silverman had the uncomfortable feeling that the man was tensed at the wheel with fear. Were they lost, hopelessly lost? "We will get there tonight?" he asked as cheerfully as possible.

Swenson giggled. "The good old off-road Saab here can get through most anything. I'm just not all that familiar with this particular road—if it is a road. What do you think, Syl? Maybe we should have forked right instead of left back there."

"I'm sure it's left," Syl answered. But she didn't sound all that certain.

"Maybe we're going in circles," Silverman suggested, pointing to another blue-ox effigy ahead.

"No, no," Swenson said. "That's another one."

Forty-five minutes later it turned out Syl had been right after all. They were in sight of the Swenson home. "We live across from the college," Swenson told him, pointing off across a frozen lake. "Most of the faculty live on campus, but we like our privacy. It's only a stone's throw. You can see the lights of the school."

While Swenson fetched his suitcase from the van, Silverman paused to look around. Frigid as the night had become, this was a sight not to be ignored. With a chill celestial light cast across it, the scene took on an austere beauty. The moon, drifting among high dark clouds, was ringed by a bright bow of frost. Where the covering snow had blown away to leave the dark ice clear, the lake—it was called Beaver Lake—stretched away like a tarnished mirror. Silverman stood on the front porch admiring the winter grandeur until he felt the cold reaching into him, searching for the bone. Then, click! he took a mental photograph, a snapshot to be used in some future story. In the basement of his mind he kept a storehouse of such snapshots: places, events, interiors, exteriors, above all people who might fit into a novel one day. Until he discovered that he was a writer, he never knew what to make of this strange childhood capacity to capture moments of living time like pictures in a secret album. Who could say? Maybe he would write a tale of the frozen north one day.

As far as he could tell in his depleted condition, the Swenson home had the feeling of a rustic cabin, small but cozy. His bed in a room on the second floor was wedged under a sloping knotted-pine roof. As soon as he saw the mountainous feather tick he would sleep under that night, he was ready to crash. But tired as he was, he couldn't let himself sleep without phoning Marty. It would be nearly midnight in San Francisco, exactly the right time to call. There was one problem. The Swenson telephone was on a hall table outside the Swenson bedroom. Silverman stretched the cord as far as he could, but he knew he was still within earshot of his hosts behind their door. With so little privacy this wasn't going to get very intimate.

"Everything's okay," he told Marty. "They're good people, but," he added in a whisper, "I'm calling from right outside their bedroom."

"What?" Marty asked.

"I can't get too loud," he said seeking a discreet volume.

"Why not? Are they holding you prisoner?"

"It's not too private. Talk for me."

"*For* you?"

"Tell me what you know I'm thinking."

"Well, you know how much I hate it that you're there."

"I do, I do."

"And I hope you miss me like mad."

"Like mad, yes. Go on."

"And you're thinking that missing our midnight kiss is practically a sin."

"Yes, yes. Go on."

"And that you're going to make it up to me ten-million times over when you get home."

"Absolutely. A million times ten-million times."

"And that I have your permission to go to bed tonight imagining any wild thing I want about you, and it won't be nearly extreme enough for what's really going to happen when you get back."

"Guaranteed."

"And that I'm going to be the last thing you think about tonight."

"And the first tomorrow morning."

"And that we're never going to let this happen again, not for millions of money. Promise?"

"I promise."

"And—oh what the hell!—that I'm the love and the light of your life, and the vice is versa."

"No truer words."

"Love you."

"Love you. I'll call tomorrow."

5

Breakfast with Richard and Syl

He awoke the next morning in the grip of a merciless hangover. He should have known better than to indulge so freely. He had neither the head nor the stomach for drinking. Too much booze set his ears roaring and his head pounding. It also tied his gut into a knot, which made it all the worse to wake up in a house filled with delicious kitchen odors. Wandering downstairs in bathrobe and slippers, he discovered that Syl had prepared a classic farmhouse breakfast for him. The table groaned with food, most of it the sort of industrial-strength cholesterol that Marty had spent years expunging from Silverman's diet.

"Happy New Year!" Syl called to him as he entered the kitchen. "If you don't see what you want, let me know." She was holding the baby over her shoulder just as she had last night when he headed off to bed. Maybe she had never put it down. The kid was still sniffling and whining.

"That's really sweet of you," he answered. "But I'll stick to black coffee. I think something I ate on the plane didn't agree with me. Sorry."

"Oh, that's all right. I didn't know what you liked, so I made a little of everything," she explained almost apologetically.

Silverman had been too groggy to give the Swenson home any aesthetic attention the night before. Now he was beginning to register the charm of the house he was in. It was small, so low-ceilinged in some corners and at the doors that its six-foot-plus residents had to stoop to move about. Cramped as it was, the house had a remarkable warmth and comfort to it; it also looked authentically old, a classic piece of prairie farmhouse Americana built of heavy wooden beams and hand-hewn stone. "This place is right out of a history book," Silverman observed. "Is it as old as it looks?"

"You betcha," Syl answered. "Of course it's been patched and rebuilt here and there, but it dates way back—middle of the nineteenth century. It was the Olafsen place, first Minnesota farm this side of the Mississippi. The school owns it now, as well as this whole side of the lake."

"Doesn't look tall enough for you."

"Oh, we've gotten used to that, though I used to take my lumps at first. Seems I've been stooping my way through life since I was twelve."

Swenson, taking his seat at the table, frowned. "Well, for Pete's sake, Syl, you might have guessed Professor Silverman can't eat bacon," he chided too severely.

"I can't?" Silverman asked. "Why not?" Bacon was among his favorite weaknesses. It had been one of Marty's proudest achievements to wean him off of it.

Swenson stared back in bewilderment. "Well, it's not, well—"

"Oh, I see. But you forget: I am a Jewish Humanist." And in order to offer Syl a small gesture of gratitude, he forked a crisp rasher of bacon onto his plate and proceeded to chomp it. God, that was good! He must have another. "Humanists are not kosher," he reminded Swenson. "Or rather they are kosher in their own way, which means they can eat anything they want except for Brussels sprouts. Incidentally, I'm not actually, *really* a professor, you know."

"I hope you won't mind if I call you professor," Swenson said, a clear pleading tone in his voice. "It'll matter to a few of our more snobbish faculty. And you are, after all, university-connected."

"In the sense that I sometimes teach in the university extension. That makes me about as professorial as I am kosher. But if you want, you can call me rabbi."

"So you won't mind about 'professor'?"

"Suit yourself. I trust you to introduce me any way you please."

"Well, perhaps we might talk about that a little," Swenson answered, pulling his chair in closer to the table as if he meant to get down to important business. Silverman could feel the man's nervous tension radiating across the table. "As I said last night, we hope to make some history here today. I guess I shouldn't expect you to know all that much about the reformed evangelicals."

"Not a thing. Do I have to?" A half-dozen rashers of bacon seemed to have migrated to Silverman's plate. Must mean his appetite was returning. Yes, it was. He chomped.

"Just so you won't be in for any rude surprises, it might help for you to know that there are some rather conservative elements in our church. Very conservative. You'll be quite challenging for them. They may bring up some pointed questions."

"As long as the points aren't at the end of sticks."

"They can seem rather narrow-minded."

"Might that be because they are?"

Swenson laughed defensively. "Yes, you could put it that way. Our church—and I say this as a loyal member, both me and Syl—has a strong dispensationalist streak running through it." Silverman's face before him was a bored blank. "Not that I'd expect you to know what that is."

"Right. I don't."

"Maybe a little theological background would help."

Shit! Silverman might have said the word out loud, but his mouth was now deeply invested in a well-buttered biscuit which, at first bite, seemed to be superb.

"Our confession derives from the Doctrine of Inspiration," Swenson began, "which, while deeply conservative, has never regarded other congregations as apostate. But there are those, well, like Mrs. Bloore for example, who are really quite rigid about the fundamentals. Whereas many of our younger parishioners want to move toward a far more ecumenical stance. Not that the Free Reformed Evangelicals will ever be liberals."

Silverman gave Swenson a comic squint. "Am I supposed to know what you're talking about?"

"Ouch!" Swenson said, stopping short and wincing as if he had made a great mistake. "I do carry on, don't I? Sorry."

"Remember," Silverman continued, "I was raised among people who think the *goyim* swiped our holy book and turned it into Looney Tunes. If you don't mind me saying so."

Swenson suddenly looked worried. "Of course I understand. But I'd like to ask you to soft-pedal remarks like that."

"Never fear, Richard. I can soft-pedal it to the point of silence."

"Because I believe our faith can be significantly liberalized without compromising its basic tenets. Like it says in Matthew, 9:17 about the new wine in old bottles. Well, I believe that's happening to our church right now."

"Believe as you please," Silverman answered. "I don't intend to say anything controversial. I'm here to talk about literature, not theology." Now that was interesting. His fork was reaching for more food: a muffin and some hash-brown potatoes to keep all the bacon on his plate from looking so lonely. And, oh yes, might as well try some of Syl's tempting, home-made jam.

"Of course. That's good," Swenson agreed. "But may I suggest— in case anything uncomfortable comes up—please feel free to circle round it as tactfully as you can and move along? If any of our more polemical elements seem to want to hold forth—and we do have a few, not many, but a few zealots on campus—I'll try to steer you clear. Because it's really the students I want you to reach. They've been preparing questions for you all last semester. Frankly, I think many of them are sincerely curious about the humanistic viewpoint. Especially our little Religious Humanism committee. They're wonderful young people. And they want so much to meet you. We'd like to spirit you away for dinner this evening, someplace away from the school —weather permitting."

"That's sort of a litany around these parts isn't it? *Weather permitting.* Like Jews saying 'God forbid.' Are you expecting bad weather?"

"Possibly. A bit of a blow this evening."

"Well, as long as we get away on time tomorrow morning." To his surprise, Silverman found his plate stacked with scrambled eggs, fruit, rolls, toast, and, yes, still more bacon.

"I think I can guarantee that," Swenson assured him. "I want to make sure you're prepared for a few, well, awkward questions."

"Awkward for whom? Look, Richard, I'm going to make some good literary talk. Books, authors, scholarly judgments. I'll answer all questions politely. Then I'm going home. That's all I agreed to.

If some of your zealots are unhappy, well, too bad. After I'm off the premises, make what you want of anything I said. If it helps punch a hole in some closed minds, good."

"That's fair enough," Swenson agreed. But he still looked worried. Silverman decided this was the time to ask.

"What went wrong with Gore Vidal?"

Swenson looked stunned. "Ouch!" he winced again. "You heard about that?"

"Mm-hm. So what's the story?"

Swenson's face went red. He looked to Syl.

"A member of the trustees found one of his books offensive," Syl said.

"Myra Breckinridge," Silverman guessed.

"No," Syl said. "It was the novel about Aaron Burr."

"Burr? They thought *Burr* was offensive?"

"Well, there are some bad words in it," Syl explained.

Silverman turned to Swenson. "I don't get it. Why are you inviting novelists? I can't think of a single novelist since Louisa May Alcott who doesn't use 'bad words.' I sometimes think bad words have become the total American vocabulary. I've heard more bad words waiting for a bus with a gang of junior-high-school kids than I've used in all my books put together. Maybe what you want for your program are Sunday School teachers."

Swenson hastened to explain. "There was simply so much resistance to Mr. Vidal. I do believe he was frankly too controversial to start our series with. I suppose if I had fought harder, I might have gotten my way, but that didn't seem the smart thing to do."

Silverman mulled this over, trying to make sense of what he was hearing. "So you invited me instead. Why? Because I'm good and safe? There are bad words in my books too."

"I know, but see, you're here as a Jewish Humanist."

"And that's why I'm acceptable?"

"You betcha. You connect much more smoothly with our program."

As he began to pack away more food, Silverman felt a better mood coming over him. All right, then. He was more than a mere novelist. He had another string to his bow. He was a humanist of the subcategory Jewish. Didn't that lend a certain breadth to his reputation? Why not make the most of his sojourn? Perhaps he could learn a thing or two, something that might work as comic relief in a future novel. "What was that about 'disposabilism'? Never heard of that." Whatever Swenson might answer, it would give Syl a chance to rustle up more bacon.

"Dispensationalism?" Swenson brightened at the question. "That's the most rigid kind of evangelical faith. What it is, you see, is a sort of Biblical timetable that dictates exactly how God relates to man, with no interpretation possible—a straight, literal reading based on the belief that the word of God is totally true and trustworthy."

"What a good feeling that must be," Silverman commented, "knowing that something in the world is totally true and trustworthy. I have friends back in San Francisco who talk about the Internet that way. They believe everything they read there. Myself, I don't think anything is totally true and trustworthy—except possibly loyalty between people."

"That's what makes you a humanist," Syl suggested. She had a nice smile, a big, warm, toothy grin that glowed with good will.

"That's a nice way to put it," Silverman agreed.

"Well," Swenson went on, "the dispensationalists believe that any deviation from the inspired and inerrant word is apostasy. And as they see it, all the major Christian congregations are apostate under the influence of Satan."

"Really?" Silverman was savoring another of Syl's biscuits. No doubt about it, these were the best he had ever tasted. "You people believe things like that, do you?"

"Oh no, not me. Not Syl. That's one of the main differences between our church and the rest of the synod. We're the most liberal of the Reformed Evangelicals, wouldn't you say, Syl?"

"You betcha, by miles and miles."

Silverman was beginning to register 'you betcha' as North Fork vernacular. Watching Syl pat her contented baby with her blouse still open from the feeding, Silverman couldn't believe she took any of this theological crap seriously. In any case, she sure baked a tasty biscuit. "What's in these?" he asked.

"Well, there's ground walnuts and cherries, for one thing." Under her breath, she added, "The cherries were cooked in sherry, so we have to keep that secret. Our home is supposed to be tee-total. I hope you don't mind."

"Mind what?"

"The sherry."

Silverman knitted his brow. "I'm glad you told me. I allow myself a teensy tipple every New Year's Day. This will take care of me for the rest of the year. Is this your own creation?"

"It's an old family recipe. But I add in extra nutmeg."

"Delicious. And the jam, that's yours too?"

"Yeah."

"What is it?"

"That's gooseberry with a little orange peel. The other's apple-cinnamon."

"You ought to take out a franchise. Seriously."

Swenson was grinding on. "But we've always had some fringe elements in the church that think we've become too liberal."

"Fringe elements?" Silverman asked. "Exactly what would that mean, viewed from the broad mainstream of the—what is it? Free Formed Evangelicalites?"

Swenson didn't bother to correct him. He raced on with mounting enthusiasm. "There are a few members of our faculty who are frankly at war with the entire modern world. They refuse to compromise with anything that deviates from a godly, righteous, and sober life. They think 'the dark side' is about 99 percent of all there is. I mean they regard drinking Coca-Cola as a mortal sin, or even coffee."

"Mrs. Bloore thinks decaf is a Satanic plot," Syl laughed. "She says there's more caffeine in decaf than in regular. Could that be true?"

"You mean this is the last cup of coffee I'm going to have in North Fork?" Silverman asked. "A refill please." Syl obliged. "So I'm up against some real Moral Majoritarians here, am I?"

Swenson gasped out an apologetic little giggle. "Oh, way beyond that. A lot of our people have given up on believing the American people care about morality at all. As they see it, the country is so deep in sin that there's no hope left for godliness. They want to separate and dig in. They think you—the secularists—represent the enemy. And they think you've won. They claim that right-wing politics, even the churches, are in the grip of political correctness."

"They call it an alien ideology," Syl said, "like it wasn't even human."

"You're kidding."

"Not in the least," Swenson assured him. "The Christian Coalition, the Moral Majority, they use television, don't they? There are people on our faculty who have never seen a television show, won't let their kids watch—not even Sesame Street. They think the Teletubbies are pushing homosexuality and that Barney the dinosaur is the great serpent himself." He leaned in closer. "Our church—now this is strictly confidential—our school hasn't cooperated with the IRS for . . . well, for as long as I can remember. They won't deduct my taxes from my salary. They think the government is a secularist plot against God's people."

"How do they get away with that?" Silverman asked. "Not paying taxes."

"They just don't pay, that's all," Syl said. "Richard and I, we send our taxes in. But we're not supposed to. We're supposed to donate them to missionary work."

"Lots of folks in these parts don't pay taxes," Swenson added. "We have a lot of independent types hereabouts ready to head for the border if the black helicopters ever arrive. I guess the government doesn't want to make too much rumpus about it."

"Disney," Syl said darkly. "They hate Disney."

"Right," Swenson agreed. "They think Disney is a cultural Marxist plot. MTV too. Television, movies, computer games, that's what we spend most of our time talking about now. And I must say that Syl and I tend to agree. TV is pretty vile. I don't know if you see it that way."

"I do have my limits, believe it or not," Silverman answered. "I think I'd agree. Vile, yes, extremely vile. Of course, I'd be more sensitive to sins of the intellect. I discovered a few years back that there wasn't anything I could think up for one of my novels that was more shocking than what you can hear people talking about on Oprah any day of the week. So I gave up trying. You know, the hardest thing these days—if you're any kind of artist—is to create something truly fine. By which I mean, at the very least, not dumb, not ugly, not crass. But that's getting off on an aesthetic tangent here."

Swenson picked up where he had left off. "So you can understand, then, as the more conservative wing of our church sees it, my worst offense is that I've been leading the charge for a television ministry. If it were up to them, they'd just as soon segregate themselves from the world and wait for the Rapture."

"Rapture? Sounds vaguely sexual." Silverman was trying his best not to seem frivolous.

"Oh, no. They mean the end of the world. The second coming. The apocalypse."

"The day of judgment," Syl added somberly.

"That's called Rapture?" Silverman asked.

"The Rapture is what the righteous will experience," Syl said, "just before the tribulation begins."

"Syl," Swenson said in an admonishing tone.

"Well, maybe not *just* before." Syl made the correction sheepishly.

Swenson turned to Silverman to explain. "Most of our congregation leans toward a mid-trib position."

Silverman shook his head as if he'd taken a hard punch. "Mid-trib?"

"Mid-tribulation as opposed to pre-trib or post-trib."

"Forty-two months," Syl added.

"Right," Swenson said. "Forty-two months into the tribulation. That's when Reverend Apfel believes the Rapture will happen, though of course nobody can pretend to know for sure."

"And then what?" Silverman asked.

"We, or the saved among us, will be swept up to eternal bliss, while all the rest of the human race—maybe members of your own family—are condemned to damnation."

"And you don't find that sort of severe?"

Syl bit her lip. "Well, yes. But, you see, damnation is what we deserve—that's how we're taught."

"Deserve? Who could deserve eternal damnation? I mean, well, Hitler maybe, or Attila the Hun."

"Oh, that's not how the church sees it." She dropped her voice to a near whisper. "When I was six years old, I remember this Christmas sermon our minister preached. Reverend Arnoldson was his name. First he asked us kids what present we thought we should give little baby Jesus on his birthday. So we each thought up something like toys or nice clothes. But Reverend Arnoldson shook his head. Then he said, 'You have already given baby Jesus his present.' And he held up a picture of Jesus on the cross. And he said, 'Here is your present to Jesus. Your sins nailed him to that cross.' I went home and I cried all day thinking about what I did to little baby Jesus." Silverman waited, wondering if she was going to cry again. She seemed solemn enough to be near tears. But instead she brightened. "That's why the Rapture is so beautiful to think about. It makes everything else that ever happened seem so small and unimportant. At least that's how our church explains it. Only I don't know. Shouldn't life mean more than that? I don't think God would have put us through so much tribulation if all that mattered was one big blast of joy."

"One big blast of joy," Silverman mused. "That's interesting. I have friends in San Francisco who talk that way about Ecstasy. That's a drug. A controlled substance. You bliss out and that's all that matters. Never tried it myself. Have you?"

Syl gulped. "Me? Us? Oh heavens, no." Then, blushing, she giggled. "We did have some Coca-Cola once, last time we were in Minneapolis."

Silverman registered mock disapproval. "Your secret is safe with me. So when exactly is this Rapture supposed to happen? Not before the Superbowl, I hope."

Swenson looked desperate. "I know this must seem pretty strange to you."

"Would you mind if I said it sounds absolutely zany? What else can you expect me to say? You did ask me here as a Jewish Humanist, right?"

Swenson's voice was now down to a near-whisper. "I think it's zany too. So does Syl. We think it's crazy. But I've lived with it all my life. It *is* my life. My parents were deacons of the most conservative evangelical congregation in western Minnesota." He swallowed hard as if he were about to make an agonizing confession. "I was taught that Jews—I hope you'll forgive me telling you this—that Jews don't descend from Adam."

Silverman found this an intriguing statement. "Of course, I'm not sure about that myself—me being so secular and all. But does that mean your parents believed Jews descended from, oh say, primates by way of evolution?"

Swenson's eyes noticeably popped. "That would have been so unthinkable that, well, nobody would even think it. What I was taught was that Jews were descended from Eve after the temptation."

Silverman thought that over. "Well, that's not so bad. I'll bet Eve was a very nice lady. I always had a pretty good opinion of her, especially after the temptation."

Swenson hastened to correct him, again in a heavy whisper. "No, no. What they believed, my parents, was that Jews descended from Eve and the serpent."

"Hm," Silverman said, having no idea what to make of this news. "I guess that's meant to be insulting."

"My God! It's like saying Jews aren't even of the human species." Looking sincerely contrite, Swenson added, "I hope I haven't hurt your feelings."

Silverman shrugged. "Well, there's a sense in which all this Biblical stuff is pretty academic for me. But I get the point."

"So you see when I went over to the Free Reformed Evangelicals in college, that was as good as apostasy as far as my folks were concerned."

Swenson was making big startled eyes at Silverman. "That's bad, eh? Apostasy?"

"It's hell and damnation."

"No."

"Really. Evangelicals take pride in believing in the reality of hell. 'Into the furnace of fire with wailing and gnashing of teeth.' Matthew, 13:42. It's one of the first things you learn."

Gnashing of teeth. That phrase always got to Silverman. It made him wonder when he had last seen his dentist. Given the precarious state of his own dentition, that was as vivid an image as he needed of perdition: an eternity of root canals. "Wow," he said, "that's strong stuff."

"Especially when it comes to, you know, well, you know." Swenson exchanged a glance with Syl. Syl's brow folded into a deep frown.

"Yeah," she said. Then looking shyly at Silverman, "Sex."

Silverman nodded gravely. "Oh, yeah, that."

"Ever since college," Swenson went on, "I've been inching toward liberalism, hoping I could broaden the school and the church about . . . that. But it isn't easy. I'm viewed with such suspicion for even hinting at the possibility of drafting a Welcoming and Affirming Statement." Silverman looked blankly from Swenson to Syl. "That's for, you know. . . ." Swenson began.

Syl supplied the rest. "Homosexuals."

"Right," Swenson said. "I mean even the Baptists, well, some of them, have a Reconciling in Christ movement for their gay parishioners."

Reconciling in Christ. That was one of those phrases. Like the Pledge of Allegiance, it came across in Silverman's ear like squeaky chalk on a blackboard, leaving his teeth set on edge. "Whoa," Silverman said. "I'm supposed to help reconcile people with Christ?"

"Not 'with' Christ. *In* Christ."

"In, out, with, over, under, between. Come on, Richard. You're asking me to help you bring the sexual revolution to North Fork?"

"No, that's not exactly why I asked you to come."

"I wonder if you're sure why you did ask me. Maybe you've been reading my books upside down."

Swenson stared at him like a man biting his tongue, trying as hard as he could to keep from speaking. Instead, Syl spoke up. When she lost the big, toothy grin, she actually looked sort of pretty. In Silverman's system of feminine beauty, that took about fifteen inches off her height. She reached out to put a hand on his arm. "Richard does need you here. *We* need you, believe me." That was so sweet. It made him feel vaguely heroic, even though, as far as he could tell, he didn't share an inch of common ground in life with Syl or Swenson. Silverman wondered when he had ever seen such a sincere expression of need and gratitude. No, he didn't understand what lay behind it, but he did believe her.

"Well, as I said, I'll do the lecture. But remember: it's in and out for me." As they were getting ready to leave the table, Silverman turned to Syl. "Any chance I could take a few of those biscuits and some muffins along for later today?"

Syl lit up. "Oh sure. I'll pack you up some things. I made cookies too. Chocolate chip and walnut. Would you like some of those?"

"You betcha."

6

When Your Peewee Is All Wrong

Back in his room, Silverman shaved and dressed for the day ahead. Preparing for events like this always posed a challenge. For some groups—universities, book clubs especially those with lots of women—he usually let his beard go to two day's growth. That was his hard-working-no-nonsense-author look. It created the impression he had rushed in from laboring over his latest manuscript, a rumpled, hard-bitten got-to-get-back-to-the-trusty-old-Underwood-before-the-inspiration-fades writer who had no time to care for anything as trivial as personal appearance. People usually liked authors to be crusty and cantankerous, still linked to an antique cultural style called "literacy." Actually, the trusty old Underwood was long gone from his life, abandoned soon after his second novel. But when asked, "Do you use a word processor?"—the question that came up next most often after "where do you get your ideas?"—he pretended to cling to his typewriter. It sounded colorfully idiosyncratic. And so, too, the look of a typewriter-loyal man of letters: no tie, uncombed hair, coffee-stained slacks. In such circles, scruffy was the official uniform of literary genius. Normally, he was much more fastidious about his grooming; Marty, a stickler for haircuts and pressed trousers, insisted on that. Silverman decided that was probably the best way to go today. With these more bucolic types, stubble would likely consign him to the category of "bum." So he went to work with his razor.

As he lathered away, he held the Swensons before his mind's eye for critical inspection. They weren't really such bad people—for Christians. If the others he was to meet were no worse, he'd get through the day unscathed. Now that he thought about it, the

Swensons were the only real Christians he had ever met. Well, there was Sally Weeks, his neighbor who worked for Planned Parenthood. Sally had once been a nun, but she claimed to have lost her faith. When it came to actual, flesh-and-blood, believing Christians, the Swensons were it. Maybe that's why they were holding his interest.

Of course most of the people he knew—those who weren't Jews—were probably some kind of nominal Christian. Or so he assumed. He never asked, and they never told, but Christianity was the country's default religion, wasn't it? Only what exactly did that mean—giving gifts at Christmas, having a champagne brunch on Easter? As far as he could tell, nominal Christians were as secular as he was, good people, but not God-fearing. He couldn't imagine any of his friends praying; he certainly couldn't imagine them worrying over hell and damnation. He did have rather a large number of acquaintances in San Francisco who identified themselves these days as Buddhists, but he had never taken them all that seriously. He assumed that claiming to be a Buddhist was nothing more than dinner-party persiflage. Buddhists liked to tell you where they had "sat" last week and where they were going to "sit" next week. "Sitting" meant meditating, which, as Silverman understood it, meant doing nothing at all. Why Buddhists had to go on distant retreats to do their nothing was more than he could fathom. Most likely it was all high-priced goofing off. Retreats seemed to involve long plane trips to places he imagined being pricey spas. Sitting at an expensive spa and eating health foods hardly qualified in his eyes as a dark night of the soul. It seemed more like a way to lose weight.

The Swensons, on the other hand—or at least Richard—seemed to be honestly suffering for their faith. Suffering was something Silverman could take seriously. Poor kids! They were young and earnest, struggling to find their own identity in life. Except for their terminal mediocrity, they might have qualified in the same category with some of Silverman's heroes—like James Joyce, fighting his way out from under a stifling church in the name of his art. "Silence, cunning, and exile." Joyce had called those his only weapons. Silverman had always liked that phrase. Sadly, it would never suit the Swensons. They surely weren't cunning or silent.

And, instead of going into exile like the great artist, here they were hopelessly stuck up to their necks in theological horseshit.

As odd a couple as the Swensons were, Silverman was surprised to discover how easy it was for him to sympathize with their plight. All he had to do was call his grandfather to mind. Grandpa Zvi, his father's father, had been the great ogre of his childhood, a sour-pussed, snaggle-toothed old man who always smelled moldy. Grandpa Zvi never looked, he glared; he never spoke, he ranted. He was the family's most fiercely orthodox member—earlocks, phylacteries, and all. He spent more time in the synagogue than he did earning a meager living as a Hebrew teacher. He even forced his wife to go bald and wear a wig, which Silverman, as a boy, had regarded as barbaric.

Relations between Grandpa Zvi and Silverman's father had been a lifelong running battle. The son, rebelling against his father's bullying, had, in his late teens, become as fanatically Marxist as Grandpa Zvi was fanatically orthodox. Things became so bitter between them that at one point, when Silverman was six, Grandpa Zvi had cursed his son, yes cursed him. That had happened after a terrific row. Oh, how the house had trembled with the fury of that epic altercation! Silverman still remembered his father screaming through the walls, "Speak English, damn it! This is America, you crazy old bug! Don't expect me to understand that stupid ghetto babble!" To which Grandpa Zvi had on this occasion responded, not in his usual Yiddish, but with an explosive stream of Hebrew, a great, boiling, guttural torrent. *Hebrew*: God's language, as young Daniel had come to believe. Though his father had done all he could to indoctrinate him with militant atheism, as a boy Silverman was secretly haunted by the dread possibility that Grandpa Zvi, with his close-set, piercing eyes and uncanny prophetical air, might be on to something. Maybe there was a God. Maybe He was always up there watching. Maybe all the smelly old Hebrew books that lined the shelves of his grandfather's room bespoke mysteries of the universe that his father was too stubborn to learn. There was always that chance.

Silverman was absolutely sure that the day his father was cursed was a decisive moment in his own young life. He remembered the

incident vividly. His father had emerged from Grandpa Zvi's bedroom in the basement of their home, slamming the door behind
him. Then he had stared in tongue-tied silence at his wife and
young Daniel, a wild, frightened expression stretched across his
face. "He *cursed* me," he reported. "My own father. The worst possible curse. 'May your son disgrace you one hundred times over.'"
Turning suddenly, he glared into little Daniel's face. "Do you hear
that? Well, is that what you intend to do? Speak up!" Little Daniel,
too shocked to know what to say, concluded that the best answer
might be to giggle, as if perhaps this were all some joke the grown-
ups were playing. So he giggled, a small, hesitant giggle, but a
giggle nonetheless. To which his father responded as he never had
before or would again afterwards. He raised his hand to slap the
boy. "You see that?" he shouted. "He thinks it's funny."

Before the elder Silverman could decide what to do with his
uplifted hand, his wife intervened. "You take that seriously, a
curse?"

"Me?" the father shouted, now at top volume. "Of course not!
Such mumbo-jumbo, I laugh in its face. Ha!"

"Then why get mad at Danny?" she asked, the voice of pure
Cartesian reason. "He's laughing already."

"At the curse, I laugh. Ha! But at disgracing his father, the son
shouldn't laugh."

Unbeliever though Silverman's father was, Grandpa Zvi's repri-
mand never ceased to make a big difference to him. For days, he
remained visibly shaken. But what had they—the father and
grandfather—been arguing over so furiously? That was the
shocker. Staring down at Daniel, Silverman's father had finally explained, "It's *you*! That superstitious old *vontz* refuses to accept
you." Astonished, little Daniel had asked, "Me? Why?" He
shouldn't have asked. The answer was jolting. "It's your pee-wee.
He says your pee-wee is all wrong."

Then the story came out. It had to do with the *bris*.

When Silverman was born, his father, as an act of defiance, had
refused to hold a *bris*. Worse, he had sent out announcements—or
rather anti-announcements—to every member of the family saying
that there would *not* be a *bris*. His father had decided to preclude

all possibility of a *bris*. So ill-informed was the elder Silverman about his faith that he believed he could make sure that nobody, not even young Daniel, could ever reverse this decision. His announcement proudly stated that the *bris* had been preempted by modern hygiene. Yes, there had been a cutting of the foreskin, but in such a way that the son of David Silverman would remain forever not a Jew, at least when it came to the state of his penis. The deed had been done by a doctor—a *schiksa* doctor named Phyllis O'Malley, no less—as nothing more than a casual surgical snip. "My son Daniel," the father declared, "has been circumcised for health, not mumbo-jumbo. Unless my son grows another foreskin, this act is irrevocable."

From Grandpa Zvi's viewpoint this meant that young Daniel wasn't a member of the tribe. "He cannot enter the fold," the old man lamented, never missing an opportunity to throw this offense up to his son or to glare balefully at little Daniel as if he were a veritable Philistine. But on one point, Silverman's father had miscalculated. There is, in fact, no way to eliminate the possibility of a *bris*. Even on his death bed, Daniel Silverman could be circumcised. "There is always something to cut," Grandpa Zvi informed his son with a triumphant cackle. "Always something, even that much you can pinch between your fingers. And he will be brought into the fold. As long as there is blood, as long as there is pain, there is a b*ris*."

Silverman remembered his father fuming. "Like a vampire, the *alter kocker* wants blood. We are living with Count Dracula. These maniacs will cut, even if they cut too much."

Thereafter, Silverman heard the status of his foreskin debated so often and so heatedly that until the age of twelve he was convinced that religion was all about mutilating genitals for the greater glory of Jehovah. It didn't help that his father had sought to calm his fears by telling him, "If it were up to your crazy *zeyde*, he would have you kidnapped in the middle of the night so some witch-doctor could chop your pee-wee. Believe me, he lays awake at night thinking up ways to get his superstitious claws on you. But don't worry. I'll never let that happen, never, if I have to fight to the death."

After that, little Daniel never went to bed at night without checking to see if this witch-doctor was lurking in the street below his window. To this day, he knew that in some dark sub-basement of his unconscious, he still believed that God was a cosmic monitor. And what was He monitoring? He was keeping an eye on your dick—and boy, it better look right.

In the years that followed this traumatic occasion, even as Daniel grew more wary of his grandfather, his relations with the old man actually became closer. At age ten, during those intervals when his grandfather and father were on hostile terms and wouldn't eat in one another's company—which was never less than months at a time—young Daniel was given the unwelcome assignment of taking his grandfather's meals to his basement quarters on a tray. He would have preferred to knock and leave the food, but his instructions were to deliver the tray politely into *zeyde's* hands. The grandfather never quite thanked him, though he sometimes mumbled something that might have been a faint word of gratitude. What he invariably did was to study the boy from under his wild, dark eyebrows with a despairing gaze, sometimes wagging his head sadly. Then once, as if he couldn't hold back any longer, he reached out to tousle Daniel's hair. In the English he rarely spoke and with a gentleness the boy had never heard before, he invited Daniel into his room. "Come," he said. "Come, come, come. I don't gonna eat you."

Daniel entered, hoping the door would stay open behind him. No such luck. Grandpa Zvi closed it, then stood with his back against it. The room had a musty, used-up odor to it as if the air had long since congealed into one funky block never to move again. "Now I gonna show you somet'ing," Grandpa Zvi announced. He asked Daniel to seat himself on the edge of his bed; then he took a heavy volume from one of the bookshelves and laid it open between them. "Dis," the grandfather said in a solemn tone, "is de Talmud. Never your father told you about dis, right?" Slowly he leafed through the pages of the book. Daniel watched a procession of black characters going by, crazy shapes that looked to Daniel like insects, but which nevertheless possessed a certain stern authority. Hebrew. The oldest language in the world, the language God spoke on the day of creation, or so Daniel assumed. "Is

it not beautiful?" his grandfather asked. "Even you don't understand, Talmud is beautiful. Glorious. Never you gonna see a book
like dis anyplace in de voild."

There were tears in Grandpa Zvi's eyes as he spoke. His nose
began to run. "Your father, he t'inks I am an old fool. But did he
never give me the chance to teach him? Maybe you vould like to
loin? You see?" He pointed out various letters with his wrinkled
forefinger. "*Aleph*. Dat's the foist letter. Now, maybe you can find
aleph all by yourself somevheres? Eh?" Nudging Daniel in the ribs,
Grandpa Zvi moved his crooked old finger to point at the letter he
wanted the boy to find.

Following the finger, Daniel gazed across the page and spotted
another *aleph*. He pointed to it. Grandpa Zvi clapped his hands in
jubilant celebration. "You see how easy? A *talmid khochem* you
could be." As he put the volume back on the shelf, the old man actually did a little dance step. The young Silverman couldn't remember seeing his sour-pussed grandfather so happy.

That evening at dinner he asked—oh so very casually—"Daddy,
what's a *khochem*?"

With a puzzled expression his father answered. "A *khochem*? A
genius-type. Like Einstein. Not you."

"Oh?" his mother interjected at once. "And how would you
know? Do you ever look at his school work, you're so busy?"

"What? We have an Einstein at the table?"

"He wrote a nice story for his English teacher. About a cat."

"We don't own a cat. What would he know about cats?"

"He used his imagination, what's the trouble?"

With mock sincerity, his father bowed over his soup bowl to
Daniel. "I'm so sorry, Professor Einstein. Where do you hear words
like this anyway? Have you been talking to your grandfather?"

"No. I heard it at school. Could you pass the potatoes?"

Following little Daniel's spectacular success finding *aleph*,
Grandpa Zvi began to invite him into his room regularly to look at
his copy of the Talmud. The old man did this with a furtiveness as
if the two of them were planning to hold up a bank. Each time he
taught Daniel one more Hebrew letter. He would point out a letter,
then ask Daniel to find that same letter elsewhere on the page.

Then over again, the same exercise, never more than one letter at a time. How dumb does he think I am, the young Silverman wondered. Can't we ever do two letters or even three—maybe a whole word? But invariably, Grandpa Zvi would yip with pleasure when Daniel found the next *beth, gimel, daleth.* He would give the boy a big, sloppy kiss on the top of his head and praise the brilliance of his little *mazik.* But even ten-year-old Daniel realized that at this rate it would take five-hundred years before he could read anything in Hebrew. And that wasn't the only problem. Grandpa Zvi's breath was pretty hard to take, a rancid aroma of bad teeth and onions. Years later, he was still able to recall the smell; in his sensuous recollection, it became intertwined with religion in general, the odor of piety—harsh, old, and sickly.

At last, Silverman's clandestine tutorials with his grandfather came to a sad end. On the day little Daniel reached *gimel,* his grandfather, with a sly wink, asked "A yeshiva boy you vould like to be maybe?" Daniel smiled politely, but shuddered inwardly. Yeshiva boys, the serious ones who dressed the part, were a familiar sight in the Bronx neighborhood where Silverman grew up. All the non-Jewish kids made wisecracks about them. In truth, Daniel himself thought they looked weird, with the funny hair and the hats. Grandpa Zvi was clearly taking this little alphabet game too seriously. He was turning Daniel into a pawn in the household battle between Daniel's father and himself. He was interpreting every letter Daniel learned as a secret victory over his son. Daniel had no choice. He had to terminate his budding career as a Talmudic scholar. He came up with a ruse. After learning to find the letter *teth,* Daniel unaccountably lapsed into Hebraic dyslexia. He began pointing to all the wrong letters. Even *aleph* he could no longer find. Told to find *aleph* he deliberately pointed to every other letter until he had made twenty-one mistakes, the most possible. Then he said, "Maybe there's no *aleph* on this page."

His grandfather gazed at him in wide-eyed amazement. "How you can forget *aleph?* Vot's de matter, you lost your brains?"

"It's hard, *zeyde,*" Daniel insisted with a pathetic whine. "I can't remember, it's so hard. All the letters look alike."

"Dey look alike? How can dat be? Every letter is different dat

ain't de same. Don't you see vit your own eyes? Look, see. *Aleph*—
de foist letter of all."

Daniel twisted himself into a small pretzel of protest. "It doesn't
look like the first letter. The first letter should look like A."

Grandpa Zvi was thunderstruck. "*Aleph* should look like A? Vy
it should look like A? Vhich you t'ink came foist? Don't you know,
aleph is as old as God, blessed be His name. T'ousands of years dere
vas *aleph* before dere vas A."

"I don't know. I get confused. It's too much to remember. It's
not like English where everything looks right."

Grandpa Zvi hunched over and buried his head in his hands.
Under his breath he was saying something, maybe a prayer for the
little Jewish boy who couldn't even learn *aleph*. Daniel could see Hebrew characters ascending from his grandfather's head like ominous black smoke as he prayed. This was a very mean trick he was
playing on the old man, but what choice did he have? If he ever so
much as mentioned yeshiva to his father, there would be an explosion heard round the neighborhood. Fortunately Grandpa Zvi
proved to be remarkably forgiving. "De Mickey Mouse ate up your
brains, dot's vot." He shrugged and sadly replaced the volume of
the Talmud on the shelf. Then bent with sorrow, he escorted Daniel
to the door. "Poor little *pisher*!" he muttered, patting Daniel's head.
"You vill be a *nebech*, a poor *nebech*, and all because. . . ." But he
never finished. With a tear in his eye, his grandfather turned away
and closed the door. As the door shut behind him, Daniel, though
he was no more than ten years old, knew he would remember what
he had done that day as one of the cruelest acts in his life.

Nebech, as he later learned, meant "nothing."

What if Grandpa Zvi had been Silverman's own father? Imagine being forced to recite all those prayers he never understood,
and to endure arcane rituals. Imagine never being able to order a
BLT for fear of angering God Almighty. So maybe that's what it
was like for the Swensons. They lived surrounded by a town full of
Grandpa Zvis, narrow-minded, vindictive people who stood ready
to condemn them for apostasy. That could be worse even than
Grandpa Zvi's curse. At least Jews didn't go on and on about fire
and brimstone.

Silverman finished his preparations for the day with a stinging slap of after-shave. Glancing one more time in the mirror, he said to his reflection, "I do not see myself. I do not know myself. I cannot look at myself truly. No one truly exists in the real world because no one knows all that he is to other human beings. "

He spoke the words, and then saw his face turn puzzled. This was indeed odd. These words were not his own, but another writer's. They came from a story. But what story? He cast his mind back and back until he reached his college years. Ah, yes. The quotation was from "America! America!" a story written in the 1930s by Delmore Schwartz. He hadn't thought about this piece of literature in years. The words were those of a character named Shenandoah Fish, Delmore Schwartz's literary alter-ego. For the life of him, Silverman had no recollection of memorizing these words, he had no idea they were rattling around in his head. But as he spoke them, he vividly remembered the effect Schwartz's tale of a troubled young writer had worked upon him when he first read it in college. Daniel Silverman, twenty years old at the time, had reached a significant conclusion. "I could say that same thing about myself. I also do not know myself. But that's got nothing to do with being a Jew. The way of the modern world is to lose one's inherited identity, to become a zero that must be filled in. And is not the art of our time grounded in that very loss and that filling-in? Of course, Schwartz couldn't see it that way, he being from another generation." Silverman took a moment to review this line of thought and, yes, he said to himself, that's still the way I feel.

As Silverman left the house with Swenson that morning, Syl handed him a good-sized brown paper bag. He glanced inside. It was packed with food: biscuits, jam jars, cookies. "Well, thank you," Silverman said. "But really, this is too much."

"Oh, if you get a little peckish on the plane home. There's a couple bottles of sarsaparilla that I made up last fall. Just in case."

"You won't be coming to the lecture?" Silverman asked.

"Gee, I'm real sorry," Syl apologized, "but Jessy's down with something. She's so cranky, I don't want her to interrupt things. But I know it's gonna be great."

Click! Suddenly and as unpredictably as ever, his mental camera took her picture. Someday, in a story he hadn't begun to imagine, Syl would become somebody's long-suffering wife or rejected girl-friend, a real American sweetheart. Silverman had a deeply in-grained dislike of any female big and strong enough to carry him off, but Syl was turning out to be a major exception. There was no question that she was the best thing that was going to come of this cold, hard journey. Syl was a *mensch*.

From the front yard of the Swenson home, Silverman could see the main buildings of the college among the trees across the lake. There were skaters on the lake and kids with sleds. Against the high banked snow and the fir trees, it might have been a scene from a greeting card. "If you'd brought your skates," Swenson told him, "we could make it across in ten minutes. With a Bloore, it wouldn't take five."

"A Bloore?"

"You betcha. Best snowmobile made anywhere. You can see the Snow Ghosts out there on the lake." He pointed toward a distant, thronging area of the ice. Several spluttering vehicles were cutting patterns in the white slopes above the frozen surface: circles, fig-ure-eights, ovals. Distantly, Silverman could hear the roaring mo-tors. "The Ghosts are our snowmobile squad, named after the company. We hope to see snowmobiling become an Olympic event. If it does, our precision team would be hot for the gold."

By snowmobile, five minutes. But by car twenty minutes, Swenson explained, "weather permitting." But the weather wasn't permitting that morning. Cutting cautiously through the last snowfall, the tire chains of Swenson's van nibbled away with a steady crunch, crunch, crunch. "Now, there's something I've saved to the last," Swenson said as he maneuvered his way around the lake. "I didn't want to mention it back at home because Syl would get her expectations up. I can't guarantee anything, but I have a promise from our state senator, Jake Dawes, that he'll make every effort to be here this afternoon. And if he is, I'm going to have him introduce you. I can't tell you how helpful he's been with the Reli-gious Humanism program. You can imagine how important it's been to have support from someone of his weight. Along with Mrs. Bloore, he's about as big a honcho—I guess she'd be a honcha, right?—as we have in these parts. Of course, like all politicians, he's got to stay connected with his voting base, which has turned pretty conservative. In fact, a good deal more conservative than some of us realized. This part of the state always had a strong farm and labor orientation; but in the 1992 elections, wow! the evangelicals really turned out the vote. It was the first time the Free Reformed Evangelical Brethren in Christ ever made political endorsements—ever. Dawes was one of eight candidates we helped elect. So he owes us a great deal."

Swenson guided the van through an intersection where there were a few clapboard farmhouses and some small stores—a Stop and Shop, a Laundromat, a feed mill with a high, weathered tower, and a saloon called the Paul Bunyan Tavern—the first sign of commercial life Silverman had spotted in the area. The outsized sign above the saloon featured badly drawn cartoons of the legendary woodsman and his blue ox. Swenson turned into a narrow side road. "This is—or rather, that *was* North Fork," Swenson announced as they cruised past the collection of stores.

"That's it?" Silverman asked, looking back.

"Yep. If it weren't for the postal substation in the feed store, North Fork might not officially exist. We're not that far from Flat Rock, which is about twelve miles further along. That's where we're hoping to take you for dinner. Best steak house in the county. Otherwise we're pretty isolated." Swenson carefully guided the van over a deeply rutted railroad crossing. "Train stopped running twenty years ago," he commented, as they bumped along at a crawl. Silverman peered down the crooked rails until they disappeared into a snow bank. There was something so desolate about the rusted and abandoned old tracks that he was overcome by a sense of nauseating depression. The last snowfall had blanked out the land in every direction, leaving it flat and featureless. The clumps of barren trees that poked up here and there out of the dead whiteness only made the vista seem more forlorn. The two or three solemn towers Silverman could make out in the distance probably had to do with farming. Grain elevators, silos, things like that. They looked antiquated and rickety. Perhaps they were as defunct as the railway. Even the ice-coated power lines that limped away over the horizon, drooping from pylon to pylon, looked as if they might be out of commission. No doubt about it, this was one dead end of a place. And despite the whirring heater in the van, Silverman could tell it was getting colder by the minute. He bent forward to study the sky through the windshield. Though it was only a little past noon, a gathering darkness hovered ominously overhead like the dirty sole of a gigantic boot that was about to squash everything in sight. *What am I doing here?* Silverman wondered. *Money* was all that leaped to mind, but suddenly money seemed like a shamefully bad answer to that question.

The road became bumpier as they headed over the tracks. "We call this the Bunyan to Bunyan road," Swenson said. Silverman returned a blank stare. "Paul Bunyan Tavern back there and John Bunyan up ahead. Do you know Bunyan, John I mean?"

"*Pilgrim's Progress?*" Silverman asked. He remembered the name from a freshman great books course. The old allegorical Christian epic that nobody reads anymore. As he recalled, three pages had been more than enough.

"It still tops our freshman reading list at Faith," Swenson told him. "Along with the Bible, of course. So the further we get from Paul and the demon drink back there at the junction, the closer we get to John and the Celestial City. An old campus witticism."

Swenson maneuvered the van around a huge frozen rut and back on to the narrow road. That took a lot of back-and-forthing. "I'm sure that by your standards," he resumed, "Jake Dawes might seem pretty right of center. But I have great hopes for him, great hopes You see, he's not a deep dispensationalist. He went to the university law school, which certainly broadened his horizons. He has as much as told me—*sub rosa,* of course—that anything I can do to help liberalize the evangelicals will not go unnoticed in his office. He agrees that conservatives are going to have to move with the times, especially on lots of women's issues. Trouble is: you don't move if you don't care about winning elections. And lots of evangelicals really don't. They want to be right and righteous. So Jake feels he can't make the first move. But I think he's prepared to soften the party line, if you know what I mean."

"No, tell me what you mean," Silverman said.

"The three Gs: God, guns, and gays."

"Oh, yes. And which of the Gs is he for and which of the G's is he against, respectively?"

"What? Oh! Very for. Very, very for. And very, very against. Which is what I guess you would expect. The gun clubs give him even more money than Mrs. Bloore. And of course there's abortion; Jake has had to be very tough on that."

"But otherwise he's a flaming radical."

"Well, no," Swenson laughed uneasily. "I wouldn't say that. But he's been moving in a relatively, more or less, comparatively, surprisingly liberal direction. Without his support, I could've never gotten the Religious Humanism program off the ground."

"But he couldn't help you get Gore Vidal here last year, right?" Silverman asked.

"It was an awkward decision."

"Not because of *Burr* or even *Myra Breckinridge*."

"Oh, that did play a part. I mean. . . ."

"But there was something that mattered more."

"Well, yes. But quite honestly, can you see Gore Vidal lecturing here?"

"Sure. For twenty-thousand dollars. I can even see myself lecturing here for considerably less."

"So that's okay with you, then, if Jake introduces you? He asked to do it himself."

"He did? I wonder why."

"You see, Jake is our local fair-haired boy. He has his eye on Congress in the next election—probably the Senate—so he wants to get in good with the Israel lobby."

"Oh, well in that case, what can I say? I'll be sure to put in a good word for him next time I'm in Jerusalem."

Silverman was making light, but he inwardly flinched. On the subject of Israeli politics, a matter he could remember being argued in his family to the point of fist-fights, he had chosen his course in life carefully. He was a *nebech*, a total and deliberate know-nothing. Perhaps genetically he had inherited his father's stance. "If you want to be an Israeli patriot, go. Fight. But keep it to yourself." His father's "leave-me-out" position was based, like so much else in his life, on a rejection of all things paternal. Whatever Grandpa Zvi might be for, the elder Silverman was against and outspokenly so. "If the Lord God Almighty exists and if He wants to promise his people a piece of real estate, why not the French Riviera? Why a piece of dried-up desert, who'd buy it for a nickel?" Sentiments like this had left Silverman's father ostracized by aunts and uncles, brothers and sisters in all directions.

Silverman's motivation for adopting his father's views was different. He fancied himself an artist, a man above politics, especially tough, nasty, violent politics. Besides, that haughty moral posture was nicely compatible with the physical cowardice that came naturally to him. If you belong to a persecuted people, why gather in one place and become an easy target? Better off with the diaspora. Scatter in all directions. Surely none of this would come up today. How much trouble need he expect on such matters in an assembly of Gentiles?

But there was something in what Swenson said that nagged at his memory. That name—Dawes. At all points east of San Francisco Bay, Silverman's political savvy shaded off sharply, but he was pretty sure he had heard the name Dawes at rallies and demonstrations back home. Determined to rise above politics, he left demonstrations to Marty, who enjoyed attending anything big, noisy, and crowded. What he remembered was a Dawes who had been barnstorming the country in behalf of the Family Protection Amendment. If the amendment ever passed, it would officially define marriage as heterosexual and require homosexuals to keep four miles away from all children below the age of twelve—or something like that. "The Family Protection Amendment, right?" Silverman asked. "This is *that* Dawes?"

"Yes, it is," Swenson answered as if he were unburdening himself of a great guilty secret. "I wouldn't have thought you kept track."

"Richard, you're a lucky man. I may, in fact, be the only person you could have found in the San Francisco Bay Area who wouldn't spit in Mr. Dawes' eye from across the room."

Swenson had the odd habit of flinching with exaggerated embarrassment when he was caught out on a point like this. He squinted, grit his teeth, and hid behind one upraised shoulder as if to ward off a hard whack. Then he would give a sheepish grin and look out of the corner of his eye, begging more forgiveness than was necessary. Silverman had noticed him going through this routine three or four times now. It was an annoyingly childish reflex for a man his size. Had he perhaps had a lot of practice in being whacked? In any case, Silverman could predict what would follow. *Ouch!*

And "Ouch!" was what Swenson did say. "Should I have warned you about Jake?" he asked.

"Doesn't matter," Silverman answered with a casual air, trying hard to make it clear that, in his capacity as hired talk-and-run lecturer, he cared nothing about these local matters. "I'm actually not all that political. But if Mr. Dawes starts pushing his agenda, well, I might have some trouble restraining myself." Which was a lie. He couldn't remember the last time he had waded into a heavy political argument.

"Well, then, one more thing I should mention," Swenson added, coyly tip-toeing up to another awkward problem. "Mrs. Bloore."

"Yes?" Silverman sighed.

"She's sort of our matriarch around here—though she'd hate to hear anyone put it that way. She claims to be firmly in favor of womanly submission. You know, Colossians, 3:18."

"Are you people born knowing all these little parenthetical citations? Because I wasn't."

"Oh. Sorry. Dumb. Wrong testament."

"Any testament for that matter."

"'Wives, submit thee unto thine own husbands.' But I can't imagine Mrs. Bloore submitting to anybody short of gunpoint. You'll find her pretty outspoken. When she's staying at the school—she has her own suite here, private elevator and all—she expects lots of deference. And she gets it. Well, after all, she's our principal benefactor. She's rebuilt most of the campus over the last twenty years. And, of course, she endowed our lecture series. She insisted on meeting you before you spoke. A private audience. She'll try to tell you what to say—she does that with everybody. Please be as forbearing as you can. I'm sure the lecture you brought with you is great just as it is."

"And the lady's money comes from where? These little putt-putt runabouts we saw on the lake?"

"Oh, yes, indeed. Winter sports are very big these days," Swenson informed him. "And the Bloore Snow Ghost dominates the market. Before that, there was the Tomahawk Motorcycle." He seemed to be waiting for Silverman to give an "*Oh, wow!*" Silverman, knowing nothing about motorcycles except that he hated them, gave no oh, wow. "The Bloores made a fortune on the Tomahawk before they went over to snowmobiles. 'Hell on Wheels, One Devil of a Machine.'"

"What?"

"That was the Tomahawk company slogan. And 'hell on wheels' he sure was."

"Who was?"

"Big Burt Bloore. Quite a rascal. Hard-drinking, foul-mouthed, and a fearful womanizer. Truth is, Mrs. B. wasn't much better—at least to start with."

"Do tell."

"I shouldn't be gossiping like this."

"Gossip is my stock in trade," Silverman reminded him. "Some people think fiction is nothing more than pretentious gossip with the names changed."

"Well, nobody's supposed to know, but everybody does. When she was a girl, Mrs. B.—a minister's daughter, no less—was a holy terror. Raised in the church, but wild as they come. During the war—World War II, that is—there was an army base at Grand Forks over the state line. The fast girls from all the surrounding towns used to haunt the place in those days. That's where the future Mrs. B. met Burt. They had one of those high-speed wartime romances—lasted all of two days—and wound up married a couple hours before he was due to ship out. She was barely old enough to make it legal."

"Ah, ha. So the pious lady was, as my Grandpa Zvi would have said, a *tsatske*."

"Pardon."

"A hot number."

Swenson pulled a worried face. "Oh, please, don't breathe a

word of that to anyone," he pleaded.

"Never fear, Richard. I'm trying to make North Fork as interesting as I can."

"Oh, I see. Well, given the cad Big Burt turned out to be, it's a wonder he came back looking for her after the war, but he did. It was a bad marriage from the word go. Years of pitched battles. Meanwhile, he got rich on the Tomahawk, and then on the Snow Ghost. But the richer he got, the more devilish he got. He supposedly had girlfriends stashed away in cities all over the country—including San Francisco. When she'd had her fill of the man, Mrs. B. came running back to the church like a fallen woman looking for forgiveness—and went on to be (now, this is strictly confidential) the most unforgiving soul I have ever met. She's been taking her guilty conscience out on everybody in the church ever since. Sorry, I know that sounds judgmental. I really have no right. . . ."

"Please, be my guest," Silverman said.

"The marriage was bound to come to a bad end. And it did. One night Big Burt got drunk as a skunk, next morning they found him dead of exhaust fumes in his own garage. He was lying pinned under his favorite old Tomahawk. Must have fallen into a stupor, tinkering with it. That was twenty years ago. Well, the long and short of it is, Mrs. B.'s been giving her husband's money to the church ever since he passed on. That is, all the money she could keep his four or five illegitimate children from getting hold of. Giving to the church was a sort of posthumous revenge, I guess. Only there's more money than she can give away. If you're in the market for a good investment, it's Bloore."

"Thanks. You actually make the woman sound interesting—at least from my corrupted novelist's point of view. I look forward to meeting her."

"I'll try to make it as painless as I can for you. But please don't let her upset you."

After about a half mile of silence, Silverman asked, "Was Mrs. B. at home the night he cashed in?"

"Hm?"

"Big Burt—the night he died?"

"Oh yes."

"She found the body?"

"Yes, she did. And never shed a tear, I understand. I've heard her call that the day of her deliverance."

• • • • •

The school, as it came into view at the end of a long double row of snow-cloaked, barren trees, was more impressive than Silverman had expected: a collection of imposing, many-gabled brick buildings centered on the campus chapel. Back in earthquake country, brick architecture of this magnitude was non-existent. "That's where the lecture will be," Swenson informed him as he parked the car. "You'll speak from the pulpit." No doubt this was intended as an honor, but it was lost on Silverman. He shuddered inwardly at the possibility that he might be surrounded by images of the weeping virgin and the crucified Christ. Did Evangelical Brethren go in for things like that? He hoped not. He hoped their tastes ran to iconoclastic austerity. Even so, he knew what Grandpa Zvi would say were he alive to hear that his grandson had preached to the Gentiles under the sign of the cross. "Dot's vot happens ven you don't chop the pee-wee right."

Making their way across the central courtyard toward the faculty residence—the name above the entrance was Gundersen Hall—Silverman felt the morning air crisping around him. The cold sliced through his raincoat, lining and all, as if he were wearing no more than a tee-shirt. Swenson, his words turning to vapor as they sailed from his mouth, was pointing out things about the campus, the men's dorm, the women's dorm, the gym, the student union. Apparently the chapel was an authentic historical monument, the highest steeple between someplace and someplace. Silverman was paying no attention. His eyes were searching the sky overhead. He didn't like what he saw, not one bit. The black and purple clouds now seemed so ominously close to the ground that Silverman wanted to stoop beneath their weight. "It's absolutely not going to snow, is it?" he asked Swenson as if he were issuing a command.

"You can never be sure. There was a hard blow last night over

Winnipeg. We often inherit their weather. Don't worry. They keep the Founder's Suite good and toasty."

But that wasn't what Silverman had on his mind.

Gundersen Hall was a rambling, renovated mansion, probably one of the great private homes of its day, displaying the sort of Robber Baron splendor that not even billionaires could afford any longer. But the splendor had turned somber and musty with age. Steeped in shadows, the high ceiling of the foyer seemed as low and oppressive as the lid of a tomb. The large windows that lined the balcony overhead were heavily draped. Perhaps that was for insulation, but it left the interior in a suffocating Gothic gloom. Silverman could make out what seemed like sumptuous chandeliers far overhead, but none were turned on. The only light in the hall came from the sconces along the corridor, dim lights in candle-flame shaped bulbs. As Silverman and Swenson crossed the floor and turned up the broad main staircase, the century-old boards underfoot groaned in an almost vocal protest. It was a sound that always froze Silverman's blood. "Like stepping on sick mice," he remarked more to himself than his companion.

"Like what?" Swenson asked, stopping to glance behind him.

"The stairs. Like . . . stepping . . . on. . . . Oh, skip it."

"Oh. The sound of tradition," Swenson suggested, and then began a small lecture on the various woods that had been used to build the campus. "This floor was made from the last stand of native maple to be found in this part of the state. They actually had to skimp on the staircase. Under the carpeting, it's cottonwood, which tends to buckle. Fact is even the cottonwood was gone by the time. . . ."

Silverman stopped listening. He had decided that, given half a chance, Swenson could qualify as the most boring man in the world.

The Founder's Suite, one flight up from the entrance hall, was surprisingly elegant. Furnished with overstuffed furniture, potted palms, and sumptuous drapes, it might have been a museum exhibition for the age of Grover Cleveland. The bed was a canopied heirloom ornately carved, heaped with embroidered silk cushions and patchwork quilts. There were still wrought-iron gas jets protruding from the wall; the electric lighting had been grafted into them and into the spreading crystal chandelier overhead. The room was indeed toasty, thanks to a well-laid fire that was sizzling away in a large stone hearth.

"This is the oldest building on campus," Swenson explained. "It's an architectural landmark, but a bit of a scandal actually. It was built back in the days of the Big Woods by one of the state's timber millionaires as a home for his mistress. If you get enough light on it, you can see a little token of their mutual affection. See, there." Swenson was pointing into a darkened corner up under the canopy. "The ornate little heart carved there and the angels? You can't read the letters from here, but it says 'C.B. + N. M.' That's Clive Benchley and Nadine Mircheson. If it were any more visible, I suspect the whole bed might have been burned by Benchley's widow. It is, after all, an emblem of infidelity. Benchley made the mistake of marrying a good, pious Norwegian girl. So when he died, Gerda, his wife, kicked the mistress out and donated the estate to our church. It was the Reverend Lucy's greatest coup."

"Reverend Lucy?"

"Ah, you'll meet her in a moment. Downstairs in the lobby."

"Well embalmed, I hope," Silverman said.

Swenson flashed a playful grin. He moved quickly to stash Silverman's bag in the closet, then, with a finger to his lips, summoned him over to reveal a secret. "I smuggled this in for you. I know you're only here for the overnight, but, well, if you need it. I didn't want us to seem too Spartan." He drew back a covering cloth to reveal a small television set at the back of the closet. "As I said, there are members of the faculty who won't have any truck with TV. Sets aren't permitted on campus, so do keep the sound down."

They were about to leave. But as Swenson opened the door into the hall, he leaped back, startled. On the other side of the door stood a large, stolid man blocking their way. He was carrying an armful of logs. Silverman was jarred as well. The man was glaring at him like a bird of prey. Silverman had never seen such fierce eyes. They stared out from beneath dark, ragged brows that were so tightly knit they must have been cramped permanently into place. The man's face, wrinkled and coarse and edged around with a chaotic beard, seemed frozen on the brink of a furious outburst. His sparse gray hair stood out in spikes around his skull, adding to his wild appearance.

"Oh, Axel," Swenson said by way of feeble greeting. "Come in," he added, standing back from the threshold. But his face was showing no welcome at all.

The man was so large he made Swenson look small. He stepped ponderously through the door, ducking to avoid the jamb. He wore a leather apron over work clothes and thick-soled boots that boosted his height by a couple of inches. For a long moment, he paused, his eyes burning a hole through Silverman. The look suggested he was sizing up a deadly enemy before battle. "This is Axel Hask," Swenson said. "Axel helps out," he added as if that explained something.

"Hello," Silverman said as cautiously as he could.

Axel said nothing. He lumbered across the room and set his load down beside the fireplace. Kneeling before the grate, he fitted a few more logs on the fire, then turned and, again pausing to scrutinize Silverman, departed.

"Axel helps out," Swenson said again. "Don't mind him."

"Was I supposed to mind him?" Silverman asked.

"I mean he's a bit dour."

"So I noticed."

"We're due in the commons room," Swenson said, ushering Silverman into the hall and back down the stairs. "But let's take a moment to say hello to Reverend Lucy." He led Silverman past a row of grim-faced portraits, all somber, clerical-looking males. The pictures segued from nineteenth-century etchings to oil paintings to photographs, but with never a smile to be seen. Instead every face seemed to be struggling to prove to God that, yes, I am a serious Christian, I am thinking of eternal hellfire. Ah, thought Silverman, the true first commandment: *Thou shalt not laugh, thou shalt not even snicker*. At the far end of the entrance lobby stood a larger-than-life bronze sculpture of a portly woman with a severe face, one hand holding out a Bible, the other raised with finger pointing skyward. The words carved below identified her as the Reverend Lucy Gundersen. Below that was the phrase: "I Shall Immerse."

"Our founder," Swenson explained.

"A woman?" Silverman was surprised.

"Oh, yes. Our denomination has always honored female discipleship. As it says in scripture, 'your sons *and your daughters* shall prophesy.' Acts, 2:17. Lucy Gundersen was quite an advanced lady. Far ahead of her time. She crusaded for breast-feeding—in public."

"Ah, did she?"

"Reverend Lucy always insisted that breast-feeding mothers occupy the first row of the church. The place of honor. And no skittishness about it. If the Lord wanted babies fed that way, there was no cause for shame."

"Well, good for Reverend Lucy."

"We like to say she was totally unbuttoned. She was arrested in Minneapolis for feeding her own children in public places. That's why she moved to North Fork. On the other hand, she could be pretty conservative. She was absolutely opposed to women's suffrage. You'll never guess why."

"Okay, why?"

"She believed women were naturally smarter than men. So if they got the right to vote, their smart votes would be offset by their husband's stupid votes. She preferred having women force their husbands to vote right. Then there would just be smart votes."

"An interesting lady. And I gather she was determined to immerse."

Swenson grinned. "Well, that was actually the issue on which the Free Reformed Evangelicals were established. Back then many Evangelicals had drifted away from total baptismal immersion. They thought it was unhealthy for the babies, especially in the winter. This is Minnesota, after all. But not Reverend Lucy. She insisted on full immersion, whether of babies or adults. And it had to be in a natural body of water. She even cut holes through the ice of Beaver Lake so she could baptize in the winter. Now that might lead you to suspect that Reverend Lucy was raised as a Baptist.

Well, you'd be right."

Swenson had finished on so gleeful a note, Silverman felt churlish to confess his flat disinterest. "You could fool me, Richard. The home I grew up in, Baptists, Lutherans, Episcopalians, it made no difference. They were all just another kind of Catholic."

Swenson chuckled feebly as if the remark must be a joke. "We were so lucky to have Reverend Lucy convert. Though when it comes to baptism, we've moved a long way since her day."

"Have you?"

"Now we leave it to the parents. And things are loosening up. Last year we had less than a half-dozen immersions. And none in the lake." In a whisper, he added, "People want heated water these days."

"Of course they do."

"So you see, if we can liberalize on an issue that was once foundational, well, why not on other things? Like, you know."

"Why not indeed?"

7

The Ambassador from Sin City

As he approached the open door of the commons room, Silverman could hear the low rumble of conversation. More than ever, he was feeling that sense of sickly dislocation he thought of as the loneliness of the long-distance lecturer. In another moment he would be in a room filled with strangers—very strange strangers in this case—making inane small talk about things of no real interest to him and soon to be forgotten. He would have to wear at least a semi-smile and repeat anecdotes he had told a hundred times in other rooms like this. People would want to know where he got his ideas, what book he was working on now, how many hours each day he spent writing, were his characters based on real people.

There was an out, but it was almost as painful. He had learned during his early years of travel that nine out of ten people he met on the road regarded his visit as an opportunity for them to talk, not him. They had hired a listener, not a speaker. So he did have the choice of laying back and letting his hosts hold forth. Any little question would do to elicit a disquisition on their project. And they all had projects, projects they had been pursuing longer than he had been writing. Do-good projects, political lobbying projects, community relations projects, gardening projects, church projects, clean-up-our-environment projects, education projects. . . . It was amazing how eager people were to talk about themselves. Even more amazing: how readily they assumed you wanted to hear all about them. Once you got them started, all you had to do was look politely inquisitive, hide behind whatever you were drinking, nod your head soberly every fourteen seconds and mutter "really," "how interesting," "I didn't realize," or "well, that's certainly impressive."

The stranger the audience, the safer it was to let them do the talking. Sometimes Silverman turned it all into a private game. At a conference of Jungian psychologists he had once managed to say nothing more than his name and a sincerely attentive "hm!" through a three-hour dinner party. In this case, he had already decided to stay as mute as he could. If everybody here were like Swenson, what did he have to tell them anyway? If he opened his mouth at all, he was apt to stick his foot in it.

Outside the commons room Swenson diverted Silverman toward three students, a girl and two boys, who were standing in the corridor. "These are my partners in crime," Swenson said under his breath. "Let me introduce you." He identified the three as his Religious Humanism committee. "To tell the truth, they had more to do with bringing you here than I did." The girl—Tilly—was small and plain with a face so narrow it might have been drawn on both sides of a sheet of paper. Her skin was so fair she seemed anemic. She wore blonde bangs long enough to mask her pale blue eyes, a style that made her seem all the more withdrawn. The boy beside her was small and dark with a rough thatch of black hair over his eyes. His name was Alex. Silverman shook his extended hand, but—there was no way he could help himself—his eyes went at once to the second boy who introduced himself as Jack. Tall enough to be a basketball player with magnificent shoulders and a head full of wild blonde curls, Jack was irresistibly gorgeous. Taking Silverman's hand, he returned exactly the shy smile that melted Silverman in his shoes. He was so entrancing Silverman had to remind himself that the boy was much, oh yes! much too young for him. Not that he really was by any prevailing San Francisco standards. The reminder was a little psychological device that he and Marty had agreed to use when temptation came calling.

"We're so honored to have you with us," the girl was saying. "We've read all your books. Well, all those we could find."

"We look forward to seeing you for dinner," Alex added.

"If the roads are still clear, that is," the girl added. "We're taking on a lot of weather."

"Are we?" Silverman asked vaguely. Even when he moved his eyes away from Jack, he was distracted by the boy's presence. He had to look again to see if he was really *that* beautiful. Yes, he was. It would be a pleasure sharing dinner with him even in a snowstorm.

As they broke up, the girl took Swenson aside to whisper, "He's *here!*" Swenson glowed. Promising the students he would meet them in the chapel, he quickly escorted Silverman into the luncheon.

The commons room might have been a cozy place for lunch. It was rich dark wood throughout with high mullioned windows and deep carpeting. There was a leaping fire in the hearth and a lavish buffet laid out on the large central table: whole hams, a roasted turkey, bowls of salad. But Silverman nearly shivered as he looked around. Every face he saw was frosted over with undisguised suspicion. This was going to be one tough audience. He at once secretly reminded himself: *You're doing it for the money. They've paid in advance.*

He hadn't taken more than three paces into the room when he caught sight of something that worried him more than the icy faces beginning to gather around him. High on the wall at the far end of the room was a scarlet banner bearing three large gold letters. JIW. Silverman stopped in his tracks to puzzle over its meaning. Could it be these people didn't know how to spell Jew? "What's that?" he asked Swenson, taking hold of his companion's arm to make him stop and look. "That's not for my benefit, is it?"

"What?" Swenson asked, looking around in alarm.

Silverman nodded toward the banner. "Jew, spelled with an i?"

"Ha!" Swenson laughed in surprise, then clapped his hand to his mouth. "That's a good one," he whispered as he guided Silverman deeper into the room. "What that is is sort of our school logo." He bent closer to mummer in Silverman's ear. "Jesus is watching." Silverman stared at him uncomprehending. "JIW. Jesus is watching. Mrs. Bloore made it up. It's her one big thing. She delivers a lecture to all the incoming freshmen every year, reminding them that Jesus is watching all the time, no matter where they are. So they better be careful. You'll see it all around the place, especially in the, you know, bathrooms. She has these little kits with JIW labels she gives us to stick wherever we go. We have a sort of reputation for that. Which reminds me." From behind his lapel Swenson retrieved a little red pin with the three gold letters on it. He affixed it to the front of his jacket. "Mrs. Bloore expects it," he explained somewhat sheepishly. "I'd offer you one, but I don't suppose. . . ."

For the first time, Silverman glared at Swenson, who mouthed a silent "ouch." *Jesus is watching. What a vile idea*, Silverman thought. Of course, he remembered Grandpa Zvi telling him that "God is alvays vatching over you." But "vatching over" wasn't the same as just watching. He was sure there was a distinction there.

Swenson made several quick introductions all around, a flurry of names that flowed past Silverman without leaving a trace. Professor so-and-so, Doctor so-and-so, a couple of reverends and deacons and their wives. Silverman shook hands and flashed a cut-rate version of his "glad-to-be-here" grin. As far as he could tell, everybody in the room was wearing little red and gold pins to remind one another who was watching. All the while Swenson was guiding him through the crowd, Silverman could hear one big laughing voice that blanketed the room. That was where Swenson was headed. "Lord! I'm so glad he showed up," he said to Silverman.

Jake Dawes stood surrounded by a small circle of admiring listeners. By the time Swenson reached him, he had already broken out in great guffaws several times, the sort of exaggerated public mirth that comes naturally to politicians. "Professor Silverman," Swenson said, "I'd like you to meet Jake Dawes, our State Senator. Thanks for being here, Jake."

"Always a pleasure, Dick," Dawes announced, as he reached out to clasp Silverman's hand. He was one of those big greeters who clutched your elbow while he shook your hand, as if he might be trying to unscrew your arm. "And so pleased to have you here with us today, Professor Silverman." As if a button had been pushed, Dawes' expression shifted from jovial to darkly pensive. "As I'm sure you know, Professor, I, along with the entire membership of Midwestern Allies of Israel, have been pressing our state congressional delegation to go on record expressing northern Minnesota's concern, our unwavering concern for enduring reconciliation in the Near East. After all, it's our Holy Land too." Still gripping Silverman at the elbow, he seemed to be waiting for applause. There were murners of approval on all sides.

"I'm glad you see it that way," Silverman said. "Though if it weren't so holy, it might not be so bloody." Dawes, clearly wondering if he should approve of this unexpected sentiment, was giving him a confused frown. "That would be the humanist perspective, you see," Silverman explained.

"Ah, yes," Dawes said, as if he were pondering the idea rather than endorsing it.

"Myself, I don't think of any piece of land as holy—except possibly Yankee Stadium. But that was when I was a kid." He did Dawes the kindness of laughing the remark off.

Uncertainly, Dawes joined in on the laugh. "But, seriously, I remain as confident as I'm sure you do that a peaceful resolution can be found if both sides meet in a spirit of Christian charity."

"You put it so well," Silverman answered. "Maybe we should let them know that Jesus is watching."

Dawes' brow folded into a thoughtful squint. "Why yes, exactly. I'll have my staff make a note of that."

Dawes, though in his later middle years, was ruggedly masculine enough to be a male model. He was athletically well built, square-jawed and endowed with a heavily gelled mountain of blond locks—altogether a figure of energetic vitality in a tailored suit. He was in the company of a strikingly lovely woman. Young, blonde, and flawlessly featured, she was favored with marvelous eyes, heavy-lidded and long-lashed. Bedroom eyes, as Silverman thought of them. His response to female beauty of this kind was complex. As if he were admiring a fine work of art, the aesthetic invariably overrode the sexual, but didn't wholly eclipse a certain yearning. All of which made him wonder if, perhaps before beauty was divided between the genders, it had been a quality in its own right, capable of intoxicating the senses as at times the birds and flowers still do. Well, whoever she was, Dawes' companion was that kind of stunner. As Marty liked to put it, "when they get that good-looking, it almost makes you wish you were a lesbian." Like Dawes, she might also have passed for a fashion model—except for the masochistically frumpy clothes she was wearing. Crossing the room, Silverman had noticed several women dressed much the same way: a black sack of a dress that seemed deliberately designed to make the female body look like a vertical mailing tube.

As if that weren't bad enough, Dawes' lovely companion sported a huge polka dot bow at the throat and ruffles at the wrist. Almost in spite of itself, the dress did offer enough indication of hips and a bust to hint at a shapely woman underneath. Silverman assumed the blonde must be the Senator's trophy wife. He was wrong. "And this," Swenson went on, "is Jake's daughter Gloria, who joined our faculty last fall."

Gloria, as sullen of face as most of the rest in the room, took Silverman's hand limply and mumbled a perfunctory welcome, then stepped back to let her ebullient father take over. "Dick and I hope this occasion will be the beginning of a fruitful dialogue among all God's people," Dawes said, sounding as if he were reading the words off a teleprompter. Then, with a wink, he bent down to stage-whisper in Silverman's ear, "Unless I miss my guess, you may be the first ambassador from Sin City to visit these parts." The Senator laughed; as if on cue, his companions did their best to echo him but seemed to run out of steam before they had done more than exhale loudly. "Only joking, Professor Silverman," Dawes added. "We must remember your city was named after a saint."

In and out, twelve thousand net, Silverman repeated to himself for perhaps the tenth time that day.

"I've been reading your books, Professor," Dawes continued, assuming a more serious air. He reached into his attaché case to pull out a copy of *Deep Eye* and, surprisingly, *I, Emma*. "Well, actually," he added with a chuckle, "I've been having Gloria prepare notes on several of your works. She's the family bookworm. She took her master's degree in . . . what was it, Glory? Comparative Literature?" Gloria gave a brief embarrassed nod. "At the University," Dawes went on, rehearsing his blushing daughter's résumé. "*Magna cum Laude*." He took Silverman firmly by the arm and drew him off as if he might be about to put the bite on him for a campaign contribution. Looking around to make sure they were out of earshot, he bent to whisper, "Now, Glory tells me there's some pretty strong language in. . . ." Holding Silverman's two novels in his hands, he was looking from the one to the other clearly unable to tell which book he meant to refer to. ". . . this one I believe." He held out *I, Emma*. "Not that I can say I approve, you understand, but of course we get a lot of that behind closed doors in the political world, enough to singe your ears. Mustn't be hypocritical about these things. In your case, Glory tells me the language, while X-rated, could be said to have a redeeming literary context. If anything comes up on that score—which I suspect is unlikely—I hope we can stick to that formulation. Agreed?"

What is this? Silverman wondered. *A deal? He's cutting a deal with me about dirty words? What dirty words?* Dirty words were a literary sore point for Silverman. His novels were so embarrassingly clean that he could recite the small inventory of expletives in them from memory and give the page each was on. As he listened to Dawes, that was what he was doing: running the list to find these offending, X-rated words. What could the man be talking about? Editors had actually warned Silverman that his fastidiousness was costing him dearly among younger readers, a demographic for whom four-letter words now functioned as punctuation. "Can't you get a couple 'fucks' in there?" Tommy Sutton had once pressed him, "just for the marketability? Think of them like exclamation points." And Silverman had tried, he really had. In *Parliament of Monsters,* he had given the gargoyle atop Notre Dame a soliloquy that led up to the line, "tonight, beneath the dismal roofs of Paris, ten thousand humans are fucking more of their wretched kind into existence." Sutton thought that was a good beginning, but wondered if the line might be improved to read "tonight, beneath the dismal roofs of Paris, ten thousand humans are fucking more of their fucking, wretched kind into existence," but no. A lot of good the line had done him anyway; his gargoyle's-eye view of the world never even made it into paperback. And *that* was his only printed "fuck."

Had the Senator's daughter found a rare copy of the clothbound edition? Other than that one pathetic attempt at high literary obscenity, the best Silverman had managed to do in other books was eight "shits," two "peckers," and three "tits," all in the mouths of very surly characters. In truth, Silverman was simply incapable of being authentically gross. These days, when he found himself buried in an avalanche of obscenity by movies produced for twelve-year-olds, he realized how out of touch he was with popular taste.

Yet here was this hick politician worrying him over a few commonplace vulgarities. But, "Yeah, sure," Silverman agreed. Why make trouble?

"That's wonderful," Dawes said, pumping his hand again as he led Silverman back to where the others were waiting. He quickly returned *I, Emma* to his daughter as if it might be toxic material. "Now," he went on, "as for your other book, the one about the dolphin. . . ."

"Whale," his daughter reminded him, offering Silverman an apologetic smile.

"Yes, of course," Dawes laughed. "Whale." He was still groping for the title.

"*Deep Eye.*" Gloria supplied the name.

"Right, *Deep Eye*—that would have to be a whale, wouldn't it? And such an excellent title," Dawes remarked as much to everybody in earshot as to Silverman. "I mean that's the whole story right there, isn't it? Glory tells me that *Deep Eye* is a distinct contribution to the ethic of stewardship that we hope all people of faith uphold."

Silverman had never been complimented by a politician before, let alone by a rabid right-winger, but as he might have suspected Dawes' comments came across as cautiously crafted sound bites. "Thanks," he answered. "The book isn't actually meant to be environmental. . . ." He saw a confused look wash over the Senator's face, as if he were worried that he might have to ask his staff to do a quick rewrite of his introductory remarks. *Oh-oh. Make trouble at this point and it might delay the lecture. Take the course of least resistance.* Silverman back-tracked ". . . on the surface, that is. I'm glad to see that Gloria got the underlying meaning—the subtext, as we say."

Dawes looked relieved. "Of course she did. The subtext. *Magna cum Laude*, didn't I tell you? She's my bright little girl. I so look forward to your lecture this afternoon. I expect Dick has told you that you will be launching our new Religious Humanism program. We've been working on the project for several years."

"Well, I intend to do my best," Silverman smiled back.

"Excellent! What else could we ask?" Then, leaning in for another private remark, "Subtext. I like that. I should mention that, shouldn't I? Do all your books have a subtext?"

"A subtext? Sure. All my books have a subtext, but you can't read it unless you hold the pages up to the light."

Swenson, who seemed eager to keep conversation between Silverman and Dawes at a minimum, tactfully drew the Senator off to work out some details about the introductions. With Dawes withdrawn, his circle of admirers closed around Silverman as if waiting for him to take up where the Senator had left off. Instead, finding himself face to face with Gloria, Silverman picked up the piece of small talk that he found closest at hand. "So, what do you teach?"

"Bible studies," she answered. "And theology for women." Silverman could see her fidgeting with discomfort. So far she was the one person he had met who seemed to feel as out of place as he did.

"Can men enroll in women's theology?" Silverman asked.

"Not women's theology," Gloria corrected him politely. "Theology for women. No, men aren't admitted."

"Too shocking for male ears to hear?" he asked.

"No, not at all."

"When God was a woman, that sort of thing?"

Her bedroom eyes lit up with quiet alarm. She shot a quick glance to the left and right to check how the others had taken the remark. "Hardly!" she answered with an unconvincing chuckle.

"It's the going thing in Sin City," Silverman rambled on. Gloria, struggling to hold back a blush, shot a disapproving frown at him. "Sorry, am I being heretical?"

Looking for help, she ran her eyes around the circle that had gathered. Hovering nearby were an older man and woman. "Oh, Reverend Berglund," she called. To Silverman she said, "This is Reverend Berglund and Mrs. Berglund. Reverend Berglund is one of our trustees. I'm sure he'll want to tell you about his travels, won't you, Reverend?" As Gloria made the introduction, Silverman thought he detected a distinctly impish gleam in her eye. She was palming him off.

The Reverend and his wife reached to shake Silverman's hand, each in turn giving him a vise-like squeeze. The Berglunds, as they were prompt to report, were in charge of Free Reformed Brethren missionary activities. They had returned for the holidays after four years of winning disciples for Christ in central Africa. Silverman might have guessed as much. For a couple in their sixties, they looked remarkably fit: lean, brawny, outdoorsy, and thoroughly bronzed by the tropic sun, exactly the sort of muscular Christians Silverman could imagine wading across crocodile-infested rivers and going without water for forty days on the veldt. Utterly positive and forceful, the Berglunds were strong on numbers. Babies inoculated, families fed, Bibles distributed, acres planted, schools built, souls saved—burgeoning quantities of good work done for the Lord, and all in the middle of a ghastly civil war. "Oh, there were bodies everywhere," Mrs. Berglund reported. "Heaps and heaps of them left to rot in the sun. Terrible stink. Mothers and babies hacked to pieces. Oh my, such a savage people. Wherever you walked, heads, hands, legs. You couldn't even wash in the morning, all the wells were running blood. Praise God, we were able to bring the loving word of Jesus to our tiny flock before they were wiped out."

"Wiped out?" Silverman asked, trying his best to sound reasonably solicitous, but wondering why he should care.

"You betcha," Mrs. Berglund replied. "Massacred, every last one of them, Lord Jesus take pity on their souls! All one-hundred seventy-four. We lost the entire mission, including our loyal Michael Mbiki, our first animist convert south of Khartoum. A true heathen. You remember Michael, don't you, Phyllis," she inquired of one of the women in the group. "He preached here last Easter."

"I do," the woman answered. "Such a polite young man. And always smiling."

"Ah, he was like our own son," Mrs. Berglund sighed.

"Disemboweled he was," Reverend Berglund recalled. "In front of the entire mission. But singing, singing to heaven all the while. I can still hear that indomitable voice of his soaring to the clouds. 'Jesus, priceless treasure, Fount of purest pleasure . . .' You remember, my love?"

"'In thine arms I rest me,'" Mrs. Berglund added. "He made it through the last stanza, God love him. Well, he is with Jesus now. Let us pray."

Heads bowed, except for Silverman's—and Gloria's. Glancing across at her, he noticed the same mischievous look he had seen before. So, she was teasing him, as if to say, *Are you happier with this subject?* Well, that actually showed some wit on her part. He gave her a wink of acknowledgement. *Touché.*

"Sounds dangerous," Silverman observed simply to have something to say when all eyes returned to him.

"Oh, yes," Reverend Berglund assured him. "We've lost four missionaries in central Africa over the last five years. Two hanged, one impaled, one eaten alive by ants."

"Eaten by ants?" somebody in the circle exclaimed. "Who was that?"

"Little Georgie Hein from Puposky, praise the Lord."

"Really? I hadn't heard," the questioner said. "Bob and Helen's boy? Did you hear that, Jeany?" he asked his wife. "Little George Hein, eaten by ants."

"God rest his soul," the wife answered.

"Was he also singing?" Silverman asked.

"I wouldn't be surprised," Mrs. Berglund answered. "He had a lovely voice."

"Oh, yes, very risky work," Reverend Berglund agreed, nodding toward his wife. "One can only trust in God. Martha was herself wounded. Brave girl!" As if on cue, Mrs. Berglund drew down her collar and turned to display a vicious scar that ran across her shoulder and further down her back than she dared show in public. "Nearly lost you that time, didn't we, my love?" the Reverend said. "It was touch and go. Badly infected, no antibiotics. Her temperature went to 104."

"106," Mrs. Berglund corrected. "I prayed to the Lord night and day. And he came to my rescue, praise be."

"Hallelujah," one of the others in the circle murmured. And all the rest did the same.

"Something that might interest you, Professor," the Reverend went on. "We came back home by way of Israel, where our efforts are bearing more and more fruit."

"Israel?" Silverman asked. "You send missionaries to Israel?"

"Oh, yes. After all, the Jews are also a Biblical people. I've always said, if we cannot convert the Jews, what chance do we stand with hard-core pagans?"

"Yes, that's a thought," Silverman said. "But you know what they say about converting the Jews."

"Yes? What?" Reverend Berglund asked, sincerely curious.

"Well, that it can't be done," Silverman answered. "Least of all by Christians. If I'm not mistaken, Jews came first, didn't they? Yes, I'm sure they did. And, as you can see, here we still are. Of course, there are these people—Jews for Jesus—they come knocking at my door every once in a while to see if I'd like to convert. I guess they do get a few takers, but in my experience most Jews are rather fond of their own religion."

"True, true," Reverend Berglund agreed, a note of sad resignation creeping into his voice. "Still, as long as there's the slightest chance to do the Lord's work. . . ."

Mrs. Berglund picked up briskly. "Now, now, no need to sound so defeatist. Remember, our orphanage in Tel Aviv has grown by over seventy percent in the past two years alone."

"And you try to convert the kids?" Silverman asked.

"We seek to bring them into the fold."

"Should I approve of that, I mean as a Jewish Humanist?"

"Ah, that is a question," Mrs. Berglund agreed. "I see your point. But we must bruise the serpent's head wherever we find him."

"You see," Reverend Berglund hastened to explain, "we are commanded to evangelize and to exclude no one, neither Jew nor Gentile. Romans, 2:10. In our eyes, a converted Jew is a completed Jew."

"Of course, we don't wish to convert all Jews," Mrs. Berglund added, as if making a generous concession. "Especially not all Israelis." Heads bobbed in affirmation all around the circle.

"Why not?" Silverman asked. "Might as well go for broke."

"Oh, no, no," Reverend Berglund insisted. "There has to be an Israel. Armageddon, you know. The way and the place must be prepared. And only your people can do it." He flashed Silverman a big encouraging smile, as if to say, *and I know you're up to it, my boy*—whatever it might be.

"Well, that's mighty white of you," Silverman said.

"Not at all, not at all," Reverend Berglund waved the compliment aside. "No need for gratitude. Frankly, it would break my

heart to know that all those sincere Jewish prayers were going unheard."

"Unheard?"

"But you see when Christians pray for Jews, God listens. As the
hymn teaches,

'Let every kindred, every tribe,
On this terrestrial ball,
To him all majesty ascribe. . . .'"

He was cut short. Swenson, having finished with Jake Dawes,
slipped up behind Reverend Berglund to touch his arm. Glancing
at his watch, Swenson apologized, "I'm sorry to interrupt." He
pointed upward toward the ceiling, "Mrs. Bloore is expecting to
meet Professor Silverman."

"Ah, well then. . . ." At once, Reverend Berglund fell dutifully silent and stepped aside to let Silverman disengage.

"Rhymes with ball," Silverman said as he drew off. "What could
it be?" he asked Reverend Berglund.

"Hm?"

"The rhyme for 'On this terrestrial ball. . . .'"

"Oh, yes. 'To him all majesty ascribe, And crown him Lord of all.'"

"I might have guessed."

"We'll remember you in our prayers," Mrs. Berglund whispered
as she gave Silverman a farewell handshake.

"You will? You mean you'll be praying for my conversion?"

"Yes we will," Mrs. Berglund promised. "Every night."

A clammy sensation crept over him. The thought that these
people would be using his name in their prayers every night from
here on made him feel vaguely sick. Did they have the right to do
that? It sounded like a violation of the Constitution. "Ah, but you
can't do that," Silverman declared with a calculated note of mock
sorrow.

"Why not?"

"Because I'm a humanist, you see. Humanists aren't even certain
God exists."

"Oh, but that makes no difference, Professor," Mrs. Berglund
assured him with swelling sincerity. "There is One who died for all
of us."

"How nice!" Silverman answered. "But I'm sure he won't accept prayers for the likes of me. In fact, I rather hope he won't."

By this time Swenson was tugging at his arm so hard he almost pulled Silverman off balance.

"Nevertheless," Mrs. Berglund called after him with a cheery wave. "No harm in trying."

8

The Matriarch

Using the same magic words—"Mrs. Bloore is waiting for us"—and the same upward gesture as if he were pointing the way up Mount Sinai, Swenson steered Silverman through the crowd and out the door. They used a private elevator to make the short trip to the second floor. "We had to put the elevator in for Mrs. Bloore," Swenson explained. "Her mobility is pretty limited. Arthritis. But she's as feisty as anyone half her age—as you'll see."

The elevator opened directly into Mrs. Bloore's private suite. As the doors parted, they were met by a small, pale woman with tired and cheerless eyes, her hands folded in front of her. She was dressed in a white, starched uniform. "Hello, Miss Bjork," Swenson said. "I think Mrs. Bloore is expecting us."

Miss Bjork nodded and admitted them, then scurried back into the room to take her place behind a lady in a wheelchair. Obviously Mrs. Bloore.

All that was missing from the scene behind the door to make it totally funereal was a Hammond organ playing "In the Sweet Bye and Bye." Otherwise, Mrs. Bloore's private quarters on the upper floor of Gundersen Hall might be the house of the dead. The curtains, drawn to let in minimal light, made the room seem shrouded. The pictures on the walls—another gallery of morose divines—might have been in deep mourning. As for the three reasonably live people who were waiting to greet Silverman, their faces were ready for the coffin to arrive. They had been having a private luncheon; now they turned from the table to make introductions. Mrs. Bloore, seated at the center of the threesome, looked like a reigning potentate waiting to be appeased. To her left

and right stood two men of vastly contrasting appearance. One
was "oh-oh, another biggy," as Silverman thought to himself, a
large, portly man with handsomely sculptured features. The shock
of white hair he wore piled high on his head added at least three
inches to his height. His eyes, deep-set beneath assertively thrusting
brows, lent him an intimidating air of magisterial arrogance. He
was introduced as Reverend Apfel, Pastor of the congregation and
Provost of the school. His companion was squat and small, one of the
few people Silverman had so far met in Minnesota who was shorter
than himself. Standing no taller than Apfel's collarbone, his build
was stunted, leaving him with a barrel chest and overly long arms.
This was Professor Jaspers, Dean of Theology. And, yes, the matriarch and her posse of two were all sporting their little red pins.

Mrs. Bloore rose effortfully to her feet. As she did so, the nurse,
in a well-rehearsed maneuver, nimbly slid an aluminum walker in
front of her. She was a large woman with broad shoulders. Her
face, deeply lined, was frozen into a baleful frown that would have
looked right on a hanging judge. She held out a quivering hand;
Silverman shook it. Though she trembled with palsy, her grip was
remarkably firm. Silverman, studying her as closely as good manners might permit, was disappointed. In this stiff and frigid face,
he could find not a trace of the *tsatske* she might once have been.

"Welcome to our school, Professor Silverman," she said, with
minimal courtesy. Her voice was as gruff as a man's. If this were
not teetotal country, one might have called it a whisky voice. Silverman, about to make a perfunctory reply, was cut short. "You are
here against my better judgment. I can only hope we won't regret
inviting you. You are a novelist. I don't approve of novels. Novels
are fiction. They are simply made up. I fail to see what this has to
do with the word of God. I'm not sure you have any business being
here. Nevertheless, I've agreed to have you visit, even though a
great deal of what you've written is deeply offensive."

Wow! Silverman thought, right between the eyes. He wondered
what parts of which books had rubbed the old lady the wrong way.
Probably the best stuff he had written. But this wasn't the time to ask.

"As I warned you, Mrs. Bloore believes in being direct," Swenson
hastened to explain, adding a chuckle that Mrs. Bloore didn't echo.

"I find that so refreshing," Silverman answered. For twelve thou he could take a few ignorant knocks. What choice did he have?

"I trust Dean Swenson has prepared you for today's event," Mrs. Bloore went on. "We expect your lecture to be in good taste. There are passages in your books that are not in good taste. Please avoid saying anything today that is not in good taste."

"Mrs. Bloore, I aim to please," Silverman replied. "Good taste is my middle name. I intend to give you a totally inoffensive lecture. If you wish, I can make it completely vacuous."

She studied him even more suspiciously. Her eyes seemed never to blink. Her voice slipped into a near-growl. "I'm not paying for a vacuum. I'm paying for a lecture, a pleasant, uplifting talk to begin the new year. While I've never heard of you, Dean Swenson assures me that you have a literary reputation. Apparently your appearance at our school will help with our accreditation. Such worldly things mean very little to me. My concern is that your remarks should be inspirational—or at least as inspirational as we might expect from someone lacking religious faith, which, I gather, is your condition."

"How well you put it," Silverman answered. "Pleasant and uplifting, of course—with no more than a soupçon of inspiration."

"We expect to hear nothing suggestive," she went on as if he hadn't spoken at all. "In particular, I ask that you say nothing about the reproductive organs. Novelists are always going on about the reproductive organs. Bear in mind that you'll be speaking to young people, young people who are not fully in control of their reproductive organs. And is it any wonder when we see the smut—the smut! that rains down on them? Do, please, restrain yourself."

"No smut, absolutely," Silverman promised with exaggerated solemnity. "Well, except perhaps a few good words about breastfeeding."

Mrs. Bloore wasn't amused. She looked at Swenson with intimidating displeasure. "He's going to talk about *that*?"

"I think Professor Silverman is joking," Swenson rushed to assure her. "I mentioned Reverend Lucy's feelings on the matter."

She sniffed dismissively. "Reverend Lucy wasn't always known for good taste."

"Well, then, I'll leave that out too," Silverman said. "Actually I'm relieved. I never feel all that comfortable talking about ladies' private parts. Mammary glands especially. They seem to link us to the lower orders. I'm sure you understand." He furrowed his brow and nodded gravely as if a matter of great importance had been settled. There was a pause. The pause grew longer. Silverman looked around the room, but found nothing engaging to ask about. His gaze came round to the second button on Reverend Apfel's suit jacket. He looked up from there into the pastor's face. As if the vacuum of silence had sucked the words out of him against his will, he asked, "Why forty-two?" Yes, he had been wondering about that. The question fell to the floor and lay there like something half-chewed that had slipped out of his mouth.

"Pardon?" the pastor said.

"Why forty-two weeks?" Silverman repeated. "This mid-trib idea. Why forty-two weeks?"

From behind him he heard Swenson saying, ". . . months."

Silverman turned to accept the correction. "Oh. Forty-two months." He looked back to Reverend Apfel, assuming one of those pleasant, small-talk expressions that are meant to indicate that one has no interest in the matter at all.

"Because forty-two is half of seven," Reverend Apfel answered as if that should be obvious.

"Forty-two is half of seven?" Silverman asked.

Swenson whispered something. He turned. ". . . years. Half of seven years."

Silverman did the math. "Hey, that's right. Forty-two months is half of seven years." Well, where did that leave him? He might try *why seven?*

"Which reminds me," Mrs. Bloore said as if her mind had been jump-started. "This Holocaust thing. I hope you will spare us any of that."

The remark blindsided Silverman. "But I had no intention of bringing the subject up."

"Good. We were discussing it at lunch—how people of your persuasion go on and on about the Holocaust, the Holocaust, the Holocaust. We've heard quite enough about that, and most of it obviously exaggerated. All very distasteful and hardly suitable for young minds on an occasion like this. We will, after all, be meeting in a church."

"What do you think, Richard?" Silverman asked, turning to Swenson. "Does Faith College need a full discussion of this Holocaust thing?"

Swenson had gone pale. Silverman could hear him ouching inwardly. "We had intended this to be inspirational and literary, not political."

"Yes, of course, inspirational," Silverman agreed. "And literary, meaning having nothing to do with real life, correct? Well, suppose I keep my remarks purely personal. My life as a Jewish writer. The pleasant, uplifting, and inspirational forces in twentieth-century life that have shaped me, with the exception of wars, revolutions, pogroms, death camps and that sort of thing? Would that be agreeable?"

Mrs. Bloore looked left and right to her two male companions, who were at last given permission to speak.

"Oh yes," said Professor Jaspers. "I think that will fill the bill more than adequately. Something not too political."

"Not political at all," Mrs. Bloore corrected him.

"Yes, not at all," Professor Jaspers agreed at once. "This being the beginning of a new millennium."

"Exactly," Mrs. Bloore agreed. "A new millennium. Doesn't that say it all? Where, after all, does this millennium, or any millennium for that matter, come from? Please try to keep that in mind, Professor. Christians have millenniums, even if others do not."

"As for myself," Reverend Apfel took his turn to speak, "I want you to know that I believe it is a brilliant stroke for Richard to think of sharing our millennium with a luminary from the Jewish community. And a humanist at that. You may not appreciate how controversial that word has become in certain evangelical circles."

"Humanism!" Mrs. Bloore snorted. "What does it mean in any case? Aren't we all human?"

"If not more than human," Jaspers corrected her. "I mean as children of God. Galatians, 3:26."

"Not always, Walter," Mrs. Bloore replied. "There are those who

have no place in a civilized Christian society. Am I right, Albert?"
I-better-be, said the look she shot off in the pastor's direction.

Reverend Apfel nodded judiciously, "Yes, of course. Romans, 1:28."

"Would you agree, Professor Silverman? We have heard of these beatnik persons that you have in San Francisco."

Silverman blinked. "Beatniks? Oh, I haven't seen any of them in years. I think they're all safely extinct."

"Are they?" Mrs. Bloore replied. "Well, that's one good thing. Had you heard, Albert? The beatniks are gone."

Apfel smiled in celebration. "I suspected as much. I hadn't heard about them for some while."

"Thank God for that," Mrs. Bloore continued. "But I'm sure there will be others every bit as obnoxious. Once you lower the standards, there's no going back. The rot keeps spreading."

"There are times when I feel that way too," Silverman agreed.

"Fruit?" Mrs. Bloore asked.

"Pardon?"

She was gesturing toward the table. "We have fruit punch," Mrs Bloore explained. "Daisy, give the man some fruit punch. Where are your manners?"

Miss Bjork, giving a cluck of annoyance, toddled over to a small punch bowl on a side table and spooned out a cup for Silverman. At the first taste, Silverman could tell it was a packaged mix, mostly water, fructose, and lurid colors. He was tempted to ask if there was something to spike it with. *Don't be childish*, his inner counselor advised him.

"Humanism," Reverend Apfel was musing. "One wonders, can there be a 'religious humanism'? Ah, now there is a great question."

"It is no sort of question at all," Mrs. Bloore snapped. "Humanism is godless, hence condemned out of its own mouth. I really have no idea why we are giving it any attention at all."

"Well, how about humanist religionism?" Silverman suggested in the spirit of helpfulness. "That sounds a little better, doesn't it?"

"Humanist religionism." Apfel's eyes squinted hard as if he might be on the brink of insight. "Ah, yes. When you put it that way. . . ."

"I see no difference whatever," Mrs. Bloore said. "You're splitting hairs. More to the point: no profanity, that I insist upon." She fixed Silverman once again with her unblinking gaze.

"You have my solemn word," Silverman said. "No dirty words. I'm so relieved you're willing to do without them. You know, publishers expect so much obscenity these days. The public simply demands it, so they put it in whether authors like it or not."

"They put it in?" Mrs. Bloore was astonished.

"There's a computer program that makes sure there's at least one dirty word on every page. It's called the smut-inserter."

"Good Lord," Mrs. Bloore yipped. "Are you serious?"

"Oh yes," Silverman nodded soberly. "It includes all the four-letter words. It even includes the ten-letter word." He noticed Mrs. Bloore making a quick calculation. She gasped. "Which I hadn't even heard of myself," Silverman continued, "until it showed up in one of my novels. I don't keep that kind of company."

"Have you no power to protest?" Mrs. Bloore asked. "These books after all carry your name."

Silverman wagged his head disconsolately. "Sometimes they run the book through the smut-inserter first. I get pages and pages with nothing but dirty words on them. They want me to write the story around the obscenities. Can you imagine?"

"I believe it," Mrs. Bloore said.

Apfel glared forbiddingly into the distance as if he were judging the world at large. "To think how Christ-denying our society has become."

"And there are those," Jaspers was quick to add, "even in our own church who would have us traffic with these very forces. The World Wide Net." He spat out the words, making no effort to conceal the mordant glance he sent toward Swenson.

More in sorrow than anger Apfel nodded his agreement. "Ministries of flesh."

"Of course, there's also the Christ-inserter," Silverman added as an afterthought. All eyes were on him at once. "Sure. You can buy a program that sticks 'Jesus Is Watching' across every page you write." The eyes turned suspicious. At his side, he could detect Swenson caught between a giggle and a groan as he prepared to make light of the remark. "Could be done. Same principle."

"What a marvelous idea," Mrs. Bloore said, her most spirited remark so far. "Richard, you should look into that."

"Yes, of course," Swenson agreed quickly.

"Richard is our school hucker," Mrs. Bloore reminded Silverman.

"Hacker?" Silverman asked.

"Well, not really," Swenson said, modestly laughing off the suggestion. "I do dabble a bit at a few programs like. . . ."

"Nobody really cares, Richard," Mrs. Bloore said, closing the subject.

"So, let's review," Silverman said, counting on his fingers. "No dirty words, no Holocaust, no sex, no politics, nothing too Jewish. Does that about cover it?"

"Excellent," Mrs. Bloore added in a flat tone that made it clear she expected nothing excellent to happen that day. She exchanged glances left and right. There were nods of approval all around.

Apfel drew a watch from his vest pocket. "I do believe it's time," he announced. Swenson, who couldn't get away too quickly, agreed at once. He shot out of his seat and headed for the door. "May I walk with you and Professor Silverman to the chapel, Richard?" Apfel asked.

Mrs. Bloore settled back into her wheelchair, gesturing to her nurse and Professor Jaspers to guide her into the elevator. Click! Silverman, watching after her, took a mental picture: embittered, bossy woman, a true dragon lady. If he ever needed an "off with their heads" female, this was it. But Mrs. Bloore was also taking stock. Glancing back at Silverman, she said, "And do be brief," not as a request. "Your fee will be the same no matter how long you talk."

"Oh? I thought I was being paid by the minute."

Mrs. Bloore stopped her wheelchair dead in its tracks and shot a dark look at Swenson, who pulled a big innocent face. "I think Professor Silverman is joking."

"Of course I am," Silverman acknowledged. "I surely agree: the briefer the better."

9

Which Holocaust Did You Have in Mind?

"I gather Mrs. Bloore has a problem with the Holocaust," Silverman observed as he and Reverend Apfel started down the stairs behind Swenson.

"Yes, don't we all?" Apfel replied.

"Do we?"

"Holocaust, Holocaust," Apfel murmured under his breath as if musing to himself. "How far we have strayed from our sources." Then leaning close to Silverman, he said with a fatherly smile, "I admit that it piques my curiosity."

"How so?"

"Are you among those of your people who have a position on the historicity of this matter?"

For a moment Silverman was caught off guard. Holocaust. Wasn't that originally a Biblical term? Was he being asked about some obscure passage in scripture? "Are we talking about *the* Holocaust?"

"No, no. I mean the event commonly associated with World War II."

"And commonly called *the* capital-H Holocaust."

Again the oily smile. "'Holocaust' properly so-called is an act of worship. It is a sacrificial rite performed to beg forgiveness from the Lord, as in Genesis 22:8. 'And Abraham said, "God will provide Himself the lamb for a burnt offering."'"

"So you do mean *the* Holocaust. Nazis, Hitler, Auschwitz. You're asking me what? If I believe it happened?"

"I am." The man seemed totally pleased with himself for catching Silverman by surprise.

"Meaning you *don't?*"

"You must be aware that this happens to be a matter of some dispute."

"Oh? Where? At the Heinrich Himmler Retirement Home in Paraguay?"

Apfel's face assumed an expression of smug reproof. "You're being sarcastic. I only wondered if a Jewish Humanist might be somewhat more open-minded about the question than an orthodox fanatic."

"What do you mean by 'question'? You haven't seen the pictures or read the accounts? I mean what basis is there for doubt?"

Apfel offered him an indulgent smile. "Of course, given the nearly monopolistic influence your people hold over the mass media, it is wholly understandable that even educated people find it difficult to believe that the evidence for this event, such as it is, might be exaggerated, if not largely fabricated. But for some of us, the testimony of those we trust must of course carry more weight."

"Like who?"

"I have an aunt who lives in the village of Buchenwald. She assures me that she never saw a camp of any kind in the area."

"I also had an aunt. . . ." Silverman began, then let the words trail off. Did he want to get into that? He glanced at the man walking beside him, the self important thrust of his jaw, the pompous arch of his brow. No, best to let it pass. "And you're sure your aunt has no reason to color the historical record?"

"Absolutely none. She is a godly woman. On the other hand, sad to say, we know of the effort that has been made to misappropriate the word Holocaust for political purposes."

"'Misappropriate'? But who are you to decide? It's not your book, Reverend. If anybody ever misappropriated anything, it's those who ripped off my ancestors' intellectual property rights. Somewhere back in the distant past out there in the desert, some gang of old Jewish guys who probably looked like my grandfather wrote the thing. I don't agree with very much they had to say. I think they were all suffering from delusions of grandeur. But it's still *theirs*. And they passed it on to people like me, for better or worse. Now whatever my people want to use the word Holocaust for, even if it's for barbecuing a chicken, that's our right. Our book, our words."

"And the low political intention behind this effort, that doesn't trouble you?"

"Sure, there are politics involved. Low politics. Hitler's politics. But what's that got to do with the truth of the matter?"

"There are other grounds for doubt."

"Yes? What?"

"Faith. Unswerving faith. You find yourself among people of faith."

"Faith in what?"

"In the unbounded love of the Lord. He would never permit so unspeakable an evil to happen, not to His people. Psalms, 89:3. 'I have made a covenant with my chosen, thy seed will I establish forever.'"

Silverman chuckled bitterly. "As I recall, He's certainly permitted us to take our lumps. Which is something, I can assure you, many good Jews have tormented themselves over to the point of going plain nuts. Or, like myself, coming to a rather obvious skeptical conclusion."

"Or perhaps, in other less principled cases, assuming the right to rewrite history."

Silverman was so puzzled by what he was hearing that he asked with honest curiosity, "So you think all the victims who survived the death camps are lying?"

"Sad to say, there are those in this world who possess the shameless duplicity to invent such a falsehood and even to exploit it for selfish ends. Christian society has always been vulnerable to such tactics. Those who believe in charity and compassion can have their best intentions used against them. Guilt, cynically used, is a powerful weapon."

They had crossed the courtyard and reached the front entrance of the chapel. Silverman, walking beside Apfel, found himself speechless. Focussed on his exchange with the pastor, he only marginally noted the chill in the air. It had sharpened its teeth still more. He had heard that there were those who dismissed the Holocaust as fiction, but he had never encountered anyone who really believed that. He had never expected to. This was like meeting someone who insisted that the Earth was flat. He was searching for some slashing comeback, but then that seemed wholly inappropriate. This wasn't an occasion for wit; true censure was required, a stinging statement of principle, but before he could find the words he needed, Reverend Apfel had asked to be excused. "And now, I'll leave you in Richard's hands," he said and was gone, satisfied that he had made his point.

Silverman started to call after him but the words, whatever they might have been, died a few inches short of his larynx. Something had taken his eye and choked off his reply. Yes, there above the entrance to the chapel was another scarlet and gold banner. *JIW, JIW, be careful!* Saying nothing, Silverman watched Apfel drift off. In another moment, the pastor had mixed in with a group of several faculty members who were entering the chapel. At some remark from the minister, two or three of them laughed, glancing in Silverman's direction. What was he saying? Probably that their visiting lecturer was one of those who believed in the lie of the six million. As the group entered the church, they were joined by the shambling figure of Axel Hask, who had put on a coat and tie for the occasion. The big, hulking man kept his eyes on Silverman until he was through the door and out of sight.

Even without looking, Silverman could imagine Swenson, walking at his side, wincing and ouching. As Apfel moved off, Swenson began an embarrassed apology. Silverman cut him short. "Don't bother, Richard. It'll all be over soon. But for an exercise like this, I should have charged you twice as much. Crucifying the intellect comes expensive."

Wanting no explanations or apologies from Swenson, he asked to be taken someplace where he could glance over his notes. He drew his lecture from his inside coat pocket. "I'd like to gather my thoughts," he said.

"Yes, of course," Swenson said and led him up the stairs into the chapel and toward a small room off the main corridor. "Sanctuary" said the sign over the door. *Boy, that's sure what I need*, Silverman thought. *Like Quasimodo running from the mob.* "Sanctuary, sanctuary!"

"I'll be back in ten minutes," Swenson said, closing the door gently. Left on his own, Silverman slumped down at the long table that filled the center of the room, only to discover that his brain was reeling so fast that he couldn't focus on the pages in front of him. That was no problem; he knew the lecture by heart. But did he care to give it? That would be the easiest way out. Do the minimum he was contracted to do, grab the money, and run. After all, what did these people mean to him, this strange species of far northern evangelicals? What did he have to win or lose on this playing field?

"You see," he said to the small, obscure figure who had appeared at the far end of the table, "it's not worth the effort. I mean, sure, I could make a few nasty cracks, but what good would that do?"

The figure wasn't placated. With his eyes firmly glued on Silverman, Grandpa Zvi, his ancient face more wizened and splotchy than Silverman could remember ever seeing it, was haranguing his grandson, no doubt in a gurgling stream of Yiddish. The old man gestured wildly and pounded on the table, railing at his grandson but making not a sound in the still room. As if between them there stood a wall of glass, none of what he had to say was getting through. But then it didn't have to; Silverman knew its import. "Okay, you were right. I turned out to be a *nebech*. Shame on me. But look, this is a new millennium, or at least that's what the Gentiles are calling it, whether we like it or not. Time marches on, *zeyde*. History has to loosen its grip."

"So you're going to let them get away with it?" said a mordant, whining voice from another part of the room. Silverman turned to face the figure that stood leaning against the wall behind him. After the incident with the mirror that morning, he wasn't the least bit surprised to discover that it was the shadowy form of Shenandoah Fish who stood there studying him with lofty contempt, with almost a sneer. Fish was a fantasy resident of Bookville. In that literary village of the mind, he lived on Gimpel the Fool Street, in a neighborhood of notable, mid-century Jewish-American protagonists. Shenandoah Fish—such an absurd name. Like his creator's own name, Delmore Schwartz, a conflicted amalgamation of the old world and the new. But Fish was special among the characters Silverman carried about in his writer's imagination. Fish had been the first to illuminate the dilemma of Jewish identity for the youthful Daniel Silverman.

When, during his college years, Silverman had read the story "America! America!," he had flashed upon the fact that Shenandoah Fish was the spokesman of his father's generation. That was why, in the mind's eye, he looked rather a lot like Silverman's father during his younger years, the child of immigrants torn between past and present, struggling to escape and yet honor loyalties rooted in their tortured history. *But I belong to the future,* the nineteen-year-old Daniel Silverman had decided. *What Fish says of himself—that nobody knows who they are in America—may be true. But this is not ethnic, it is existential. It is everyman's fate to grow away from origins. In the modern world every thinking person becomes a* nebech, *and welcomes that fact because this is what frees us from the past, and so we become ourselves.*

"Oh, that's a cute one," said Shenandoah Fish, who had come upon all this before as he wandered among Silverman's thoughts. "A brilliant and impregnable defense you've designed for yourself, a Maginot line of the conscience. Congratulations, Mr. Modern American Obfuscator. But what you're up against here, this isn't a matter of ethnicity, it's common decency." Like Silverman's father, Fish spoke with a heavy New York accent.

Silverman knew at once there was no point in arguing. The outcome was certain. Anyone who could twist his conscience like Shenandoah Fish was bound to win his point. Still, because the fear and the reluctance he felt were so oppressively real, he would do his best to squirm out of his responsibility.

"Look, these people who brought me here are hard to take," Silverman argued feebly. "Believe me, they gripe the pants off me. I mean, every night of my life from now on, I'm going to hear them praying for my conversion. 'Lord, help us to wash this stiff-necked Jew in the blood of the lamb and bring him into thy fold, yada, yada, yada.' You think I like that? But as anti-Semites go, they aren't the worst."

"Oh?" said Fish. "And what could be a crueler act than to deny the reality of a people's suffering? To say it never happened? In this you wish to participate?"

"Of course not," Silverman protested. "I care deeply. I mean, in principle I care." He turned back to his grandfather, who, with his face screwed into a knot, was struggling to understand what was passing between his grandson and Fish. "I do care, *zeyde*. But these people—they aren't worth the trouble. They're minor, backwoods bigots. Who cares about them, stuck up here in the north woods brooding over their sins?"

Fish was unimpressed. "You think it's smart to wait until the rednecks put on black shirts before you spare them a few fine words of criticism?" His tone was turning more sardonic by the moment.

"What would it get me?" Silverman asked. "A small charge of vindication. I couldn't change their minds. In fact, arguing with them could make things worse." His grandfather made a disgusted face and waved him aside with a dismissive gesture. "It's true," Silverman insisted to Fish. "They're fanatics. It would be like talking to a stone wall. Is it worth the grief?"

"Have they no souls?" Fish asked. "Don't they deserve whatever chance you can give them to learn the truth and show compassion?"

"Oh, come now!" Silverman scoffed. "I should care about that?"

"In any case," Fish went on, "in a situation like this, you are called upon to be a public Jew."

Silverman cringed at the phrase. That was how his father had many times described himself. He moved closer to Fish, lowering his voice. "I know what this looks like to him," he said, nodding over his shoulder toward his grandfather, who sat silently muttering to himself. "But you should understand. You remember in the story where it talks about your family? About how little they understand what you write? It says, 'Whatever he wrote as an author did not enter into the lives of these people, who should have been his genuine relatives and friends.'"

"You remember so much word for word?"

"Yes, isn't that remarkable?"

"Well, actually, wise guy, you got it wrong. The exact words are '*true* relatives and friends.'"

"No, I'm sure it says 'genuine,'" Silverman insisted.

"Well, you could be right," Fish admitted. "It's been so long."

"Wait, there's more. And then it says you were a 'monster' to your family. Why? Because, it says, you were 'a certain kind of au-thor.' A *certain* kind, meaning sophisticated and deep and searching."

"Flattery will get you nowhere," Fish replied sharply. "Espe-cially since I'm a fictitious character. I never wrote a word."

"Okay," Silverman agreed, "but you do say—or Delmore Schwartz says—that this separation between you and your family was totally irrelevant when it comes to what really matters, which is the work itself."

"Oh my! This is worth a trophy," Fish commented. "Such excel-lent casuistry! I could almost *plotz*. You went, maybe, to a Jesuit college? And do you recall it also says in this story, which you are twisting into an ethical pretzel by now, that this gulf between me and my family fills my work with denial and rejection? You think that's good? Maybe you should re-read the text, smarty pants. And maybe you should remember one more thing." Fish's expression shifted from frowning disdain to true melancholy. "Everything you're quoting was written before 1940."

Silverman sighed. "Well, yes, I see that. But look, give me a break here. I'm not political, I'm not."

"Which is why you aren't in any of your books," Fish replied. "I mean not really *in* them, but always floating above the story, at a distance. The whale, the various women, the gargoyles even—you write from everybody's viewpoint except your own."

"A writer has to be able to see things from all sides."

"Which is not the same as refusing to take sides." Suddenly, Fish stepped forward aggressively, fixing Silverman with a sly look. "Tell the truth. When the good Reverend Apfel crapped all over the suffering of millions, what was the first word that popped into your ever-so-literary mind? The very first."

"I . . . I don't remember."

"Get off it. You remember, because I remember. I heard. '*Oy*,' you said. Am I correct?"

"Yes," Silverman relented. "But. . . ."

"'*Oy*,' you said. See? Case closed."

"So exactly what does that prove? *Oy*."

"Say a guy named O'Shaughnessey claims he's an atheist. But in a foxhole with the bullets flying, he makes the sign of the cross.

What does that tell you?"

"It's not the same!" Silverman insisted. "*Oy* is part of the American vernacular. Everybody says it."

"You can imagine Fitzgerald, he ever said '*Oy*'? You think John Updike, he's in a pickle, he says '*Oy*'? Please."

"We're not dealing here with anything that important," Silverman pleaded. "This is one of those things where the best response might be to rise above it all."

"Rise above it? You're good at this rising-above-ness, aren't you? You're a fucking balloon, already, is what you are. Your pen name should be Daniel Helium."

Behind him, Grandpa Zvi, his hand cupped at his ear, was trying for all he was worth to make sense of what Fish and Silverman were saying. His expression made it clear that he trusted neither of these *gonifs*. And now, indeed, he was beginning to fade away. He was less than a shadow.

"Look," Silverman pleaded, "this trip was meant to be in and out, a soft touch. I didn't come here to play defender of the faith. I agreed to come as an author, to talk about literature, you know? I'm here alone, for God's sake! I'd like to get out of here with as little hassle as possible. Now that's perfectly reasonable, isn't it? Isn't it?"

"Of course," Fish said. "But answer me one thing. How does that differ, may I ask, from simply being a lily-livered *schtunk*?"

Mercifully, before Silverman could be expected to answer, Swenson was at the door. "We're ready for you," he said.

Silverman, preparing to leave, searched the now-empty room. He was on his own. He turned away and closed his eyes."Oh, Marty, you were right. I should have told you to bake more Madeleines."

He wished, he wished, he wished—that he were anyplace but here. But in another moment he would be still deeper into the ordeal. He would be in the pulpit.

10

The Blue Tattoo

It was, after all, a church. And so, as they entered, people fell into a hush. But Silverman knew this wasn't a hush of eager expectation; he wasn't in the company of literary fans eager to hear their favorite author. Row after row, students, faculty, and parents filed into the pews and took their seats as solemnly as witnesses at an execution. Even before all the seats were filled, Silverman realized that this was the largest audience he had addressed in years. At a bookstore, it would have qualified as celebrity-level attendance. Seated in the front row, he was thumbing through the pages of the lecture he now knew he wouldn't give. But what would he do? He had no idea. Two thoughts loomed large in his mind. One: *Hanna has their check.* Two: *I have my plane tickets in my pocket.* Those were such beautiful, reassuring thoughts that he simply kept rolling them around in his brain.

On the other hand, Swenson, seated beside him with his three young humanists, was percolating with nervous anxiety. The twitchy little smile he kept flashing at Silverman did nothing to reassure either of them. It didn't help that Mrs. Bloore was taking her time reaching the chapel. If she didn't arrive soon, Swenson might very well collapse of terminal tension. Her seat, Silverman gathered, was one of the three that remained empty on the front row aisle. What were Christians supposed to be thinking about in church, Silverman wondered. He picked a hymnal off the seat beside him and browsed through.

> Evil world, I leave thee
> Thou canst not deceive me,
> Thine appeal is vain.

Sin that once did blind me,
Get thee far behind me.

The name "Jesus," the words "love," "grace," "sin," and "forgiveness" leaped out on every page, and, strangely, the word "blood." Songs imploring mercy and consolation. A grim vision of life afflicted by misfortune all around and infinite, gnawing guilt within. He thought back to the Berglunds, intrepid Christian soldiers. How casually they had prattled on, describing the horrors they faced in their work. Silverman couldn't get a fix on such people. Had their faith made them cheerfully courageous? Or had it blunted their ability to experience life?

At a signal from Swenson a group of students took their place at the front, facing the congregation. They were carrying various rustic instruments, banjos, a fiddle, a harmonica, even a Jew's harp. They started in on a bit of gospel music that had a faint bluegrass tone to it. The style was modestly upbeat, but the words remained dire, a lament about fallenness and the faint hope of redemption. A girl with a tambourine took up the song. "Peace perfect peace,/ In this dark world of sin,/ The blood of Jesus whispers love within." At Silverman's side, Swenson beamed with proud delight as he discretely clapped hands. Silverman gathered this was another of Swenson's major concessions to youthful modernity: morbid teachings set to a whining country tune.

Suddenly Swenson stood up as if he had been yanked from his seat. He had spotted Mrs. Bloore entering at the rear. The singing stopped. The congregation turned and watched. With Professor Jaspers at her side and Miss Bjork pushing, the great lady glided down the center aisle in her chair and pulled herself into her seat. If there was anyone who knew how to upstage God Almighty, it was Mrs. Bloore. She glanced at Silverman as if he were a stranger, no smile, no nod. But then, Silverman was giving no smile, no nod. *Twelve-thousand bucks for forty-five minutes,* he was thinking, and that was all he was thinking.

When the chapel doors were finally closed, Swenson rose to take charge. "Pastor, will you lead us in prayer?"

Reverend Apfel, who had slipped in at the side of the pulpit, stepped forward, bowed his head, closed his eyes, and raised his right hand high over his head. In a richly orotund voice that was nothing like his normal tone, he commanded, "Everybody stand and say 'Jesus.'"

"Everybody" presumably included that day's Jewish guest, who, nevertheless did not stand and say "Jesus!" But everybody else did. The entire congregation rose, raised their right hands, and intoned "Jesus!" at top volume, stretching the first syllable as if to see who could make it last longest. Some people might have added six or seven "sus"s before others had finished the "Jeeeee."

What a nice welcome, Silverman thought, he being conspicuously the only person in the church who kept his seat and uttered nothing. *What next? Shall we all immerse?*

"Hallelujah," Reverend Apfel whispered with quiet authority. He lowered his hand and opened his eyes; the congregation sat. After a moment of silence, he spoke again. "We thank Thee, Lord, for the fruit of Our Savior's atoning sacrifice on the Cross. We stand before Thee, Thy loving disciples, with sinners' hearts that beg for Thy forgiveness. At the beginning of a new millennium, fill our minds with Thy teachings so that we may clearly discern truth from error in all that we hear today. Guard us from false doctrines, no matter how they please the ear. Strengthen our resolution so that we shall not be swayed an inch, even by the Devil's eloquence. Let the power of Thy spirit enfold this gathering for the edifying of the body of Christ till we all shall come unto the measure and fullness of Thy Kingdom. And let Thy saving grace infuse our guest so that his words may serve Thy glory. In Jesus' name, Amen."

And everybody said "Amen."

Now that's what I call warming up an audience, thought Silverman. *I'll be lucky if they don't throw rocks at me.*

Swenson rose again to speak. This time he introduced Jake Dawes, "the Senator who has served our district, our church, and our Lord so well." Dawes, wearing a well-practiced smile, took over the gathering with consummate political ease. "As the first speaker in our millennial Religious Humanism lecture series, we are delighted to have the distinguished Jewish Humanist—and number one best-selling novelist—Professor Daniel Silverman."

Silverman would have been happy if Dawes had stopped there, but he of course continued offering a deluge of adulation, the mark of a host doing his best to sell the crowd on a dubious speaker. The introduction went on and on, listing every book Silverman had written and numbering among his bibliography various reviews and articles he had written over the years as if these also might be novels. Dawes' remarks, a prepared text he was obviously reading for the first time, even included excerpts from reviews, some of them slashing comments. "Well, I guess *The Boston Globe* wasn't too high on that one, eh, Professor? But the *Des Moines Press-Register*—now that's right here next door to us—felt that Professor Silverman 'deserves credit for an engaging tale well told.' I'll bet that warmed your heart. Now more seriously, my friends, as we gather here today to welcome the religio-humanistic perspective into our understanding, I ask that you try to see all that Professor Silverman says and all he has written, both the rough and the smooth, in its proper and redeeming literary context, remembering that the Holy Word of God is also literature and that the life of our Lord is also a story, and that for some who travel through this vale of tears in search of the road of faith, a work of fiction may lead them to the one true Word. And let that be our subtext for today. So to speak. Hallelujah and Amen."

When he was finished, Dawes took his seat beside Swenson and the three students Silverman had met outside the commons room. They offered him the only friendly faces he could see as he mounted the pulpit.

Silverman took a moment to adjust. He was relieved to see no graphic symbols of the faith. The chapel was, in fact, graceful of design and mercifully unadorned—well, except for the stained glass windows, but that wasn't too bad. In fact, most of those looked like scenes from the Old Testament. Drawing a deep, steadying breath, Silverman began by holding up a sheaf of papers. "I did bring a lecture with me. This is it. All about books and authors—Jewish authors, Bellow, Mailer, Roth, Malamud—all the guys you've been waiting with bated breath to hear about, I'm sure. Writers of social alarm, they've been called. I guess that qualifies them as Jewish Humanists, though they might be surprised to find themselves so classified. They'd probably rather be called, well, writers. And they are all fine writers, every one of them. Nothing makes me prouder than occasionally to see myself mentioned along with them. I don't deserve that, but it makes me feel great.

"I thought I might be telling you about them today, because, after all, that's how Richard persuaded you to spring for the very generous amount of money I'm being paid here. It's a chance to show how tolerant the Free Reformed Evangelists can be. I'm sorry, maybe I got that wrong. Is it Reformed Free Brothers? Well, mix and match as you wish. But I gather I'm here to give you a chance to be 'ecumenical,' is that the right word, Richard? Sort of 'take a Jewish guy to church this Sunday.' And that's good. It's good for people to be tolerant. Or as some might say, 'glass-nosed.' Have you heard of that? 'Open?' 'Unbuttoned,' the way Reverend Lucy was in some respects. But I digress. Suffice it to say, while I can't claim to know as a matter of certainty, I'd like to believe that God approves of tolerance. It would mean He bears with His troubled children as they pick their way through His big, confusing world. And if He doesn't approve of tolerance, if He prefers the Spanish Inquisition, well I would say 'shame on you, you big bully!'"

He could hear rustling in the pews and some whispers. *Get on with it*, he told himself.

"Am I wandering here? I guess I am. Sorry. Maybe I'm trying to work up some speed. I won't take much more of your time. I'm not going to give the lecture I brought with me. Instead I'm going to tell you about a much more important example of Jewish writing than our great novelists. I'm going to say a few words about the most important piece of Jewish writing ever. No, I don't mean the Bible. Not something written *by* Jews, but written *on* Jews. I came across it when I was five years old, before I could even read. I didn't know what it meant, though it was pretty simple. One line. I memorized it. B742365. That's it. B742365. It was written by hand in little blue characters. It was written on my Aunt Naomi. Right here, on the inside of her left arm. B742365. 'What's that?' I asked her one day. She was holding me on her lap at the time, and her sleeve slipped up and I saw this odd mark. And she said, 'That was written on me by Adolf Hitler.' Now, in my family that name

Hitler was what I guess Gog and Magog or the Great Beast or the Antichrist might be for you. A name rarely mentioned, and when mentioned only in a certain tone, a combination of fear and fury and disgust. I certainly didn't understand why that man should be writing things on my Aunt Naomi. So she explained. And when she was finished explaining, she wept. Not for herself, but for me. For the sheer surprise and horror she saw in my five-year-old face. She wept as if she was apologizing to me for the way of the world— that she should be the one to tell me. She said, 'Some people have already forgotten about what I told you. Some people refuse to believe. That's why I don't take it off, that mark. I keep it there, so I will remember and so I can show them so they will remember.'

"Will you understand what I mean if I tell you that Aunt Naomi's little blue tattoo is the most important work of Jewish literature ever written? Those who wrote it testify to the greatest evil imaginable. And those, like Aunt Naomi, on whose flesh this work was published and who have survived and carried on, testify to the greatest courage, the greatest humanity, the greatest love of life I can imagine. What else can anybody expect of a work of literature than that it should contain so much of the good and the evil?

"I've been in North Fork for only a day now, but I've learned that there are some people in these outlying regions of the country who can't believe such evil was ever done. Perhaps they think God would never let such a thing happen. I guess they feel ashamed of God, but they can't bring themselves to say so. They want to get God off the hook. So they try to deny the truth, as if that's what their faith demands. I wish I could introduce them to Aunt Naomi, who is dead now. I wish they could read her blue tattoo. They might believe her. Aunt Naomi was a deeply religious person. She said the prayers and lit the candles and went to the synagogue. Aunt Naomi went through it all, things I cannot bring myself to tell you, things I should not have to tell you, because you should all know them. But she never stopped believing in God. She never let Hitler take God away from her. But Hitler did take God away from my father and my mother and from me.

"To some degree I am here under false pretenses. I am not actually much of a Jew—not when it comes to all the religious things a

good Jew should know. Not as Aunt Naomi understood being a
Jew. In that area, I'm pig ignorant. My father refused to have the
Bible in our house. He was an orthodox atheist and wanted me to
grow up to be the same. Instead I grew up to be, I suppose, a
nebech. That means 'nothing' in Yiddish. Not a Jew, but not anything else either, not even an atheist. Maybe that's what a humanist is: someone who tries to find the worth of life without asking
God to give it to him ready made.

"I wasn't sure I wanted to give this talk today. I came, frankly,
because the money was good. But now, right now as I stand here,
I'm glad I came. I think I told you something important. And even
if what I said didn't mean much to you, it has made a big difference
for me. Today, maybe for the first time in my life, I feel very Jewish. Because I've been reminded that I'm Aunt Naomi's nephew,
that I have had this chance to defend the dignity of her life, and to
associate myself with her. I could never have endured what she endured. In that sense, I cannot even claim to represent her. But at
least I can remember what she told me and defend its truth to
those who would wish it away or lie it away. What could be a
greater blasphemy than that people should suffer for their religion
and then have others say their suffering was a hoax?

"Whatever you believe about God, about His love and mercy
and goodness, you must also believe this. That He let Adolf Hitler
etch an obscene little blue tattoo on my aunt's arm. And that He
let others who wore those tattoos perish by the millions. I leave
you to make whatever sense of that you can. As people in my family used to say, 'So go figure.'

"That's really all I have to say, all I feel like saying. I don't know
if this was of any value to you, but it was to me. There's something
Bernard Malamud wrote. It comes at the end of one of those long,
dreary sagas of Jewish suffering and injustice. 'One thing I've
learned,' he wrote, 'there's no such thing as an unpolitical man, especially a Jew. You can't be one without the other.'"

He let a pause settle in, then added, "So okay, that's it. I think
Richard wants to have a question period now, so ask away."

11

A Good Word for the Monkeys

On a few fondly remembered public occasions Silverman had been
greeted by the tribute of delighted silence after a lecture. That was
the sound of an audience moved too deeply to want to break the
spell of the moment. There were passages in his books—not many,
but a couple—that produced that delicious effect. Now what he
faced was another kind of silence, the silence that settles along the
tracks after a train wreck when the last voice stops calling for help.

What he had done was so unexpected that Swenson, his only
sure ally, was caught off balance. Instead of stepping forward as he
had promised to field questions, he sat trapped between pathos
and astonishment, staring stupidly at Silverman. Silverman felt
himself beginning to sweat. Perhaps he should simply leave the
pulpit with an air of injured dignity. At last Swenson shook himself alert and rose. Turning, he looked out over the audience. "Are
there any questions?" he asked, stumbling over every word in the
sentence. "If not. . . ." He was obviously trying to close fast. But
before he could, a small, red-haired girl in the middle of the
church stood up. Silverman nodded at her. Taking at least one
question before he walked away seemed the most graceful thing to
do in the circumstances. Besides, he was curious to know what the
girl had to say. She appeared to be bursting with eagerness.

"Do Jews believe that we come from monkeys? Thank you," she
said, in the cadence of a well-rehearsed question and at once sat
down.

Silverman stared at her. His mind went blank. "What?"

She bounced back to her feet. "Do Jews think we come, you
know, from monkeys?"

"I . . . well . . . I have no idea what Jews. . . . Well, yes, I think, well, at least most Jews I know, most people I know believe. . . . Actually, I think you have that wrong. I don't think anybody believes we come from monkeys." Glancing toward Swenson, he caught sight of Tilly. Her face burning, she was staring up at him in a silent panic. But on the other side of the aisle, Mrs. Bloore was holding him in a cold, punitive stare that meant *twenty lashes well laid on*.

The girl who had asked the question had fixed Silverman with a look at once quizzical and suspicious. "Didn't you ever hear of Darwin and like that?"

"Of course."

"Well, isn't that what secular people believe? That we came from monkeys?"

"'Secular people'? Odd, I never thought of myself as representing anything that large. But, let's see, as I recall from my high school biology, the correct phrase is: we and the monkeys descend from a common ancestor. Common ancestor, yes, that's right."

"So, does that mean we come from monkeys?"

Silverman wanted to chuckle her inquiry away, but he sensed that nobody would chuckle with him. It was clear from the faces he surveyed that the audience was behind this question. "You know, I think this is really inappropriate. I didn't come here to teach a class on evolution. And I certainly can't speak for all secular people, whoever they are."

That only encouraged the girl to become more dogged. She apparently felt she had him on the run. "Well, is that what *you* believe? That we come from animals?"

Silverman blew off a frustrated breath. "Yes, in a sense. Common ancestors would be animals."

The girl stared at him with honest horror. "How can you believe that? I mean where are our tails?"

Around the room Silverman saw smiles and nods passing down the aisles: people agreeing that he was indeed an imbecile to think people came from monkeys. For indeed where were our tails? With hundreds of eyes upon him, Silverman tried to keep his cool. Affecting a breezy little grin, he resorted to literature. "Let's see. . . .

There's a short story by Philip Roth. It's about this little Jewish boy, a real pesky kid, who gets his whole school, including his rabbi, to agree that Jesus might have been the Messiah. Because if God can do anything—He's omnipotent, right?—then why couldn't He arrange for a virgin to have a baby and make that baby the Messiah? You see the point? Once you make a virtue of believing the unbelievable, where do you draw the line? Of course, in the story, the little boy has to threaten he'll jump off the roof and kill himself if the rabbi doesn't agree. But now you—and I guess everybody in this room—have no trouble believing in the virgin birth, do you? Easy as pie for you to believe that, even though it seems pretty far-fetched to me. So if you can believe that, why not that God could turn an amoeba into a man—in easy stages, of course? I mean, who's to say God couldn't do life on Earth that way? That'd be quite a trick. In any case, I can tell you for sure that Jews are pretty clear about the difference between religion and biology."

The girl was totally unimpressed. Looking around for support—and finding it—she answered, "It can't be that way because the Bible doesn't say so. It doesn't say God turned a smelly, dumb old monkey into a person with a soul and all. And the Bible is God's holy Word." Nods of approval all around. Somebody added a "hallelujah."

The girl's tone was so smarmy that Silverman decided to counter-punch. "So you prefer to think you're made of dirty old dirt?"

"Huh?"

"I recall that the Bible, which some people regard as totally true and trustworthy, says we were made from the dust of the Earth. Reverend Apfel might correct me here, but I think the Bible says, literally, that God made Adam from dirt. Yes? No? Is coming from dirt better than coming from animals?"

Reverend Apfel, who was standing at the rear of the church, arched his brow smugly. "As you say yourself, Mr. Silverman, you aren't all that proficient when it comes to scripture."

"I'm willing to drop the point." Silverman sighed. "I don't frankly care what we're made of or where we came from. I have no objection to being related to animals, especially since I believe that to be true. Animals are pretty good, better than a lot of people I know. There's a poem by Whitman about the dignity of animals. You should look it up. Animals, he says, "don't make me sick discussing their duty to God. They don't lose sleep weeping for their sins." I like that. In any case, I write stories about people, wherever or whatever they came from. But I guess I'm willing to put in a good word for the monkeys."

"Shall we move on?" Swenson said, again rising to his feet. "If there are no more questions. . . ."

But Swenson wasn't moving fast enough. He was leaving just enough of a pause to let another question sneak through. A girl rose to speak. Like several others in the audience, she held a card in her hand, apparently to make sure she wouldn't forget the great point she was about to make. Reading stiltedly from the card, she asked, "If Jewish people wrote the Bible, how come they don't believe that Jesus is their personal savior like it says in the Bible? Thank you." And down she sat.

Take a deep breath, Silverman advised himself. "Well, one simple answer would be that if Jews did believe in Jesus, then they wouldn't be Jews. And if there weren't any Jews, who would Christians have to kick around for the last couple thousand years?" That drew a few frowns and gasps. Silverman let a small glow of delight show in his expression. *Good! That's one for our team.* "Or another answer might be that the people who wrote the Old Testament didn't feel the addendum quite measured up. You do know that we're dealing with two different—very different—books here? The old and the new? Even a humanist knows that much."

The girl stood up again. "But the Old Testament prophesies Jesus as clear as day. Thank you." And she plumped down looking quite pleased with herself. There was a stirring around the chapel that suggested the room might burst into applause.

"Are you sure about that?" Silverman asked, fighting back a surprising wave of sorrow he could feel rising inside him. The truly pathetic thing about this question was its bouncy, bright-eyed sincerity. This kid really believed what she was saying. Everybody in the room was with her in that belief. In all their lives, these people would probably never once stand face to face with their own entrenched ignorance. He was talking to an audience that was at the absolute limit of its intelligence. "Do you know what language the Bible—I mean the *real* Bible, the Old Testament—was written in?" he asked.

The girl frowned back at him suspiciously. "Jewish? I guess?" she replied nervously.

"Okay, that's close enough. Well, can you read Jewish?"

"No," the girl answered, now looking severely annoyed. "But you don't really have to, because God put it all into English."

"Oh, I see. Well, you have to understand that Jews are very dubious about this idea that the Old and New Testaments belong between the same covers. My father, who incidentally went to Hebrew school and actually learned to read 'Jewish,' used to say that every time he thought about the Old Testament getting teamed up with the New Testament, it reminded him of a comedy act. You have the straight man, you know, who keeps trying to explain things to the little boob. And the little boob keeps getting it all wrong." Again there was a rustle of annoyance in the room. "Anyway, that's how my admittedly irreverent father saw it. Myself, I say if you want to borrow our book, be my guest. It's out of copyright, so do as you please. Incidentally, you do know that the Muslims also got in on the act. They added quite a bit more to the Bible. Have you ever considered believing in the Koran?" The girl frowned with bewilderment, looking all around her for support in the face of this apparent insult. "I'm not being facetious," Silverman hastened to add. "That's the way a humanist sees things. Read the book, sample everything, make up your own mind. Maybe you'd make a great Muslim. How can you tell until you try it out? Life is an adventure. Live it."

"Thank you, Professor Silver. . . ." But before Swenson could cut the meeting short, three more students were on their feet, each holding a card. Silverman sensed there was blood in the water and the sharks were circling. Shrugging and hoping for the best, he nodded toward a lean young man with a ruddy, earnest face. He seemed the least aggressive of the students before him, but once he was called on he turned a challenging gaze on Silverman as if he were drawing a bead. He was wearing a tee-shirt under his suit jacket. There was something written across it that ended with "Jesus." As the boy spoke, Silverman tried to read the rest of the message. "Sir, in your book about Emma? When she has this baby coming, she has an abortion?" The kid paused, then hit the word "abortion" hard, giving it an explosive emphasis. At the same time he twisted his face into a disgusted grimace. A mediocre piece of amateur dramatics, Silverman thought, but it had the desired effect. At once, there were sounds of audible surprise from several quarters in the hall. As Silverman suspected, most of those present hadn't read any of his books. So now they knew: this guy writes about "things like that." The kid went on. "And the way it says in the book, you make that seem like it's. . . ." Another histrionic pause. ". . . okay. Do you truly approve of Emma murdering her child, sir? Thank you."

Swenson rose to intervene. "*I, Emma* wasn't one of the assigned texts for this lecture. I believe we should move. . . ."

Real Men Love Jesus. Silverman had finally worked out the phrase emblazoned across the boy's tee-shirt. "He's asking about one of my books, Richard," Silverman said, cutting Swenson off. "That's fair enough. In fact, that's what I thought I came here to talk about." He turned to the boy who was still standing. "Yes, I approve of what Emma does. I believe a woman has that right. Most of what troubles Emma is that, in her time, women had so few rights and no power over their lives. They bore the babies, but men owned the babies—and their wives' bodies. Literally so. So Emma is fighting her way free of centuries of male domination, as women were doing in her day. But I hope you noticed how she suffered over that decision. You see, I wanted to show. . . ."

There was a sudden disturbance at the rear of the church. Somebody was making his way rapidly out of one of the pews, scrambling over the knees of those who were in his way. It was Axel Hask. Clear of the pew, he lumbered rapidly up the center aisle and out the door as if the building had caught on fire. Silverman interpreted his departure as furious disapproval. *Ah well, you can't please everybody.*

"As I was saying, I wanted to show the full moral tension of that decision."

"And you think what she did was *right?*" the student asked on a rising note of incredulity.

"I would place what Emma does in a category that deserves more understanding than dividing the world between right and wrong. I'd call what she did an emotional miscarriage." The student was making an expression of painful incomprehension, looking right and left for support. "Okay, let me explain," Silverman said. "You see, human beings—well, women, that is—don't experience pregnancy the way other animals do. Shouldn't that be obvious? I mean, as far as we know, animals can't take an attitude toward their pregnancy, can't have an emotional response. It's a purely physical process. They're very obedient to their anatomy. But a woman gets pregnant with her total being, her heart, her conscience, the full force of her life. That's what I was interested in at that point in my book. So when Emma gets pregnant by the lover who has spurned her, she feels. . . ."

At the rear of the church, there was another commotion. A door slammed, there were raised voices. Axel Hask had returned, with blood in his eye. He was struggling to drag a huge bundle through the door. Reverend Apfel, standing at one side of the entrance, rushed to lend a hand. Together he and Axel at last yanked the cumbersome object into the chapel. Hefting the load on his shoulder, Axel trundled down the center aisle. Behind him trailed a rotund woman with a face as scowling as Axel's. When Axel and the woman had reached the middle of the chapel, they unrolled the bundle between them. It was a canvas scroll. At first, Silverman couldn't make out the picture it carried, but he could clearly see the words spelled out in large, crooked red letters: "Holocaust USA. One Million Per Year." Squinting at the image on the scroll, he finally made out its meaning. It was a blown-up, blurred photograph of a dismembered baby, the head, the arms, the legs scattered across a blood-smeared sheet. It was the ugliest thing Silverman could remember seeing since, well, since the last time he had seen a photograph of the death camps.

"You want to talk about Holocaust?" Axel called out in a voice that rumbled across the church like thunder. "I give you Holocaust. Humanist! Baby butcher! You think this is okay?" He had a strong guttural accent, but whether German or Scandinavian, Silverman couldn't tell. More likely it was Neanderthal.

Axel and the woman stood glowering at Silverman. He had never seen such fury directed at him; it pressed against his brow like a physical force. As he scrambled in his mind to deal with the situation, he caught sight of Jake Dawes leaning toward Swenson to whisper in his ear, then excusing himself and rapidly exiting through a door at the right. The Senator was no doubt cutting his losses. He would probably have his staff at work on damage control before the end of the day. The remainder of the audience seemed unmoved by the outburst, as if Axel and the woman—probably his wife—had done no more than raise a reasonable point. Mrs. Bloore, her eyes still more fiercely riveted on Silverman, now added a sharp, approving nod to all that Axel had to say.

In that moment, for a split-second as if by an act of black magic, Silverman was inwardly startled to see the audience before him turn into one great glaring face, its eyes burning into him with a monstrous hostility. The terrible vision came and went in a second, but before it faded, Silverman clicked it into his literary memory, an image so ugly he couldn't imagine ever wanting to confront it again. *Think fast!* his mind was telling him. At once a clever strategy presented itself. *One: get into some warm socks. Two: get the hell out of here right now, even if you have to run all the way to Minneapolis!*

Well, fat chance of that. He had hoped that Aunt Naomi's story would soften their hearts, but apparently not. Where did that leave him? Could his allies help? Silverman glanced over at Swenson. Two of his student allies, Alex and the girl, were hanging their heads. Jack was watching Silverman with an expression of profound sympathy. Swenson rose to speak. Before he could open his mouth, Axel shouted him down. "No! You sit down! Let *him* answer, the Jew that comes to ask pity for the Holocaust. Here is Holocaust. Do you approve, Professor?"

And Swenson sat down. *Thanks, pal,* Silverman whispered under his breath. Then, forgiving the man, he looked away. This wasn't Swenson's fight, after all. *You're a big boy now,* Silverman said to himself. *What would Marty tell you to do? Of course.* No way out but to face down the true believers.

Silverman allowed a long pause. He was frankly amazed at how calm he was becoming. Acquiescence in fate, perhaps. Or maybe it had something to do with Jack's eyes being on him. They reminded him of things that mattered more than whatever was going on in this sad, tortured space that was meant to be a house of God. "Mr. Hask, is it?" he asked at last. "Mr. Hask, I wish I could respect your feelings, but I can't. You simply have no right to the word 'Holocaust.' It doesn't suit your cause. You should really find your own tragic imagery rather than hi-jacking from others for whose suffering you seem to have no understanding. Do you know what you mean by Holocaust as you are using the word? You mean a troubled woman, maybe a deeply shamed or frightened girl, ending her pregnancy with fear and trembling—because that's what most abortions are, a sad, desperate last resort in life. If you can't see the difference between that and the deliberate extermination of millions of people by a well-oiled war machine under the control of cold-blooded, ideological fanatics, well, then, we don't share the same moral universe." Somebody in the audience hissed. That rattled Silverman. He had never been hissed at before. But his composure held. "Or maybe you'd prefer to have a lecture from Mr. Hask on medical ethics."

The student who had asked the question pointed to the banner that Axel and his wife still held unfurled. "Well, in words of one single syllable, what do you have to say about that picture? Is that okay with you, the way they murder babies? Do you approve of that?"

"It's a very ugly sight," Silverman conceded. "I wish Mr. Hask would remove it, though, frankly, I don't know what this picture represents. I don't know where it comes from. I don't believe it's a real photograph. It looks like a full grown baby that has been hacked to pieces. Or maybe it's a picture that has been cut up and pasted on the banner. As far as I know, most aborted fetuses are terminated before they are more than a few unformed cells."

Somebody called out, "Life is life. Size does not matter."

"Well, okay," Silverman agreed. "I take your point. Ethically speaking, maybe it doesn't settle anything to count trimesters. I think I understand the moral position of those who reject abortion.

But then, nobody favors abortion, you know. I don't, certainly. People favor the right to choose. Isn't that a sensible distinction? We agree that people have certain rights—to speak, to worship, to invest their money, to decide things about their bodies—but not on the assumption that we'll always approve of how they use those rights.

"I have a neighbor back in San Francisco who works for Family Planning. Sally Weeks. Sally used to be a Catholic nun, a pretty rebellious nun. She still opposes abortion. When she deals with a woman who wants an abortion, she tries to offer her some alternative. But if the woman finally chooses an abortion, that's what Sally helps her find. She believes we're living in a time when women have to be regarded as responsible adults. It's a matter of their moral dignity. That's pretty much my view. I don't object to people like Sally trying to talk women out of having an abortion. But I do want to see women left free to make the ultimate choice. See, that's the trouble with Mr. Hask's banner. It's not the whole picture. There's no womb there, there's no woman there, just an isolated baby suspended in space. Fetuses exist inside other people. That's why there's an ethical problem. Whose body is it, after all? Whose future is it? Not just the baby's. Anyway, try to understand that I'm a novelist. I don't like talking about things like this in the abstract. That's why I sink these big ethical questions into stories and surround them with as much human warmth as I can."

Silverman was frankly amazed at how sweetly reasonable he was trying to be. Shenandoah Fish should be pleased. He was trying to appeal to the conscience of these hostile people. But, alas! Axel Hask was having none of it. Pointing to the scroll, he bellowed, "Murder! Murder! You say okay."

Turning to Axel, Silverman said, "I get your point. Do you want me to stop or go on?" Axel and his wife didn't budge. Silverman took a deep breath and went on. "All right, then, Mr. Hask. Let's see if I have an answer for you. I think you're as phoney as your picture. I think anybody who uses guilt the way you're trying to use it here today has something to hide. Good people, honest people, don't use conscience on each other to draw blood. You're a fake, Mr. Hask."

"So? We will see who is the liar here," Axel roared back, still not budging.

Swenson, burning with embarrassment, stepped forward to bring an end to the meeting. In a voice that sounded as if he had been chewing on sandpaper, he said, "I'm sure we all appreciate what Professor Silverman has had to say to us today as we move into a new millennium. It gives us much food for thought." He began to clap, hoping to stir up a round of applause. The three students he had been sitting with joined him, but only briefly. The faint applause chilled into a solid, icy block of silence.

A few people rose to leave. Instead of beating a quick retreat, Silverman held his place in the pulpit. To his own surprise, he found himself opening his mouth to speak again. Courage, he was discovering, takes on momentum. "If I may," Silverman called out, "I want to add one more autobiographical detail that neither Richard nor Senator Dawes mentioned." The general commotion in the chapel came to an abrupt stop. Row by row, surprised faces turned toward Silverman. "Richard and the Senator couldn't mention this because they didn't know about it. If they had, today would have been an even greater test of your—shall I say your Christian charity? I mean all that about not casting the first stone. That's my favorite part of the New Testament. Back in San Francisco, or Sin City as some of you think of it, I have a lover. We aren't married because the law won't let us be married. That's because my lover isn't a she; he's a he. And incidentally, he's black— though I hope that makes no difference one way or the other. In fact, I think I may have gotten that one right. Isn't there a line in the good book somewhere . . . 'my lover is black and comely'? And he is—both of those."

This isn't smart, a voice inside him said. *It sure isn't necessary.* No, but it was certainly exhilarating. It was a way of giving this gang of bigots one swift kick before they saw the last of him. Sort of like spilling soup on someone who had insulted you at dinner. Hell, what did he have to lose? He was enjoying the dizzy surge that was welling up from some place below his diaphragm. Once the courage-juice starts running in your veins, it can be intoxicating—especially when you can see a clear route of escape: out the door, down the highway to the airport, grab a seat on the red-eye for SFO. Why wait until tomorrow? He could see the good old red-eye winking through the night at him from where it stood warming up on the runway—like that plane at the end of *Casablanca*, the last chance to escape. Wasn't it great to be a novelist? You could turn anything into a story.

He expected his remark to produce a stir, maybe even some cat-calls. Perhaps because his audience was gasped out, not much happened. The silence, already hostile, might have tilted a few more degrees toward revulsion. But he did get a detectable rise in one predictable quarter. Mrs. Bloore, for whose reaction he made a special point of watching, at last changed her expression—from frozen disdain to rigidified shock. Staggered to learn that she had, only an hour before, served fruit punch to a homosexual, she signaled at once for her wheel chair. Nurse Bjork went scurrying.

But there was another response Silverman hadn't anticipated—a gasp that could be heard around the room. It was Tilly, supposedly his humanist ally. Apparently his confession was too much for the poor pious girl. Her eyes popped and her hands went to her mouth as if she might be on the brink of vomiting. She rose as if she wanted to bolt for the door, but Alex and Jack held her back and set to work trying to calm her. Silverman had never witnessed such a look of wounded amazement. She looked as if he had just shot her in the stomach. And though he knew the girl not at all, her response jarred him. He felt hurt, perhaps because he recalled her saying she had read all his books—or at least as many as she could find. Well, that was one customer lost.

"So you see," Silverman continued, fixing Tilly with a sullen stare, "not only am I a Jewish humanist, I'm a homosexual humanist as well. I didn't have to tell you that. I actually make a point of not bringing it up. I like to think of it as private and, even more important, plain irrelevant. As irrelevant as how I brush my teeth or what I eat for breakfast. But at some point, after I leave, somebody is sure to find out. And if I didn't tell you, you might think it was a guilty secret. Or you might think Richard—and his young friends—were trying to cover it up. Well, it's private, but it isn't secret. So now you know. Whatever you think 'gay' means, I'm it."

"Ha, now we know the truth," Axel growled. "The baby killer is homo." He turned to glare at Swenson, "Homo abortionist. That is what you bring here to preach to us. Sodomite, Sodomite, be gone from this holy place!" Here and there around the chapel, Silverman saw lowered heads wag in resignation as if at tragic news. Nobody wished to make eye contact. *They're either praying for my soul,* Silverman concluded, *or imploring God to strike me dead.* Axel's appeal did, however, produce a rousing show of approval that was especially wounding. Tilly, her face now livid with repugnance, was on her feet applauding to beat the band at Axel's words. She was carrying on so wildly that her male companions, offering Silverman apologetic expressions of embarrassment, hastily intervened, all but dragging her out a side door. Slowly, the room emptied until, besides Silverman and Swenson, only Axel and his wife were left with their banner. Finally they folded their butchered baby out of sight and left, leaving behind a funereal quiet. Silverman stayed in place. If anybody was going to throw anything or make a remark, he wanted to be in the pulpit when they did.

As the last few people filed out at the rear, Silverman rushed to buttonhole Swenson like a cop pulling a suspect into a corner for questioning. He even slipped a hand under Swenson's lapel to get a firm grip. "Look, Richard, this has been a big mistake. I'm sure you agree. I want you to get me out of here pronto. I want you to take me back to your place now. Right now. And I want to be on the red-eye for San Francisco tonight, okay? I don't care what it costs, get me on board. I'll pay."

"Oh, please don't feel you have to rush away."

Silverman was hanging tough. "I have to and I want to. Tonight. The red-eye."

"I don't even know if there's a red-eye out of Minneapolis."

"Of course there is. There's always a red-eye."

"But we'd have to leave for the airport in. . . ."

"I won't unpack. I'm ready to go."

A voice called sharply from the back of the church. "Richard! May we see you please?" Silverman turned to see Reverend Apfel standing in the door to the lobby. Behind him he could see Mrs. Bloore surrounded by a half dozen members of the faculty, their faces a solid wall of contempt. Dawes was among them, no longer his smiling and jovial political self. Clearly he was prepared to terminate his Israeli connection. All were doing their best to avoid seeing Silverman, even though he was positioned between Swenson and them. "*Now*," Mrs. Bloore called in a voice more commanding than Apfel's. "I want to see you *now*, Richard."

"As for Mrs. Bloore," Silverman added, turning back to Swenson, "she didn't get the lecture she paid for, so she can have her money back. It was a free shot for me."

Swenson looked as if he were on the point of crying. "I'm sure there's no problem about the money, really."

"Yes, there is a problem. I don't want this money. I'm refusing it, understand?" He released Swenson and stepped away. Smoothing his hair back, Swenson moved toward Mrs. Bloore. "The red-eye, okay?" Silverman reminded him. "I'll be up in the room."

"I'll do what I can," Swenson answered without much conviction. "But it looks as if we may be having some weather. We'd need three hours to make the airport, if there's a flight, that is." He glanced at his wristwatch, peered out the window, and shook his head. Then, like a beaten dog at its master's heel, he followed Mrs. Bloore and her retinue out of the church.

Silverman stood in the chapel waiting for his nerves to unwind. He could tell that wasn't going to happen—not until he was 35,000 feet in the air, thoroughly sloshed and headed due west. As he waited, his heart hammering in his ears, an eerie sense of desertion descended upon him. With Swenson gone, he was alone in the chapel, abandoned to his fate like a wounded soldier left for dead on the field of battle. And then—wham—without warning, the lights went out. At once, shadows swept down from the ceiling like a quick curtain at the end of a performance. The gloom that closed upon him was unnerving enough, but worse, it called to his attention how little light there was filtering through the stained glass windows. Though it was only mid-afternoon, what remained of the day was being submerged in storm clouds. He shuddered. Even with the chapel empty, echoes of hostility hung thick in the air as if the very bricks and boards of the place were telling the Sodomite to be gone. Gathering up his coat and his lecture notes, he quickly headed up the center aisle for the door. There was so little light that he might have rushed by without noticing that there was, after all, one remaining presence in the chapel. But as he passed, a voice he couldn't ignore called out to him.

"Mazeltov! I knew you had it in you."

"Thanks a lot," Silverman answered, giving the words a hard sardonic twist. "But I was right, wasn't I? It was a waste of breath."

"You think so?" Shenandoah Fish asked. Despite the deepening shadows, Silverman could see the smile that stretched across Fish's lips, a lop-sided grin that revealed his broken front teeth. Silverman remembered that smile, though he had seen it rarely. It was his normally-grouchy father's smile, which always looked more like a sneer. "At least you got a good literary incident out of it, didn't you? That was impressive, how you stood up to the resident Nazi there. Don't tell me you haven't salted that away for future reference. Watch how it will grow in drama and eloquence. A whole novel it could become."

"Well, maybe, maybe."

"The story about your aunt—was it true?"

"Of course it was. Would I make up something like that?"

Fish shrugged maybe-yes, maybe-no. "With writers, how can you tell? They can't tell themselves. And in this case, you would have been justified to fabricate the story so you could stick it to the *goyim.*"

"Oh? Well, the pastor here, he thinks we made up the whole Holocaust. You think I should feed his skepticism?"

"The Holocaust nobody could make up. Aunt Naomi it would be okay to make up. The pea brains you're up against here, she's about as much as they can take in. And listen, refusing the fee, that was a magnificent gesture." Fish bunched his fingers at his lips and kissed the tips like a man savoring fine wine.

"Casting pearls," Silverman answered sourly.

"Ho-ho! Careful there. You're quoting from the opposition. Matthew, 7:6."

"Cut it out! Anyway, what good will it do? You saw how they applauded for the *gauleiter* with the banner. You think they're all going to have a change of heart when they get home?"

"That's not the point," Fish assured him suddenly turning stern.

"Oh? So what is the point?"

"You're down among the Christians, *boychik*. The point is to keep the first commandment of a public Jew. Thou shalt not fink out on your people—even if you are a world-champion bacon fresser."

12

Video Nirvana

Silverman wondered if there might be a lynch mob waiting for him in front of the chapel—or at least a few lingering hecklers. He paused in the doorway of the chapel to peer this way and that. The only people he could spot in the courtyard clearly had no interest in him. They were scrambling to leave as if they were running for shelter. As he stepped into the open air, he realized why. A gust of wind caught him at once, delivering a hard, cold punch. Snow, frigid and gritty, swirled around him like a swarm of angry white bees waiting to attack. At once his glasses were plastered over as if they had been whitewashed. He took them off and slipped them into an inside pocket, then pulled his coat tight at the neck. That did absolutely no good; the wind slashed through his flimsy garments like a rapier, chilling him down to his toes. Which way was the hall where he had left his suitcase? He couldn't remember. The darkness and the snow were closing down visibility by the minute. People rushed past him, apparently heading for the parking lot. The surrounding campus was streaked with the moving headlights of cars jockeying to find their way home.

Silverman headed one way, then another and at last lost his footing on the slippery ground. As he fell, the wind ripped the cap from his head. Spotting it on the ground, he crawled toward it only to lose his grip on his lecture notes. Cap and notes, all were swept out of his reach as if by a roaring prankster. He watched the scattering pages as they whirled off into the snowy chaos. Fine. The wind itself was trashing his work. The lecture he hadn't given became his free gift to the raucous Minnesota elements. *Hey, this is serious*, Silverman thought to himself as he struggled to get back on his feet. Another reality was aggressively impressing itself upon him, replacing the anger and anxiety he had carried with him out of the chapel—a wind strong enough to knock him off his feet, a cold that had already turned his fingers and feet numb.

Luckily, Gunderson Hall was still barely visible against the storm-darkened sky. Silverman fought his way in that direction against the buffeting wind. Once inside, he stamped his feet to bring the blood back, then rushed up the stairs to the founder's suite gasping for breath. There he stood for several seconds with his back against the door, his breath fluttering as if someone had chased him home. Rage, insult, alarm spun in his head. He was in a state of barely controlled detonation, a slow explosion of the rib cage that might get out of hand at any second. He made at once for his overnight kit and dug through, looking for his pills. What had he brought? Good old Restoril. Never leave home without it. One tablet would probably be enough to settle his nerves tonight. He downed two, swallowing without water. And what else? Paxil? He had three, four, five of those. No, takes too long to kick in. Ah, yes, Xanax would be just right. Superb for panic attacks. He shook the bottle. Not many of those left. He took one.

Then he went for the phone. What he needed now was all the warm, mothering friendship he could find—even it had to come via long distance. He punched in his home number, hoping as he did so that Marty would be home. Of course, he'd be watching the Rose Bowl, the Sugar Bowl, something that had a football in it. The real problem might be getting him to pick up the phone. Before Silverman had finished dialing, he got premature bleeps, then a recorded voice. "Please dial 9 for an outside line." He hung up and started over. This time he got a different recorded voice. "We're sorry. This telephone cannot accept long distance charges. Please dial the operator to place this call."

This wasn't helping. He was growing more agitated by the moment.

He dialed 9, he dialed operator, he prayed for connectivity. What he got was endless, endless ringing. As minutes passed, he could feel his nerves burning and curling and crisping. The result this time was the phone company's rising three-note theme that meant *Out of luck,* followed by the voice from another planet saying,

"Your call cannot be completed as dialed. Please check your telephone listing."

Silverman tried 9 and O for operator again. After many rings, an old, foggy, female voice answered. "Faith College."

"I want an outside line to place a collect, long distance call. What do I dial?"

"Who is your long distance carrier?" the voice croaked.

"I use, what is it? Shit! I just changed over. I can't remember."

"If you curse, sir, I will not be able to help you."

"What? Oh, sorry, very sorry. My long distance carrier—it's one of those cut-rate operations."

"Is it AT&T, MCI, or Sprint?"

"Oh, God!"

"*Please*, sir!"

"What?"

"You mustn't curse. This is a holy line."

"Oh. Sorry. Listen, Sprint, Shprint, I have no idea."

"Do you have a calling card?"

Calling card. Where was his calling card? In his wallet. He tugged his wallet out and began fingering through it. "Look, I'll take anything you can connect me with, okay?"

"Wait a moment. I'll give you an outside line. Dial 011." There was a click and a buzz, and finally a genuine dial tone. All the while, Silverman felt his blood bulging in his arteries. He dialed 011. More ringing. And more . . . and more. New Year's Day. Everybody was reaching out to touch their loved ones. Everybody but Daniel Silverman. After several minutes he wanted to smash the phone to pieces. With maximum self-restraint, he eased it back into its cradle. Okay, time to get that bottle of booze working. He tore open Marty's Canadian Club and sucked down a deep swig. It sent a shiver down his spine. Man, that was good! Pure liquid fire. It burned away the foul taste in his mouth. Now all he had to do was hang on until the pills and the whisky zombified him. Twenty minutes should do. Ah, but how was he going to get through those twenty minutes without climbing the walls and screaming? Diversion, he needed diversion, something to hammer his brain into numbness. The ideal thing!

He went to the closet and lifted out the little television set Swenson had stashed there. He plugged it in, positioned it at the foot of the bed, and lay back across the quilts. The set was practically an antique. Rabbit ears for an antenna and push buttons to switch the channels. Silverman kicked off his shoes, removed his right sock, and pressed his big toe against the control pad. Click, click, click—he was soon skimming round the dial. No sound, just pictures—and no picture on screen long enough to register its meaning. The tuning was so bad most of what he saw was a smear of crazy color. That didn't matter. Vertigo was the objective. Video nirvana was a trick he used when he was in the grip of writer's block. For Silverman, writer's block took the form of hyperactive neurons, a bubbling cerebral stew that had to be chilled. The spinning images on the flickering screen never failed to do that. They worked by deep-tissue boredom, stroking his brain into a relaxing stupor.

He fixed his gaze on what northern Minnesota television had to offer that late New Year's Day. Of course, football. Games on two channels, the action on the field, garishly colored and grudgingly squeezed between all the familiar commercials for beer, pizza, cars, beer, and more beer. What else? Not much. Some grainy, ghostly images that looked vaguely like a talk show: a very large black man seated between two even larger women, one black with a mile-high hairdo, one white wearing tons of cosmetics. All three were mouthing away in anger trying to shout over one another. Hadn't he seen this threesome before? Maybe the show was a rerun. What else? Gophers mating. Obviously PBS. What else? Something even less visible in grainy black-and-white. Was that Bette Davis? In what? Marty would know. Marty knew all the Bette Davis roles; at parties, he did such a great imitation of the lady. Who was the man in the scene? Looked like Claude Rains. What was that movie? Too late. The dial had to spin. And spin. And spin. He was amazed at how well he was managing to do this with his toe. Push, click, push, click. And then every other number: 2, 4, 6, 8. Television toeing. Someday it might be an Olympic event. Push, click. Football. Beer commercial. Yes—the fat threesome on the talk show were now socking and kicking each other. He had seen this before. One woman was going to tear the other's clothes off.

Copulating gophers, now with a curious bird watching . . . Bette Davis . . . round and round in a blurred cycle. It was working. His brain was going comatose. Restoril and the good amber whisky of Canada were beginning to wilt his synapses. He was unwinding, forgetting, floating away. Bliss.

At some point, as he sank deeper into welcome quiescence, the television screen began to blur before him. His hardworking toe slipped down and rested on the mattress. A moment later, not wanting to fall asleep, he shook himself awake and stared harder at the screen. What he saw was a face staring back at him, a large malevolent dead white face: a face that seemed to be shaped out of snow, an ice creature with great blazing eyes. It was growling at him. He knew this face. It was . . . Axel Hask! He was on television made up as the abominable snowman. No, he wasn't on television; he was climbing through the frame of the television. He was wriggling out of the set and into the room, a gargantuan white figure wielding a club. Silverman struggled to get off the bed and flee, but his legs had fallen asleep and wouldn't move. In a minute the murderous iceman would be on him. Then he heard a dull ringing somewhere across the room. The telephone. Suddenly he was wide awake, standing in the middle of the room. Axel wasn't there. The television was still running its silent pictures. A football game. No snowman. Silverman had been having a nightmare. The phone had awakened him. But now the phone was quiet. Had it really rung? Who was calling? Was that Swenson? Had he booked a flight?

Silverman raced over to the phone. He groped through his trousers for his pocket diary, found it, and flipped it open to Swenson's number. He punched it in and listened for the ring. Somebody said "Hello." The voice was distant, almost inaudible, but he knew it wasn't Swenson.

"Hello, Syl? This is Daniel Silverman at the college."

"Hello," the voice said again.

"This is Daniel Silverman," he shouted into the receiver.

"Oh, hello. I can hardly hear you."

He raised his voice still louder. "Is Richard there?"

"Richard? No. He's with you at the school."

"He's supposed to arrange for plane tickets."

"Plane tickets? I believe he sent you your tickets. For tomorrow at ten."

"No, for tonight. I want to leave tonight. On the red eye." There was long pause. "I can't stay here. I want to come back over to your place."

Then Syl said, "Was it that bad?"

"Yes, I'm afraid so. I really must leave. Must, must, must."

"I'm sure Richard can make everything all right. He does want you to meet the students."

"I'm sorry, Syl, it's too much for me to handle. Please understand. If it were mild dislike. . . . But there's this man here. Axel. He frightens me."

"Axel? Oh, yes. Be careful with Axel." There was honest fear in her voice.

"Careful? Why?"

"Be careful. Don't get him angry."

"Angry? The man is erupting like Vesuvius. It's about abortion."

"Oh, my Lord, did that come up? You should have avoided that. Axel has a thing about that. I mean we all oppose abortion, but Axel, it's different with him. He's, well, a fanatic."

"Tell me about it. He broke up the lecture. They *let* him break up the lecture. That's why I have to leave. Please, Syl, let me come back to your place."

"Yes, that would be best. Can Richard get you the reservation?"

"That's what I'm calling to find out. Where is he?"

"He hasn't come . . . as far as I know . . . should call later. . . ." Her voice was fading out.

"Syl? Syl? I can't hear you."

Her voice came back, then began to fade and return. ". . . a meeting with . . . last I heard . . . everything he can . . . depends on . . . does seem to be a storm . . . any flights tonight."

"Listen, Syl, when you hear from Richard, tell him to call. Right away. Tell him I'm waiting. We need to leave soon. Can you hear me? Syl?"

But the line was silent. Turning from the phone, he went to the window. There were now sheets of snow whipping in the air. The sky was already black. He knew there was no chance Swenson would get him on the red eye. He wouldn't even get to the airport tonight. He went at once to the door to check the lock. Then he listened to hear if anyone was in the hall. Maybe Axel was loitering there, waiting to finish the argument. He heard nothing. Well, one night on his own would be bearable. Except for food. Was he being left to starve? Then he remembered Syl's package. He fished it out of his bag and opened it eagerly. Good old Syl. It looked delicious: biscuits, jam, cookies, and of course that good home-brewed sarsaparilla, which he intended to lace liberally with Canadian Club. He spread the food on the bed and began to eat. She had even included a cheese-ball coated with walnuts. And the cookies—they were heavenly. Marty would love this woman. She was a baker after a baker's heart.

Dare he try to reach Marty again? He placed the phone on the bed and went through the drill as precisely as he could. Dial 9, dial O, dial 011. After a few rings, he reached a working human voice. "I want to place a collect call to—"

"Can you speak louder please?" the voice said.

Speaking at a near-shout, Silverman managed to place the call. He waited. He prayed. Then, like the Red Sea parting, a miracle. There was a voice. Marty! Silverman began to blubber.

"Danny? Is that you?" Marty asked. His voice was riddled with static.

"We have to speak louder," Silverman called down the failing line.

"So what's going on, baby? How are you?"

"I'm okay, I'm really, actually okay. I'm . . . I'm . . . oh, God! It's terrible, it's so terrible!"

"Terrible, did you say?" Marty shouted. "What's goin' on?"

Silverman was talking through his tears now. "They're vicious bigots . . . practically Nazis. I can't tell you . . . there's this one monster . . . he's practically pathological. He called me a baby-killer. Oh, Marty, I'm stuck, scared, and freezing. I feel so alone." Actually, he wasn't freezing. The room, warmed by hot-air vents and a healthy blaze in the fireplace, was oppressively over-heated. His shirt was clinging to his back.

"I'm not hearing you too well, honey," Marty shouted back

along two thousand miles of fragile phone line. "Did you say Nazis? What about Nazis?"

"If these people had their way, they'd send us all to the gas ovens, the Jews, the gays, the humanists."

"Nazis? Listen, Danny, don't let on you're gay, understand?"

"Too late. They know."

"They know you're gay? How'd they find that out?"

"I told them. I had to tell them. I . . . I felt forced to tell them. He was pounding away at me, pounding and pounding with this bloody, ugly, bloody . . . thing. I couldn't stand it anymore."

"They forced you to tell them? What the fuck is going on there? Who's beatin' on you?"

"I'm trapped in my room here. They're letting me starve. They don't care. They hate me, except for Syl. Syl is great. Axel—he's the brute."

"Danny, I'm not reading you. You're locked in your room? Baby, get out of there. Get out of there fast."

"I will. I'm going to try to take the red eye. But I guess it's too late now."

"The red eye? You're taking the red eye?"

"If I can— "

"Hello? You'll be on the red eye, right? Danny baby, talk to me! Can you call—"

"Hello? Marty? Can you hear me? I'll be okay. I'll leave tomorrow."

"Hello? Danny baby . . . I can't—"

"Hello? Marty . . . Marty, sweet . . . I can't. . . ."

After another half minute of silence interrupted by static, Silverman hung up. *I'll call in the morning when the line clears*, he decided and turned his attention to digging his pajamas and toothbrush out of his suitcase.

By ten-thirty, the tranquilizers and the liquor had reduced him to a near-hypnotic languor. He no longer had to spin the television stations round. He was taking nothing in, nothing at all. On PBS, somebody was getting on and off trains, on and off, on and off. He got up enough energy for one more punch of the toe. He aimed, missed, and fell back on his pillow, dead to the world.

13

They Hate Jumanistic Hews

That night the gods of the north gathered in Valhalla, rank upon rank of fair-haired, blue-eyed Aryan specimens, uniformed in Gestapo black leather. And Odin, his hawk-beaked cap set at a jaunty angle, asked, "Und vhere is Daniel Silverman, who fancies himself a hero of his people?" And the wily Thor answered, "He is in North Fork frolicking among the Christians." And Odin said, "Hi-yo to-ho! He is within our power. Let us make sport with him." And all the gods, looking more and more like a room full of German body-builders, beat on their shields in assent. And so it came to pass in the early morning hours of January 2, a billion billion tons of snow were unleashed upon the author Daniel Silverman where he lay, together with much wind. And what resulted would be remembered as the blizzard of all blizzards. And there was great laughter in Valhalla.

The laughter descended upon Silverman like a discordant Wagnerian blast, as if there might be a hundred drunken orchestras rehearsing *Siegfried* on the roof above his bed. His dream of malicious Nordic deities suddenly dissolved into a deafening crescendo. He was on the floor groping and scrambling in the dark before his brain came awake. "Holy shit! What was that?" he cried out loud, though he couldn't hear his own voice above the sudden din.

It was the wind. It was the wind howling with such volume, it couldn't possibly get louder. And then it got louder, and louder still. So loud, it no longer sounded like wind but like an army of Valkyries screaming for blood outside the walls. Gundersen Hall palpably shuddered.

Staggering to the window, Silverman stared into the night. He
could see nothing. Some prankster had painted the windows
white. They were totally opaque. Staring more closely, he realized
the window before him was plastered solid with blown snow. A
glacier the size of Canada was leaning against the building, pressing at the glass, trying to capsize the school. Silverman had never
experienced weather like this, a living malignant force. Like a
frightened child he retreated to his bed and drew the covers up to
his neck. In search of sustenance, he reached for the bottle of Canadian Club, upsetting the bedside table in the process. He groped
on the floor for the fallen lamp, found it, but it wouldn't turn on.
Busted, he decided. Groping further, he found the bottle and took
a long swig, then settled in to wait for morning. In the morning,
Swenson wouldn't even have to stop the car to pick him up. Silverman would be out front waiting. All Swenson had to do was slow
down; the Jewish humanist would board on the dead run. And
"Drive!" he would shout. "Drive!"

The White Giant who trounced North Fork that night was des-
tined to rush forward like an atmospheric *blitzkrieg* to conquer the
airports and main highways of eight states. He would ice-bomb
powerlines into submission as far south as Little Rock and Atlanta.
He would leave the suburbs of Philadelphia and Buffalo besieged
for days by wave upon wave of driving snow. But of all this the stu-
pefied Silverman knew nothing as he dozed through the rest of the
night, consoling himself with the conviction that storms were
creatures of the dark. Did they not pass with the coming of dawn?
So he had always assumed. But not this storm on this dawn. When
he woke again, the Valkyries were still riding full tilt round the
college, shrieking as fiercely as ever. The room was filled, not with
daylight, but with a faint, sickly, swirling glow, a light from the
netherworld that seemed to teem with writhing bodies. Silverman
groped along the floor beside the bed. He couldn't find the alarm
clock that had fallen from the table, but he did discover his wristwatch. Again he tried to switch on the lamp, but with no success.
Inching as close to the shuddering windows as he dared to stand,
he stared at the face of the watch.

8:20. *8:20!*

He was supposed to meet Swenson at 8:00.

Wrapping a blanket around himself, he rushed barefoot from his room and down the stairs. The hall outside his room was unlit, a shadowy dungeon. Skipping and sliding down the stairs, he lost the blanket, but didn't turn back. Spotting the door to the commons room where Swenson said they were to meet, he lunged toward it, pulling up at the last moment to make sure his slipping pajama bottoms were buttoned and drawn tight at the waist. The last thing he needed now was to rush in pantsless. "Christians Attacked by Crazed Faggot," the newspapers would report, explaining how Daniel Silverman had died riddled with bullets in the Faith College commons room. Inside the nearly lightless room he could make out figures at the table gathered around a kerosene storm lamp. "Richard? Swenson?" he called from the door.

The figures turned to regard him. Even without his glasses on—he hadn't taken time to find them—he could recognize Mrs. Bloore. He couldn't make out her expression, but he had no doubt her look was intended to produce sudden death. The others—two, three, four, five of them—were faculty members he remembered from the lecture, some who had left the chapel early in clear disgust. One was Jaspers, recognizable by his bald head and shrunken stature. They were here, but Swenson wasn't among them.

Silverman stepped further into the room. As he approached, Mrs. Bloore rose, her hand clutching theatrically at her bosom as if she were being stalked by the Mummy. The males in the room rose gallantly, positioning themselves between her and the semi-clad pervert who had invaded the premises. Mrs. Bloore, her face dark with anger, was speaking to him. Silverman stared at her stupidly, unable to hear a word she said. The wind was making it impossible to pick up more than scattered words. "Please leave! You are not welcome here," Mrs. Bloore cried, upping the volume of her command. "You are *unclean*. Leave at once!"

"Gladly," Silverman replied. "All you have to do is show me the way."

"It may be the custom in the city you come from to flaunt your obscene personal habits so shamelessly. How dare you bring such filth into our school!"

As he strained to bring this repellent woman into focus with his blurred vision, Silverman, his head swimming, his heart pumping, his pajama bottoms slipping, realized that he was balancing on the brink of a steep slope preparing to release an avalanche of invective on its way. But did he want to do that? *I'm too groggy for this*, he told himself as he rubbed the sleep from his eyes with his free hand. In a surprisingly dignified voice he replied, "I don't believe I was flaunting anything. If I was shameless, it's because I have nothing to be ashamed of."

Mrs. Bloore was now stiff with rage. "Indeed, I'm sure you're *proud*. Isn't that what your people celebrate in San Francisco? Your pride? Pride in defying the law of God?"

Silverman pawed wearily at his brow. "Please, Mrs. Bloore, all I want to do is find Richard Swenson. The sooner I do, the sooner I'll be out of here."

"Swenson, ha!" said Mrs. Bloore, making a wildly dismissive gesture with her free hand. "The two of you must feel so very clever, to have taken advantage of our trust." Then, with her anger mounting, "You will not be allowed to proselytize at this school, do you understand? Not as long as there is breath in my body. We will defend our boys." And then she screamed. She actually screamed, a good loud operatic shriek as she reached to cover her eyes.

"In God's name, man!" one of the professors shouted. He was pointing at Silverman's midsection. Silverman glanced down. In his distraction his grip had loosened. His pajama bottoms had slipped to reveal a few inches of bare, hairy belly. "For Pete's sake," he said as he tugged the garment back into place. And then, for a fleeting moment, he was tempted to let it slip all the way. But no. Clutching at her chest, Mrs. Bloore spun around on her walker, and began to shuffle rapidly toward the door at the far side of the room.

"Oh, come now," Silverman called after her, his temper rising. "Enough melodrama. Do you really think I came to...." And there he stopped. Inside his head a voice was warning, *Careful! Don't hit if you can't run.* Right. He must make sure he had an escape route. At the very least he had to catch sight of Swenson. In any case, why should he waste his time justifying himself to this old harpy? Biting his tongue, he fell silent long enough to let her hobble out of the room. *Hey, that's pretty good*, he said to himself, admiring his self-control. But inside his head, the rest of what he had to say raced forward: *Do you really think I came to this hellish place to pick up one of your little evangelical prigs? If I was playing that field—which I'm not—I could do better in any bookstore or coffee house along Fillmore Street—without leaving home.*

After Mrs. Bloore was gone, Silverman turned to the phalanx of blank faces that were left regarding him. "Look, Richard Swenson is taking me to the airport this morning. Where is he?"

Professor Jaspers rose to answer him. "Not here, as you can see."

"But where is he, then?" Silverman demanded.

"At home, I suspect. You may have noticed we are experiencing a blizzard. Like the rest of western Minnesota, Dean Swenson is no doubt snowbound and like us without electricity."

"Snowbound? But he's supposed to drive me to Minneapolis."

"That would probably require access to the roads, don't you think? Which, as you can see from any window, does not exist. For that matter, if you got to the airport, no planes would be leaving or arriving. It has been shut down."

"Then we have to go to some other airport. Any place. I'll pay."

"There is no other airport, none that is working. As I said, we are having a blizzard. A white out, in fact. It will not lift until tomorrow."

"Tomorrow?"

"Wasn't that the forecast?" Jaspers asked one of the other professors. Oxenstern, was that the man's name? Silverman remembered that he had sat through yesterday's lecture with an annoying grin on his face.

"Tomorrow at the earliest," Oxenstern answered. Again the grin, as if he were mulling over some private joke.

"You mean I'm stuck here?" Silverman asked in a tone of outrage.

"We're all stuck here," Oxenstern replied.

"If you're here, why isn't Swenson with you?"

"I happen to live here," Jaspers answered, "as do Professors

Oxenstern and Halstadt. As for Dean Swenson, who prefers his familial privacy, Mrs. Bloore asked him to leave last night so that we might discuss his future at the school. He left, we stayed, long enough for the rest of us to be snowed in."

"Aren't there snowplows, snow blowers?"

"That is for *after* the blizzard," Oxenstern said, as if he were explaining the matter to an idiot. "Now we are *in* the blizzard. First the snow falls. It can't be either blown or plowed until it has stopped falling. In any case, we don't expect the state to send us any heavy equipment until they've cleared the main highways."

"How long will that be?"

"There's no way to tell," Jaspers answered. "Perhaps a few days after the blizzard blows over. We do intend to start up the school's electrical generator any moment now, so there will be basic electricity."

"What about the phones?"

Jaspers shrugged. "The campus switchboard has been experiencing difficulty, as always happens in bad storms. Have you tried the phone in your room?"

"It was working, then it stopped."

"Perhaps you have a cell phone? I believe that Professor Haseltine may have one. But I haven't seen him this morning. Do you carry a cell phone?" he asked Oxenstern.

"Of course not," Oxenstern replied, almost sneering.

Silverman was beginning to feel like a cornered animal. Between him and all avenues of escape there stood a White Giant who looked like Axel Hask. The Giant had conquered the roads, the airfields, the vehicles. *This is the modern world*, Silverman kept reassuring himself. *There are rocket ships, space shuttles. There's got to be a way out of here.* But he kept drawing blanks. Nothing that would get him from here to Minneapolis—automobile, dog sled, feet—seemed the least feasible. His brain was screaming, but he couldn't think. He was sodden with booze, tranquilizers, and self-pity, and his thinly-clad bones were beginning to shiver with the morning cold. The room was reasonably warm, but his pajamas were California thin. There were also buttons missing and snaps that wouldn't snap. He had no choice but to keep one hand at his waist holding on tight. Across the room he spotted a buffet with what looked like food. "May I have some breakfast, at least?" he asked. "I haven't eaten since yesterday lunch."

"What there is left," Jaspers answered. "We didn't know if we should expect you. I can have Mrs. Hask put out some more."

"Mrs. Hask?"

"The cook."

"Never mind, I'll make do." Summoning up as much dignity as his makeshift attire would permit, he strode to the buffet. There he found scraps of things, rolls and some jam and butter, a cold pancake with congealed syrup, no juice, but an urn of hot water. "I don't suppose there's any coffee."

"It is a polluting beverage," Jaspers answered.

Silverman was studying a small bowl of brownish powder. "What's this?"

"A roasted barley extract," Oxenstern answered. "My own mixture."

Silverman mixed some powder into a mug of hot water, crammed bread and rolls into his single pocket, and turned to head back to his room. Now, with both hands occupied, in order to keep his pajama bottoms up he had to walk in a sort of squat, his legs spread, his bare feet taking mincing little steps. Even so, the bottoms were working their way down one buttock. And, oh God, there were people watching this performance. Catching sight of himself in the mirror above the buffet, he winced. His eyes were blurred and his hair was sticking straight up. He looked a sight. Why was he letting these people see him this way? *Swenson,* a voice in his head kept saying. He must get through to Swenson.

As he left the room, Jaspers called after him. "You may want to take a flashlight with you. We turn the generator off for a few hours at a time."

Silverman noticed a small pile of flashlights on a table near the door. He managed to cram one under his left arm. He left without saying thanks.

Mounting the staircase, he drank off as much of the hot brew as he could, spilling more than he consumed. It had a muddy taste. He was moving as fast as he could, but half way up the stairs the

mean little guy with the ice-pick was waiting in the shadows. He
attacked like a cat. Wham! a merciless thrust straight up the nose.
That was the way the flu always started with Silverman. The little
flu demon delivered him a stinging jab through the sinus into the
optic nerve. After that it was totally predictable. Headache, runny
nose, fever. He stopped short to let out a Herculean sneeze. Then
he panicked. Flu meant: *call Dr. Kirchner, get antibiotics, send Marty
out for chicken soup, otherwise you will die.* But Dr. Kirchner and
Marty and chicken soup were a million miles away, blocked off by
the White Giant. All he had was Canadian Club. In his room, he
reached for the bottle before he went for the telephone. A good
big swallow. Then he turned to the phone, silently praying that it
still worked.

He picked up the receiver as if it might be a small wounded animal and listened for its heart-beat. It was there! The dial tone,
faint and flickering but a sure sign of life. Setting the phone down
ever so gently, he hunted up Swenson's phone number, then
punched it in. He waited, clinging to each buzz-buzz as if it were
another rung on the ladder leading him out of the snake pit.

Finally, there was a voice. He rushed to answer. "Hello! Hello!"
But the voice continued. "We're sorry. We cannot complete your
call as dialed. Please check the number and dial again. We apologize for the inconvenience. Thank you for using AT&T." He
pressed the hook down and repeated the procedure with the same
result. "Later." How much later? He tried again to connect. Then
he realized that the problem might be the dial tone, which was
coming and going like a weak pulse. If he waited to press each button until the tone was there, he might get through. *Slow down*, he
said to himself, as he waited after each number for the tone to return. This time the ringing continued. Three rings, four, five . . .
and then a voice. "Hello." It was Swenson. Silverman felt his blood
heating up at once.

"Richard? This is Daniel Silverman. Where are you?" His voice,
he noticed, was already becoming harshly nasal.

"Oh, Professor Silverman. I've been trying to reach you. The
line is— "

"Where are you?"

"Snowed in, I fear."

"Don't you realize that we're supposed to be at the airport?"

"I know. But everything's closed down, including Minneapolis-St. Paul International. The blizzard covers eight states. It's a real doozy."

"I wasn't warned about this."

"Nobody was. The weather is like that in these parts. Last year we were—"

"Snowed in for four days. Yes, I've heard that bit of folklore. Well, I don't give a good God damn. Did you hear that? *God damn.* That's the Lord's name taken *not* in vain. I want you to get me out of here. I will camp out at the airport if necessary."

"But, you see, I can't. I can't even get out my front door. There's four feet of snow on every road."

"Well, can't you order a snowplow or something?"

"There are no snowplows working in this area. I imagine they're all out on the interstate. There's been a terrible pile-up. We couldn't get through there even without the blizzard."

"So exactly what does this mean?"

"Well, it means we're . . . snowed in."

"What about a helicopter?"

"How would I get a helicopter?"

"How should I know? Call 911. Tell them I'm having a heart attack. I need to be rescued."

"Are you having a heart attack?"

"I might. I could. I could say so."

"But then they'd take you to the hospital in, I guess, Fargo, not the airport."

"Use your imagination. Once we're on board, we can hijack the thing."

There was a long, clearly horrified pause. "You can't be serious."

"Does that tell you how desperate I am? Look, I'll settle for getting out of this hell-hole of a school. I'll stay at your place."

"You're more than welcome, but there's no way to get here. I'm twelve miles away and all the roads are blocked."

"You said you were just across the lake. A stone's throw, you said."

"But, you see, there's a blizzard. You can't skate in a blizzard."

"All right, forget the skates. I could walk across, like Jesus crossing the Dead Sea."

"The Sea of Galilee, actually. Matthew, 14:25. But that was a miracle."

"Where's this lake? Which direction out the front door?"

"Oh, please don't try that! You could get lost. It's a mile and a quarter across the lake. There are channels where the ice won't hold you. You have to be familiar with the— "

"Put some coffee on. Unless you come for me, I'm on my way across the lake. I mean it. I'm coming. Do you hear me? I'm on my way."

He hung up with a decisive click, taking satisfaction in the fear he had inspired in Swenson. Serves him right. And for that matter, if the wind lets up, why not try jogging across the lake? Mile and a quarter—that was a short Sunday walk through Golden Gate Park. He lay back savoring whatever consolation he could from the thought that he might be able to escape across the lake like Eliza fleeing from Simon Legree over the ice floes. As if to shatter his hope, the wind flung a shuddering salvo against the wall, reminding him that the blizzard was still raging full blast. Unless the weather cleared, he could never find the lake.

He reached again for the phone and spent several minutes trying to call through to Marty collect. He had always regarded the telephone as a sort of life preserver. In trouble, reach for it first. Now he was learning, in the day of oh-so-many features and options and services, it was a leaky raft. He dialed O for operator, expecting no more success than in the past. The ringing went on interminably, finally yielding a syrupy recorded voice. "We're sorry, we are experiencing an unusually high volume of calls. All of our representatives are busy with other customers. Please hang up and try. . . ." His heart sank. But as he lowered the phone from his ear, there was another voice. A woman's voice.

"U. S. West operator. May I help you?"

A real voice! Was it? "Are you there?" Silverman asked. "I mean are you *real*?"

"May I help you?"

"Yes, yes, please! I want to place a call to San Francisco. The number is—"

"Who is your long-distance provider?"

"What?"

"Who is your long-distance provider?"

"Aren't you?"

"This is U. S. West. We are not your long-distance provider. If you would like us to be your long-distance provider, I can put you in touch with our business office."

"Can't you place the call now and bill me?"

"Surely, if you wish. One moment while I transfer you to the long-distance operator."

"No! Don't go away!"

But she had. The ringing commenced again. Many minutes of ringing. And then the familiar voice from the grave. "We're sorry. Your call cannot be completed as dialed. Please check the number and try your call again."

He set the phone down and finished his now cold barley brew and as many crumbs as he could salvage from his pocket. The butter he had spread on one of the rolls had soaked through to become a big stain on the front of his top, and this was his only pair of pjs. How much Restoril did he have with him? He found the little bottle next to the bed on the floor. Uh-oh. Eight tablets. He decided to take one of them before attempting the phone again. Ever so delicately, he tapped in a 9 and O and waited. There was a ring. He waited through a dozen more rings. Finally there was a voice, a human voice, a man sounding bored, but definitely alive and there.

"May I help you?"

"Oh, God, I'm so glad to hear you. I want desperately to place a call to San Francisco."

"You can dial that directly."

"Not on this phone. It's about to die."

"Do you know the number?"

"Yes I do. But will you please not go away?" he added. "Can you stay on the line while I talk to my party?"

"Stay on the line?"

"I want to be in touch with you."

"I'm sorry, sir, but I do have to take other calls."

"Please! I'm trapped here. I can't get away. There's a blizzard."

"Tell me about it. I don't expect to get home tonight."

"Where are you?"

"Minneapolis, where, believe me, it is a sheer white Nordic hell outside. How I hate this city."

"Isn't it going to let up ever?"

"In these parts, when the iceman cometh, he god-damn cometh. Last year we were snowbound for four days, and that was in the actual civilized metropolis where we have machines. In the boon-docks, they were tramping around in snow up to their kiesters for over a week."

"So I've heard."

"Of course they didn't care, the natives. Some of them love it, the hardship, the misery. They think of it as a testing. Norse, you know. Dour, very dour."

Silverman felt the liquor beginning to colonize his larynx. He was now backed into the closet with the phone cord stretched to its limit as he tried to get as far from the wind-battered windows as possible. Even so, in order to hear he had to press his hand against his free ear to shut out the storm. "I should never have come here, never, never," he moaned.

"You're from San Francisco?" The man's voice was softening, growing warmer.

"Yes, Fran Sancisco."

"God! You left San Francisco to come to Minnesota? Whatever possessed you?"

"I came to lecture."

"Where are you?"

"Faith College, it's called. North Fork. They think I'm a Hewy Jumanist. I'm not. I'm a fake. But they're worse." And then it came pouring out. "They hate me here. They hate Jumanistic Hews. They want me to go away. I want to go away. But I'm trapped. They're a collection of religious, white-ring, ultra-conversative, anti-Semite bigots. I think they'd like to skin me alive."

"So what are you lecturing on?"

"Nothing important. I did it for the money. I'm a novelist."

"You are? Who are you?"

"Daniel Silverman. I wrote—"

"Daniel Silverman. I know you. I read one of your books last week. The one where you rewrite Madame Bovary. Oh, this is truly Kismet." Silverman was stunned. It was like manna from heaven in the desert. One of his readers. Someone who actually bought his books. "I picked it up in this little thrift shop for a dime. They have a great paperback bookshelf. I buy all my books there. I loved *I, Emma.*"

"Oh, thank you."

The man's voice dropped to a whisper. "And I did get the message."

"The message?"

"Come on, Daniel. You don't mind if I call you Daniel?"

"No, not at all."

"Well, anybody who can be that convincing as a woman. . . . You're very good. You should write another book."

"I did. I have. Several."

"Wonderful. I'll look for them at the thrift shop."

"What's your name?"

"Jerry Simon. I was in Frisco three years ago."

"We don't call it Frisco."

"I know, but I do. It was terrific. God, it was like a jailbreak. I tell you if I lived in Frisco, I'd never leave, not for a million bucks."

"How right you are. Good old, good old Frisco! I don't see why Nimesota was ever invented."

"Oh, not that we don't have our own little entertainments in the Twin Cities. But it's not to compare. Of course you're getting the worst of it up there near the line."

"The line?"

"The border. You're within spitting distance of Canada, you know. The closer you get to the line, watch out! It gets very ethnic."

"I made the mistake of letting them know I'm pro-choice."

"Fatal error, my friend. In those parts, they immolate girls who get prego out of wedlock. They stone them in the streets. Or they would if they could. Of course, I'm pro-choice myself. Who isn't? Fact is, I never did understand how women could stand having something so alien growing inside them. Yik. It's a wonder they don't *all* choose, if you follow my meaning."

"If they all chose, how would any of us be here?"

"Now, that's very logical. I didn't know novelists were so logical."

"Listen, Jerry, I'm in a real pickle here. I'm going to be snowed in with these Evol-genical creeps for who knows how long."

"My advice is, don't let on about your predilections."

"They already know about my prelidictions. I told them."

"Uh-oh, bad move."

"I know, I know." His voice was filling with tears of self-pity.

"Why'd you do that?"

"I wanted to show them I had nothing to hide."

"Dumb. When you're surrounded by homophobes, hide. That's my advice."

"I should've, I should've, you are so right." Thanks to the booze, Silverman was descending toward mental age eleven. "I've never been through anything like this. I live on Fillmore Street, you know, in wonderful San Fran, fransan frisco. I have friends who think I'm nice. A nice little guy. As far as the good Christians of Forth Nork are concerned, I'm no better than a cockroach. You know how they spell Jew around here? With an i. JIW, JIW all over the place."

"Oh, that's the crowd you're with. Lucky you. But, listen, not to worry. JIW is for 'Jesus is watching.' It isn't anti-Semitic. It's just generically revolting."

"I know, I know."

"They've become famous hereabouts as the Church of the Peeping Jesus. They put their nasty little red stickers everywhere. Mainly they put them in toilets, can you imagine? It's actually very self-defeating, if you ask me. I mean you're standing there peeing and not even thinking about jerking off or hitting on the guy next to you. And then as soon as you see that JIW, you begin thinking of all the things Jesus might be watching for—and bingo, next thing you're doing it." Jerry's voice dropped into a confidential tone.

"And you know what the irony is? The irony is that Jesus himself and his boyfriends would have been on our side."

Silverman's brain, already sluggish, had to grind away at that one for a while. "They would?"

"Oh, yes. What do you think was going on there with all those yummy young guys in robes eating and sleeping together and having love feasts and all like that? Listen, in ancient times, almost nobody was straight."

"Whose idea is this?"

"It's all based on, you know, research. There are these censored books, which were found in a cave or somewhere. Don't tell me you've never heard of the Church of the New Testicle?"

"No."

"We even have a congregation here in Minneapolis. It's a real fun scene. I mean not like religion at all, which is so, you know, dour. Brother Jerome, that's the pastor, he was a Catholic priest before they defrocked him for preaching about the gay Christ. Now we get together and we all defrock. I thought that would be big time in Frisco."

"For all I know, it is. Frankly, I don't keep up with the latest."

"Well, you tell those Christian creepos that the only way they ever got Jesus to be straight was to nail him down." He snickered. "Brother Jerome has these counter labels he's printed up. Whenever we see a JIW, we stick our label right under it, which says 'And we hope he enjoys what he sees.' "

Silverman's mind was getting cloudier by the minute. "All I know is, my partner back in SF must be frantic by now, wondering why he hasn't heard from me. I've been trying to get through to him but the system keeps glitching on me. Can you help?"

"Of course. What's the number?" Silverman gave the number, feeling all the gratitude of a drowning man who has been thrown a life preserver. Jerry went to work punching it in. "And I will stay on the line to make sure we get through. What's your friend's name?"

"Martin Foxwell. That's his stage name."

"An actor?"

"Yes."

"Good friend?"

"Very good."

"How long together?"

"So long we don't keep track any more. Over ten years."

"That's beautiful. My companion and I have been. . . ."

And suddenly the line was dead. Not even a crackle. Nothing but the sound of Silverman's own heartbeat echoing against the earpiece.

Stunned, Silverman stared at the phone, then called into it. "Hello? Hello? Hello?" No response. Did Jerry have his number? Could he ring back? Of course he could. But when? What if the system was out for days? Would his message get through to Marty? Oh, God, how he missed Marty! If he were home now, he'd be banging away at the old Macintosh and in another hour Marty would bring him tea—that good yogi tea he liked with extra cinnamon—and a fresh Madeleine. And later in the afternoon, they'd take off for an hour and meet the gang at the Annex for a beer. He felt tears brimming under his lids. He was never, never, never going to leave San Francisco again, not even to receive the Nobel Prize.

He fell back against the pillows, suddenly depleted. He could feel steamy little germs on the march through his bones and sinews. He could tell this was the sort of flu that normally knocked him out for a week. But he couldn't afford to be knocked out for a week. No, no, no. He mustn't sleep. He must plan. Yes, that was it. So this is what he would do. And at once he was asleep, a deep, dizzy sleep shot through with fevered aches and pains.

When he woke, he wasn't sure where he was. Then a blast of wind at the window reminded him. The sleep had cleared his head a bit, but he was still running a temperature. What time was it? After one in the afternoon! He should be hungry, but he wasn't. The flu was keeping his appetite minimal.

Weak as he was, he wasn't going to play prisoner. He rose, shaved, and dressed. Here's what I must do, he counseled himself. Let's say I've been washed ashore on an uncharted island. I fall in with a primitive tribe, worshippers of a strange god. I'm the first person from the outside world they've ever seen. Let's say I'm an anthropologist doing research. I'm among a savage people. We have to communicate by grunts and gestures. *Ugga-bugga*. As long as they aren't cannibals, I'm safe. I'll survive. I'll get back to civilization. Stay cool. Rescue is on the way. Meanwhile, take notes. *Ugga-bugga*.

He slapped on some aftershave and wandered out to meet the natives.

14

Male and Female Created He Them

The commons room had brightened up, though only marginally. The daylight at the windows was still grayed with storm. But with the generator running full blast, the lights were back on and the central heating was roaring almost loud enough to drown out the gale that was battering the walls. At the center table, now cleared of food, sat Professor Jaspers absorbed in a book. He looked up at Silverman's entrance, tilted his head back to squint through his bifocals, then glanced at his watch. "Two o'clock. I was about to give up." He rose to fetch a plate, an apple, and a bottle of orange juice from the buffet. "We put aside a lunch for you."

"Thanks," Silverman said and sat down to the meal, which was no more than a dry turkey sandwich on soggy white bread with poison-green pickles and wilted potato chips. Still it was more than he expected. As Silverman started eating, Jaspers resumed his seat across the table, folded his hands, and watched. Seated at the table, the little man showed only from the collarbone up. He was bald as a doorknob with a scraggly beard sprouting from below his jowls that looked as if it had been stuck on with glue. It was the worst-looking beard Silverman had ever seen. Altogether the man was totally unnerving.

"I have been delegated to speak with you," Jaspers announced. He had a raspy voice that grated on the ear.

Ah, thought Silverman, an emissary from the tribe.

"My charge is this," Jaspers continued. "For as long as we are confined here, I must ask you to honor some rules. Mrs. Bloore wishes me to request that you take your meals in your suite or that you wait until after she has finished before using this room, where we shall be serving meals until the storm lifts. She also proposes that, in so far as possible, you remain in your suite between meals until we can deliver you to the airport."

"First of all, it isn't a suite. It's a room, just a room," Silverman protested. "Second, that's practically solitary confinement. There isn't even decent television reception."

Jaspers knitted his brows. "There isn't supposed to be any television reception at all. You have a set in your room?"

"I won't give it up," Silverman announced emphatically. That television set might be all he had to save his sanity, especially if his supply of tranqs ran out.

"You brought a television with you?" An expression of surprised disgust passed over Jaspers' face, as if he were hearing an alcoholic confess to overpowering addiction.

Careful, Silverman warned himself. Swenson had asked him to keep the television set a secret. "Yes. It's very compact. A Sony mini-mini-micro-portable. No bigger than a . . . tiny TV set. Not even that large."

"You always bring this device with you?"

"Always. I can't miss *Jeopardy*."

"I have no idea what that is. But if it is your set, then you may keep it, though I must ask that you conserve as much electricity as possible. Our generator has fuel for about six days. As for the reception, we can do nothing about that, nor would we care to. We try to keep the students free of these influences. We regard television as an ever-widening sewer."

Silverman flinched inwardly. How he hated it when these people were right. "Okay, so you're isolating me. The fact is I'm as eager to avoid meeting you as you are to avoid meeting me. So I agree about the eating arrangements. But do be reasonable. I'll go stir-crazy confined to one room."

Jaspers pondered the question judiciously. "We might include the faculty library across the hall. It has a fine small collection, mainly classic works. But that would pose a problem."

"Yes? What?"

"There are bathroom facilities on this floor."

"Yes?"

"We would have to place them off-limits to you."

"Meaning?"

"Simply that we ask that you use the bathroom connected to your suite, which I believe is adequate for all human purposes."

"Is that because Jesus is watching in the downstairs bathroom?"

Jaspers dismissed the remark with a derisive twitch of the lip. "I think you understand the concern."

Silverman, the blood rushing to his face, felt tempted to stomp out of the room in outrage. But then, *Ugga-bugga!* he remembered: he was on an expedition. *Retreat to anthropology. Take down what the savage is saying.* He at once became intrigued. He tried seeing this wretched, grim-faced man before him as a grass-skirted native with a bone through his nostrils. What might Professor Jaspers become one day through the alchemy of his literary imagination? Could he ever be anything besides a figure of fun? *Let's wait and see*, his writer's curiosity whispered.

"Of course, I understand," Silverman replied. "I was going to raise the point myself. You see, I'm a stickler for clean bathroom facilities. You never know what you might pick up from strange toilet seats. I mean you can't tell what sexual habits people may be into these days. So I would like you to agree that no one will be using my potty while I'm here. Especially Mrs. Bloore. And since we're being frank about these things, I do hope your kitchen staff washes its hands before it handles the food."

Jaspers' expression was growing more and more caustic. "You have no fear on that count. In any case, your sarcasm is uncalled for."

"All right then. We all agree to be really, really clean." He turned back to what was left of his meager lunch, which was now engaging his anthropological curiosity quite as much as Professor Jaspers. This white bread he was munching, it tasted like . . . well, it had no taste at all. It was like eating a sheet of paper. So, too, the turkey lunch meat; in his mouth, it was turning as gummy as paste. His teeth were now coated with a pulpy residue that reminded him of the plaster dentists use to take an impression. A childhood memory returned: the first time he realized one of the great differences between Jews and non-Jews. Bread. There were Irish kids he once knew who ate spongy flour like this. Whereas Jews ate good rye bread and challah and bagels. Now nearly everybody ate bagels. In San Francisco, you could even find cinnamon kiwi bagels. Ugh! Perhaps only here, in this strange uncharted tribal society hidden away in the snowbound wilderness of northern Minnesota, could food like this still be found.

Across the table, Professor Jaspers was still in his seat. Behind his thick glasses his enlarged eyeballs looked like exotic fish staring out of their bowl. Apparently he intended to count every last potato chip. "Is there something more?" Silverman asked, his feverish head growing more swampy by the minute.

"May I make one comment on your lecture yesterday?"

"Yes?" Silverman felt his gut muscles tighten.

"I would like you to know that I found myself quite moved."

Surprise! "Did you?"

"I hope you understand that not all of us question the historical reality of the Jewish Holocaust. I realize a few members of our community—Pastor Apfel and of course Axel—have peculiar views on the matter. Others, like myself, are completely sympathetic. Especially with respect to Israel. We understand that Israel is part of the Lord's plan. The way and the place must be prepared."

"I've heard that remark before," Silverman said. "And it means? . . ."

"Armageddon," Jaspers answered, as if the one word sufficed. "Revelation, 16:16." Silverman stared back blankly. Jaspers's face twisted into an expression of painful incredulity. "Surely you've heard of Armageddon." He parsed the words out carefully.

"Only in connection with the end of the world," Silverman answered. "Is that important?"

Jaspers rolled his eyes. "The time of the second coming."

Silverman felt as if he had clicked the last piece into a jigsaw puzzle. "Oh, I see. This isn't about Jews. It's about Jesus. You think he's coming back. And his first stop is what? Tel Aviv?"

Jaspers removed his glasses and wiped them with a table napkin. Apparently they had fogged over with emotional heat. His voice fell into a tone of infinite resignation. "I wouldn't expect you to understand. I would simply like you to know that I found the story about your aunt most touching. I confess to having no explanation for the Lord's decision to allow such things to happen. It is a testing of one's faith. It forces us all to ask Job's question. If you had stopped there, I don't think we would have any difficulty relating to one another for as long as you must remain here. But you must have realized that intruding your personal s-s-s . . ." Jaspers, hissing like a steam pipe, paused, closed his eyes and took a breath as if he were resorting to a practiced discipline. ". . . personal sexual preference into the situation was totally uncalled for. As for associating that preference with scripture, that was offensive in the extreme."

"I wanted to be candid about something that was bound to come up."

"You might at least have referred to your companion more discreetly."

"More discreetly? What did I say?"

"You know full well. You did it deliberately."

"Did what? Really, I don't follow you."

"Oh, come now! You referred to this person as your . . . l-lover." The word had to fight its way out between Jaspers' teeth. After it was out, he made a sour face as if at a nauseating taste.

"Oh," Silverman said, not quite seeing the point. "That upsets you? It's the usual term."

"'Usual'? Even if your companion were a female, it would be an improper word. It may, of course, be the vernacular in your part of the country, perhaps even a source of pride that you can be so blatant."

"No, I'm not proud either," Silverman hastened to assure him. "I don't think anybody's sexual orientation is a subject for celebration. As far as I'm concerned, sex is beyond shame or pride—as long as it's kept between consenting adults. It's simply *there* like the nose on your face. Myself, I don't give it a second thought."

"'Simply *there*.'" Jaspers sneered. "Yes, that would be the next step beyond flaunting one's sins. Taking them for granted as the usual thing. At the very least, I hope you will bear in mind that nothing that may be usual in San Francisco is apt to be usual any place else in the world—least of all in a pious community. You must know that sodomy is regarded by our faith as a profound offense."

"There's something I've always wondered about," Silverman remarked, looking for a way to change the subject as he worked his way through the last of his lunch. "Maybe you can enlighten me. The word 'sodomy' comes from the city of Sodom, am I right?"

"Yes. 'Sodom and Gomorrah, their sin is very grave.' Genesis, chapters 18 and 19."

"So everybody in the city—in both these cities—was gay? But if they were all Sodomites in that sense, how did they reproduce?"

"You are, of course, being frivolous. The evil for which these cities were punished was moral degeneracy in general, not any one act. Sexual perversion was, however, the worst offense of the Sodomites."

"I see. It's a blanket term. Well, if that's so, why do you always use it for homosexuality in particular? I mean, maybe God was punishing all those Sodomites for other things. Maybe it had nothing to do with sex."

Jaspers let out a weary sigh. "There is a vast literature on this subject, Mr. Silverman. I happen to be our church's leading authority on s-s-sexual morality, so you can hardly expect me to clarify a matter of such complexity in a brief conversation."

Bop! Silverman felt as if somebody had bounced a basketball off his forehead. *This* was Faith College's authority on sex? This was the guy who was telling a schoolful of randy kids what they could and couldn't do with their private parts? Silverman struggled to keep from yipping with derision. If there was ever a compulsive non-masturbator, this was the man. "But I am right," he went on, "in thinking that sodomy might include lots of things. Like cheating at cards or forgery."

"No. In the fullness of time, it has come to mean specifically homosexual fornication.'"

"Who decided that?"

"We take our guidance from scripture. 'Male and female created He them.' What could be clearer?"

"But can't you see male and female being something like roles in a play? Isn't there room for interpretation?"

Jasper's jaw actually dropped open. A visible shiver of indignation passed through his body. "Interpretation? Mr. Silverman, do you take life to be some sort of farce? Have you never heard of obedience?"

Silverman backed off strategically. "We all do our best, Professor."

"Yes, and that's not good enough. *All* have fallen short. God does not give a B+ for effort. There you have the difference between the godly and the reprobate. *I* know I have sinned. *You* apparently have no such conception." Jaspers voice suddenly rose to a trembling high pitch. He sat bolt upright in his chair, glaring with conviction. "Even after justification there is sin. There is always sin. *Simul justus et peccator.*" Then, as if embarrassed by this outburst, he slumped back and covered his lips with his hand.

"So what is it you would have gay persons do? Kill themselves?"

"The rule is simple and merciful. Repent, resist, and restrain. We have methods that can help with each. Where the effort is sincere, redemption follows."

"And all this, you're saying, is because there's a place in the Bible where it says that homosexual sex, this particular use of the sex organs, is specifically inappropriate?"

"*Inappropriate?*" Jaspers gave a sniff of contempt. "The word is far too mild. It is referred to as 'an abomination unto the Lord,' which means a hateful action toward God. And I assure you, scripture leaves nothing to guesswork. In the book of Jude—Jude 7 to be exact—sodomy is referred to as 'going after strange flesh.' "

" 'Strange flesh,' that's how it's put? I find that rather poetic, but isn't that really sort of vague—I mean as a basis for damning somebody forever? That is the penalty, I assume."

" 'The vengeance of eternal fire,' yes. If you require more clarity, Leviticus tells us that 'if a man lie with mankind as he lieth with a woman, both have committed an abomination' for which the punishment is, of course, death." The look in his eye was a headhunter's look, no mistaking.

"Of course. Well, I guess that's pretty clear. I didn't realize God got into those details."

"Detail is what religion is all about," Jaspers said, his eyes taking on an aggressive sparkle. The man was clearly warming to his task. "I like to say that true faith is in the jots and tiddles that most people have no time to honor. When it comes to moral guidance, God is not a prude. He gives us the particulars with no room for personal interpretation. 'The woman shall not wear that which pertaineth unto a man, neither shall a man put on a woman's garment.' Deuteronomy, 22:5. What could be clearer?"

"You mean cross-dressing qualifies you for damnation?"

"In that case the punishment is unspecified. But for graver offenses, there is no guesswork. Thus, in first Corinthians, Paul declares that both participants of the male pair bear equal guilt, the catamite as well as the abuser—both he who enters and he who is entered. Both shall be damned."

"'Enters'? No! The Bible actually says 'enters'?"

Jaspers was pleased to see he had gotten a rise out of Silverman. "In the original Greek, the phrase is *arsenokoitoi*: he who enters by the buttocks."

"And that's why God wiped out the whole city, two cities? For entering by the buttocks?"

"Precisely. He rained down fire and brimstone on the cities of the plain, on everything living there and everything growing there."

"The people, the plants, the grass and the insects, the whole works? All the children too? Isn't that called visiting the sins of the father upon the child?"

"Even unto the third and fourth generation. Evil requires a stern rebuke."

"Come now! Wiping out a whole city?"

Jaspers leaned forward, reaching across the table to tap out his words with his finger in front of Silverman's chest. "Mr. Silverman, you simply don't know the facts. The events that led to the destruction of Sodom are numbered among the darkest deeds in the history of our world. We are told that the men of Sodom, these sex-crazed degenerates, had become so bold in their ways that they besieged Lot and his family in their house and cried out for him to send forth the men so that they might fornicate with them. With the men, and only the men."

"This is the same Lot whose wife turned into salt?"

"The same."

"I've always wondered what that was all about."

"The woman, as women are prone to do, disobeyed a clear command *not* to look back."

"Was that so bad?"

"Indeed it was. She showed no proper revulsion for what the homosexual mob had done. Even when Lot offered these raving perverts his own daughters for sexual satisfaction, they wouldn't be satisfied. They wanted the men. Is it any wonder the Lord turned his wrath on them, one and all?"

"Lot offered his daughters?"

"The man was desperate. From this we can conclude that even rape is a lesser sin than sodomy."

Silverman felt his anger rising, but quickly backed off. What was there to argue about here, after all? Some lurid piece of mythology that probably never happened? Women turning to salt, cities destroyed by fire and brimstone. Arguing about such things was like arguing about Jack and the Beanstalk. The objective observer merely notes down the folklore; he does not critique it. Still he couldn't resist toying with Jaspers a bit longer. "Well, one consolation. I have some women friends back home who'll be relieved to know they have nothing to worry about, damnation-wise. You'd be surprised how angry it makes lesbians to have the gay-male model imposed on them. But if I understand you correctly, queer ladies are free and clear in God's eyes."

Jaspers flinched with amazement. "What can you possibly mean? L-l-lesbianism falls under the ban quite as unambiguously. Romans, 1:26: 'for even their women did change the natural use into that which is against nature.' "

"But I thought you said it all had to do with illegal entry."

Jaspers groped for words. "But surely, coming as you do from that community, surely you know about the practice of tribadism."

Silverman assumed an expression of sincerely puzzled innocence. "Tribadism. Now that's a new one for me. Could you describe what you mean?"

"I certainly won't. This is a religious institution. Religious people eat at this table."

"I wasn't asking for a demonstration. Just a little hint."

"I refer to the use of . . . devices."

"Devices?"

"Instruments."

"Instruments?"

For a long moment the two men stared across the table. Silverman, affecting dense bewilderment, wondered how long he could keep this going. It was like teasing a scrappy little dog. "You don't expect me to draw you a diagram, do you?" Jaspers snarled at last.

Silverman patted his pockets as if he were searching for a pencil. "Actually that might help."

Jaspers leered at him. "Come now. I think you understand quite well."

As if the light had dawned, Silverman pulled an *a-ha!* expression and pointed a finger at Jaspers. "I think I know what you have in mind. Toys. That's what we call them in San Francisco. Oh yes, we have stores full of them. Of course you probably know a great deal more than I do about all this, but my impression is that women don't really go in for the nastier forms of entering. I'm sure you have that wrong."

"That is a fine point," Jaspers snapped.

"But didn't you say it's the details that matter? So if women use devices in ways that avoid. . . ."

That was it. Jaspers had reached his limit. He bounced from his chair and drew himself up to his full four-foot-nine height. "You're trifling with me," he sniffed. "Yes, you are. That's more insulting than frank opposition." Displaying all the hurt feelings he could muster, the little man headed for the door.

The son of a bitch, Silverman said to himself. *This preposterous runt is trying to guilt-trip me.* Before Jaspers could make an indignant exit, Silverman stopped him with a question. Reverting to his role of make-believe anthropologist, he asked, "May I ask you something, Professor Jaspers? Am I the first gay man you've ever met?"

"Face to face, yes. To the best of my knowledge."

"That's important to add, of course. 'To the best of my knowledge.' Because you might be surprised to know how many of us there are all around you. We're everywhere, you know. You may have friends who are gay and you never knew it. Your doctor, your grocer, your mechanic, your barber, any number of them might be gay. Ordinary people getting along."

Jaspers' mouth curved into a wry, bitter smirk. "But I agree completely. You *are* everywhere. We are surrounded, permeated, and saturated by sodomy, by the flesh pots of secularism. And we cannot even speak out against sin for fear of being 'insensitive,' or 'homophobic,' or—God forbid!—'judgmental.' I freely, if sorrowfully admit that we have lost the culture wars, as many of us suspected we would. The sin-cursed race of man is simply beyond redemption. I cannot think of a single institution in our society that hasn't been captured by the enemy. But the fact that sin has become publicly acceptable and now abounds alters nothing regarding God's law. It only serves to remind us that we are living in the last days. Sodomy is, in fact, a prime measure of our fallenness. You may applaud what you call 'coming out.' But every homosexual who comes out of the closet to spread his vice proves we have moved one step closer to the final reckoning. The fate of Sodom impends."

One thing I have to grant him, Silverman thought, *he isn't simply laying on the rhetoric. He's genuinely scared.* "How odd this is," he observed out loud. "Back in Sin City we spend a lot of time fretting about what the radical right is going to take over next. We think you're riding roughshod through the country."

"Ha!" Jaspers sneered. "Perhaps you enjoy the sense of victimization. But turn on your television set, look at any popular magazine, go to the moving pictures. Do you think *we* are producing the filth you find there? Come now! You do recall that not long ago we had a president of the United States who was a documented lecher, pervert, and fornicator. And what happened when his debauchery stood revealed? Did the public even care? Or did it salivate to hear more of the revolting details? What you mistake for power on the part of God's people is simply that they are at last being heard, crying out in pain. The little we have done to clean out the cesspool of modernism is as nothing compared to the flush that will next arrive to cover us. That we should even have to embarrass ourselves speaking out against things that were once unspeakable is already a victory for your side. To condemn you is to advertise your vice."

Silverman was astonished by the tone of sincere sorrow he

heard in Jaspers' voice, but even more so by the barely disguised desperation. How could anyone bear to live in such a state of moral despair? "Have you ever been interested in learning more about gay people?" he asked. "Like me, for example? I don't know what you think gays get up to, but I actually live a pretty normal life with my partner Marty. We work, we shop, we cook, we pay our bills, we have tiffs, we make up. We're simply loving friends."

"No one questions friendship. That is not the basis of the offense."

"It's what we do physically—or what you imagine we do, isn't it?"

"As C. S. Lewis has put it so aptly, sex outside of marriage is like chewing up your food to get the pleasure of the taste and then spitting it out undigested. All the worse, I must add, when the sex is unnatural."

"Well, that's mean enough. But when it comes to questions about natural and unnatural, would it make any difference to you to know that homosexuality and bisexuality are more common among animals than heterosexuality? It's a fact, Professor. Ask any zoologist."

"Our church doesn't derive its sexual ethics from zoology. When I speak of 'nature,' I have human nature in mind. And that, we believe, derives from a higher order of being. Of course, if you wish to base your conduct on the rutting beasts of the world, you're free to do so."

"Would you consider it fair or even proper if I were to make judgments about your private sexual conduct with Mrs. Jaspers?" *Uh-oh, bad question.* What could be more tactless than asking about this man's sex life? For that matter, how could there possibly be a Mrs. Jaspers?

Jaspers didn't miss a beat. "In this case, the judgment is not mine, but God's, and it is unmistakable, a chastisement of historic proportions."

Silverman knew what he had in mind. "Come now, AIDS isn't a specifically homosexual disease."

"There is a plague abroad in the world," Jaspers insisted, "Can you really deny that people of your kind have visited it upon us?"

"Yes, I can. Why not say the judgment in question has to do with promiscuity? I might go along with you there. Africa is being ravaged by AIDS. The carriers are prostitutes of both sexes. If AIDS had existed during the days of World War II, one hard-working whore like Mamie Stover could have wiped out the entire Pacific fleet. She was servicing a couple hundred customers a night."

"You're quibbling, always the sign of a guilty conscience. The issue you raise is rather like debating which was the greater enemy of Christ, Judas Iscariot or Simon Magus. But if it is of any comfort to you, where AIDS is concerned, I will grant that the whore is a worse offender than the homosexual. I suspect, however, that the matter is wholly academic, since I assume that, like all humanists, you favor the legalization of prostitution. Am I right?"

"As a matter of fact I do, in order to protect the women."

"As I thought. Well, then, what is there to argue about? You may not even realize how much is at stake in the matter, but between the two of you, the prostitute and the Sodomite—both of whom enjoy your high opinion—what chance has Christian marriage to survive?"

"Didn't Christian marriage have its chance for centuries?" Silverman asked. "It left us with puritanism, repression, hypocrisy." He scratched his brow in an effort to recall something Marty had mentioned a few months back, an item from the gay press. "I'm not strong on statistics, but I think there are studies that show lesbian couples are doing a better job of staying monogamous than heteros. So if we legalized same-sex marriages. . . ."

Jaspers made a sound. He was hissing again, this time gagging on "same-sex." Unable to get the words out, he bowed his head and made a heroic effort to regain his composure. Silverman could hear him murmuring under his breath. Was he praying, Silverman wondered. At last, looking up, Jaspers replied with admirable calm. "You may be right. Many have given up on marriage, perhaps most have. These are not matters where statistics settle anything. The simple truth is: you are the ally of a curse—a curse!—that could well wipe out our entire corrupted civilization. If you cannot see that, you are willfully blind."

With that, Silverman's anthropological patience was exhausted for the day. If anybody was going to leave in a fit of indignation, it might as well be him. "Thanks for the sandwich. I suppose I should be grateful that you're not leaving me to starve—as a stern rebuke." He tried to close the door gently as he left, he really did. But it slammed loud enough to echo through the building.

15

The Mad Bomber

With no place else to go besides his room, Silverman, his brow feeling more fevered by the minute, went looking for the library as if to test the perimeters of his confinement. Waiting for his anger to cool, he searched the shelves of the small, dark-paneled room. What could Jaspers have meant by "classics"? There wasn't a title here he knew other than the *Encyclopedia Britannica*, and of course the Bible, of which there were a few dozen copies. The rest were obscure theological or homiletical works, many dating back to the nineteenth century. There were several yellowing works by Lucy Gundersen, all having to do with the vital issue of immersion. He took one down from the shelf. *In Charitable Refutation of Those Who Teach that Non-Immersion Can Quench the Fires of Hell, Together with Seven Joyful Sermons on Baptismal Sanctification*. A real winner of a title. What he found inside was page after page of exegesis on Biblical passages, a genre that left him stiff with boredom.

On another shelf he discovered that the college itself published a monographic series dating back to the 1890s called *Battlelines of Theological Warfare*. At the far end of the room he came upon a shelf lined with works on the dreaded sin of sodomy. One, published in 1922 by the Sweet Heart of Jesus Press in Dangerfield, Texas, was titled *Lusting After Forbidden Flesh: The Abomination of Unnatural Love Fully Documented in Divine Law* by a Reverend Gideon L. P. Pickett. Its frontispiece showed two long-haired gentlemen in Victorian dress holding hands. Obviously the Sodomites. Both were staring upward in stark terror. Above them hovered an angry angel wielding a flaming sword. Below were the words: "I will come unto thee quickly and will remove thy candle-stick out of his place, except thou repent. (Revelation, 2:5)" Where was this candlestick? he wondered. Nowhere in sight. A metaphor no doubt. He was touring the inside of an alien intelligence.

He continued scanning the shelves, and at last came upon a title he recognized. *Pilgrim's Progress*, several editions in fact. Well, it was better than nothing. He tucked it under his arm and moved to the other side of the library. There he came upon a shelf that held copies of the college yearbook reaching back to 1874. He pulled out a few volumes at random. On the cover of one of them, the 1992 edition, was a photo of a campus event. It showed a cheering throng of students with signs and placards, the school band, the faculty with beaming smiles. Across the front of Gundersen Hall—the building he was now in—there was a banner: "Welcome Home, Axel! With violence shall Babylon be thrown down."

He flipped the book open and found a newspaper clipping pasted inside. The date was May 16, 1992. The story featured a photograph of the always scowling Axel Hask looking fit to be tied, lip curled, eyes afire. There was a headline: "Faith College Custodian Cleared in Bombing Case."

The story read:

> Axel Hask, groundskeeper at Faith College in North Fork, accused of bombing a Fergus Falls Planned Parenthood clinic last May, has been cleared of all charges in the case and released. Hask, 52, has been a leading figure in the western Minnesota Right to Life campaign for several years. He was identified as one of three men who set off an incendiary device at the clinic on the night of September 12 last year. A doctor and three clinic staff members died in the ensuing blaze. The trial, whose venue was moved to Thief River after a vigorous appeal from Hask's attorney, lasted only one week. Despite evidence against Hask given by two eyewitnesses, the not-guilty verdict was swift and unanimous. A Planned Parenthood official who wished to remain anonymous denounced the ver-dict as the work of a runaway jury. Hask, who has

been arrested on several occasions in the past for aggressive picketing of family planning clinics, was detained in connection with a bombing incident at a Duluth facility in 1988 in which three people were injured. No charges were brought against him in that case. He will return to his position at Faith College, where he and his wife Helga have been employed for more than twenty years. At a spontaneous victory rally outside the courthouse following the verdict, Hask vowed to resume campaigning against what he calls "the true Holocaust." The Faith College Associated Students Organization, which paid for Hask's legal defense, issued a statement Sunday applauding Hask's acquittal and welcoming him back to his campus home. Said Arnold Stitch, the Faith College studentbody president, "Axel has long been a beloved figure at our school and a source of moral inspiration for our campus community. We are pleased to see that justice has been done not only to Axel, but to the anti-abortion movement, which continues to enjoy the support of our church and our school."

Silverman stood staring at the page. *Jesus! The man's a mad bomber!*

Before the shock of this revelation had worn off, he heard a door creak behind him. He darted behind a chair and began to look for something—a fire poker, a broom, a paper-weight—to protect himself. Two people entered the library, a man and a woman, faculty members he had met at the New Year's Day luncheon, but whose names he had forgotten. He recalled that they had been among the people he saw when he blundered into the commons room that morning. He assumed they were trapped by the storm like the others. When they spotted him, they stopped short, probably wishing they could withdraw. "Have you seen Professor Oxenstern?" the woman asked. "We were to have a meeting."

"Not since this morning," Silverman answered. Then, before they could leave, he asked, "May I have your help about something?"

"Yes?" the woman said, her face stiffening.

"Excuse me, I know we've met. I've forgotten your names."

"Erika Halstadt," she answered. She was in her late middle age, a tall, handsome woman with good bones in her face, but wearing her hair drawn back so tightly that her eyes were slanted. The man, probably in his late thirties, already balding and broad of build, introduced himself as "John Hoff." Neither stepped forward for a handshake.

Silverman held out the yearbook he had been reading. "I came across this book. There's an article in here that says your groundskeeper, Axel Hask, was on trial for murder."

"That's true," Professor Halstadt said. "He was acquitted."

"But there were eyewitnesses," Silverman said.

"Yes, but the jury didn't believe them," she answered. "They were convinced that abortion is a crime."

"But that wasn't the issue," Silverman corrected her. "This was a case of murder."

"Of course we know that, like many humanists, you don't regard abortion as murder."

"But I do regard murder as murder. And four people—grown people—were murdered in this bombing. That's what the trial was about."

"And as I said, Axel was acquitted."

"By a runaway jury," Silverman added.

"That's what you would expect the liberal press to say," she replied.

"But you did see how he behaved at my lecture," Silverman reminded her. "He certainly looked ready to knock me off."

"But he didn't, did he?"

"No, but if he had, would you have regarded that as justifiable homicide?"

"Of course not," she answered in a wounded tone. "Axel is a man of great religious passion and he allows it to show. We regard him as one of the treasures of our campus."

Professor Hoff added, "You have nothing to fear from him, if that's what you're asking about."

"That's right," Professor Halstadt concurred. "It really shouldn't be that hard for you to understand his point of view. After all, you told us how strongly you feel about those of your people who perished in the Holocaust, as it is called. Axel feels the same way about the innocents who are being slaughtered even now as we speak."

"In Axel's eyes," Professor Hoff said, "you look like the Germans who stood by and said nothing while millions died."

Silverman, at an impasse, tried to summon up an *ugga-bugga*. But his situation was beginning to seem too precarious for playing games. Axel Hask had succeeded in rattling him in the chapel; the violence of the man's temper had been on open display. But that was merely an unpleasant encounter. It was quite a different matter to discover that Axel had very likely acted on that impulse, had deliberately planned to kill, and carried out his plan without remorse—more than once. Yet here were the Professors Halstadt and Hoff telling him that Axel had every excuse to treat people like himself the way a Nazi sympathizer might be treated—and why didn't Silverman understand that?

"But you have no reason to be afraid," Professor Halstadt assured him. "Axel is a good Christian. He is a zealous believer, but he would never harm you."

Not to worry, says the fond dog owner. The growling pit bull at his heels never bites. Silverman shrugged his shoulders and replaced the yearbook on the shelf. "Emotional miscarriage," he groused loud enough for the professors to hear. "I should have known better than to try to make a point as sophisticated as that in a place like this."

"Oh?" Professor Halstadt said, sounding a note of pique. "Are you under the impression that sophistication is what's at stake here? You're quite mistaken."

"Am I?" Silverman answered sullenly. "All I meant was taking a larger view of things. I don't think there's much of a market for that in North Fork. You seem to be pretty ingrown about certain issues and—frankly—pretty close-minded."

"You're not being at all fair," she protested. "I actually found myself interested in your ideas about abortion, as shoddy as they were. Professionally interested I might say. I thought I'd heard all the clever humanistic arguments on behalf of abortion, but your remarks were new to me. Professor Hoff and I teach family values. I'd actually like to talk more."

"I'm not an authority," Silverman reminded her.

"That never stops people from holding forth on great moral issues. May I ask you a question?" She raised the query aggressively, something that had been rankling for the past few days. With nothing back in his room waiting for him except the story of Christian the Pilgrim, Silverman saw no reason why he shouldn't play anthropology with Professor Halstadt. The truth was he felt safer in the company of other people. He moved away from the windows, where the storm made speech almost inaudible, into the farthest corner of the room and dropped into a chair, careful to make sure he could keep his eye on the door.

The two professors took seats opposite him. "What exactly do you mean by this remarkable concept 'emotional miscarriage'?" Professor Halstadt asked. Curious as she might be, her manner was stiff and standoffish.

Emotional miscarriage—what did Silverman have to say about that? Nothing all that original. He had picked up the idea from his neighbor Sally Weeks. She had parted company with her church on the subject. Her view was based on a simple perception. Silverman wondered if he could explain it. "Well, lets see," he began as they settled into their chairs. "Suppose we start with pregnancy. Pregnancy isn't uniquely human, is it? I mean it happens to all animals. So what's the difference between a woman's pregnancy and a dog's pregnancy—I mean from the pregnant female's viewpoint?"

"Quite a lot, obviously," Professor Hoff answered. "A woman knows she is pregnant and understands her responsibility. That's why the pregnancy is a matter of moral theology."

Feeling the professors were seated a bit too far away, Silverman moved his chair a few inches closer. He noticed at once a simultaneous expression of discomfort on both faces. "Right. And because a woman can know she's pregnant, she can have feelings about it. I mean I assume so, never having been pregnant myself."

"Feelings? Yes, joy, anticipation." As he answered Professor Hoff moved his chair back about as far as Silverman had moved his forward. Professor Halstadt made the same adjustment.

"As well as fear, shame, disgust," Silverman added. "All of the above, right? A woman might know that the pregnancy will kill her. Or she might feel ashamed because she was raped. Society does make women feel that way, you know—as if rape is some sin on their part." Once again, without quite thinking about it, Silverman edged his chair closer. "Some women may feel too tired and overworked in life to have another baby. Or the baby may be deformed in some way. Lots of feelings."

"True," Professor Hoff replied as he once again backed his chair off, "but all beside the point. The only feeling that matters is gratitude to God." Professor Halstadt also quite casually worked her chair back a few inches. This time Silverman registered the movement. He realized that his interlocutors were keeping a fixed distance. He wondered if this was a sort of intuitively defined homosexual safety zone: *no nearer than thirty inches.* Or maybe it was his cold, though he hadn't shown any symptoms.

"Well, suppose the woman has a miscarriage," Silverman continued. "Is she supposed to be grateful for that? Because some women do have miscarriages, you know."

"That's true, and very sad," Professor Hoff admitted. "It is God's will."

"Would you blame God for that and call God a murderer?"

The two faces across from him chilled by several degrees. "Of course not," Professor Halstadt snapped. "We are not to question God's will. James, 4:15."

"Or perhaps Romans, 12:2," Professor Hoff suggested.

"Oh, yes," Professor Halstadt agreed. "Much better."

Silverman cocked his head and squinted. "You make those things up, don't you."

"What things?" Professor Halstadt asked.

"Romans, 1:2:3, Matthew, 4:5:6, Peter, Paul, and Mary, 7:8:9. You don't really have the whole Bible memorized."

"These are scriptural citations learned from many years of study. No, we don't make them up. That would be blasphemous."

Growing more anthropologically curious, Silverman asked, "So when you throw out one of these parenthetical zingers, that means what exactly?"

The professors were looking a bit testy. "We are citing the Word of God."

"And that means you've proven your point?"

"Obviously, yes."

"Well, then tell me, if it's so obvious what God says on the matter, how come there isn't one big Christian church where everybody believes the same thing? Why is it Christians have been at each other's throats for centuries? You know what I mean—the inquisitions, the persecutions, all like that."

"Unfortunately," Professor Hoff explained, "not all ministries are instruments of the Holy Spirit. We are warned that even the devil can quote scripture."

Silverman decided to stop working that front. "Okay, then, let's go back to miscarriage. Am I being naive here? Couldn't God prevent that if He wanted to? Couldn't He make sure every woman has a perfect delivery?"

"And why that's not so is a mystery that lies beyond us," Professor Hoff answered before Silverman had even completed the question.

"All right, then," Silverman agreed, "so we don't blame God for miscarriages. But we don't blame the mother either, do we? We don't condemn her because her body couldn't go through with the delivery?"

"No, of course we don't," Professor Hoff conceded.

Silverman thought: *once you get into these things, it's sort of like a game, isn't it? Talking about what God thinks and does and wants.* He couldn't remember ever having a conversation like this. But here he was, holding his own better than he expected he might. Of course, look at his opposition. "Okay," he went on, "so now let's talk about abortion. Some women, maybe most women, when they get pregnant, feel pretty happy, or at least they go along without complaining. But God allows some women to have very big doubts about having a baby. He lets them feel afraid for their lives, He lets them feel ashamed and guilty, He lets them feel regret, or maybe anger and resentment. *Madame Bovary,* page 324."

"What is that?" Professor Halstadt asked.

"That's a literary citation. I thought I'd throw that in on my

side. I'm not actually sure about the page, but I did write a variation on *Madame Bovary* that was based on Flaubert's account of
her pregnancy. It works up to an abortion."

"Novel? If you intend to be frivolous," Professor Halstadt said
with a clear caustic edge, "we may as well have done right now."

"Sorry. I'll avoid literature. Anyway, feelings like that—fear,
guilt, anger—can be overwhelming. They drive some women to
end the pregnancy. Now that's a peculiarly human kind of miscarriage. A dog can't have those feelings, but a woman can. If a
woman isn't emotionally ready to have a baby, I think that's the
same as a purely physical miscarriage. Sad, but not sinful. That's
what I meant by an emotional miscarriage."

The two professors exchanged disapproving glances. Professor
Halstadt's face assumed a wry smile. "That's all very clever, Mr.
Silverman. I might call it diabolically clever."

Silverman secretly took that as a compliment, but aloud he said,
"No. Just humanistically merciful."

She continued, "You overlook the fact that all these doubts that
may plague a woman issue from the devil. They are temptations."

The woman said this so coolly that she might have been reading
the weather report: *and the midwest remains covered with snow.* "Of
course I might say," Silverman commented, "that it's the devil who
is encouraging you to take a harsh, self-righteous attitude toward
the troubled women we're talking about. I'm inclined to think the
devil is on the side of unkindness. But look, let's suppose a woman
has good medical reasons to fear that she will die in childbirth.
That's the devil speaking?"

"Of course," Professor Halstadt answered. "A good Christian
woman trusts in God."

"Who sometimes does let her die in labor."

"For His own good reasons. One can only trust."

Was it his job, Silverman wondered, to speak for the women of
human history? Well, why not? "You're saying, you're *really* saying
that emotions like anxiety or shame or disgust are not to be taken
seriously?"

"They are to be stilled by prayer."

"So what you're really saying, then, is that a woman *does* get pregnant the same way a dog does. Or at least you believe she should. Flush your head and go through the process by instinct, no personal emotions allowed."

"There are other emotions," Professor Halstadt reminded him. "Elation and pride."

"As for taking charge of her own body?" Silverman asked.

"But it's *not* her body," Professor Halstadt protested with a sudden show of temper. "Especially not when it's the vessel of another life. She is consecrated to God then more than at any other time. These ideas about 'her own body' are simply the tempter's rhetoric."

"In contrast to what?" Silverman flashed out at her. "Her husband's rhetoric, or her father's, or her male minister's? You don't see any possibility here for what I've heard some women call 'patriarchal' behavior?"

Professor Hoff intervened, "But of course it's patriarchal. This word carries no pejorative meaning for us as it does for the feminists. Patriarchy is explicitly approved in scripture. It is, in fact, ordained. Man is the image of God, woman is man's complement. It's the most obvious fact about our religion. Professor Silverman, patriarchal is normal. It stems from a perfect creative act which established the roles of man and woman. On the other hand, unisexism is strictly forbidden."

"You really believe God is a man?"

"Not a man," Professor Hoff corrected. "Masculine. A totally masculine being."

"Is that simply because the Bible refers to God as 'He' and 'Him'?"

"And are we to regard that as a sloppy mistake? A misprint? A bad translation? Hardly. In any case, if there were any doubt in the matter, it was set to rest by our Lord Jesus, who was indubitably a man as revealed in hands-on, true-life, experiential knowledge. So you see, since Jesus was the express image of God incarnate, God must be masculine."

Professor Halstadt nodded in firm agreement. Silverman had to admit these people could make a solid legalistic case when they had to. All you had to concede was the authority of the book, leave out history, sociology, and the vagaries of poetic license, and the rest followed like a geometrical proof. "Does that mean," he asked, "you believe God has a penis and testicles?"

Professor Hoff pulled a sour expression. "Of course not. We aren't dealing here in crude physical terms. Biologism has no role to play in these questions, which is one of the main reasons that we reject the lies evolutionists tell about our own nature. God's masculinity has to do with the higher powers—intellect, will, dominion, especially fatherhood, with all its disciplinary responsibilities. How could all this be conveyed by a female image?"

Silverman turned to Professor Halstadt, who had been punctuating every word her male colleague spoke with expressions of absolute approval. "You go along with all this?"

"Of course," she answered, seemingly puzzled that he would ask.

"You don"t mind being a second class cosmic citizen?"

"Oh my!" she burst out. "How little you understand. There is no implication of inferiority here. Woman is a full member of Adam's race. But there's a precious distinction, one that unisexists fail to appreciate. If you wish to know, I revel in woman's status as helpmeet. It's my highest identity and calling. Abortion strikes at the very core of my womanhood."

Silverman blew out an exasperated breath. "Look, Professor, as far as I'm aware, nobody thinks abortion is a good thing. Maybe your people assimilate it to sexual license in some way that makes it seem enjoyable. But I can't imagine that ever being the case. The women I know who've chosen to have abortions agonized over their decision long and hard. They really did. If I felt this was any of my business, I think I'd feel sad about it, as I would about an ordinary miscarriage. Beyond that, I guess I see pro-choice as part of what's going on with women, which is that they want men to stop bossing them around and kicking them around. Abortion may be the price we pay for centuries of putting women down. Maybe once we get past that, things will change. Maybe women will make other choices."

"How very reasonable you sound," Professor Hoff said, wagging his head. "And how very kind. I'm sure you're totally unaware that what you're saying is diabolical."

"Moral theology has never been my forte," Silverman explained. "I'm a novelist, Professor, a storyteller. Saying the devil made me do it isn't a very interesting motivation. It's got no human content to it. As I see it, there are miscarriages. Some are physical, some are emotional. If God wanted to, He could change all that with a literal snap of His literal fingers. No miscarriages, nothing but guaranteed happy motherhood. Let me put it this way: If you were God, wouldn't you make it work like that?"

"The woman who thinks the way you suggest is being tempted to doubt God," Professor Halstadt answered. "She's presuming to pit her judgment against His. You seem unable to accept the reality of temptation."

"Maybe so. That might be because I can't imagine God Almighty playing such cruel games with something as basically human as childbirth."

"You're also overlooking the fallenness of man," Professor Halstadt added. "'In sorrow thou shalt bring forth children.' Genesis, 3:16. You see, we have brought this suffering upon ourselves, the price of disobedience."

Silverman studied her closely. "You don't find it hard to say that, you being a woman? You don't feel that's a raw deal?"

She blinked with surprise. "Raw deal? In heaven's name, Professor, we're talking about God's sovereign will.

'For contemplation he and valor formed,

For softness she and sweet, attractive grace.

He for God alone and she for God in him.' "

Silverman gave a big, resigned sigh. "Well, one thing I'll grant you, Professor. Between the King James Bible and John Milton, you've got some great, wrong-headed literature on your side."

• • • • •

You seem unable to accept the reality of temptation, Professor Halstadt had said. And she was right. He was among people who thought in categories he had never learned: temptation, damnation, sanctification, repentance. Even sin, when you came right down to it. Though he had known shame—who hadn't?—he never

imagined his transgressions were being chalked up by an angry
God Who was keeping score. As alien as all these items were, he
could sense the drama that lay behind them, the picture they drew
of life as . . . well, the pilgrimage John Bunyan had taken it to be—
a quest filled at every turning with dread possibilities, eternal implications. It wrenched his mind, trying to return to a time when
the world was a stage at the center of the universe, when human
beings acted out the drama of salvation on that stage. But he had
also learned something else. Though Christians occupied center
stage, that had nothing to do with pride. Rather, they thought of
themselves as damaged goods, flawed through and through. Oh, a
few of them might slip through to enter the Celestial City, but far
and away most of them were so wretchedly bent out of shape that
the God who was their maker stood ready to consign them to everlasting perdition. Silverman couldn't put out of his mind how
readily Erika Halstadt had assented to bearing the pains of childbirth, accepting punishment for a legendary transgression she herself condemned. Guilt seemed to be her habit; she was *comfortable*
with it, as if it were the skeletal structure of her life. Take away her
sense of sin and she might collapse like an empty sack. And being
convinced of her own guilt, she had little trouble reviling others
for their sins. Christians were such good revilers! Like all the other
godly folk he had met at the college, when Professor Halstadt
looked at him, she saw a damned soul before her, a *justly* damned
soul for whom she felt not a lick of pity.

Perhaps it was theologically incorrect to ask, but where was love
in all of this? Where was kindness, pity, compassion—all those
things Christians liked to sing songs about? *Jesus loves me, yes I
know, for the Bible tells me so.* Words like that had a strangely
skewed meaning for these people. Whereas Silverman found it all
very simple. Love meant not hurting, it meant accepting, it meant
feeling for. Isn't that what "compassion" meant? *Feeling for?* Come
to think of it, that's what novelists did as second nature: they got
inside somebody else's life and experienced the emotional turmoil,
the heartbreak and craziness—the *mishegoss*, as his people would
put it—that went with fighting to hold on to as much of your dignity as life allowed. Yes, but could Daniel Silverman the novelist

do that for Axel Hask? Could he feel for the mad bomber who had publicly reviled him and might even now be plotting to plant his woodsman's axe in the faggot's cranium? No, he couldn't. Absolutely not. Right now he wanted to put as much physical and emotional distance between Axel and himself as he could. But at least he wasn't pretending there was any love to be lost between them. And that's what irked him about these Christians. Pretending love when there was none, or often exactly the opposite. When you're making somebody feel like dirt, don't pretend you're playing Jesus on the cross.

Maybe he wasn't picking up on the theological fine points, but as he thought back over the last few days, Silverman couldn't remember hearing anything at Faith College that remotely resembled love, if "love" were more than a word in a hymn. Instead, he was hearing vindictive things left over from some distant age of dismal hardship, when people expected life to be nasty, brutish, and short. A time when there was little to share, little to lift the spirits. A time when heavy fathers had to whip their kids into shape fast so they could get out and earn their daily bread. And going all the way back, a time when pharaoh battered his people into a state of blind, self-loathing obedience to get those pyramids built. In the world as seen from North Beach and the Fillmore and the Castro, that distant age of squalor and despair seemed light years away. Yet here it was, only a few hours distant as the airlines fly from New York or San Francisco, that same bleak teaching, still being voiced with total conviction: hate yourself, squelch yourself, apologize for being alive. Guilt: the great ego-cop was still on the beat in North Fork.

Things were coming back to him, uplifted voices, snatches of angry contention he had left behind him in his childhood, his father's many bitter tirades against his father and his father's Bible—"that piece of moral pornography," as Silverman's father called it. "Who wrote this ugly thing, eh? Some self-righteous, freeloading ratfinks, never worked a day in their lives. Why should we care what they thought back there roaming the desert before anybody even invented the wheel? Bunch of bearded bums always beating up on the poor working-class slobs down below. Think of the satisfaction! '*You* are no damn good! But, hoo-hoo, *I* am so holy, I go up on the mountain and talk to God personally. And He told me that He is sending you to hell because you ate the wrong food, because you had it off with your neighbor's wife, because you can't keep your pecker in your pants. Unlike holy *me* who has a room reserved at the Ritz Paradise.' You know what this is, this whole misbegotten book? Moral sadism. I'll tell you why Ezekiel and his crew of miserable grievance collectors were always so pissed off. They were scared that, God forbid! somebody, somewhere, should be happy. They stayed awake nights worrying. 'Wipe that smile off your face,' that's what your *zeyde* used to tell me. 'You think life is some big joke?' Joke! In this whole miserable book there isn't one laugh, not one. That says it all, kiddo."

Maybe that's why gays were so offensive in these quarters. Because they were, after all, *gay*. That strange word. Whoever decided that was the right word anyway? Whoever it was, they sure pushed the hot button. They had dared to send up a cheer for joy, or at least that one kind of joy, the most forbidden. Especially the drag queens, who carried on as if life were one big giggle. Outrageous! They got their rocks off with no promises and no apologies. For them, sex meant freedom, self-worth, community. They let their hormones govern them, not rules carved on stone. He thought of Jerry Simon's Church of the New Testicle. Humor in religion. That was like thumbing your nose at old Yahweh.

When Silverman first came to San Francisco, erotic free fall had all but become a religious cause. The gay neighborhoods were swarming with Dionysian revelers who had busted out everywhere, Rabelaisian crusaders championing the inalienable rights of the prick. He had been swept up in the frenzy, though only for a few dizzy weeks. Coming out of a lifetime of baffled, resentful virginity, that brief interval of sex in the moral void had been sheer intoxication. Let your cock lead the way. Enjoy, and let there be no hang-ups, no shame, no commitments—and no consequences. That was the wild time before the bad news came down and the bathhouses were closed and the most important four-letter word in town became "safe." Which—and this was an authentically troubling thought—might have been God or Mother Nature or somebody on high having the last laugh.

As a brainy guy who found more exuberance in his writing than in polymorphous perversity, Silverman hadn't found it all that difficult to bail out of the fast-lane gay scene. The depletion, the compulsive transiency, the exaggerated physicality, worse still the mutual exploitation—it was more than he could handle. With the benefit of hindsight, he now realized he had escaped not a week or a month too soon. At some point not much more than six months after he arrived in San Francisco, dark rumors of the Plague began to circulate, and soon after the chill descended. Thank God he had found Marty, who had also burned out on cruising and anonymous sex. They met and created a pact. Marty, two years older on the calendar than Silverman and a lifetime savvier on the streets of the Castro District, found the right words at the right moment. "Dear friend," he said one night, "you and I have slipped under the wire. The lights are going out all over the Castro. Either we are true to one another or we die. Which for me is a no-brainer of a choice. I've seen it all, I've done it all, and, man, I love being alive. How about you?"

The wild time now seemed like some mythical golden age, so obscured by clouds of wishful longing that it was impossible to tell if it had ever really happened. But after only a few days among the Lord's sour-pussed people, Silverman was beginning to see the point of that bizarre moment in modern history more lucidly than ever. It was the exodus of the despised, the outcast, the downtrodden. Who could say what it might look like a hundred years from now? Possibly a grave mistake, or possibly a necessary chapter in the human story, something yet to take its place alongside the *Declaration of Independence* and items like that. A Symposium of the Whole, that's what the good gay San Francisco poet Robert Duncan once called this strange episode in his city's history, a time when "all the old, excluded orders must be included, the female, the proletariat, the foreign, the animal and vegetable, the unconscious and the unknown, the criminal and failure—all that has been outcast and vagabond." Everybody welcome. Though he had never seen things that way before, Silverman was glad to have been some small part of the show.

16

The Troubled Pilgrim

Five pages of John Bunyan, Silverman soon discovered, was almost as effective a tranquilizer as Restoril. He read, he dozed. Several times he woke to read again, then tried to write, but his mind was too unsettled for that. The wind alone was relentlessly unnerving. It wailed and wailed, hurling itself at the windows like some horror-movie monster determined to break in and slaughter everybody it found inside. He had quickly developed a subliminal habit of listening for the wind, always an ear out for the least change in the intensity of the storm. Not that there was much variation to hear. The wind speed seemed stuck at a hundred miles an hour, with scarcely a fluctuation. As long as that kept up, he was too paralyzed with anxiety to put pen to paper.

Writing, at least for Silverman, required peace and contentment. A quiet place to work at his own pace, his own special chair, his own special music in the background—the Debussy Preludes to set one mood, Errol Garner to set another. Also, his own special coffee (Charlie's Choice, a mixture of Jamaican and Kenyan blue, from the cheese and coffee shop down the street) brewed and served in his own special cup—the Japanese raku mug Marty had bought for him in Tokyo while he was shooting a Toyota commercial, the first serious gift they had exchanged. How he missed all that. How he missed his midmorning break for fresh-baked Madeleines, that mellow interlude when he and Marty would shuffle through the news and gossip of the day.

In the course of twenty-some years, writing had taken on a seamless, organic quality for him, an intricate bio-psychological texture woven into a time and a place. He had become part of a fabric of affection and respect that reached out through his neighborhood. Wrong-headed and corrupted as the world around him might sometimes seem, there was this one good place on the planet where he was "Danny the writer" and valued for who he was. That was the other side of not being so famous and well-heeled that he might long since have moved into the glitteratti. Instead, he was Danny the struggling Fillmore Street man of letters everybody was proud to know as if they played some role in his work. And they did. When Silverman brought out a new book, Lisle and Jason at the Midnight Bookshop, now the last independent bookshop in the area, always filled the front window with copies, and even hosted wine-and-cheese signings that might not sell five books. And Angus at the Annex, his favorite watering place, would throw him a party to celebrate what he insisted on calling Danny's "latest best-seller." Kathy at the library was sure to post reviews of his books (but only good ones) on the bulletin board in the fiction section. Bob behind the counter at the post office sometimes shaved a few ounces off the price of the manuscripts Silverman sent out, a sort of unofficial NEA grant to the cause of good literature. Greta at the bank had even let him off the hook for the cost of a few bounced checks because, after all, he was "our novelist."

Every day he lived among people who thought a writer was a rather remarkable person. And that was why, hard-pressed as he was for money, he refused to scuffle like so many of his colleagues, for whom writing was like toiling in the mines. He and Marty were doing well enough. Not great, but well enough. True, with his advances and lecture fees diminishing at about the same pace as Marty's television earnings, they were becoming ever more dependent on precarious sources of income, mainly the university extension and Madeleines by Maurice. But month by month, in some combination, literature, acting, and gourmet pastry were keeping their heads above water. He would have loved to come home from Minnesota with enough money to pay off Marty's cruelly expensive bridgework, but even so, they were going to make it. That was how he felt when he was at work in the right place at the right time—which emphatically wasn't here and now.

Trying not to hear the White Giant's steady roar, he rubbed his eyes and returned to his copy of *Pilgrim's Progress*. It was an impossible old book, a childlike allegory of the religious life that clashed with modern taste at every level. Between himself and old John Bunyan, the inspired tinker, there stretched a distance of seeming millennia. How remarkable that, once upon a time, this quaint book had been among the most widely read in the world, there beside the Bible in every English-speaking Christian household. Generations of true believers had been raised on the spiritual adventures of Christian the troubled Pilgrim. A couple of Bunyan's images, Silverman had to admit, were priceless. The Slough of Despond, well, that's where he was now. And Vanity Fair, that's where he lived with Marty, surrounded by the crass whirligig of fad and fashion that every modern city had become. What would we do without a phrase like that? Bunyan the Puritan would have seen most of what Silverman thrived upon as soul-killing idolatry, and maybe he was right about that. There were times when Silverman felt that the whole foolish rat-race for recognition and success was a test of character. Could he walk away from it? Could he?

Well, no. It was too exhilarating. So there was a hopeless divergence between Silverman, whose eyes were on contracts and critics, and Bunyan, whose eyes were on the Heavenly City. On the other hand, the preface to the volume Silverman had picked up in the library told how Bunyan and his kind had suffered for their faith. The evangelicals with whom Silverman was keeping company had apparently forgotten how detested and outcast their religious ancestors once were. The history of Christianity seemed to be an infinite regression of persecuted minorities suffering the oppression of the dominant self-righteous. And often the issue in question was so silly that nobody could understand it any longer. Blood had been shed over trifles, a word, a phrase, a ritual gesture—like to immerse or not immerse. To his credit, Bunyan the martyr had fought for religious freedom. He had certainly paid his dues. Twelve years locked up in a cell barely big enough to walk across. That was when he wrote the book. Quite a life.

Had Bunyan ever thought of himself as a queer, Silverman wondered. Could he have imagined a day when something as trivial as the private uses of the genitalia would produce the same heated controversy, the same acts of narrow-minded cruelty? Probably not. When you think you're on God's side, you become the standard of normality, even as a minority of one.

Toward six that evening, there was a rap at the door. Silverman waited till he heard nothing in the hall, then cracked the door open and peered out cautiously. No one. But there at the threshold lay a covered tray. He brought it into the room and inspected his dinner. A thick, pasty soup and crackers, some cold cuts with bread, a little container of mayo, another of catsup, a limp salad, a Hostess cupcake, apple juice. With a few additions from Syl's lunch bag, it would do. He really had no appetite.

As he set the tray down, he paused to do the telephone thing. The telephone thing was becoming a ritual observance. In his room, whenever he passed within a certain distance of the phone, he would stand before it, utter a prayer to the inscrutable god of telecommunications, then gently, ever so gently raise the receiver to his ear, hoping to detect a dial tone. But this time there was nothing and when he tapped the hook, again nothing, and when he tapped the hook again, still nothing. So he adjusted the tray on his increasingly rumpled bed, freed his big toe, and got ready for another night of spin the dial. Talk show—nobody he recognized—commercials, commercials, commercials—an auction, a barely visible movie (something with Rock Hudson and, what was her name? Right. Dorothy Malone.)—car chase—back to the talk show. . . .

Wait a minute! Go back. He big-toed the button for the channel he had shot past. Yes, he was right. The car chase! A ghostly blur drained of color, but recognizable as a re-run episode of *Chopper Patrol,* Marty's old show. A totally characterless cops and robbers mediocrity, it had starred Marty as Lt. Mel Collier, the requisite black cop. It had run for three seasons, and then was dropped five years ago, the best-paying gig Marty ever landed. He was still collecting from re-runs like this. The show's only distinction was the chopper. Every installment was built around it. Trick flying, chases, crashes, lots of aerial acrobatics performed by the stunt crew. Marty appeared mainly in close-ups looking intense or worried inside a fake helicopter cockpit. He had to sweat a lot as he pretended to maneuver the chopper over moving cars on the highway or under bridges or between high-rise buildings. He would set up the scene, then the camera would cut to a long shot and the stuntman would take over. Marty's lines, bellowed into a headset mike, rarely amounted to more than "Let's get out of here," "Let's move," "Watch it," "I need more lift," or "We're going down." And, oh yes, "Go! Go! Go!"—which had since become a favorite phrase during their love-play.

Sharpening the television image as best he could, Silverman waited for Marty to appear, then turned up the sound. Ah! there he was now on the screen: sleeves rolled to show his excellent biceps, teeth on edge, brow gleaming with glycerine spray, mad as hell and shouting, "Get closer so I can jump." Cut to a from-the-bust-up shot of the deep-cleavage blonde who played his chopper partner—Silverman could never remember her name—as she grimaced at the controls, doing her very best to act. Then the long shot of Marty's stunt-double leaping from the chopper to the top of a truck racing down the Santa Monica freeway. Then a shot of Marty clinging to the roof of the truck, his shirt blown open, his hair torn by the wind. Silverman remembered this episode; he remembered all the episodes. Marty leans down through the side-window to shove his Magnum 45 into the truck driver's ugly mug. "Pull over!" he shouts. "Pull over or you're road-kill."

If only he could pause the television or play the program back. He would have watched Marty over and over again that night. With that build, those steely eyes, that snarling baritone, Marty looked like such a tough guy. That was the way he always got cast: black, intimidating, and hard as nails. Marty could put on a look that would stop a charging rhino in its tracks. Who would ever guess he spent most of every week in their tiny, funky kitchen on Fillmore Street baking San Francisco's best Madeleines? "How can you play these roles so well?" Silverman had once asked, early on in their friendship. They had been watching a show where Marty was cast as the brutal boss of a crack-cocaine syndicate. In the previous scene, he had gunned down four rivals and then yawned. "It's nothing like you."

"Sure it is," Marty corrected him. "Because what I am is an actor. And macho is all acting, don't you know? Maybe so is being female, but men got it harder, because macho is so dumb. You gotta be careful you don't do yourself in. No animal as stupid as your typical macho guy could have survived in the evolutionary zoo, believe me. So underneath the macho there has to be minimal intelligence, though sometimes you meet guys who make you wonder— like those football players who like to butt their heads against one another. Oh, man, that is so brainless. See, macho is all on the surface. You know: the glare, the swagger, the trash-talk, the chest-beating. What's that basically all about? We know, don't we? Getting it up. Some guys, they can't get it up unless they got everybody in sight, especially the females, groveling at their feet. It's an act, man. It takes an actor to act. Until I learned that, I was a scared little boy, ran home from school every day. Then, when I hit age eleven, I started to get a build. Right off I knew that if I muscled up and talked dirty, I could be as manly as any guy around. You know what the first macho thing was I learned? How to spit. No foolin'. In the fourth grade, I could spit farther than any guy in my school. Also I could pee farther. That really commanded respect. It's all like that, see? Dumb. Grow muscles and act like mental age twelve. And then you will be a man, my son."

Oh, God, how I miss him, Silverman moaned to himself as he stared through the rolling credits for the last, most important image of the show: a triumphant Captain Mel Collier giving his buxom leading lady a big bear hug. Marty once told him, "Every time I get into a clinch with her, I make believe it's you." It was enough to start him blubbering.

But the next moment, with the good Canadian corn mash beginning to sizzle along his veins, a giggle erupted from out of nowhere, and then another. "Imagine, just imagine," he found himself saying as he slid away toward stupor. A faded memory bobbed its way to the surface of his mind, a bit of boyhood flotsam floating out of the watery depths like a scrap of clothing that had worked itself free from a long-drowned corpse. "For this," he heard himself saying, "gird thyself with sackcloth, lament, and howl: for the fierce anger of the Lord shall not be turned back from us." And

again he broke out in giggles. *Tisha B'av*. Of all things, he was remembering *Tisha B'av* and quite inappropriately he was bent
double with hysterical laughter. *Tisha B'av* was the day set aside to
commemorate every knock and bruise, every lousy, low-down, outrageous thing that had ever befallen the children of Israel, starting
with the fate of the great temple in Jerusalem, which had been reduced to rubble not once, mind you, but twice. Who but the Jews
could have such a holiday? *Tisha B'av* was called the darkest day in
the Hebrew calendar. Originally, it had been enough to mourn the
fate of the temple. But then, as if to cover all the bases, other ca-
lamities had been added to the main event. Persecutions, massa-
cres, expulsions, rapes, depredations, failed rebellions, defeats at
the hands of crusaders and infidels, along with the deaths and torments of several famous martyrs. After all, as long as you're down
there in the depths of despair, why not get as much *tsouris* out of
the way at one shot as you can?

Once, at the age of twelve, Silverman had been smuggled out of
the house by his ultra-orthodox Uncle Seymour to observe *Tisha
B'av*. Next to Grandpa Zvi, Uncle Seymour was the elder
Silverman's greatest adversary in the family. Uncle Seymour could
never have gotten away with taking little Danny to a religious ser-
vice if Danny's father knew what was going on, but there was a
cover story. Once every year, Uncle Seymour treated his nephew to
an educational outing, sometimes the Bronx Zoo, sometimes a
movie and stage show at Radio City Music Hall. The elder Silverman knew his brother used these occasions to talk up the faith, but
what could he do? This was the boy's uncle. That year, Daniel had
been promised a movie. But Uncle Seymour decided it was time
for Danny to learn that life was no joke. So instead of seeing John
Wayne in *True Grit* and the high-kicking chorus girls, uncle and
nephew wound up in a stuffy synagogue where the windows had
been covered with heavy black curtains. The room was sweltering
in the August heat of a bad Bronx summer. In the near pitch-
blackness, people were huddled on the floor, their heads covered
with rough cloth as they read prayers by candlelight. At the front
of the room a cantor was wailing away in Hebrew. Without explanation, a cloth was draped over Daniel and he was handed a book.

Lamentations read the title on the cover. It was an English translation for Hebrew-illiterates like himself. "This we do in remembrance of our common misfortunes," Uncle Seymour told him solemnly. "Read this to yourself. Read with your heart and let the sorrow emerge." And he ran his finger underneath a text: "gird thyself with sackcloth, lament, and howl." Except for that one line, Silverman had long since forgotten the rest of the occasion. He certainly couldn't recollect the catalogue of catastrophes under review that day, but he retained a blurred *gestalt* of surpassing wretchedness. When it came to tribulation, he would never have reason to doubt who held the world's record. Christians might argue about pre-trib, mid-trib, post-trib, but Jews were already veterans of extra-, hyper-, multi-, and ultra-trib. Yet here was Uncle Seymour's nephew caught up in a drunken laughing jag as he tossed this way and that on his bed in the Founder's Suite at Faith College. For who would have guessed that in the fullness of time Daniel Silverman, so sadly lapsed from his faith, would make his contribution to *Tisha B'av?* Definitely, if he ever got out of this predicament, he was going to nominate himself for inclusion in that long litany of martyrdoms and misadventures. "Honest to God," he laughed, "if you think four-hundred years in Babylon was bad, try overnight in North Fork."

17

Concerning the Reality of Satan

By his second morning in Gundersen Hall, Silverman had learned the importance of getting down to the commons room early to scoop up as many supplies as he could carry. If he was lucky he might get in and out before he had to cross paths with anybody besides Mrs. Hask. Mrs. Hask might have been a monster but, Silverman had to admit, she made great buttermilk pancakes, especially if you got them hot. And that was as good as it got at Faith College. After breakfast, it was white food all the way. White bread, mashed potatoes, off-white gravy, various faded gray meats, bleached vegetables, vanilla sponge cake.

With lunch, avoiding resident faculty got more problematical. The buffet might be set out any time between noon and one. Trying to evade encounters, Silverman waited on the landing outside his room until he heard sounds of activity behind the closed door. That would be Mrs. Hask putting out food. Then, checking in all directions, he made a dash for it.

Ah, but he arrived before Mrs. Hask had finished. She made no mystery of her feelings. She instinctively positioned herself between Silverman and the buffet as if she planned to deny him access. She could have done it; she was a big woman, a half head taller than Silverman and twice his size across. Still he wasn't going to let her intimidate him. He casually walked round her to the buffet and started loading up. "You going soon?" she asked with a hiss in her voice.

"No, as a matter of fact I thought I might settle down and open a family planning clinic right here in North Fork. Your coeds wouldn't have to leave town to arrange their sex lives."

"It's a joke for you?" Her face was turning beet red. "You think—"

He cut her short. "I don't usually answer questions from the hired help. Will you be setting out any cold-cuts?"

She made an evil face, spun on her heel, and headed off toward the kitchen, giving the door a hard thump.

As he waited for Mrs. Hask to return, he quickly wolfed down some crackers and cheese. He was beginning to stuff more cheese, fruit, and biscuits into his pockets when Professor Oxenstern entered and stood eyeing him with contemptuous amusement. Silverman slowed down and then slacked off. He spread a glop of mayonnaise on a slice of bread, arranged a few tomatoes on his sandwich-to-be, and waited. Oxenstern forked some food on a plate, then sat down at a table. "No need to hoard, Professor," he said, "Our school has been through all this before. We keep a well-stocked larder. We could hold out for a month."

"That's good to hear," Silverman answered, "but if it comes to rationing, wouldn't I be at the end of the line?"

Mrs. Hask at last brought in a plate of lunch meats and set it in place. Silverman at once shoveled several slices on a plate and mixed a cup of barley brew.

"Do you like the barley tea?" Oxenstern asked. "It's my own concoction. A family recipe from the Black Forest."

"It grows on you," Silverman answered. "Especially if you stop thinking of it as coffee."

"Good. That's exactly the way to think about it. It's a thing in its own right." He noticed Silverman was struggling to juggle all the food he had collected. "You don't think we would starve you?" Oxenstern asked.

"Professor, I really have no idea. I'm at your mercy."

Oxenstern was the oddest of them all. He was the only person at the school whose face didn't turn instantaneously severe when Silverman appeared. Instead, his mouth seemed perpetually curved into a wry smile that was more arrogant than friendly. He was a lean, wispy man, balding and stooped. He might have seemed an ineffectual old geezer, were it not that, from time to time, a malicious gleam flickered through his pale blue eyes. It was there now. "I wonder, Professor, are you keeping a busy social schedule this afternoon?"

"Hardly."

"Would you enjoy a game of checkers?"

"Checkers? Is that permitted?"

"Why not?"

"I didn't think games were permitted in these parts."

"Games of chance, no. They would be a blasphemy. But games of skill are, of course, permitted."

Silverman couldn't remember the last time he'd played checkers. It may have been in his childhood. Did he still remember the rules? Move on the diagonal, take by jumping—something like that. "I warn you," Oxenstern added. "I'm the northern Minnesota champion."

It was a small, curious offer of friendship. Silverman wondered what lay behind it. "Sure, why not?" he said. "We're in for a long blizzard."

Oxenstern suggested they take their food into the library. There he moved the checkerboard to a table well away from the windows where the ever-raging wind made it difficult to talk. The light, Silverman noticed, was low and dingy this afternoon. "The generator is running at half-strength," Oxenstern informed him. "It may be shut down to conserve fuel. Best to be prepared." He placed a kerosene lamp beside the checkers board and lit it.

Most of the first few games were played in silence. Silverman munched away at his modest lunch and tried to recall the rules. He had always thought of checkers as a children's version of chess. Which meant it was just right for him. He qualified as the world's worst chess player, regularly beaten by nine-year-olds. Once, when a boy of about that age challenged him to a game in Golden Gate Park after he had finished an aerobic run with Marty, Marty had threatened to disappear. "Man," he said, "you are not just a bad player, you are embarrassingly bad. I'll bet five bucks the kid beats you with fool's mate." Fool's mate: three moves and checkmate. Silverman could never see it coming. Nor did he that time, after which he vowed never to try chess again. But checkers—that had to be easy. Still, by the fifth game, though he now knew all the rules, he was still getting easily beaten by the ever-grinning Oxenstern.

At the opening of the sixth game, Oxenstern asked casually, his eyes on the board, "Have you ever heard, I wonder, of the ontological proof for the existence of God."

Was this the real agenda, Silverman wondered. The question caught him off guard. "The what?"

"It's credited to Anselm, the eleventh-century Catholic theologian. It holds that God's essence necessitates existence. Now what is God's essence?" Jump-jump. Oxenstern took two of Silverman's pieces. He was eyeballing Silverman now with a hungry intensity.

"I have no idea what you're talking about," Silverman replied in a grumpy voice, as if he had lost the pieces because Oxenstern had distracted him.

"I'm talking about perfection, Professor Silverman. Perfection is, of course, God's essence. Now, what does perfection entail?" He was actually waiting for an answer, this insufferable twit. He sat there, his big blue eyes goggling at Silverman with a gleeful exuberance. Hardly looking at the board, he jumped Silverman again. "King, please," he said.

Silverman crowned the piece that had reached his back row with a second checker. "I frankly plead ignorance," he said, pretending he was concentrating on the board.

"Why, *existence,* of course. For, after all, which would be more perfect, a being that exists or one that does not exist?" Silverman stared at the board, refusing to reply. Damn! He didn't see a single piece he could jump. On the other hand, he was sure—he was absolutely sure—there wasn't a single piece Oxenstern could take. "But of course a being that does exist," Oxenstern continued, answering his own question. "Hence, God, who is the perfection of being, *must* exist." How pleased the man was with himself. Jump, jump. He took two more pieces.

Why didn't I see that? Silverman wondered. "Isn't that some kind of logical fallacy?" he commented morosely. "Defining something into existence doesn't seem convincing to me. Why couldn't I define a perfect second baseman into existence? A perfect second baseman is a second baseman that exists, right?"

"Because, obviously, a second baseman is not a *necessary* being. But God being necessary to the very existence of the world. . . ." Jump, jump, jump. "I believe you've lost," Oxenstern added. On his side of the table, he had a small pad of paper on which he was keeping track of the games. It now had six marks for Oxenstern, zip for Silverman. Outsmarted! At checkers! By a hick bigot! How had he let this happen? He was showing up as a bicoastal imbecile.

Silverman wondered if Professor Oxenstern was finished. Had he proven himself as both philosopher and checkers-genius? "Now then. . . ." Alas, no! He was going on. ". . . consider the devil. Is not the devil the perfection of evil?" He had quickly set up the board for another game.

Silverman waited. A long wait. He carefully pondered his first move, which made him feel all the stupider. By now he should at least know how to start. Oxenstern invariably moved his pieces as soon as Silverman took his finger off his checker. "I ask again," Oxenstern said. "Is not the devil the perfection of evil?"

"If you say so," Silverman muttered.

"Then by the same token, must not perfect evil exist?"

"All right, let's say so." Ha! Silverman made a jump, and then another. His first double take.

"But of course you, as a conventionally educated modern man, don't believe there is a devil, do you?" Jump, jump, jump, jump. "King, please." Oxenstern requested.

"My education was hardly conventional." Silverman sullenly crowned the king. "I went to Brandeis."

"But in this most important respect I wager that it was. For I would bet anything—were I a betting man, which I am not, gambling being a form of idolatry—that you don't believe in the existence of Satan."

"Do you mean the literal, physical existence of Satan: horns, a cloven hoof, and a tail?"

"The Bible says nothing about hooves, horns, or tails. That's all folklore. Let's think of Satan as a person, in the same way we speak of God as a person." Jump, jump.

Shit! Why don't I notice these things? Silverman wondered. "Isn't that a bit abstract for people who believe God walked the Garden of Eden in the cool of the evening, left foot, right foot, clump, clump, clump?"

"We needn't be that precise, though do bear in mind that to believe in the inerrancy of scripture doesn't rule out metaphors and similes. I'm willing to concede—for the sake of the argument—that neither God nor the devil are fleshly entities. By which concession I don't mean to imply they are merely symbolic inventions. I mean they are persons in the same sense that we are persons. They are real spiritual entities. In the case of Satan, I mean a personal agency who is responsible for making evil things happen, someone whose temptation might be heard as a voice speaking in one's ear."

"No, Professor, I don't believe there is a person called Satan who makes evil things happen and speaks in our ears."

"Good! Then will you let me show you the error of your ways? You did say we were in for a long blizzard. Ah! It seems I've won again." He made an eighth mark on the little paper pad. "Again?" With a silent shrug, Silverman agreed to another game. Oxenstern continued. "I wouldn't be far wrong, would I, if I assumed you consider Satan to be gross superstition? Don't hesitate to be frank."

"Yes, I believe it's superstitious."

"Even grossly superstitious?"

"Sure, grossly superstitious."

"But now think: wouldn't the most perfect of all evil entities also be the most cunning? Can we doubt that?"

"Whatever you say." He saw a jump, but dare he make it? Or was this a trap? He drew back from the move.

"The rule is," Oxenstern said, "that you must make the jump." Silverman did. "And now, finally, tell me: what would be the most cunning thing that the most cunning of all evil entities might do?" Oxenstern performed a triple jump, seemingly without even glancing at the board.

"I'm sure I don't know."

"Why, to convince all learned fools that he didn't exist, that he was a mere superstition. And since that is exactly the consensus of all conventionally enlightened moderns, QED!" He actually clapped his hands in glee.

Learned fool. I guess that's me, Silverman reflected. He saw a jump and made it. In turn, Oxenstern took four pieces in one maneuver. "Okay," Silverman said as if he were rolling up his intellectual sleeves. "Let me try an idea on you, Professor. If there is a devil, what would his best strategy be for obscuring God's glory?"

Oxenstern frowned with honest interest. "Do tell me."

"Well, the guy would be hopelessly outclassed, wouldn't he? I mean look at all these wonders of nature, the stars, the sun, the moon. What could old Beelzebub do that compares to all that? Wouldn't his best move be to distract attention, by, say, keeping people's noses buried in one very old book filled with a few good stories and a lot of nonsense? And might he not tell them that God wrote the book?"

Oxenstern emitted a contemptuous sniff. "Clever, Professor Silverman, but not at all convincing to those of us who find the Bible to be self-validating."

"In what way?"

"Prophecy, of course. Prophecy is what proves the Bible's divine authority."

Silverman was ready to call it quits. "If you can find me a clear prediction in the good book of who'll win the Superbowl next year, I'll be impressed, Professor. I might even join the church."

As if he were validating his superior theological skill, Oxenstern cleaned the last three of Silverman's checkers off the board. "My mind isn't on the game, I guess," Silverman confessed gloomily, pushing the board away. "Must be this head cold." And he gave a validating sneeze. "Actually, chess is my game."

"Is it? We might try a few games, if you wish, though I'll admit I'm not all that proficient."

"No, no. I never play simply to pass the time."

"Well, do you have any more time for the devil this afternoon?" Oxenstern asked. He was holding up a key on a chain. The twinkle in his eye had grown menacing.

"In what sense?" Silverman asked. The man was playing with him. He resented it, but his curiosity had been aroused.

"Demonology is my special interest. I have a small collection in my office. Would you like to see it?"

"A collection of what?"

"Why, devils. Lost souls. The terrors of damnation. Fire and brimstone. The perfect way to warm one's thoughts on a day like this, don't you think?"

"Where's your office?"

"Where else? In the crypt."

18

The Underworld

Oxenstern was being facetious. By "crypt" he meant basement. Taking up the kerosene lamp that had lit their checkers game, he led Silverman through the kitchen, down a flight of stairs, then along a badly lit corridor.

"Tradition tells us there were 133,306,668 angels who fell from grace with Lucifer," Oxenstern said as he led the way. "Another theological census counts trillions. So, of course, my little collection hardly does justice to the variety. Still it serves its purpose."

The basement was quite warm, but the hard-working generator seemed to be weakening by the minute, dimming the light steadily. Oxenstern unlocked a door that bore his name on a silver plaque and ushered Silverman into a cheerless and cluttered office that might have been made over from a storeroom in the original building. The walls remained rough, old brick. As an office the room was spacious enough, but it was queerly shaped and poorly lighted. Its high and narrow fan-windows would have left the room steeped in gloom even if they hadn't been covered over by snowdrifts. The few dim bulbs in the ceiling, flickering precariously, did nothing to dispel the sepulchral atmosphere. Oxenstern turned up the kerosene lamp and held it as high as he could reach. The first thing Silverman saw by its unsteady yellow light was an oversized woodcut that filled the wall above Oxenstern's desk. It showed a ghastly, horned figure with the lower part of a human body dangling from its jaws. *Lucifero* read the name scratched beneath the monster in a broken Gothic font. Looking more closely, Silverman saw that the figure had three faces, each stuffed with a writhing human form.

"A recent acquisition," Oxenstern explained. "Early sixteenth-century German. This is an enlargement I had made from the original block." He pointed to a blackened square of wood attached to the wall beside the picture. "Mrs. Bloore was kind enough to make the purchase. Satan dining on Judas, Brutus, and Cassius, the classic great traitors."

With Oxenstern carrying the light, Silverman stepped further into the room. There were some half-dozen bookcases; among them works of art covered all the available wall space. "What purpose?" Silverman asked.

"Hm?"

"You said the collection serves its purpose."

"Oh, yes. Literally, to scare the hell out of our students, if I may use so vulgar a phrase."

Wherever Silverman looked he saw depictions of devils at work punishing damned souls. Some were primitive, childlike renderings from a more innocent period; in these, the devils were cartoon-like meanies with pointed ears and pitchforks. Other, later pictures were graphically sadistic depictions of diabolical cruelty. Along one wall hung several of Gustave Doré's familiar illustrations for Dante's Inferno, all richly framed. "We have eighteen Doré first prints," Oxenstern informed him. "I bought them from a dealer in Geneva about ten years ago."

"All very morbid," Silverman commented.

Oxenstern chuckled. "So Mrs. Oxenstern believes. She made me move the collection out of the house. She had every justification. This isn't domestic decor." He bent close to the Doré prints, studying each one. "Yes, here's one you may find worth closer inspection." He tapped a knuckle against one of the Doré illustrations. Silverman came closer to see. The picture showed a dismal landscape filled with writhing bodies under a constant rain of fire. "This figure here," Oxenstern explained, "is Brunetto Latini, one of Dante's teachers. Note how friendly Dante seems to be with this fellow. You might wonder why Signore Latini was condemned to so terrible a fate."

Silverman knew why. "I spent my sophomore year in Florence. Dante was my special interest," he said. "This is the seventh circle of the inferno. The damned souls were condemned for their *mal potesti nervi*. That might be translated as 'their wicked pricks.' They're homosexuals—Sodomites, as you prefer to call them."

"Correct," Oxenstern said in a schoolteacherish tone. "'The violent against nature.' See how well the picture catches the agony and despair of their condition."

"I know something about Dante's treatment of homosexuality," Silverman commented as he scrutinized the image. "He actually thought of Brunetto as a noble soul. He had fond memories of him as a poet and a philosopher."

"But he does, nonetheless, condemn him to eternal torment."

"Yes, but Dante deals with all the sins of love and passion as if he thinks God might have been rather too severe. They're hot-blooded sins, sins of the heart. I'd agree with him. Sins of passion deserve a certain latitude. None of these people did anything that hurt another person."

"Except God, who took deep offense at their unnatural lust. And you must admit, the punishment you see Brunetto suffering is rather horrendous. Can you imagine putting up with those flames for as long as five minutes without screaming in pain and possibly begging forgiveness? But it would be to no avail. The flames will continue forever."

"Well, let's hope God has learned better since then. I'll bet if Dante were writing today, he'd allow gays at least to make it into Purgatory."

"These are matters of eternal law," Oxenstern insisted. "We must remember that Dante is not God. If he forgave people like Latini, that was a matter of fallible human judgment."

"Nor are any of us God, Professor. Not you, not me. Not even the guys who wrote the Bible." He crossed the room to view another picture that was little short of pornographic. It showed a naked, voluptuous woman being sexually tormented by a team of demons. They were leaving no orifice unattended. "I can see why Mrs. Oxenstern wanted these out of the house. She shows good taste."

Oxenstern beckoned him to one of the shelves. "This is one of the largest demonological libraries in North America. I've spent forty years assembling what you see here." The books were clearly collector's items, many of them leather-bound and worn with age. Silverman pulled down a few volumes and flipped some pages. There were several studies of witchcraft and sorcery, works on possession and exorcism, several monographs on unnatural sexual practices. One, titled *The Abomination of Self-Abuse*, was filled with the most bizarrely contorted images Silverman could remember seeing. The illustrations purported to be forms of masturbation, all of them roundly condemned in the text—as if to make the point "And don't try to get away with *this* either!" But a great deal of what the pictures showed was, Silverman judged, physically impossible.

"Shouldn't it be a sin to imagine sins that can't possibly be committed?" Silverman asked, showing one of the pictures to Oxenstern. "Nobody could do *that*."

"It's my understanding," the professor answered, "that the study of yoga, so popular in your part of the country, is designed to enable people to assume these very postures—and for that very purpose. Which is why our church condemns the practice."

"That's news to me," Silverman admitted. "I thought yoga was all about curing constipation." He thumbed through a few more books. For the most part, the pictures were grotesque depictions of infernal horrors, some so extreme as to seem comic, but none pleasant to see. As he moved through Oxenstern's dismal office, he wondered whether he had entered a time warp. It was the beginning of the twenty-first century, but in this shadowy Minnesota basement, he was surveying an iconography that dated back to the days of the Roman catacombs when the people called Christians gathered amid the cultural rubble of the day to raise their incantations to a strange god. Here he was in the company of a man who would have been perfectly at home among them, praising Jesus and ejecting demons.

"The collection is a lot more cramped than it was in our home," Oxenstern apologized, "but I can make better use of it here on campus."

"What use is that?"

"I think of it as a teaching device that conveys the true meaning of our faith."

Silverman sensed that he was about to find out Oxenstern's reason for inviting him into this chamber of horrors. "How so?" he asked, eager to move things along.

"Consider what faith means to most people," Oxenstern began. "Believing in God, correct? But believing in God is little more than minimal and hardly that much of a challenge. After all, here we are, we exist, and so too the sun and the stars, all pretty clear evidence of divine power. I've always thought that even professed atheists must have some appreciation for the miracle of creation, even if they won't admit it. Don't you think that's true? But believing in God isn't nearly enough, not at all; it isn't even a beginning. It doesn't bring repentance and true conversion—not unless one dreads the pains of hell. If faith is going to touch the heart, there has to be fear, fear of damnation, fear of everlasting anguish, fear of the devil's cunning. Ah, but believing in the devil, as I hope I've shown you, is far more difficult than believing in God. For most modern people like yourself, it's nearly impossible. Satan is so absurd, damnation is so absurd. 'God,' says the reasonable humanist, 'if there is a God' (for he isn't even sure of that) 'God would never let there be a devil. God is nice, He is reasonable, He is fair.' Even for liberal Christians, Satan is an embarrassment, a vestige of ancient superstition. Away with all that! It's almost as if Satan were at our ear night and day, whispering, 'Don't believe in me! Don't believe in me! Only a fool would believe in me.' And yet our faith requires us to believe in evil as well as good, the devil as well as God."

Silverman's eye fell upon a series of woodcut illustrations that might have come out of an S&M magazine: a tangled heap of naked male and female bodies undergoing excruciating agonies, many of them blatantly sexual. In this case, the demons were apparently working for Jesus, who was shown high above egging them on. "Strong stuff," he commented. "But I gather Jesus approves."

"That's from the Counter-Reformation period," Oxenstern told him. "The Last Judgment as seen by a Spanish artist. This figure may interest you particularly." He pointed to a shapely, half-clad woman. "This is Belphegor, who is actually a man. Thus, a transvestite devil. He's credited with being the guardian of Paris, in its time an even greater city of sin than your San Francisco. The damned are, for obvious reasons, all Protestants."

"So once upon a time, people of your faith were counted among the reprobate."

"Yes, by an apostate church ruled over by the whore of Babylon."

"Does it ever trouble you that Christians seem so eager to damn and punish one another? I mean you can't all be right because you swear by the Bible and claim to be Christians. Doesn't it worry you that your judgment may be as bad as that of the Spanish artist there?"

"Not at all. Faith requires us to fight against such doubts. That's why our church insists on staying as close as possible to the clear and simple meaning of scripture. There is no more certain basis for belief."

"So you teach a class in all this—the suffering, the sadism?"

"More than a class. What you see here is my way of inculcating the reality of Satan. We've made it a requirement that every student at our school spend one day each year studying these pictures. They have to write an essay on some form of torment they see here, preferably the one that they would find most unbearable. We want them to know the cost of disbelief. We want them to tremble with dread, wondering if their faith is strong enough to save them from eternal retribution."

"And does it work?" Silverman asked. "Do things like this teach them Christian love?"

"Oh, no, not love. You misunderstand. Love is another lesson entirely. But love is really no challenge. Have you ever heard anybody reject or revile love? The modern world is in love with love. Love is warm and comforting. What students learn here is fear—as in the phrase 'God-fearing.' They learn the meaning of judgment and the wages of sin. And they learn something else, something that has always meant a great deal to me. They learn the satisfaction of knowing that all those who doubt and mock, those like yourself who are so proud of their intelligence and their worldly accomplishments, all of you will come to this." He stepped over to one of the woodcuts and tapped on a picture of bodies enveloped in flames.

"To this, where you will be as nothing but a howling heap of rags and bones. All the enemies of God will finish in the lake of fire, not one will escape, not even the virtuous heathens or the most saintly humanists. This is your eternal future, Professor."

"You believe that? That it makes no difference how good people have been?"

"Not the slightest. Because all have sinned and fallen short. Nobody works the sins off their souls, Professor. That's the bedrock of our faith. 'The Scripture hath concluded all under sin,' *all!* 'that the promise by faith of Jesus Christ might be given to them that believe.'"

"Wait. Let me guess," Silverman interrupted. "Romans, two for a quarter? Matthew, 7 come 11?"

For a split-second Oxenstern's smile slipped, a small show of temper, but quickly overcome. "Galatians, 3:22 actually. Of course, there are those who believe otherwise, the champions of easy religion and guaranteed salvation. They exist even in our own church, like your young confidante Swenson, and they seem to be gaining the day steadily. But that is apostasy, for which they will be punished as severely as the infidel and the heretic. Those who don't throw themselves upon God's mercy and accept the salvific promise of Christ will burn, all of them. You will burn." There wasn't the least hint of anger in Oxenstern's words; he uttered them matter-of-factly. All the while he spoke, the smug little grin that lent him such an uncanny air remained locked in place. Now Silverman understood what that smile was. It was a sign of deep inner consolation. It meant, "You will go to hell and I won't. Ha-ha-ha."

Ugga-bugga, Silverman reminded himself as his thoughts tipped toward outrage. *I am learning the articles of the savage faith.* "Is it okay for Christians to gloat?" he asked.

"If by gloating you mean enjoying to see justice done, then yes, it's among the rewards of the faithful. Hence, Luke 16:22-26."

"Sorry, don't know that number," Silverman answered.

"Here, let me show you." Oxenstern searched one of the bookshelves. He found the book he wanted and flipped it open to an illustration. The picture showed a man writhing in flames, reaching upward to another man who was apparently in heaven surrounded by angels. The heavenly soul was looking down in cold contempt. "It's the story of Lazarus the beggar and the rich man. Both of them die. Lazarus is swept up into Abraham's bosom; the rich man, being a sinner, descends to hell where he suffers all the horrors of damnation. The flames burn the flesh from his bones, but the flesh comes back to burn again the next day. At one point, he looks up in his misery and sees Lazarus enjoying eternal bliss. He begs Lazarus to dip his finger in the water and offer him one cool drop. One drop. At which point, Father Abraham intervenes to say: Now is the time for Lazarus to be comforted and you to be tormented. He reminds the rich man that 'between us and you there is a great gulf fixed.' You see, the rich man had his chance to win Paradise. Is he to be pitied for damning himself?"

"Have you ever read *Pilgrim's Progress*?" Silverman asked as a thought entered his mind, something that might catch the man by surprise and at least stop the flow.

Oxenstern gave a small, amused gasp. "*Read it?* I had all but memorized it by the age of twelve. I can still see the pages as if they were before my eyes. Page 67. 'In this combat, no man can imagine, unless he had seen and heard as I did, what yelling and hideous roaring Apollyon made all the time of the fight, he spake like a dragon.'"

That almost stopped Silverman dead with pity. The image of this little kid having to learn Bunyan by heart. He sighed and moved on. "Well, I've been leafing through it, for lack of anything better to read in your library, which, incidentally, is not as well stocked as my local Christian Science bookstore back home. Of course, Bunyan is probably best seen as children's literature now and not worth the analysis. But at least from my whimsical viewpoint, the man got everything upside down."

Oxenstern was looking more amused by the second, as if he were watching an animal act: a dog or cat pretending to deliver a lecture on algebra. "How so?"

"Well, it's an allegory, you know."

"Oh, yes, I had noticed."

"Bunyan has all these outdated allegorical figures. Faithful, Evangelist, Holy-Man. Well, guess what? I find all his good guys hard to take. They're too smug. But I like an awful lot of his bad guys—the ones like Heedless and By-Ways and Pliable. Not to mention Madam Wanton and Lechery, with whom I have a certain special sympathy. Because all that's wrong with them is that they admit to having a certain human latitude. You know, weakness, vacillation, uncertainty. Maybe that's where you people have gone wrong. You can't see that basic decency can walk hand-in-hand with human fallibility."

Oxenstern's expression of amusement was descending rapidly toward deep sadness. "'Decency,' he repeated with a dismissive wag of the head. "What use do you think God has for such cheap wares? The decent man can't even imagine the true cost of redemption. Do you recall a section of the book dealing with a character called Ignorance?"

"Not off hand."

"Ah, well, it is one of the best passages. Even you may be able to grasp it. And it's not written with the least hint of vituperation. As I recall, the Pilgrim asks Ignorance why he is so sure he will be saved when he has deliberately turned from the chance to cure his fallibility. And Ignorance says, 'my heart and life agree together, and therefore my hope is well grounded.' And the Pilgrim asks, 'Who told thee that thy heart and life agree together?' To which Ignorance answers, 'My heart tells me so.' " After a pause, Oxenstern added, "Rather penetrating, don't you think?"

Silverman sighed. Dropping his guise of anthropological objectivity, he wagged his head in resignation. "I guess Christianity is whatever Christians want to make it. Who am I to tell you that you've got it all wrong? Myself, being a non-believer, I think of Jesus as a nice guy who wanted people to be good to each other. 'If I had my life to live over, I'd try to be a little kinder.' Aldous Huxley said that."

"Huxley?" Oxenstern mused. "The novelist? A Hindu of some kind, wasn't he?"

"A Vedantist, I think. And an excellent novelist, which comes closer to my religion. Anyway, I like to think that's what Jesus believed. But somewhere along the line his followers decided a nice guy wasn't good enough. They wanted a miracle-maker. So they turned him into a god. And once he was a god, he became less and less human, less and less kind. Professor, all I can say is I think your religion is obscene."

Oxenstern was unfazed. "I'm sure you do. Humanism is a soft faith. It lacks the stomach for accepting God whole. But that makes no difference. I meant this little visit as a favor, please know that. It may be the greatest kindness anyone has ever shown you. Something is happening to you here, in this room, now, at the hands of a stranger. This may be the most consequential moment of your life. I ask you only to remember what you've seen here. Accept it as evidence for the reality of hell. Weigh the authority behind that teaching. If you find yourself saying, 'that could never be,' remember: You're hearing the voice of the devil. But when you hear that voice, know that there is a way even for you to avoid the fires. It could happen ever so quickly. I don't expect you to acknowledge it, but how much kinder could I be than to offer you the chance to return home redeemed? Take your time, as much as you please. I'm in no hurry."

"Take my time? To do what?" Silverman asked.

"Pick one."

"One what?"

Oxenstern gestured to the pictures all around them. "One of the torments. Pick the torture you could least endure, even for a split-second. Fire, filth, suffocation, the whip, the blade. Tonight, when you retire, keep that image before you. Try to imagine suffering that torture for eternity. For eternity, Professor. And then know: *that's* what awaits you. But you can also be absolutely certain that there is a way to escape that fate. What a balm that will be for your troubled soul. I'm offering you the chance to be sanctified. Please, look around. Pick one."

Silverman rose from his seat and backed off. There was a gleeful brightness in Oxenstern's eyes that both disgusted and frightened him. "You're crazy," he said. "You're an absolute sadist."

"Oh no, please," Oxenstern replied calmly. "I may be the most loving man you've ever met, the only person to care for your eternal soul. Others you have met here might despise you. Some, I know, find you personally disgusting. One of our teachers claims she hasn't been able to hold down any food since you arrived on campus. But I'm not among those people, who've forgotten their mission in this world. *I care*, Professor Silverman—Daniel, if I might so call you. My appeal is sincere and whole-hearted. In your pride, please don't be hasty. It's simply your carnal mind that blinds you. As we sit here, we're struggling for your soul. It's never too late. 'Repent and be converted, that your sins may be blotted out.'"

But Silverman was already backing toward the door. If he didn't leave at once, he knew he would be sick. "Don't come after me," he warned Oxenstern. "If you ever try to talk to me again, so help me, I'll flatten you."

Oxenstern rose to call after him, still wearing the smug little grin that stuck to him like a tattoo. "I'm offering you sanctification. This may be your only chance. Daniel, don't go. Don't go, please. This is your chance to enter the kingdom."

But Silverman was already inching away, his stomach wreathing itself into a tight knot. In another moment, he was out the door— but not before he had clicked a mental photograph of Oxenstern. Where would that face and that voice surface some day in his writing? A Grand Inquisitor, perhaps. Or a Gestapo interrogator. Then he was down the corridor and up the stairs to the kitchen two at a time, fleeing as if a horde of demons might be at his back.

• • • • •

A half-hour later, he was in the library seeking to make sense of his visit to the underworld. Oxenstern thought he had done his visitor a kindness. But Silverman may have done Oxenstern an even greater favor. This may have been the first time Oxenstern had known the pleasure of trying out his chop-logic on someone he regarded as a true secular humanist. And he had, to his own giddy satisfaction, totally humiliated his opposition. Of course he was free to think so; it was as if he and Silverman had been conversing in different languages, each free to impose any meaning they wished on what the other said. Silverman sat marveling over the abyss of understanding that separated him from the people he was meeting. Talk about "a great gulf fixed."

But why, he wondered, was Oxenstern, this stupid, stupid man, trying to sound smart? How could anyone so doltish even have formed the impression that he could think? Here was Silverman, a well-educated man, a novelist who knew a reasonably good amount, who had traveled, met significant thinkers, tasted of many societies, but who also knew his limits. There were millions of things he didn't know, millions of things he was unsuited to judge. He accepted that. He didn't pretend to know the deepest secrets of the universe. Yet here were these boobs—Oxenstern, Jaspers—carrying on as if they had a brain, and as if that brain were the privileged receptacle of truth. Anti-intellectualism was bad enough; pseudo-intellectualism was far worse.

Still, if he controlled his most spontaneous impulse, which was to ridicule and reject, Silverman was learning from these bizarre encounters. His brief discourse with Oxenstern left him reflecting upon the times he lived in. So much was churning through his mind. He didn't fancy himself a political person; in fact, he found politics nauseatingly phoney. Yet he had often wondered about all the rabidly conservative politicos who had been storming around the country for the last several years talking about "cultural war," troglodytes like Jake Dawes who were hell-bent on hammering gays into the ground and beating women back into the kitchen. Was it possible they were taking their cues from the likes of Oxenstern and Jaspers? Was this the brains trust behind the loud-mouth reactionaries he sometimes heard blabbering away on the radio?

When the mindless and moneyed few begin aspiring to intellect, that was getting beyond plain public-be-damned viciousness. Like Herr Rosenberg and Herr Goebbels before him, Oxenstern actually cared about being *right*. And when it came to being right, the trump card was God. Now that he thought about it, Silverman felt a queasy wiggle in his stomach at the possibility that he might be living in an era when asshole politicians were actually trying to recruit God for their agenda.

And where did all this crusading confidence come from? Fairy tales about Sodom and Gomorrah, arguments for the literal existence of a devil who whispers in your ear. Maybe that was why he and his friends were being pounded by the power elite of the nation. He had always assumed that conservative types were no more than arrogant, profiteering sons of bitches who were out to dodge taxes and screw the public. The occasional few richies he had met at author's parties were spoiled-brat rich kids who hadn't read a book since college. Why should they? They had no need of intelligence. If they did, they hired somebody to be intelligent for them. He assumed the moneyed few spent their time lunching at swanky restaurants, drinking the best Scotch, peddling influence, and humping each other's wives at luxury resorts. But perhaps it went deeper than that. Maybe the marauding rich had taken on intellectual pretensions. Now they wanted to own ideas as well as dollars. That made Professor Oxenstern's lumpen-intellectualism truly scary—in the same way that the Nazis got scary when they started hoking up theories of the master race and measuring skulls and noses. He recalled his father once saying, "It wasn't enough they should slaughter us like in the past. No, these Aryan goons had to convince themselves they had a scientific right to genocide us. They had to quote from books!"

Books. Silverman winced at the word. So much of what he was up against had to do with books. Or rather one book, one, old, uneven text, a hodge-podge anthology that deserved mixed reviews. Maybe that's what produced this sickly roiling in his stomach. Books were his life. He had never once found occasion to call their value into question. But here were people for whom the written word had a wholly different purpose. In North Fork, things written on paper were still surrounded by a primitive sense of awe that lent the words a supernatural authority. Quote the words and you acquire the authority. That was why they were all so glib when it came to citing scripture, Jaspers, Apfel, Oxenstern and the rest. Bunyan too—always so fast on the draw with chapter and verse, faster than Silverman could be with . . . well, with anything he had ever read. He had never committed more than a few poems to memory—"Dover Beach," some A. E. Houseman. Even the things he loved with all his heart, great passages from favorite authors—it had never occurred to him to memorize them, let alone to whip them out like an ace in the hole to play against an opponent. It seemed such a demeaningly adversarial use to make of literature, especially great literature—using it to score points. Who would ever think of doing that with Proust or Lawrence? But, of course, if you believed God Himself had written all this stuff, that would make a difference, a difference that Silverman had never been forced to take seriously.

The feeling he would have named as rage only a few moments ago was taking on a distant hint of nauseated fear—the kind of fear he might feel for a loved one who had been taken hostage by a merciless enemy. But in this case it wasn't a person, it was literature that was endangered—the entire population of Bookville, all his lifelong companions. The dour prophets of North Fork, this belligerent tribe he found himself among, were making him doubt all he held dear about writing. They had turned this thing they called the Word of God into an object of worship. Between the covers of this single work they purported to find all that anybody needed to answer the great questions of life. All that had ever happened or would ever happen had been prophesied by a small band of underfed, know-it-all *schnorers* dragging themselves around the deserts of Palestine five thousand years ago. For all he knew, the evangelical brethren believed they could find next year's world series scores hidden in Isaiah or Ezekiel. For them there was nothing that wasn't known, nothing strange, nothing new, nothing startling. Their book was all science, all history, all law, all politics enshrined in the quaint, often inscrutable English of seventeenth-century divines, most of whom still thought the world was shaped like a pancake and that women were the vessels of Satan.

Silverman recalled books he had read that left him dizzy with surprise, books that had left him breathless with unexpected delight. And there were other books—stories that had threatened to tear all his convictions to pieces. Camus' *The Stranger* had sent him into a tailspin of despair that wrung every last drop of meaning out of his life. And Kafka's Joseph K. had taught him that life could be a waking nightmare. That was what he went to literature for—the risk. Not so these Bible thumpers. Scripture was their cosmic security blanket; they looked to it for certainty guaranteed on the highest authority. Instead of opening the heart to free experience, their one book had slammed shut all the doors and windows. They had walled off doubt and with it, all that made living in the world an adventure. That was where they found the confidence to revile and condemn and reject. Words in a book, words written by men. *This, too, literature could do.* It could devour the mind and chew it into mush, harden the heart and make murder legitimate. Worse than any physical threat he felt, this dim-witted idolatry of the book made him wonder if the written word, however dear it might be to him, was worth all the misery that had come of it.

19

The North Fork Gay and Lesbian Alliance

As he was leaving the library, a fit of sneezing came over him. His cold was still working out its physiological destiny, through the sinus into the throat, then onward to the chest. The outburst must have covered half the room with flu virus. Good. Germ warfare. He wished he could coat every sanctimonious tome in the room with influenza. He was feeling mean.

"God bless you," a tiny voice said.

Silverman spun around. While he had been sneezing his head off, he had been joined in the library by Faith College's three student humanists. The girl had wished him the *gesundheit*, the two boys nodded their endorsement.

"Professor Silverman?" the girl said, asking permission to approach.

"Yes?"

"I'm Tilly Schurz. This is Alex and Jack. Remember? We're the committee." They came into the room struggling out of snow-dusted coats and scarves. Silverman could feel the aura of frost they brought with them into the room. The cold had reddened their faces like ripe peaches. Where they stood to take off their wraps the floor quickly formed a spreading puddle.

"What committee?"

"For the Religious Humanism Studies program."

"Oh, yeah."

"We wanted you to know, we think you were great," Tilly bubbled as she rubbed her frozen fingers. "You were so brave and strong. Just like we knew you'd be."

Silverman gazed at her in total bewilderment. "I don't get it," he said. "Yesterday you were leading the applause for this thug

Axel. Today you're throwing flowers at me?"

The girl's jaw dropped. "Me? Applauding for Axel? You thought that?"

"You mean you weren't?"

A frantic glow was coming over her. "That vicious asshole? I was clapping for you. For *you!*"

Silverman gave her a skeptical look. "It sure didn't look that way. You were applauding in his direction, not mine."

"That was us," Jack explained. "We sort of turned her that way so people couldn't tell what she was doing."

"You had no business doing that either," Tilly protested.

"That's why we had to hustle her out of there," Alex said. "before she started mouthing off. She was busting."

Tilly looked as if she might bust now. "I was going to grab that ugly banner of his and . . . and . . . I don't know what. Trample it to pieces."

"Yeah," said Alex, "and then we'd really be fucked."

"As it is we're fucked anyway," Jack added. "Nobody thinks the three of us would be cheering for Axel."

"Oh, I bet they had it all planned," Tilly insisted. "Axel and Apfel and Oxenstern. They were out to get you right from the start."

"If anybody had warned me something like that was going to happen," Silverman said, "I'd never have come, no matter how much you paid me."

"But that would've been awful," Tilly exclaimed. "Whatever happened, we don't have any regrets about asking you. We know Richard feels the same way."

"I wouldn't be so sure. Last I talked to him, he sounded pretty morose."

"Well, yeah," Alex agreed. "What with getting fired."

"*Fired*? He lost his job?"

"Yeah, last night," Alex answered. "The trustees had a special meeting. It was pretty ghastly. They—mostly Mrs. Bloore—really raked him over the coals. They want to take back his house and everything. And he's spent his whole life in the church."

"Christ," Silverman moaned. "This is a train wreck all around."

"We don't think so," Tilly insisted, putting on a feisty expression.

"That's right," Alex chimed in. "You were our idea. We're glad you came."

"But why me?" Silverman asked.

"We saw your show," Jack answered.

"Show? I don't have a show."

"The one you did about Castro Street."

"That wasn't *my* show. All they did was interview me—and not use most of what I said."

"Well, you were on it," Jack replied. "It was so cool."

Silverman wagged his head incredulously. "That was years ago."

"We saw it on a cassette," Jack said. "We watched it over and over. That's when we decided to invite you."

Silverman was baffled. "His" show, as they called it, was several scattered minutes of an interview he had done five or six years ago for the local San Francisco PBS station. Far from it being "his" show, he was only one of several people who agreed to talk about the city's famous gay neighborhood. He was an odd choice for an interview. He had never lived in the Castro District. Until his impromptu lecture at Faith College yesterday, he had never publicly identified himself as gay. But the clear assumption behind the show was that everybody who appeared was gay. That was what all the questions were about—the gay lifestyle of San Francisco. On camera, Silverman had made a point of talking about the subject as impersonally as possible. He had discussed the contribution the Castro community was making to tolerance, the role it had played in the AIDS crisis, its political and cultural influence across the country—things like that. He hadn't even been one of the main interviewees, which was appropriate enough since he wasn't active in gay politics. He considered his appearance to be a minor stint, not worth mentioning. It certainly hadn't upped the sales of any of his books. "I don't get it," he said. "I thought I was invited here because of my novels."

"Oh, that too," Alex assured him. "We've read all your books— well, almost. Some are hard to get."

"But it was the program that really opened our eyes," Tilly added.

"To what?"

"San Francisco. What it could be like," she answered.

"Yeah," Jack echoed. "San Francisco." He named the city with exactly the wistful intonation a director might try to elicit for "Shangri-La!" in a remake of *Lost Horizon.*

"So mainly what you wanted was to hear about the Castro?" Silverman asked.

"Right," Alex answered.

"From me? Because I was on that show?" He wanted his resentment to be noticed, but he was being stymied by their obtuseness. Were they too young, perhaps, to know how much it hurt to have his creative identity treated as something beside the point, something as secondary as the color of his hair or the size of his shoes?

"Right," Tilly said. "The show was never on television around here, not that anybody on our faculty watches television anyway. They think it's Satanic. So nobody would know about you, see? Only us."

"And then when you got here," Alex went on, "we could get you all to ourselves—we hoped. And you could tell us everything."

Well, well, what d'you know? It was the look in Alex's eyes that sent the message. Lonely, longing, fearful, bordering on embarrassment, but too stubbornly curious to draw back. Couldn't be more obvious. Silverman turned to Tilly. "You too?"

She blushed gorgeously and withdrew into her veil of hair. "I think so . . . sort of."

"Sort of?"

"I don't know for sure."

"She is," Alex said. "She really is."

"I've never tried it out," she confessed. "I mean, how would I around here? But these are the only guys I've ever been comfortable with, so I guess— "

"And the two of you," Silverman asked, glancing from Alex to Jack. "You're an item?" Alex gave a quick nod. Lucky Alex, Silverman thought. He slumped into the nearest overstuffed chair, asking, "So what've I got here? The North Fork Gay and Lesbian Alliance?"

Tilly laughed. "I guess so."

"San Francisco, that's what we wanted to know about," Alex explained. "Do they really have parades there—for gay people?"

"And all those bars," Jack added. "Do you know all of them? Can you really hang out and not have to worry somebody's gonna hassle you—like at that place Elephant Walk?"

"Elephant Walk?" Silverman shook his head. "That closed up four, five years ago."

"Oh."

"Not to worry. There are plenty more like it."

"Hey, that's so great." The three of them were beaming at each other.

Silverman felt his bones go weary. Back home he was known as a curmudgeon on these matters. Even Marty called him a curmudgeon. "List me as the third sex," he once said. "the sex called 'none-of-your-business.'" He had long considered the more ostentatious behavior of the gay community an obnoxious sort of theatricality. "Yes, they have parades," he said to Alex. "And carnivals, and festivals, and block parties, and Mardi Gras, and banquets, and award ceremonies. And that only gets you from January to March."

"That's incredible," Jack and Tilly said simultaneously. "The women too?" Tilly asked, "There are bars for the women too, aren't there? They showed this one—the Chi Chi Club. Have you been there?"

"Women's bars? Of course. In fact, you betcha," Silverman answered. "But we're way beyond that. We have now refined divergent sexuality in San Francisco into fifty-seven varieties. Let's see, the last official category I remember receiving representation on the City Council was handicapped, Native American, transgenderized grandmothers. They have their parade in April, I believe."

"You don't think this is a good thing?" Tilly asked, puzzled by his flippant response.

Silverman sighed. "The way I see it: parading for your sexual orientation is like taking pride in being bow-legged or left-handed or red-headed. Dumb."

"Oh, I don't know," Alex piped up. "They practically force you to be sensational."

"Who does?"

"People like Professor Jaspers," he replied, "who want gays to not exist. The way they see it, if you're normally gay and not out there parading, well, you must be ashamed of what you are."

"If you're coming to San Francisco to get in the parade," Silverman said, "that's a pretty meager reason."

"It's to be free," Tilly insisted, as if that ought to be obvious. "It's to be with people who don't think you're a freak. We thought you'd understand that."

Silverman, suddenly aware of how smug he must be sounding, backed off. "Well, I do. Maybe I've been spoiled or jaded. I suppose if I lived here as you do. . . ."

"It gives you some idea of what we're up against," Jack said.

"So you can see," Alex went on, "when Richard got this money for the program and the lectures, we told him we wanted you to be the first to come. Well, he wanted to get Gore Vidal for starters. We didn't think that was going to work. And it didn't."

"God! That almost killed the program right there," Tilly added. "We had to pay $20,000 for a no-show. Mrs. Bloore nearly went through the ceiling. After that, we had to be careful who we asked. What was good about you is that your books are lots harder to find."

"Yes," Silverman agreed, "that is a blessing, isn't it? Being out of print. It's next best to not getting published at all." He found himself caught balancing painfully between outrage and compassion. Here he was trapped among the evangelical headhunters, and it wasn't even his books that had gotten him into this pickle. It was the sexual orientation he had always insisted was nobody's business—not even other gays. But how could he blind himself to the desperation of these kids? They stood before him like three Anne Franks trying to escape from that attic. "Look, what do you expect of me? Counseling?"

"No, just to maybe talk," Jack answered. "God! Just to talk!"

"But why me? I'm not a crusader."

"That's why," Jack went on. "We could've never gotten away with bringing somebody who had that kind of reputation here. We could pretend you were a novelist."

Silverman's eyes flashed at him. "I *am* a novelist, damn it!"

"Well, yeah, that too," Jack agreed. "But, see, we could work you into the Religious Humanism program, you being Jewish and all."

Silverman winced extravagantly to make his point. "I'm not Jewish. I mean not in any important way. Notice how I didn't say '*Oy!*'"

"Well, that wasn't what we really cared about anyway," Tilly explained. "There are Jewish people around here we can meet any old time. There's like a Jewish dentist in Flat Rock. I mean, we've met Jewish people. Being Jewish isn't our problem, which wouldn't be much of a problem anyway."

"Oh, I think it would," Jack disagreed. "I've heard lots of anti-Semitism around here ever since I was a kid."

"Yeah, but like that's of a lower order of cruelty, don't you think?" Tilly explained. "Nobody thinks of Jews like gays. I mean, there's nothing like 'the demon of homosexuality' for Jews."

Silverman interrupted. "Wait a minute. I'll agree, I'm more of a gay than I am a Jew. But I'm more of a novelist than I am a gay or a Jew. In fact, when I write about anything Jewish, some people say I'm anti-Semitic. Go figure."

Alex squinted at him with a puzzled expression. "So if you wrote about gays, you mean it would come out homophobic?"

"I don't know. The issue has never come up. I've never created a gay character."

"Why not?" Tilly asked.

That was a good question. So good that Silverman could only answer, "What a dumb question!"

"I'm sorry," Tilly apologized. "But why?"

"Welcome to Creative Writing 1A," Silverman said snidely. "'Write about what you know.' Correct? Well, I know about a great deal that goes beyond my sexual identity. Anyway, what is there to say about being gay—besides all the angst and the guilt and the struggle and the persecution?"

". . . and the friendship?" Jack suggested quizzically. "I think people should know about the good times, the fun, how much it means to have someone there with you when it gets tough."

"Yes, that too," Silverman admitted. "Sure, the pleasures, the joys. . . ."

"The love," Tilly added.

"Okay," Silverman agreed.

"The tragedy, if you don't play safe," Alex observed.

"Yes, sure," Silverman went along with that. "Heartbreak, loss, grief."

"And the anger that so many gay people feel for, like, why the hell don't they leave us be?" Tilly put in.

"Right," Silverman said, "there's that. Anger. Fury. Outrage."

After a pause, Jack asked, "Isn't that just about all there is?"

"True," Silverman agreed again. "There's a lot. Okay. Agreed." And . . . so? They were waiting, but he kept his answer to himself. The truth was, he had once started a story that cut close to the bone of his identity. It was set against one of those blowzy San Francisco events: Gay Pride, Gay Life, Gay Achievement. Two men, partners of a few years, one white, one black, go to an event, tire of it, decide to leave, go to a movie. Nothing happens. That was the problem. He couldn't develop anything beyond that point that might not have been the story of a hetero couple. There was no spark. Nothing came alive in the story. He had put the problem down to a temporary lack of inspiration, but now he had to wonder if there wasn't more to it than he wanted to admit. As Shenandoah Fish would have put it, he was too good at rising above—a convenient defense. "Look," he said at last, "I didn't come here to discuss my literary career. Well, as a matter of fact, I *did* come here to discuss my literary career—but not in those terms. And anyway, I don't feel like it now. The point is: I don't trade in being Jewish or gay. What I am is a novelist. That's all I want to be. You brought me here under false pretenses, Goddamnit! Why did Swenson go along with you on this?"

"He knew we needed to meet somebody like you, from outside," Alex answered.

"He understands what we're up against," Jack added.

"He does? Why?"

Alex gave a wry smile. "Can't you tell?"

No, apparently he couldn't tell, not unless he thought about it twice. Silverman hadn't even thought about Swenson once. "Come on!" he said. "He's married. He's got a kid."

"So?" Alex asked. "Isn't that how it is when you're in the closet?"

Tilly explained. "See, in the church, you *can't* be gay. I mean you can't. Richard is as liberal as it gets—or tries to get. He's been struggling for years now to create a Reconciling in Christ program like the Methodists have. That means. . . ."

"I've heard, I've heard," Silverman waved her off. "'In' Christ, right? Not 'with' or whatever. Sort of an amnesty for homosexuals, I gather."

"Yeah," Alex said. "And even if he got an RIC going, which he never, never will, it's all this icky stuff about 'healing the pain of doubt' and 'witnessing for Jesus.' I mean you still wind up feeling like a damn freak."

"Spare me," Silverman pleaded.

"Poor Richard," Tilly continued, "He's been pretending all his life. He had to go all the way pretending, even to himself. Until he couldn't do it any more."

"What about Syl?" Silverman asked.

"Syl," Alex said with honest admiration, "is an absolute saint."

"How long has she known?"

The three students looked at each other as if comparing notes. Tilly said, "I think probably since right after they got married, eight or nine years ago."

"Probably," Alex agreed.

That settled it. Now Silverman knew for certain that Syl was going to get into one of his stories. This qualified as more than long-suffering. This was championship class-A masochism. "So Swenson's what? Your protector?"

"No, he couldn't be that," Tilly said. "I mean, not openly. None of us could be what we are. North Fork is one big closet. If they even so much as suspected anything, they'd force us to go through a shaming."

"What's that?"

They looked from one to another to decide who should speak. Turning to Alex, Jack said, "Well, you've been through one. You tell."

Alex swallowed hard. "It wasn't for being gay. It was, well, for. . . ." He looked away, then back. "Okay, like it was for, you know, masturbation. I got caught at it and was shamed. I was eleven. It's supposed to be loving counsel, but I don't think so."

"What happens?" Silverman pressed him to say more.

"You have to sit with your parents and the minister and some other older kids—who supposedly never do it—and beg God's forgiveness in their presence. Worst thing is you have to tell all the details, like what was in your mind. Everybody gets a chance to condemn you out of scripture and then to bring you back into the fold. God, it was awful."

"They do those things here?" Silverman asked.

"Oh yeah," Tilly explained. "That's why we call this place Persecution U. And then there's worse."

"Worse?"

"The church has psychiatrists," she said, a grave look coming over her. "They do things to de-demonize you. They use electricity and things you drink to make you vomit."

"It's called aversion therapy," Alex added. "It's supposed to make you hate the sight of your own genitals."

"They still do that?" Silverman was amazed. "That's illegal in California."

"Well, maybe it is here too," Tilly said. "But they do it anyway. I know, if they did that to me, I'd break, I'd break all in pieces."

"No you wouldn't," Alex insisted. "You're tougher than you realize." He explained to Silverman. "Her father locked her up once. For two weeks on practically no food."

"For what?" Silverman asked.

Tilly mimicked a suffering martyr's face. "My great moment of mortification. I was taking a bath with a girlfriend. I was only ten. I knew I liked it, but we didn't, you know, do anything. We never even touched. But my father threw a fit. He didn't even believe I should see myself naked in a mirror." She dropped her voice and added, "I've heard people say that Professor Jaspers went through therapy when he was in high school."

"For being gay?" Silverman asked.

"Uh-huh. I don't know if it's true."

Silverman wagged his head in disbelief. "This is medieval."

Alex corrected him. "No, what's medieval is a demonic exorcism.

If they found out about any of us, that's what they'd probably do. And our parents would go right along, at least mine would."

"What the hell is that?" Silverman asked.

"It's a kind of ritual to drive out the devil."

"Who's in charge of that?" Silverman asked, wondering if he already knew.

"Professor Oxenstern," Alex answered. "He's an authority on demons and devils and all that. He knows all the rules about damnation. He's got this. . . ."

"I know, I know," Silverman cut him off. "My head is still swimming. I just got back from Professor Oxenstern's black museum."

The three exchanged worried glances. "Oh, poor you!" said Tilly.

"Actually, it was quite illuminating," Silverman reassured her. "Gave me a much clearer idea of what passes for religion on the righteous wing of our culture."

"We have to walk through that place once every year," Alex said. "I try to report in sick."

"What makes me really sick," Tilly said, "are the kids that get off on that stuff."

"And Oxenstern is the head exorcist?" Silverman asked.

"He's got this robe," Jack said, "and all this equipment, you know, bells and incense."

"You've been in on this?" Silverman asked.

"No, but Richard has had to help exorcise a couple students. He told me what goes on."

By now, Silverman could feel waves of sympathy for the three kids sloshing around the edges of his mind. Yes, he felt for them, but he insisted to himself that North Fork was *their* problem, nothing for him to get sucked into. The best advice he could give them was: "Why the hell don't you clear out of here? You're old enough."

"Well, barely," Jack said. "When I hit eighteen, I started thinking about it. But that's a big step. And we've got families. They'd be horrified. I'll tell you the honest truth. I don't know how to do that. That's where we thought you could help us."

"Me? How?"

"You must know how. Didn't you break out?"

"That was years ago. It was all different then." He made it clear he would tell them nothing more. Subject closed.

Alex said, "Well, when we do leave someday, we thought you might help us get located."

"Where? In San Francisco? You think I'm running an underground railroad? Give me a break."

Just then there was the creak of a hinge. The four of them flinched as if an electric current had run through them simultaneously. The door swung open and Gloria Dawes entered the library. She was as startled to see Silverman and the students as they to see her. She stopped indecisively, then came all the way in. "Excuse me. I came for a book." She was once again wearing a drab, shapeless dress, but this time had her hair skinned back into a hard little knot. She moved to a bookshelf at the far end of the room. Silence followed her all the way across. Then Silverman realized how suspicious the silence must seem. For the students' sake, he rushed to fill in with innocent conversation. "Normally I keep two or three books going at the same time until one of them reaches a sort of critical mass and presses to be finished. The one that looks as if it will become my next completed work is. . . ."

Miss Dawes was loitering at the shelf, taking down one book, then another.

". . . is called *Man Friday*. It retells the story of Robinson Crusoe. But this time, Friday is the narrator."

"Hey, cool," Alex remarked. "That's a really neat idea. He's black, right?"

"I don't actually identify him except as native, but, yes, definitely a person of color."

Gloria finally pulled down a large volume, thumbed some pages, and turned to leave. She crossed the room without making eye contact. Watching her out the door, Silverman went on, "After all, it's Friday's island, isn't it? So you get these overtones of colonialism." Then, under his breath: "Is it safe to talk anymore?"

Alex grimaced. "That's bad luck."

"Why?" Silverman asked.

"That's Professor Dawes. She's about the worst person to see Tilly here."

"She teaches women's studies, doesn't she?" Silverman asked.

Tilly gave a sarcastic little laugh. "Women's studies? What she teaches is the Christian Submissiveness course for the girls. 'Get married, stay married, have babies, stand by your man.' She and I are on real oppositional terms. Last year, she gave me a D in submission because I asked why God made Eve out of a miserable old rib. I mean that's a pretty dispensable part of the body. Why didn't God make women out of at least a kidney. She thought I was being facetious."

"Well, you *were* being facetious, weren't you?" Alex asked.

"If you ask me, the whole Bible is facetious. That's what I think."

"The way you bait her all the time like that," Alex said, "you're lucky she hasn't had you up for shaming."

Tilly sighed. "She bugs me so much. I don't think she believes half of what she teaches. She doesn't have the balls to stand up to her jerk of a father." In a whisper, she added, "I think she knows about me. She's been asking me questions, you know, about my social habits. My parents told her all about that bathtub thing. She's supposed to keep an eye on me. Yuk!"

Silverman gave a cluck of regret. "Well, sorry she spotted you. Are you going to be in trouble?"

"We're in trouble already for inviting you," Jack said. "Maybe you didn't know what set Tilly off in the chapel yesterday, but everybody else in the room did. They know we think Axel is a monster. I doubt any of us have much of a future around here."

Alex resumed their conversation with a hushed urgency. "I don't care about anything they think or say anymore, not if we have someplace to run when we have to. That's why we needed to talk with you today. When you get back, you wouldn't mind if we sort of dropped by some day?" A pleading note had entered his voice. "At least if maybe you could help us get oriented. Though I suppose there are lots of people we could get help from in San Francisco."

Sure, Silverman thought. *You parade sweety-pie Jack here down Castro Street and you'll have help all right, like hungry sled dogs after raw meat.* What innocents they were! They had known the guilt that comes with their identity; they were preparing themselves for the rejections that would follow. But they had yet to learn about the dark, predatory side of the life they were choosing. Sexual orientation, they would soon find out, guarantees practically nothing about character. They were three friends bound together by affection and trust; they had yet to meet a rogue or scoundrel who shared their interest in "strange flesh." "Okay, look, I'll make you a deal. You get me out of here any way you can. Hire a snowplow, whatever. And I'll be there waiting with open arms when you arrive."

"But there's no way out," Tilly protested. "Not till the storm ends."

"What about walking out?"

"Oh, no, you can't do that. You'd be frozen stiff in a minute."

"Did you bring boots?" Alex asked.

"I have rubbers."

"Ordinary rain rubbers? There's no way."

Silverman waved the yearbook at them. "What choice do I have? As far as Axel's concerned, I'm a marked man. The guy is a homicidal maniac."

"Oh, right, Axel," Tilly said. "Be careful about him."

"My advice is don't rile him up," Alex added.

"Don't rile him up? He's riled to the max. He's ready to kill me right now."

"I'm sure Mrs. Bloore will keep him under control," Tilly said. "He listens to her, sort of like a big hound dog. 'Down, Bruno!' she says, and he listens."

"Listens? He needs to be tied down. I'd as soon freeze as wait for him to gun me down. Incidentally, how did the three of you get here through the blizzard?"

"Our dorms aren't far away. Over that way across the courtyard. Even so, we had to follow the ropes."

"Ropes?"

"When we get a big blow like this," Alex explained, "they set up ropes between the buildings. And the rule is never to go out in the storm alone."

"The snow blinds you," Jack explained. "You can't see your hand in front of your face. And it's fifteen below zero outside."

"We had a storm like this a couple years ago," Tilly added. "One of the teachers—Miss Henreid, she taught Creationist Biology—tried to make it back to her house about a mile down the road. She never got off the grounds. She froze right out there by the front gate. Actually froze. They buried her in the courtyard. She lived here all her life and even so she couldn't find her way."

"What about cutting across the lake to Swenson's place—if the snow lets up a little?"

Tilly shook her head emphatically. "Please don't try that. You have to know the ice. It can be treacherous. There are channels that never freeze over."

"Okay, I believe you," Silverman admitted. "But the first break in the weather you see, promise me you'll be here to rescue me." Vaguely they promised to do what they could, but Silverman felt no closer to home. "Meanwhile, do any of you have a cell phone?"

Alex did, but he explained as he held it out, "It won't work. The cell phones go down first. All the antennas are on top of telephone poles."

Nevertheless, Silverman snatched the phone away and punched in Marty's number. At his ear, the receiver was silent. He turned away from the three students, walked off toward a corner of the library and whispered into the phone, "If you can hear me, I'm here, I'm trapped. Keep calling. I miss you so much."

It was like sending a message out to sea in a bottle. He returned the phone, fighting down a wave of emotion. "Is there some way you can tie me a rope from here to the Golden Gate Bridge?" he asked.

They offered him a collective pitying look: six sad eyes, three sad mouths. Then, "Would you sign our books?" Alex asked, as if to brighten things up. Silverman nodded not too grudgingly, only to be amazed at what they meant by "books." Between the three of them, the students had all but two of his collected works, some in both hardcover and paperback. And they all looked well read by somebody. "Well," Silverman said, and "well" again as he started in autographing the small hill of books on the floor before him.

"I looked up all your reviews too," Alex added, and he pulled out a folder filled with photocopied newspaper clippings. "You got a lot of good ones."

"Oh, yes. And a few not so good. But you learn to take the bitter with the sour."

"There's one I didn't really get," Alex said. "From *The New York Times*. It's called 'All That Blubber.' Is that meant to be snide?"

"I'm afraid so," Silverman answered, signing away.

"What does it say?" Tilly asked.

And Alex started to read. And continued reading. "'Let us grant that Daniel Silverman had to begin his parody of *Moby Dick* with the line, "Call me Shirook-Han-Omura" (thereafter mercifully shortened to Shirook) which, he assures us, when freely translated from the Whalish, means Snow Mountain.' Now here's where I think he wants to get really nasty. He says. . . .'"

Silverman paused in his signing. He couldn't believe his ears. Alex was reading the most damning review he had ever received. He was reading the whole thing. When he got to ". . . unquestionably the worst line to be found in any novel this year," Silverman spoke up. "You see, he's taken the line out of context. Take any line out of Hemingway, say, or Faulkner and see how ludicrous you can make it sound. Go ahead, try it. Of course the line he quotes sounds absurd. 'If it weren't for all this blubber.' But the context clearly indicates that the line is meant to be absurd, you see. And, incidentally, the book is not a parody in the first place." Why, oh, why was he explaining himself to this gang of young philistines?

"What he actually says," Alex was about to continue.

"Please. Stop," Silverman said. He finished signing; the three students thanked him and rose to start pulling on their coats and boots.

"That's a neat idea about Robinson Crusoe," Jack remarked.

"What idea?" Silverman asked.

"*Man Friday*, the book you're writing."

"Oh that," Silverman answered. "I made that up while Miss Dawes was in the room. I'm not really working on that."

"You mean you made that up right on the spot?" Alex asked.

"Yeah."

"Wow, you're some kind of genius! That'd make a great book."

"You think so?"

"Oh, yes," Tilly chimed in, adding under her breath, "You could even put in sort of a gay theme. The white guy and the black guy, they could become like intimate friends."

Silverman shrugged off the suggestion. "I'm sure it's been done. Anyway, I have other things going."

When he finished the signing, the students went for their heavy gear. "Let us slip out of here first, okay?" Tilly said, giving him a sly wink. "Bad enough Professor Dawes saw us together."

"Sure," Silverman agreed, sinking back in his chair. When the students were gone, he sat sorrowfully remarking how the gay awakening they so poignantly displayed had to fight its way through such a weight of disapproval. It was, or at least it should be, so utterly ordinary, even banal—really the same adolescent hormonal eruption you found in every straight kid. He wondered how many gay authors over the centuries had dressed up their own impermissible passions in a heterosexual disguise. Probably hundreds, going all the way back to the troubadours, every one of them reinforcing the fixed idea that only the sexually straight experience the agonies of young love.

He was about to leave when the library door inched open again. It was Alex. He stole across to Silverman.

"God, this is hard to do!" Alex said under his breath.

"Yes?"

"It's really impossible to buy condoms around here," he whispered close at Silverman's ear. "I can't beg them off of the guys for obvious reasons. And the school has all the merchants carefully patrolled."

"Is it illegal for students to buy them?"

"No. But you have to get way out of town before you find a store that won't report you to the provost."

"Really? So Big Christian Brother is watching all the time."

"Yeah. They actually search your room if they get a report."

"I wish I could help you," Silverman said, "but you've come to the wrong man. I'm in a stable relationship, absolutely monogamous. I stopped carrying six-seven years ago."

"Wow!" Alex was impressed. "You and your partner, you trust each other that much?"

"Yep."

"That is so cool."

"But in your situation, you've got the right idea."

Alex turned to leave, then turned back. "It's hell the way you get treated. But, you know, it's also exciting."

"Oh?"

"I mean, we're overthrowing the last bastion, aren't we? We're up against the ultimate taboo. It's sort of historical."

"If you can see it that way," Silverman said. "Get a good grip on that rope."

He waited until he heard the front door swing open in the roaring storm and then slam shut. Then, beset with reflections, he fell back into the nearest chair. They had asked about his coming out. He had passed the question off impatiently, but not because it was a painful memory. Rather it was so sentimentally sweet he feared he might choke up to remember what had happened. It all had to do with Marty.

As Silverman liked to remember it, he hadn't "come out." His story, when he told it—which was rarely—had hardly any drama to it at all. Instead of coming out, he simply moved away—from New York to San Francisco. He had met Marty at a dinner after one of his readings, the last stop on a coast-to-coast book tour. In the course of casual party-talk, he discovered that Marty had grown up in the Bronx, not far from where Silverman still lived with his parents—a neighborhood off the Grand Concourse that had shifted from Jewish to black during Silverman's childhood. They wondered if perhaps, as boys, they might have passed on the streets or rubbed elbows in the same candy store. Well, one thing led to another: from matinees they remembered at Loew's Paradise (they were all but totally certain they must have been there on same day when *Lawrence of Arabia* opened; they may have even simultaneously formed a crush on Peter O'Toole during the train wreck scene) to shared tastes in books, theater, art—a long, rambling dialogue that covered two lifetimes in a single night. Marty knew all the right things to say. An avid reader, he knew as much about fiction as Silverman, perhaps more.

"Oh, yeah, I can see the influence of Bellow on your writing," he commented. "That nice loose, slangy kind of style. Love that man.

Augie March? He was my first white-guy hero."

"Me too," Silverman said, thrilling down to his toes. "Well, of course, for me white didn't enter into it."

"Yeah, so you get the point. I mean is that radical or what? The way I went for Augie, I even renamed my dog Caligula."

Silverman was enraptured. Something was going on here that was lighting him up like a Roman candle. Something of the mind, of the body—he couldn't tell which. Intellectual love, that was it— and he was beginning to sense with a delicious eagerness that it wouldn't stop there.

"Augie March," Marty was saying. "That's what got me through my Malcolm X. phase." He twisted his face into an angry scowl. "That was me. Oh, boy, was it. But then, remember what Bellow has Augie say there about 'the laughing creature' he wants to be? That's what I said to myself. I can be a laughing creature. That's how I wanna survive."

"But I'll tell you a secret," Silverman said, shifting into a glum register. "When a writer's that great, like Bellow, it almost makes you. . . ."

Marty cut him off in mid-confession. "But you're way better than Bellow, way better than all those other Jewish guys."

"Come on!" Silverman protested, yet rising to the compliment.

"Sure," Marty insisted. "I mean those guys are good, but, man, they are so stuck, know what I mean? There's this stuckness in whatever they write. Like take Salinger. Terrific writer, but that man is plain stuck. That Glass family of his is supposed to be half-Irish. Sure, sure. Which half? That man can't help being Jewish all over the page. Squeeze the book, it just drips *Weltschmerz*. I mean it's like going to a picnic in a cemetery. See, your stuff—it's got wit and *joie de vivre*. You're life-affirming, man. You know how to get out of yourself and enjoy the world. Does the heart good to read you. You are one hell of a storyteller. That's what I always liked about Frank Yerby."

Here was a comparison Silverman had never heard. "Frank Yerby?" He couldn't remember reading anything by Frank Yerby since he was a kid. "You mean *Foxes of Harrow* Yerby?"

"That's the guy. How many people know Frank Yerby is black?"

"He is?"

"There, see! You didn't know. That's what I mean. Who knows Frank Yerby is black? Who knows Silverman is Jewish? Well, maybe the name. But otherwise, you've got that transcending power, which is what art is about, right?"

"Transcending?"

"Right. You see the world from all these other angles, like you're everybody you write about. That makes you real mysterious." He gave a rumbling laugh. "Course, you can go too far. Like me. When I started acting, I was fanatic about goin' against the stereotype. What acting meant was I could step right outa my skin. I swore I was never gonna let myself be typed as black. When I went to auditions, know what I'd bring for my piece? Blanche DuBois."

"Blanche DuBois?"

"Blanche DuBois."

"You mean from *Streetcar Named Desire*?"

"You know another Blanche DuBois? Wouldn't change my voice or anything like that. What I was after was the essence of the character, you see? Actually I'd assume the stage all macho. Tee-shirt, showin' lots of muscle. I'd say 'I'm reading from *Streetcar Named Desire*.' So of course everybody thought I was gonna do Stanley. Then I'd start in on Blanche. There I was, big and black, digging the part of a fragile white southern chick. Man, did that attract attention. That's what I mean about transcending. Trouble was, that audition piece wasn't doin' me any good when it came to casting. I was showin' up as too eccentric. And no matter how much I got my voice into the Paul Robeson register, which I can do, I kept comin' across as gay. The only part that piece ever got me was, well, Blanche DuBois."

"Come on! You were cast as Blanche DuBois?"

Marty burst out laughing. "It was some gay theater group. I didn't realize until they told me they were planning to do *Streetcar* and they wanted me for the part. Man, I got out of there fast. Because that wasn't the point. Point was creative freedom, breakin' loose. Now that's what you got. Nobody who reads your books is gonna know who this guy Silverman is. He's takin' the whole world in and makin' it part of himself."

All the while Marty was talking, there was a voice inside Silverman's head that was saying, *Lie to me some more.* Not that he believed a word of it, but he was sure Marty did and it warmed him to the bone. "You really think so?"

"Hey, that first book you wrote, man, you really hit the bull's-eye about psychoanalysis. How long were you in shrinkage?"

"Not at all," Silverman answered.

"No. Really? You were never in analysis? That's fantastic."

"Were you?"

"Was I? Oh, man, three long, dismal years. I was shooting every cent I made actin', nearly went broke before I realized that this bozo who was drumming on my skull was nuttier than I was. You know what they say about analysts? In med school, any guy who starts telling people the Pope is talking to him through his mattress, they send him over to specialize in psychiatry. Well, this dude was laying a castration complex on me like you never saw. I had to check three times a day to make sure it was still there, know what I mean? He was so phallocentric, I started thinking of him like this big, walking erection, you know, tall as Coit Tower hangin' over me. I swear, I was sure that when that man went out in the rain, he pulled a condom over his head."

Silverman relished every word he remembered from that night, every warm, laughing, flattering thing Marty told him as they walked the streets of North Beach, stopping for drinks and food until the city started to close down around them. Looking back, Silverman could see more clearly now than he had at the time how purely flirtatious that first, all-night conversation had been. The long night ended with Marty offering to show him the city the next day, a sightseeing tour that segued gracefully into a whirlwind romance. When Silverman returned to New York at the end of that week, it was simply to pack and fly west. That was the story of his coming out, nothing more strenuous than falling in love and following his heart.

A few years later, when he visited home, his mother found the occasion to ask, "How's your boyfriend out there, what's his name? He *is* your boyfriend, isn't he?" The curve she put on the phrase made it clear what she meant by "boyfriend." Silverman, quietly surprised to hear his mother refer to boyfriends of that kind, answered "Yes," and that was that for her. Not one small drop of *angst*, not a hint of heartbreak.

How his mother knew he was ready for such a relationship he never learned and never tried to find out. She had asked him more than once during his high school years about girls, dates, social life, always as if she thought a mother ought to care about such things, never with any real urgency. In high school, he had gone on a grand total of three pleasant but uneventful dates. On each occasion he had been polite to the point of being boring. Oh yes, Silverman would answer when his mother asked, he *liked* girls, he definitely did. But secretly he knew that what he liked wasn't what other boys liked, nor, it seemed, what girls of that age wanted boys of that age to like. He liked the emotional warmth of girls, their gentleness, their softness—or at least that was the kind of girl he chose to go out with. But he and his mother never went into that. *Liking* was good enough for her. Once he heard her tell a family friend that Daniel was a "late bloomer." That seemed to satisfy her, as it did Silverman through his college years. *I'm a grind, that's what I am.* That was how he explained his celibate habits. No dating and no dating and no dating in the midst of a sexual revolution. *Well, I'll get around to it*, he promised himself. *What's the hurry?*

True, his father and mother were well-read professional people, a lawyer and a schoolteacher. But people of their generation were supposed to be shocked when they found out who he was and how he lived. Instead, his mother showed no sign of sadness, surprise, or shame. Perhaps it was because she had lived her life in a kind of reverie, preoccupied with other matters—a book, a crossword puzzle, a deep personal meditation. She had no expectations of him. She wrote poetry, but she had never shown him a single line of it. Maybe somewhere in a drawer there lay a sheaf of tear-stained poems about her gay son, but he doubted it. Her mind was always adrift elsewhere, needing to be brought back to the kitchen or the living room. She seemed to have had her only child in a fit of distraction. Years later she had a way of scrutinizing him that seemed to say, "Oh, so you're still here. So you really do exist."

Silverman remained puzzled to this day where his parents had found the tolerance he enjoyed from them. Didn't they care what became of him? No, that wasn't so. He was sure of that because several years later, when they paid a visit to San Francisco, his mother had raised the delicate question. On the day she and his father left for Los Angeles to visit Disneyland, she had paused on the front porch to ask discreetly, "The two of you, you can trust each other? You're safe? Because, you know. . . ." Again, he answered, yes. Again, she was satisfied. "He's a nice young man," she said as they kissed goodbye. "Be happy."

As for his father, his complacency was easier to understand. Years before, when young Daniel was still in high school, the elder Silverman had made it glass-clear that he didn't care what his son became as long as he didn't become a professing Jew. Daniel might have decided to become a practicing cannibal, and his father wouldn't have lifted an eyebrow. In fact, he suspected that his father regarded it as a plus that his son had turned into something that would have sent Grandpa Zvi into a tizzy. By the time Silverman took up with Marty, his grandfather was dead and gone, but he knew his father would have relished telling the old man, "Your grandson is a queer, how do you like that, you vicious old bug?" One thing was for certain. However he truly felt, never, absolutely never, was Silverman's father going to let on that his gay son might have disgraced him a hundred times over, because that would be to admit that Grandpa Zvi's curse had prevailed.

A sudden blast of wind against the library windows brought him back to the present. The blizzard didn't hit and run; it hit and pushed. It was pushing at the windows now, like a thief who intended to break in. Silverman sat and watched the glass panes across the room strain in their frames. Were they going to break? And then the wind gave up, reverting to mere gale force. He realized he had been holding his breath, waiting.

At the door, he listened to hear whether the coast was clear, then headed upstairs. Along the way *Man Friday* popped back into his mind. A white guy and a black guy, two castaways, getting together. Well, he knew a thing or two about that. But somebody must have done that one already.

20

Murdering Mrs. Bloore

Though his visit to the Faith College underworld left a bad taste in his mouth, Silverman was haunted by the story Professor Oxenstern had brought to his attention, the allegorical encounter between the Pilgrim and the character Ignorance. Back in his mad man's cell, he paged through his copy of Bunyan until he found it, part of a much longer dialogue that had a few intriguing twists. Ignorance was actually a likeable guy, one of Bunyan's many appealing lost souls. Not that Bunyan gave him any Brownie points on that score. At the end of the book, poor Ignorance is the last guy to be damned eternally. Silverman saw that as the cruelest moment in the story. After all, what was the man's great sin? Ignorance thought well of himself. He thought well of people. He cultivated good thoughts and good deeds. He couldn't think of himself as evil. But that was exactly what the Pilgrim held against him. "Every imagination of the heart of man is only evil, and that continually. Evil from his Youth."

Wow. Who could believe such things? Well, obviously, Bunyan did. And quite as obviously, if Silverman didn't, he was a local minority of one.

How does anybody know what to believe anyway? What was wrong with Ignorance's answer? "My heart tells me so?" What else can anybody go by? Bunyan says the Word of God. But as every author knows, words never speak for themselves, especially not The Word. Words get turned and twisted in people's minds. After all, think of that lousy review the *Times* gave him for *Deep Eye*. How Silverman wished that critic had shown a bit more heart. Talk about misunderstanding Normally, at this point, Silverman would press a mental button and self-justification tape number 25 would run for the next few hours. Instead, another thought intervened. *You know, I'll bet I could rewrite that part about Ignorance and make it come out just the opposite. Wouldn't that be interesting?*

But a little bit of Bunyan went a long way. So did the next hour of bad television. Like the ache of a decaying tooth, boredom re-emerged. Silverman decided to check his private pharmacy. One more tranq to go. He decided to save that the way a frontiersman might save his last bullet to use before the Apaches got to him. Instead, he took a few swigs of the Canadian Club—less than a half-bottle left—lay back in the dark, and fell to taking a survey of his emotional resources.

What did he have, alone in this strange room, in this strange town, in the dead cold of winter—what did he have to sustain him? Of course. Like the imprisoned Bunyan, he had his writer's imagination. Start there. Mental movies, a favorite pastime, usually reserved for the dentist's chair or long check-in lines at airports.

So what was uppermost on his mind tonight, something he could sharpen his storytelling wits on? *Mrs. Bloore.* He could still see her bitter, disdainful face gazing at him as if he were a leper. "A great deal of what you've written is deeply offensive," she had said. *Okay, you miserable bigot! I'm going to kill you. I'm going to wring the chicken-plucking life out of you.*

And he set to work.

In his mind's eye, a scenario was forming. His novels often began this way, with movie stars appearing as his characters and a camera-eye following the action. Though few writers would admit it, Silverman suspected many novelists now worked this way, hoping it would, like some voodoo magic, draw movie money their way. In his case, the magic obviously wasn't working—but it had become his habit nonetheless.

This time, the film that was being projected on the screen inside his skull was something very *noir*, very Hitchcock, a study in female evil. He had the perfect villain. Could there be any doubt whatever—that is, in the mind of a savagely hostile and paranoid observer like himself—that Mrs. Bloore, revered matriarch of the Fat Free Evangelical Brethren, had bumped off her husband? Of course not. Go back to when she first met Big Burt. What was she then? A minister's sex-crazed daughter, a small-town tart with a heart of ice. No question but that Big Burt deserved what he got. The man was a rat with women, a home-wrecker and a cad. With good cause, she hated his guts. Finally, after years of humiliation, she reached her limit.

It is a cold winter's night at the Bloore mansion, the richest estate in northern Minnesota. Big Burt comes rolling home—"drunk as a skunk," wasn't that how Swenson put it? Mrs. B., sleepless and seething with repressed fury, has been pacing her bedroom, smoking cigarette after cigarette. Then, well past three, she spots a light in the garage. Her man is back from carousing with his floozies. She creeps downstairs and out the back door barefoot and clad in no more than her silken negligee, which, of course, the wind pins against her flesh. The night is cold, but her blood is colder. Numbed with hatred, she feels nothing. Peering through the garage window, she sees Big Burt tinkering away. She sneaks in and whacks him over the head with a monkey wrench. Then, with a strength born of vengeful ire, she wedges him underneath his favorite Tomahawk and turns on the engine of the BMW. Back in her bedroom, she stares down at the garage as it fills with exhaust, her face a pitiless mask.

Who plays Mrs. B.? Silverman ran down his list of favorite *femme fatale* actresses. Yes, that's what he wanted: someone like Barbara Stanwyk in *The Strange Love of. . . .* What was it? *Martha . . . Martha?* . . . Ah! the perfect choice. Rebecca De Mornay. And for Big Burt, the brute, the rogue, the hell-on-wheels womanizer: Bruce Willis? Or maybe Alex Baldwin. *God*, Silverman thought, *I'm such a natural for the movies. Why isn't anybody in Hollywood paying attention?*

Okay, so Mrs. B. knocks off her philandering hubby, inherits millions, and gets away with it. Nobody in North Fork dares to say what everybody suspects about Big Burt's death. After all, Mrs. B. is giving away the Bloore fortune. Oh, what a good touch! She's buying the community soul, corrupting the entire congregation. Time passes. One year, two years, five years. Mrs. B., now the town tyrant, grows older and meaner, but no less beautiful. (This is a movie, after all. Maybe Faye Dunaway would be a better choice.) Then, one day, a stranger shows up in North Fork. A young clergyman out of the West who's been preaching at churches in the region. People in town have heard about him. Quiet, gentle, very praise-God pious—a Montgomery Clift type, wide-eyed, innocent, and slightly ominous. (Though he remembered Montgomery Clift—that sensitive mouth, that expressive brow—only from videocassettes, Silverman invariably cast him in all the roles he wanted for himself in the theater of his mind.) The mysterious cleric is invited to preach. There's a big scene: the Sunday sermon on sin and deliverance and all that Christian stuff. "We all carry murder in our hearts," the preacher says in a soft, dark tone. And his eyes, moving through the congregation, fall on Mrs. B. Women are reduced to tears; men shout "Hallelujah!" North Fork takes the personable young minister to its heart. Everyone, that is, except Mrs. B., who finds him menacing. As well she might. Because he is not what he seems. In reality—yes, that's it—he is Big Burt's secret lover from San Francisco.

Now there's a twist. Flashback of Big Burt and his San Francisco partner in better days, walking the city, sharing tender moments. That's why Big Burt was getting the old Tomahawk in shape. The very next morning he was going to dump Mrs. B., ride west on his favorite bike, and settle down with his one true love. But instead—whack!

Back in SF, the lover—Montgomery Clift-Silverman—has suspected all along that Burt was murdered. He is heartbroken. He broods, he weeps. At last, gentle soul though he is, he decides on vengeance. A life for a life. He travels, he reconnoiters, he snoops, he lays plans, he perfects his disguise. He is in no hurry. He scouts out some small midwestern churches, fakes a conversion, becomes an itinerant preacher. Montgomery Clift could do it. Those soulful eyes could fool anyone. Finally, in the depth of winter, he travels to North Fork. When he meets Mrs. B., he knows he's right. She's exactly the cold-hearted wench Big Burt always said she was. He can see it in her eyes. And she can see that he sees. But what can she do? He is a man of God. The congregation idolizes him. But what she hears in his voice is her own doom.

At last, safely ensconced in his room in Gundersen Hall—in this very room, in this very bed, in this very blizzard—Montgomery Silverman plots his revenge. The perfect crime. He finds a blunt instrument. The fire poker. He waits until everybody in the building is asleep, then sneaks down the dark corridor and up the stairs to Mrs. B.'s room. Is the door opened? Locked? Does he knock? Does he force his way in? Let all that wait. He gets in. The bitch is in her bed, her hair tied up in curlers, cold cream smeared over her aging kisser. She is reading *Mein Kampf.* She looks up in horror. Her voice freezes in her throat. Whap! Whap! Whap! He bludgeons her to death.

How good this felt! The pleasures of literature.

For the next hour he went over and over the plan, running scenarios, fine-tuning the details. When it came to plotting a story, Silverman was a stickler. He worshipped narrative coherence—some critics felt too much. So suppose Mrs. Bloore's door was locked. How would he get in? He might knock and beg in a hushed whisper to see her. Come on! What chance is there that she would open her door in the dead of night to a faggot she loathes?

Ah, here was an idea. Suppose he disguised his voice to sound like the angel Gabriel—sort of deep and spooky—stood outside her door, and quietly announced that the Rapture was at hand, behold! Now this sounded zany enough to work. He was dealing with a pretty superstitious crowd here. Everybody on this campus probably went to bed at night waiting for Gabriel to come blow his horn.

He wrote himself a little speech. "Helena Bloore, this is the Angel of the Apocalypse. Hoo-hoo!" That was meant to be a trumpet. Not too convincing, drop it. "I have come unto thee to announce the Coming of the Lord. The end is nigh. It is time, Helena. The Rapture approacheth. Savior Jesus awaits thou . . . thee . . . thou in the downstairs hall. Open up thy door. Salvation is at hand."

He liked that one, especially the bit about pretending to be an angel. Of course, she might look out before she opened the door all the way. He had to make it convincing. Allowing himself a ration of three of Syl's chocolate chip cookies, he went back over it again and again. But suppose she had a chain lock on the door? She would be just the kind. He wouldn't be surprised if she slept with a shotgun to defend her virtue.

Maybe if he wrapped himself in a sheet, he might pass for an angel in the dark hallway. He pulled up the bed sheet and, wrapping it around himself and over his head, posed before the mirror on the dresser. He added a lit candle held high overhead and tried his speech again in a slightly wailing tone. "Helena Bloore, this is the Angel of the Apocalypse." Oh, this was a truly macabre Hitchcock touch. The pious old lady peeps through the door, she spots this ghostly figure in the bed sheet. Her eyes pop. An angel. "I welcome thee . . . thou, my Lord," she cries. She flings open the door to receive her savior, and whack. There's Rapture for thee, thou vicious, dried up old bitch. No, don't kill her all at once. Make her suffer. Ha-ha. Silverman gloated. Now that might almost make this miserable trip to Minnesota worthwhile.

But, ah! out of the blue came the inevitable Hitchcock twist. The big screw-up. Miss Bjork. Silverman had left her entirely out of account. For all he knew, Miss Bjork shared the bedroom with Mrs. Bloore. Shit! She would be there to see the whole thing. He reran the scenario. He whacks Mrs. Bloore, tortures her to death, drowns her in the tub, and then, as he is about to make his getaway, he turns—and there stands little Miss Bjork in the middle of the room. Close-up of the wide-eyed, scared-stiff nurse, screaming for all she's worth. Well, it actually makes a better story that way.

Mentally murdering Mrs. Bloore, whether he got away with it or not, had a tonic effect. It restored his self-confidence; it also roused his appetite. He glanced at his watch. Five past midnight. An excellent time for a snack. Not many of Syl's goodies left. Well, there was no way around it. He would have to exercise a guest's prerogative and raid the refrigerator.

Where had he stashed that flashlight he borrowed from the commons room? Ah, yes, under the bed. Slipping his raincoat over his shabby pajamas, he stepped into the unlit hallway. Not a creature was stirring. In the downstairs corridor, there was a small night-light that lit the stairs enough to let him move quickly and silently. Actually not so silently. He had forgotten how distressed the floor underfoot had grown over the past hundred years. It squealed with every footfall. That slowed him down while he tested each step. It was like crossing a mine field. Each time the boards under foot squeaked, he stood frozen to see if anyone might have heard. No, no, no . . . and finally he was through to the kitchen. So far so good, but the kitchen, where he now stood, was *terra incognita*. He had only caught a quick glimpse of it when Oxenstern had taken him through to the basement. The kitchen wasn't large, but he had no idea where anything was. He would have to use the flashlight. That might attract somebody, but he had no choice. He spotted the refrigerator across the room. He cracked open the door and the light went on inside. It was well-stocked. There was cheese, butter, milk, eggs, juice, fruit, jam. Ah, peanut butter, a favorite food. Using the light from the fridge, he found his way to a bread box and to silverware in the sink. He spread some peanut butter and jam on a few slices of bread, cut some cheese, stuffed an apple in his pocket, and decided to appropriate what remained of an open carton of pineapple juice. He would have preferred to cook himself some bacon and eggs, but that would be pushing his luck. He piled his provisions into a bowl, tucked the juice under his arm, got a clear bead on the door, and started back.

"Silverman!"

He was on his way out of the commons room when he was certain he heard a shrill voice somewhere call his name. It seemed to come from across the entrance hall of the building. He was sure somebody said "Silverman." Or was it the wind? The blizzard was still blasting away outside, sometimes taking on an almost articulate whine. No, this was definitely a voice; and now, listening keenly, he could hear it was saying things. He paused, closed his eyes, and struggled to sharpen his hearing. The voice was saying . . . *something . . . something. . . .* "Silverman." Instinctively, he turned in the direction of his name. One step, another, and then he was in the foyer of Gundersen Hall, moving toward the voice. But by the time he was across the hall, the shrill voice had stopped talking. Now he heard other voices clashing with one another. An argument. The door at the far end of the hall was open; he peeked in.

Across the darkened room, he saw another door, this one closed, its frame outlined in light. The voices were behind that door, rising and falling. Then the shrill voice sounded again. It was unmistakably Mrs. Bloore. She was shouting in anger over others who were trying to make themselves heard. "Gone, I want him gone. Don't try to confuse me. How can you bear to have him under this roof one more instant?"

Well, there was no mistaking what this late night pow-wow was about. He didn't have to hear another word. Apparently the governing powers of Faith College were reviewing their Silverman policy. Under his breath, he said, *Gone? Lady, I would be so glad to be gone. Tell me how.* He crept closer to the door, feeling his way with an outstretched hand to avoid knocking against furniture in the unfamiliar interior. Halfway into the room, he was brought up short by a thundering voice. "She is right. There is no other way. Why are we talking? Under our roof is the abomination of desolation."

Axel!

Axel was cut off by three or four competing voices out of which the booming tones of Reverend Apfel emerged. "This is absurd. It isn't worth the risk. The weather report says that in another day at most the storm will clear. There is even a chance it will pass over tomorrow. Surely we can put up with. . . ."

Another voice: "We can't be sure of that. And even so, it could be days before the roads are clear. This person might be on our hands for. . . ."

Another voice, a woman's: "Exactly. How long can I go on vomiting every time I think of him? I'm starving."

Another voice, a man's: "I have noticed a distinctly strange taste to the water since this person has been with us. Do you think? . . ."

Axel: "Yes. They will stop at nothing, the homos. We are under attack."

Mrs. Bloore: "We cannot endanger the boys. If he disgraces one of our youth, think what might happen. Suicide. Somebody could wind up drowned."

Axel: "Him. The Sodomite, let him drown. Who would care?"

Apfel: "Axel, be reasonable. There would be an investigation into any mishap on the ice, whoever got drowned, even if it was

Silverman." At last, a note of Christian compassion. Apparently the pastor was Silverman's main supporter. But what was it the others were proposing?

Axel: "And so? So? Who would not sympathize with us? If we say he is seducing the students. He is. He is. He is making them all homo abortionists."

Another voice; it was Oxenstern: "You overlook the power of the Sodomite political interest in this nation. If anything went wrong on the lake, if he should meet with any injury, we would have the FBI swarming over us."

Mrs. Bloore: "I have no interest in politics. My sole concern is for the purity of our church and our school—as should yours be. I want this person, this plague-carrier, this infestation removed."

Another voice, a woman: "I absolutely concur. The lake is our only solution. It isn't as if we were planning for anybody to come to harm. Nobody would ever dare to say that. We are solving a problem. We are protecting our students."

Mrs. Bloore: "Exactly. The man is a public health menace. He is a child abuser. We have no choice."

Another voice, this was Jaspers: "I actually believe we could entice Silverman to do as Mrs. Bloore wants. I've spoken to the man. I've shown him the shame of his condition. He's as eager to depart as we are to have him leave. He would leap at the chance to be taken away. I'm sure he would be willing to take the risk, especially if we don't exaggerate the danger."

Apfel: "But the danger is very great."

The woman: "Others have made it across."

Apfel: "Not in a blizzard like this."

Another voice: "If he decides to leave on his own, if he is the one who decides to cross the lake, how can we be responsible?"

Apfel: "But it wouldn't simply be him that ran the risk, it would be all the boys."

Mrs. Bloore: "The Snow Ghosts would volunteer to do it. They are courageous soldiers of Christ. They know the ice."

Another voice: "We could ask for volunteers. Then we could tell them that if anything goes wrong, if they lose their way, if they have to turn back, they are to put their own interests first."

Apfel: "You mean they should leave Silverman?"

Axel: "Yes. Tell them: leave him. Who would know? Who would care?"

Another voice: "There have been misfortunes on Beaver Lake in the past."

Mrs. Bloore: "In this case, it would be good riddance."

Apfel: "I refuse to pretend we wouldn't be responsible. In any case, we could never get away with it. You forget that he has some allies among the students. They would speak out against us."

Oxenstern: "The Sodomite-Zionist powers would never believe it was an accident, even if it was. We would be a choice target for recrimination. We all know we have enemies who would be delighted to investigate us into oblivion. I needn't tell you what sources those enemies draw upon."

Jaspers: "We have nothing to fear as long as we battle on the side of the Lord."

Mrs. Bloore: "Exactly so."

Apfel: "Aren't we in enough trouble already about the taxes? Twenty-seven years of back taxes. If we attract any more attention to ourselves, they could confiscate the whole school."

Mrs. Bloore: "Not one penny will I pay to lechers and perverts."

Apfel: "But one battle at a time, Helena. We can surely put up with the Sodomite until the weather lifts—a few more days."

Mrs. Bloore: "We're wasting time. I didn't come here to argue. I want you to go to the Snow Ghosts. Tell them that we want this scourge eliminated. Tell them it is my wish and it is their Christian duty."

Axel: "They will do it. They will love to do it. I will go with them."

Apfel: "If you go along, Silverman will never come. He doesn't trust you."

Axel: "Why should we ask him even, this California fornicator? We pre-empt him. We go to his room and take him, I say. Right now."

Apfel: "Kicking and screaming? You intend to drag him across the lake kicking and screaming?"

Axel: "He will not kick if I am there. He will not scream." Somebody struck a thundering blow on the table.

Mrs. Bloore: "Axel, will you shut up! We don't need such dramatics here."

Jaspers: "I think we're getting carried away. Silverman will raise no questions about leaving. But I believe it would be best if you didn't get involved, Axel. If something should go wrong while you were with him, you would be under suspicion."

Silverman, standing in the dark, realized he was dripping with nervous sweat. He began to draw off backwards across the room toward the door behind him. With his adrenaline pumping, he was less cautious. Instead of feeling his way back across the squeaky floor, he moved too fast. Underfoot the very boards of Gunderson Hall called out against him. *Queee, queee, queeer,* they seemed to be whining. *Kill, kill queeer!* Suddenly, at the sound, the voices in the next room stopped dead. *They had heard!* In a moment they would be in the room and upon him. In addition to being a Sodomite-Zionist federal agent, he would be revealed as an eavesdropper. And a refrigerator raider. He froze, not with caution but terror. He could see them stretching him across the table he stood beside and . . . and . . . what? Oh, these Christians had some pretty nasty tortures up their sleeve. They were past masters. Drawing, quartering, flaying alive. He couldn't tell if the drops running down his face were flop sweat or tears of fear. And then, mercifully, the voices resumed, barking away as fierce as before.

Now with all the care of an escaping convict, he made his way out of the room, measuring each step he took, a man in slow motion, standing stalk still as each foot found a quiet board to walk on. How weird this was! Daniel Silverman, loaded down with stolen food, making his way as slowly, slowly, slowly as a Bhutto dancer through the dark, chilly halls of Persecution U. He made it through the door, across the lobby, and then, in risky quickstep, up the stairs to his room. "You got away this time," whined the guardian floorboards, "but wait!"

He didn't simply lock the door, he jammed a chair under the handle and went for the fire poker, the only facsimile of a weapon at hand. Laying it across his lap, he said his telephone prayer and lifted the phone. Nothing. He tried three more times over the next few hours.

Well past two in the morning, he was still seated rigidly in his dark room, his fire poker at the ready, straining to hear an approaching step over the gusting wind. "Take him, right now." Axel had said. "Kicking and screaming." On the dresser sat the snack he had brought with him from the kitchen. He had no appetite for it. His stomach was a solid lump of anxiety. For the first time in his life, here among the Lord's people, he wished he carried a gun.

21
The Voice of the Devil

At some point in the course of the night he nodded off in spite of himself. When he woke in a gray, hazy dawn, he hoped that what he remembered of last night had been a bad dream. No. There on the dresser were the provisions he had raided from the kitchen. It had all happened. But here he was, still alive and locked in his room. Apparently Axel had been voted down. The light of day restored his confidence that nothing hideous could happen. What choice did he have but to trust in the minimal sanity of these people? In any case, he wasn't going to leave his room again until he felt safe.

He was hungry enough to polish off the food he had pilfered the night before. By now his bed, where he sat to eat, had become a rumpled linen sty of stains and crumbs and crusts. That concerned him less than the sad fact that Syl's cookies were now all gone. There were only a few of her biscuits left, and they were going stale. When he got back to San Francisco—and someday he was going to get back to San Francisco, yes he was—he would order more from her, if he could find her. No doubt by then, the Swensons might have been driven away into outer darkness, exiled from their church for bringing the curse of God to North Fork. How sad that would be. Silverman had someplace to go in the greater world beyond white food and the fear of God. But Swenson and Syl were delicate flowers. They needed this (currently sub-zero) evangelical hothouse to stay alive. For the life of him, Silverman couldn't imagine either of them walking the streets of San Francisco or New York—or any city he knew. Every billboard, every newsstand, every window display they laid eyes on would be the devil's handiwork.

Seeking to divert himself, he began to flip through Bunyan. He had finished the book, but he was now pursuing an odd line of thought. While much of the Pilgrim's adventures bored him, he wondered if there might be some way a clunky old classic like this could be resurrected. Was there any life left in the allegorical genre? Or was it the relic of a naive and bygone age? Maybe the best you could do would be to turn it into a parody—the way Max Beerbohm once poked fun at great masters of the past—only with a crueller edge. On the other hand, if the image of Vanity Fair still spoke to people, what about Bunyan's other inventions? What about the City of Destruction? Worldly Wiseman? Giant Despair? And then there was the marvelous innocence and sincerity of the Pilgrim's great lamentation, "*What shall I do?*" How often had Silverman asked that question from the bowels of his soul? Wasn't life still like that, when you came right down to it? Suppose we all admitted that we face the same ordeal the Pilgrim once faced? What if Christians—especially these scorning folk he was trapped among—recognized that fact, honoring the real travail of the soul, instead of demanding the right credentials?

To pass the time, he had been trying to imagine an updated *Pilgrim's Progress*. Not easy to do. Maybe if that tiny Wicket Gate where the Pilgrim sets out upon his journey were to be labeled "Tolerance" instead of "Salvation." Or maybe "glass nose," to borrow Swenson's quaint image of the humanist project: Openness. Throw open the gate, take a chance, see what happens. That might make the terrible City of Destruction look like something a bit more human: our common crippled condition. Of course, working from tolerance would muck up the basic allegorical structure of the work, because Pilgrim's way to salvation has to be a road, *one* road—and a very narrow road at that. Grandpa Zvi would have agreed: just enough room for the chosen people. Bunyan's Pilgrim starts off on his way carrying a heavy burden of sin. But *One*— that's the burden all of us are carrying in our modern pilgrimage. The idea that there is one God, one people, one law, one way.

He was letting his mind rove along byways he had never explored before. Strange to say, he felt implicated in his own dilemma; he shared the fault that he condemned. Somewhere, thousands of

years in the past, the oneness of God had been the great achievement of his people, their pride, their solace. *One* was the idea
Grandpa Zvi and all those loyal to the tribe could never relinquish.
Not hard to understand. A bruised and battered people looking for
some dignity in the world, they put their heads together and decided on the one thing they could claim as theirs. The right God,
the only God there is. How often had he heard his grandparents
reciting the great prayer with such heartfelt conviction? "*Shma
Yisrael*, the Lord is one."

Boy, if ever an idea had backfired, this was it. Because just look
who claimed to be the chosen people now! The fanatical little
gang that ran Faith College, and scores of other sectarian zealots
like them. *One* had become a battle-axe in the hands of the worst.
From Bunyan on, the *goyim's* version of *One* was turning out to be
an even narrower road than Grandpa Zvi's. Grandpa's road had
been wide enough to accommodate the whole nation—or at least
all those whose pee-wees had the right shape. Also the females
they brought along with them, who didn't even have to be circumcised—wasn't that generous? But by the time Bunyan and his Puri-
tans took over, the road had been downwardly resized by several
centuries of inquisitional zeal; it was now just barely wide enough
for the elect, a mere handful. Until he had suffered through great
travail, Bunyan wasn't certain that even he qualified as one of that
handful.

Silverman thought: It makes you desperate and nasty to see the
world that way. Look at all the *tsouris* that comes when you assume
there is only one way to get from here to wherever. Only the most
paranoid and self-righteous could believe they were heading in the
right direction. Assume that, and most of the world looks as if it's
off course—which may well be the case. Silverman was prepared
to believe his fellow humans were poor, lost, and wandering sheep.
Which meant—block that metaphor!—we're all in the same leaky
boat and mercy was requisite.

In the mid-morning, there came a knock at the door. Silverman
startled and went stiff. "Who's there?" he asked, then tip-toed to
the door.

"It's Professor Jaspers. May we meet with you?"

"'We'?" Silverman asked. With his nose flattened against the door, he was trying to see into the hall through the crack.

"Pastor Apfel and myself."

"About what?"

"I think we may have found a way for you to make your departure."

"In this weather?"

"Please, can we talk? We can use my quarters. Room 6 on the ground floor."

"Not if Axel is there."

"Axel? Of course he won't be there."

"Swear on the Bible?"

"But I don't understand."

"Just swear, that's all."

"We swear."

A half-hour later, Silverman was in Professor Jaspers' room, a dark scholarly chamber lined with books and smelling as if the windows hadn't been opened for fifty years. He had brought the fire poker with him. Jaspers and Apfel eyed the object as he laid it ostentatiously across his lap; he made no explanation. Though he was trembling inside, he did his best to hang tough. He tried to remember how Marty had played scenes like this in his television series: trapped by the bad guys, tied in his chair, beaten to a pulp, but still feisty. Usually Marty was scripted to take a couple of hard knocks for talking back. *Oh, a tough guy! Whack. So you wanna mouth off, do ya? Whack.* Silverman didn't expect that would happen here, as long as Axel the Mad Bomber wasn't around.

"Well?" he said, sounding as hard-boiled and growly as he could. "I hope you don't intend to send me out into this blizzard to drown in the lake." Both men went stony-faced. "I'm a human being, you know. There's a commandment I remember. What is it? Number four or five? Whichever. 'Thou shalt not kill queers either.' I'm sure it says that somewhere, right?"

"Whatever are you talking about?" Jaspers asked, dripping with compulsive innocence.

"We were merely wondering," Reverend Apfel said, fighting down his obvious jitters, "if you might not prefer to wait out the remainder of the storm at Richard Swenson's home across the lake. You'd be so much more comfortable there."

"Across the lake?" Silverman answered in a tone of exaggerated amazement. "And how do you expect me to get across the lake in this weather? There have been accidents on Beaver Lake, I understand."

"We wouldn't want you to try it on your own," Jaspers said.

"Oh? Who would you send along with me? A suicide squad of Snow Ghosts, the loyal soldiers of Christ? Ha!"

Again both men looked stymied. "As a matter of fact, we were thinking of. . . ."

"Asking for volunteers, I'll bet. It's their duty to the school to take the homo out on the frozen lake and leave him there to turn into an ice cube."

"Professor Silverman!" Jaspers objected. "What are you suggesting?"

"That you're very eager to get rid of me—the abomination of desolation, the public health menace," Silverman answered. "Especially Mrs. Bloore. I don't think she'd care if I sank through the ice and vanished forever. She'd say good riddance."

"Oh, come now!" Apfel said.

"I want you to remember one thing," Silverman said, leaning into the remark with all the conviction he could muster. "We homos have a lot of support in the right places. The Sodomite-Zionist connection—perhaps you've heard of that. If I disappeared on that lake, the FBI would be swarming all over this place. *And* the NEA. *And* the ACLU. *And* B'nai B'rith. My friends at *The New York Times* have been looking for an excuse to investigate you into oblivion. As you may know, my Uncle Isaac owns CBS. He knows all about the little tax dodge you've been working here for the last twenty-seven years. Shame on you!"

Each time he echoed a phrase he remembered from last night, he could see his two interlocutors wince with bewilderment. Apfel, now clearly backing off, explained, "We merely felt there was some good chance that a group from our snowmobile team could guide you across to the Swensons. They're very rugged young men. At least it might be worth the effort."

"Oh?" Silverman came back. "And suppose we got halfway there and the blizzard was too much? Then what? Can you guarantee my safety? Ha!"

"Well, if you feel that way," Apfel rushed to assure him, "perhaps we should drop the whole idea."

"Perhaps we should," Silverman said. "Please remember, I am not without friends in official circles. Every room in this building might be bugged. Now if you don't mind, I'd like to have some lunch."

Once he was back in the corridor, Silverman felt just great. This was the high point. He had faced them down, even put a scare into them. Bluffed them with a pair of deuces. For all they knew, he was psychically gifted. They might have thought he was reading their minds.

His appetite was returning. A good sign. Despite a large, if irregular breakfast, he was hungry again. It was too early for lunch, but there was usually some fruit left out in the commons room. Or he might be able to mooch something from the kitchen. He had begun to feel a great deal bolder about dealing with members of the staff and faculty, especially now that he knew how intimidating his presence could be. Backed by the full force of the Zionist-Sodomite conspiracy, what did he have to fear?

There was indeed a bowl of miscellaneous fruit in the commons room; not the freshest, to be sure. But he might get a few good bites out of the one remaining banana. There was a tray of ginger snaps, some bread sticks, pretzels. And there was some hot water bubbling away on a hot plate. He took the banana, scooped up some miscellaneous munchies, and brewed a cup of Professor Oxenstern's roasted barley.

As he stepped out of the commons room, he caught sight of somebody dodging back into the library, trying to elude an encounter with him. But she wasn't moving fast enough to avoid recognition. It was Gloria Dawes. As she drew back out of sight, he heard two or three loud thumps: things falling to the floor.

Had it been anybody else, Silverman would have been grateful to do without meeting. But he was curious about Professor Gloria Dawes, BA, U. of Minnesota, *Magna cum Laude*. There was an air of unease about her that hinted at vulnerability, a rare quality at

Faith College, where conviction was worn like body armor. In his role of improvisatory anthropologist, he felt certain that nobody so young and vibrant could tolerate keeping company with troglodytes like Jaspers and Oxenstern. He had also assumed, along rather sexist lines, he had to confess, that a fair young female might be the only person near at hand whose sympathies he could win over. She hadn't been in on the midnight meeting, at least as far as he could tell. At a minimum, he might be able to turn her into a helpful witness. He could let her know he had no intention of leaving before the blizzard lifted.

He budged the library door open to look in. Just behind the door, he discovered Gloria on her knees picking up several books she had dropped in her haste.

"May I come in?" Silverman asked, already halfway through the door. "Here, I'll help you with those."

"It's all right," she protested, quickly sweeping all the fallen books toward her as if to defend them.

No question about it. The closer he got to Gloria, the prettier she became. She had delicate features and sleepy eyes that might have passed for seductive in any context besides Faith College. Her hair fell across her face as she scrambled about to recover the books; she brushed it back behind her ear with that cute, futile, feminine gesture that Silverman assumed was meant to be flirtatious. No sooner was the hair back than it fell forward again. She was once again wearing ultra-dowdy clothes, but as she clambered about on the floor, her skirt had worked its way well up her thigh. Silverman, kneeling to help her, couldn't help noticing her well-exposed knees, nor could she help noticing that he was noticing. That raised a question he was curious to pursue. Does a woman, should a woman care if she finds herself exposed to a homosexual man? Clearly Gloria did. Which created a weird dynamic between them, a kind of impossible, interspecies eroticism filled with miscues and twisted signals. But God, was he enjoying this. There was something about being inside her defenses that he found supremely entertaining, though it was, he had to admit, mean of him to be playing with her this way. It put him somewhat in the category of guys he knew—usually good-looking, bodybuilder types—who got a mildly sadistic thrill out of coming on to women, then revealing themselves to be gay. Maybe this was something like that. He was certainly puzzling the daylights out of poor Gloria. But he had to admit: if heterosexuality were his game, he'd be hitting on her for sure. Instead, he had another interest.

"May I ask you a question?"

"Yes?" Her answer had reluctance written all over it. She sat back on her heels to hear him.

"Am I right in assuming that you wrote that introduction for your father?"

"Yes. He has so little time. . . ."

". . . to find out what he's talking about. I understand. He's a busy man. But you rather worried him about the—how did he put it?—'rough language' in I, Emma. I think that was unfair. For the life of me, I can't think of what you had in mind."

She tossed her hair. "Oh, really nothing. Nothing at all."

"Come on. There must have been something. Between us professors, what was it?" No answer. She went back to arranging the books into a stack. "Just say it," Silverman encouraged. "Think of it as a test question. 'Some critics believe Daniel Silverman uses too much obscene language in his novel I, Emma. Discuss.' Now you'd have to begin by finding the words, wouldn't you? So what are they?"

She swallowed hard. "Quim," she answered in a whisper. And then she blushed the way only a very blonde, very fair female can: a deep, fiery crimson. People who blush like that get caught in a feedback loop. Realizing she was blushing, she blushed still more. She quickly turned away and let her hair hide her face.

My God, she's blushing, Silverman thought. He had never made a woman blush. What an intriguing experience. "Quim? That's it? Quim?"

"Isn't that enough?"

"But quim isn't obscene."

"Of course it is."

"Oh, really. Quim? Most people don't even know what quim means. It's prehistoric. When I put it in the book, I wasn't even sure the word would have been current in the 1880s."

"It's obvious from the context what it means."

"Oh? All it says, as I recall, is that Rodolph asks Emma if she'd like him to touch her quim. And she says yes. And he says something like, 'Oh ho, so you know what that means, you vixen.' But I'll bet most readers wouldn't know."

"How could they not? Rodolph and Emma are in bed and. . . ."

". . . naked, that's true. But it's a pretty innocent word. Quim."

"Would you please stop saying that?"

"Stop saying quim? Okay. But you really can't consider that obscene. Quaint maybe, but not obscene."

"It's an obscenity by any Christian standard."

"Ah, well. By that standard even exact gynecological terminology would probably be obscene. Because sex organs are obscene, right?"

"You're exaggerating, of course. In the appropriate place, there's nothing inappropriate about using the . . . appropriate word."

"Well, how about two lovers in bed naked. What's the appropriate word?"

"These are unmarried people, this is adultery. The entire scene is inappropriate, from a true Christian perspective."

"Well, since I'm a godless humanist. . . ."

"Exactly."

"Please know that I don't consider 'quim'—sorry!—that word— to be obscene. It's meant to be sort of cute, as used between Emma and Rodolph. Love banter, you know. Haven't your boyfriends used stronger language than that?" She shot him an insulted look. "Sorry, again. I mustn't be so presumptuous. But I'm sure you've read worse in any number of books."

"I don't read books like that."

"A major in Comparative Literature, and you don't read books with four-letter words? You must work from a very short list."

"I don't believe good literature needs to be sensational."

With Silverman's help, Gloria had managed to get her stack of books under control. She sat hugging them to her chest. He glanced at the last book as he handed it to her. It was one of the Reverend Lucy's works: *Her Husband's Helpmeet: Inspirational Instructions from Scripture for the Modern Christian Woman.* Another real winner. "I guess that's 'modern' as of 1890," he commented with what he hoped she would recognize as a friendly chuckle. No such luck. Gloria was frowning hard. It was a frown of consternation. With her arms filled with books, she couldn't think of how to keep her skirt down and get back on her feet all at the same time. "I'll hold those for you," Silverman offered. Reluctantly, she handed him the books, then quickly got to her feet.

"Thank you," she said with minimal gratitude as she took the books back.

"Do you live in this building?" Silverman asked.

"Yes," she answered. "On the top floor."

"So you're as snowed in as I am?"

"Yes."

"Damn! Oops. Sorry. I'll wash out my mouth. Anyway, I keep hoping to meet somebody who knows the way out of here."

"There isn't any way out—not until the storm passes."

"Do you have any idea when that will be?"

"By tomorrow, I've heard. Or even later today."

"Thank God. You know, I really do want to get away—though not in this weather. I'd never try crossing the lake in a blizzard, please remember I said that. Even if I had a whole troop of snowmobilers with me, I wouldn't try crossing the lake." He verbally italicized the final sentence.

She was giving him a puzzled look. "Has anybody proposed that? You certainly shouldn't try anything so dangerous."

She was going to need help getting the door open. Silverman put his hand on the knob, then asked, "May I ask about one more thing?"

"Yes?" she answered, twisting her wrist to glance at her watch as if to prepare her getaway.

"There was a student here yesterday named Tilly. She was telling me how much she enjoyed your course on — what was it? Womanly submission?"

"Yes?" Same tone, another glance at the watch.

"I've never heard of that subject. Can you tell me something about it?"

"I don't really have that much time right now."

"It must be such a difficult course to teach these days. Don't you find that women are becoming very unsubmissive?"

"Tilly Schurz told you she liked my class?" she asked, a suspicious squint in her eye.

"Oh, tremendously. She said it was the coolest." He hoped he was putting in a good word for Tilly. Probably not. Gloria looked totally unconvinced.

"I find that hard to believe," she said.

"Well, frankly, I did too. But then, I'm from San Francisco, you know. I haven't met a submissive female in at least twenty years. Even my mother wasn't submissive, for that matter. Of course, she was a schoolteacher. She had a career."

"Submissiveness doesn't rule out an education or a career," Gloria said.

"It doesn't? So submissive wives can still work?"

"Of course."

"So in what sense are they submissive?" He had straddled a chair and was sitting between her and the door. Gloria was doing her best to avoid eye contact.

"The Bible teaches that a woman must put her interests second to her husband's. That doesn't mean she can have no interests."

"But they have to come second."

"Yes. But that's true of any relationship, isn't it? I mean, you have a relationship—so you said in your lecture."

"Yes, I do."

"And has it lasted long?"

"Approaching fifteen years."

That seemed to impress her. She was frowning again, but this time with concentration. "With absolute fidelity?"

Why did she want to know that, he wondered. "Absolute."

"How would you know for certain?"

Silverman tapped his heart. "There are things you know. You'd bet your life on them."

"But can you really be sure?"

Her questions were coming across with sincere curiosity, so he did his best to give non-flippant answers. "Think of it this way. There's heterosexual and there's homosexual. That's a difference.

Then there's monogamous and promiscuous. That's another difference. I happen to know for a fact that these four possibilities don't pair up in any predictable way. Then if you add smart and dumb, careful and careless, or even sadistic and masochistic, look at all the combinations you have to work with. And every person, every couple comes up with a different mix. Me? I'm homosexual, monogamous, smart, careful, and, well, I don't figure at all in the S and M category."

"But isn't there always. . . ." She tossed her hair again as if to get back on track. "Well, in your relationship, don't you put somebody's interests first?"

"Not at all. Marty is an actor. He does his thing. I work at home, I write, I do my thing. We help each other along. It's a household of equals."

"And you never argue?"

"Sure we do. But not about who's dominant and who's submissive. We work things out about fifty-fifty."

"But of course your relationship isn't a Biblically sanctioned one."

"Excuse me."

"All I meant was, it isn't covered by divine law."

There was a quizzical tone in her voice that hinted at an honest desire to understand. And for reasons not all that clear to himself, he wanted her to understand. "I don't know about divine law," he said, "but I do know there's a relationship in the world called friendship, loving friendship. It has nothing to do with raising children or property rights—though there are some activists who'd like to see such friendships become some kind of civil union. In any case, it can be just as binding as marriage. Maybe that's what homosexuality is all about, friendship pushed to the maximum—or at least it can be that. It is with me and Marty. Have you ever wondered if marriage, family, all the extra baggage that comes with those institutions—maybe all of that blocks out another possibility in life? The possibility that two people can simply care for each other passionately."

She seemed troubled by the idea. "But that's something secular people have made up. Husband and wife are bound by God's word."

"And the wife has to be secondary."

"As Eve was to Adam, subordinate but equal."

"One thing I remember about that part of the Bible. Do you know how long those two lived?"

"Adam lived nine hundred and thirty years. It doesn't say how long Eve lived."

"Maybe that's because she was secondary; nobody kept track. But say she lived just about as long. That's a nine-hundred-year relationship. And how much does the Bible tell us about what went on? A few pages. So there must have been a lot that was left out, don't you think? For all we know, they battled every day. And maybe Eve got her way most of the time."

"It doesn't say that," she snapped. He saw she was getting steamed up.

"It doesn't say anything. Maybe that means we're on our own to figure things out."

"It says Eve was created second, that she was made from a part of Adam. Adam was God's first created. And when Eve was left on her own, she disobeyed because she was weak and foolish. Doesn't that clearly show that the woman was meant to submit?"

"Do you like believing that about yourself?"

"It's not a question of what we like."

"I guess you never heard the story of Lilith."

"That's not in scripture. That's made-up apostate deception."

"Have it your way," Silverman said with a resigned sigh. "But if I were a woman, I'd look for another set of rules. Look, Gloria, here you are: bright, educated. The men I've met around this place are brainless farts—excuse the expression. If you were teamed up with some guy like Apfel or Swenson or—God forbid!—Axel Hask, how long could you put up with being submissive? How could you do that to your intelligence and your vitality and everything in you that's young and alive? In the world outside North Fork, these ideas you're carrying around are laughingstock. Do you think anybody wastes time worrying about whether our ancestors had tails? Or if the world was created in six days? You're taking orders from a bunch of stone tablets a million years old. Did you ever read *Pilgrim's Progress*?"

"Yes, I have."

"Remember how the poor Pilgrim walks around the world bent double under a burden of sin? Well, that's you, walking around with a couple tons of superstitious *drek* on your back. '*Drek*,' do you know what that is? In my people's vernacular, that's shit. How can you stand this life you're leading? It's so damn *small!*"

She was blushing again, but not with embarrassment. "I can't listen to this," she blurted out.

"I wish you would, if not for your own sake, then for these kids. What you're doing to Tilly Schurz ought to be classified as child abuse. You're closing down the girl's life."

Her eyes had stopped being sleepy. They were flashing with anger. "How dare you say that! All you people want to do is seduce the innocent and infect them with disease. My father is right. Every one of you should be locked up. Locked up and . . . and. . . ." Too flustered to say more, she pushed past him toward the door. Once again the books began to slip, finally cascading to the floor. This time she let them lie. He let her pass. At the door, she turned, her face afire, "You are the voice of the devil."

As she rushed away, her heel caught on the threshold. She tripped out of the library leaving her left shoe behind like Cinderella fleeing from the ball. Silverman picked it up and went after her. But she was well up the stairs by the time he got into the corridor. He considered using the shoe as an excuse for following her, but dropped that idea when the commons room door opened. It was Mrs. Hask looking out to discover what the rumpus was. She was holding a large steaming bowl of something. She gazed up the stairs at the fleeing Professor Dawes, then back at Silverman. Silverman held up the lost shoe. Heading up the stairs, he dropped the shoe in Mrs. Hask's bowl as he passed. "Professor Dawes," he announced. "She lost her sole."

22

Blood

Silverman returned to his room assuming he would soon forget his conversation with Gloria in the library. Another fruitless confrontation. Another stone wall of prejudice. But an hour later, he found himself going back over the encounter again and again, and each time feeling more depressed than before. At last it came home to him. *Damned if he hadn't been proselytizing.* For what? Not for the gay way, but for life, freedom, joy. Even now, in his thoughts, he was struggling to win her over. But he had failed miserably. If anything, he had confirmed her worst fears and strengthened her most foolish convictions. *Oh, shit*, he thought, *I'm a lousy missionary.* He had pitched his strongest beliefs and left her more certain than ever that he was the devil's spawn.

Why did that make such a difference to him? Perhaps it was merely vanity. He had wanted to score some points against his self-righteous opposition, but he hadn't been persuasive enough, not even with a *Magna cum Laude* graduate. She had read his books, but what she found there was not humanity, not wisdom, not depth of character, just dirty words. Did he have any Xanax left? Nope, all gone. How about Paxil? Yes, three tablets. Well, this was a depression worth one of them.

That together with four or five pages of Bunyan was enough to bring on a heavy snooze. He might have slept until dinner time behind his locked and barred door, but something woke him. Not a noise. Silence. A big hole of silence opened around him. For the first time in four days, the wind wasn't there. Even in his sleep, he had been waiting for that. He noticed the hush as soon as his eyes blinked open: a deafening calm. He rushed to the window and gazed out. There was still a great deal of snow in the air, but it wasn't blowing; it was falling. Falling snow does not a blizzard make. A blizzard is wind that knocks you over. The blizzard wasn't there. The White Giant was moving on.

Lest he be wrong, he decided to check his only connection with the outside world. He flicked on the television and looked for a weather report. The forecasts up through last night had said nothing about the storm lifting. It took twenty minutes for him to hit upon a report. During that time, the wind moaned and groaned a few times, but otherwise stayed quiescent. A cheery blonde weather girl on the television screen was showing maps that placed the blizzard farther east, out over the Great Lakes. The prediction was for continued cold, occasional snow flurries, but diminishing wind and precipitation. "So we may begin to clear the roads—especially that big pile-up on the interstate—and get the planes flying again," said Miss Bright Eyes with a Hollywood-sized grin.

The weather was breaking. In a few days that might mean he could be out of North Fork on his way home. But it meant something even more immediate. He could get out of the school. All he had to do was get to Swenson's place across the lake. One mile, more or less. How long could that take, if the wind stayed calm, even allowing for walking on ice? Even if the snow kept swirling, all he had to do was move along the trees on the near shore until he got within sight of Swenson's house. An hour at the most. He would leave his luggage behind—get that later.

He put on all the clothes he had to provide warmth and slipped down the stairs to the entrance hall. There were several pairs of heavy boots there, but none he could fit into with his own rubbers on. Should he swap footwear? It would take time. Gamble on the rubbers. Even if his feet got wet, he could dry them out when he got to Swenson's place.

He took a breath, opened the door and stepped out into the weather. The chill was startling. It went for him with an edge that sliced through all he was wearing. By the time he made it through the courtyard and down to the lakeside, he couldn't feel his feet in his shoes. He paused on the small slope above the lake, staring into the still swirling snow on all sides. Somewhere farther off than he could see he heard uplifted voices rising and falling on the wind. People frolicking out on the lake. Squinting hard, he could see no farther than where the next several steps might take him. Looking for the opposite shore was pointless. But if he got off in the right direction, wouldn't that be good enough? All he would have to do was keep the trees in sight and move at the same distance from them. If the wind blew from the left, he would bear right. And *vice versa* if it blew from the right.

Inching forward down the sloped shore, he felt the ground beneath his feet become smooth rather than lumpy. Did that mean he was on the lake, standing on ice? He stepped again cautiously and then again, as if he were testing his footing. Hoping to spare his feet from freezing, he lifted each shoe out of the snow and shook it, then thrust it back in, each time feeling around to see if the ice was there and firm. He couldn't have gone more than several yards when the full risk of his situation suddenly took hold. A sharp blast of wind slashed at his back; behind it, another gust came and then another. Was the White Giant doubling back? Now, in the blowing snow, he really had no sense of direction. And the frosted air, already cruel, was honing its blade; it now hurt all the way down to his diaphragm to take a breath. There was no chance he could make it more than a mile across the ice in this cold.

Surrendering, he turned in what he thought was a 180-degree half circle to make his way back. Now he was walking into the wind, his head lowered, leaning hard. Under him, his feet slid and stumbled as he battled for every inch of ground he covered. But after a minute or two of walking, he had still not reached the slope that would take him off the frozen lake. He tried a slightly different direction. As if it might make him more secure, he dropped to his knees and tried to feel all around him. The shore couldn't be more than a few yards one way or the other. He crawled forward against the wind, then slightly to the left, then to the right. No sign of the shoreline. He began to crawl faster in what he was sure was the right direction. Nothing. Well, if he wasn't getting closer to shore, then he must be getting farther away. He turned around and crawled back the way he had come, speeding up as panic rose inside him.

Then, behind him there was a muffled roar. He turned. A form shot past him in the falling snow. A voice, not obviously human, called out, a yowling scream: "Woo-hoo!" Then another figure rocketed by on his other side. Again, the cry went up. "Woo-hoo!" Then he heard a shout floating on the wind. "Did you see that? What the hell was it?" Somebody else was shouting, "Was that a bear? Hey guys, I think there's a bear on the lake!"

The wind fell and for several seconds the snow thinned. He saw forms, helmeted people on vehicles, riding in circles, zig-zagging, bellowing. Six-seven-eight of them riding snowmobiles. He stood up to watch them. They were whizzing back and forth at high speed in a maneuver that seemed to have some meaning. Then he saw one of the machines shoot forward toward a small, still form that lay on the ice, something that looked like a brown sack. The sack moved, grew legs and ran, keeping its belly close to the ice. A dog? Or maybe a fox, judging by the bushy tail. The snowmobile, weaving and swerving, was chasing it. The animal spun round and scurried to escape, but another snowmobile took off after it, turning it back toward where the riders were circling. Now surrounded, the animal cowered, then bolted blindly. One of the riders headed it off, cut sharply and struck it. The fox tumbled and skidded as a whoop of human triumph went up. The dazed beast, now slowed to a crawl, did its best to escape, but had no place to shelter. Another snowmobile bore down on it and sent it skidding across the frozen surface. This time it didn't move but lay inert until one of the riders, taking careful aim at the limp shape, slammed into it. Then another did the same. As the riders sent up a howl, the form burst apart. One piece rolled toward Silverman and landed a few feet to his left. He bent to see what it was. It was the animal's head, definitely a fox. Where the head had struck the snow and bounced there was a smear of blood.

Try as he would, he could make no sense of what he was seeing. Several men on snowmobiles were smashing into the dead body of a fox, rending the corpse to bloody pieces. The madness of what he saw suddenly chilled him more than the cold. He was in the presence of maniacs who were performing some hideous ritual. Not knowing which way to run, he turned from the scene and began sliding and slipping away hoping to escape before the snowmobilers saw him.

Too late. One of the riders came skidding up to him and, mis-judging, nearly swiped him on his left side. Skipping out of the way, Silverman took a hard fall, catching himself at the last moment on one hand and one knee. He felt the concussion in his shoulder, but not in his hand which was now frozen to the point of insensibility. The rider circled sharply and pulled up beside him. "Hey, guy!" he barked from behind the dark visor on his helmet, "You crazy or somethin'? What're you doing out here? Was that you crawlin' back there? Damn! I might have rammed you."

"My hand," Silverman squeaked. "You're on my hand." The rider had pinned him under one of its runners of the snowmobile.

"You hurt?" the rider asked, as he backed away.

Silverman was too numb to know if he hurt. He pulled his hand free and immediately thrust it into his coat. "Which way is the college?" Silverman asked, with barely enough breath to make himself heard. His teeth were chattering so fiercely, he was grow-ing inarticulate. "I'm lost."

Straddling his vehicle, the cyclist walked his snowmobile closer and raised his visor. "I never seen you at the school."

"'Saw' me."

"Huh?"

"You never *saw* me, not 'seen' me. Oh, never mind! I'm freez-ing."

The cyclist peered closer. "Oh, it's you. You're the guy, the lec-turer. From Frisco. What're you walkin' around out here?"

"I thought I could make it across the lake," Silverman answered. He could now see the words that stretched across the rider's chest: *Snow Ghosts, Faith College Snowmobile Squad—State Championship.* "Loyal soldiers of Christ," Mrs. Bloore had called them. Dark, grim, and faceless behind black, opaque visors, the helmeted men who now surrounded him looked for all the world like the Faith College Gestapo.

The rider gave an incredulous sniff. "Cross the lake on foot? In this storm? No way."

"I thought the blizzard was over."

"Maybe, but that don't mean it's springtime. It's fourteen below. Man, you don't have the gear."

"So I see. Will you take me back? I think I'm going to faint." He was trying to huddle deeper into his own midsection, thrusting his frozen fingers into the pockets of his raincoat until the lining ripped. In the background he heard snatches of conversation blowing by on the wind. "It's the fag, that San Francisco guy, what's he up to? Could get us in big trouble." Somebody in the back was wondering if they hadn't found something "better'n the fox."

His desperation rising, Silverman shouted at those nearest, "Get me out of here, you bloody assholes!"

"Hey," answered the nearest angry face, "don't you mouth off about bloody assholes around here. You can take your own bloody asshole back to Fairyville with you. We could just leave you out here, you know." The student turned to call out to the others, "How about it? Should we leave Professor Pansy Ass out here?" A few voices said "damn right, okay."

Silverman, shaking with the cold, struggled to clear his head. *Concentrate!* he ordered himself. *You are in the hands of the enemy. Survive the encounter.* "I'm sorry," Silverman apologized. "I'm freezing. I'm not thinking straight. Please help me."

"Watch your mouth," the student admonished. "We didn't ask you to come here."

"I said I'm sorry. Hasn't anybody got a blanket?" One of the students stepped forward to wrap his parka around Silverman's quivering shoulders. It was a generous gesture, though grudgingly performed. "Thank you, thank you," Silverman muttered, feeling weaker by the moment. Another Snow Ghost brought his bike in close and grudgingly offered Silverman a place to stand on the rear of the sled. There was barely enough room on the sled for Silverman's feet. He wedged his shoes in tightly behind the rider's boots and put his arms around the student's torso. He heard wolf-whistling all around. "Hoo-hoo! Watch out, Anderson! Never let one of them get behind you." Another said, "Hey, Anderson's gettin' off on it. Look at him." Another said, "Anderson, yo, man! You wanna borrow my KY jelly?"

Anderson, the driver, turned around to shout, "Shut up! Just

shut up!" Then, turning to Silverman, he muttered, "Don't try anything, okay? Keep your distance."

Distance? Silverman had no choice but to lean into him as they
drove. As it was, hanging on for dear life, he wondered if he could
keep his footing on the sled. "Please drive slowly," he begged the
student, who gunned his motor and took off at once, a jarring start
that nearly threw Silverman from the snowmobile. Gasping with
panic, he put all his remaining strength into gripping the driver's
jacket and pulling himself in close. The sputtering machine delivered them to the edge of the lake in only a few moments. With a
supporting student on either side and the parka pulled up around
his ears, Silverman let himself be half-marched, half-dragged back
to Gundersen Hall, up the stairs, and into the foyer. He felt like a
fugitive from Devil's Island being returned to his cell.

By the time the Snow Ghosts got him indoors, his lips were
trembling too much to speak. The commotion in the entrance hall
soon brought out everybody left in the building. On the second
floor landing, Silverman could see Mrs. Bloore looking down like a
vulture, her face filled with hatred for all she saw below her.

"For some reason," one of the snowmobilers explained, "he was
trying to cross the lake. We almost ran into him. He could've been
killed."

Professor Jaspers, looking on, fixed Silverman with a stare
colder than the weather outdoors. *Troublemaker*, his eyes said.
When will we be through with you?

The students unwrapped Silverman, peeling the already frosted
parka from him. As they did so, one of them let out a yip as if he
had been bitten. "Blood! He's bleeding! He's bleeding on me!" Sure
enough, there was a streak of fresh blood across the back of the
student's hand. At once all the young men sprang back, so rapidly
that Silverman, at their center, lost his balance and reached out to
support himself on the nearest shoulder. His hand, groping,
brushed the neck and cheek of the person he held. That student
rubbed his hand over his neck and also gave a cry. "Me too. He's
bleeding on me, Godammit. He got blood on me." No sooner had
the profanities burst from him than the panicky student clapped
his hand over his mouth like a naughty child. On the sleeve where

Silverman had grabbed him there was a red smear. The student began to rub at it with his scarf as if a burning coal had landed there.

Silverman, still too cold to speak, looked from the one student to the other, then down at his own body. Yes, there was a gash along the side of his left hand from the fall he had taken on the ice. The hand, until now numb with cold, was just beginning to drip blood in the gathering warmth.

Professor Jaspers, livid with fright, blurted out, "In heaven's name, man, you are bleeding. Look."

From high above, Mrs. Bloore, hearing the announcement, gave a shriek. "Remove him! No blood. No blood."

At his feet, Silverman saw one, two, three drops of blood. His first emotion was a wave of embarrassment, like a high school girl surprised in public by her period. Still dazed and mute, he dropped to his knees and, using the corner of his raincoat, scrubbed at the drops. He succeeded only in smearing the blood. And then more drops fell. He tried to wrap his injured hand in his coat to staunch the flow, but that made it impossible for him to keep his balance. He slipped forward almost hitting the floor with his cheek, caught himself, and looked up. Surrounding him was a ring of students and teachers, their faces rigid with disgust, many on the edge of bolting from the room. Slowly, in what might have been a choreographed movement, they drew away from him, one step, two steps, three steps. He turned in a slow arc to survey the widening circle. Jaspers, Oxenstern, Apfel, Mrs. Hask, all there. And Gloria, she too was looking on, an expression of near nausea on her pretty face. Reflected in their eyes, he had become a monster fallen to Earth from outer space. No, worse than that. He was Satan's secret agent, an object of total human rejection. They loathed him, they feared him. He couldn't help feeling guilty under their stare, but he was also incensed. Above him, he could hear Mrs. Bloore still insisting that he be removed. "No blood," she kept saying. "Clean after him. We will all die."

"Please, I need help," Silverman said quietly. "Help me to my room."

But nobody moved, nobody spoke. The second student to find

himself blood-stained was still standing frozen in terror. Rushing to the head of the crowd, words burst from him. "Nobody's gonna help you, you rotten faggot! I'm gonna die because of you."

"You won't die," Silverman snapped. "Believe me." But of course they wouldn't. Very well, then, he would make it on his own up the stairs. He lurched forward, then stood a moment to regain his composure. When he felt his lips were under control, he turned. "Yes, it's true. I'm a liberal, Jewish faggot. I'm sure other words leap to mind. Queer, perhaps. Or cocksucker. A Jewish cock-sucking liberal. Or maybe you prefer a cock-sucking liberal yid. Take your choice, mix and match. And yes, I am someone who believes there was a Holocaust. And yes, I am someone who believes a woman has a right to abort. And yes, I am someone who believes our ancestors hung from the trees by their tails. And no, I am not someone who believes we need Satan to spread evil across the world; we can handle that very well on our own. But I am also, like it or not, your guest. And as long as I'm around, I expect you to keep your fucking, vicious opinions to yourself, because . . . because. . . ." *Because why? Think, you idiot! Bicoastal intellectuals are supposed to be able to think.* But his mind was spinning away into deep vertigo. At the rock bottom of desperation, he had no choice but to resort to the unscrupulous. "Because *Jesus is watching.*" For the first time in his life he felt like biting his tongue.

But, by God, it worked. With a look of shamed amazement, the raving student backed off as if he had been slapped across the face. Then one by one the crowd around him moved away, a receding wave of scowling human faces.

Turning with whatever composure he could muster, Silverman made it up the stairs with more agility than he expected. And he was lucky; he managed to unlock the door to his room and reach the bed before he fainted.

23
Quarantine

Dead tired and still hurting after several minutes of blackout, Silverman had barely enough energy to wash his wounded hand and wrap it in a face cloth before he collapsed back on the bed. He kicked off his rubbers to discover his shoes, like his coat and pants, soaked through. He rubbed vigorously at his feet but could barely scare up a spark of sensation. Though he felt like a chunk of ice, he was blazing inside with anger. He had let them see him humiliated. That hurt more than his bruised hand.

Furious but helpless, he let himself doze. His futile effort to cross the lake had left him totally depleted. He slept. When he woke, he once again heard the wind hammering at the walls. The White Giant—he had returned. No, it wasn't the wind he heard. There was someone knocking at the door. He rolled off the bed and pulled the door open. There was a man with a tray of food standing in the hall. He was a slight, young man with sharp, intelligent features, but his face wore the same cold, impassive expression that had surrounded Silverman for the past four days. "I'm Dr. Sorensen," he said. "I was sent for."

Silverman admitted him, then sniffed at the air in the corridor. There was a pungent odor: clearly some ambitious cleaning had been done through the building. He returned to the bed, where he now saw several streaks of blood. So did the doctor, who placed the tray on the dresser and came to the bedside. "May I see the wound?" he asked.

"What time is it?" Silverman asked as he held out his hand.

"About seven-thirty," Dr. Sorensen said. "You seem to be bleeding at the knee as well," he observed.

Silverman looked down. His pants were torn at the knee and matted with blood. "I didn't even feel it," he said. He lowered his trousers to discover that the gash along the side of his leg looked worse than the wound on his hand.

The doctor had brought a small bag with him. He opened it and took out bandages. "Is there some hot water in the room?" Silverman gestured to the bath. The doctor went and came back with damp gauze. Ostentatiously pulling on a pair of latex gloves, he started to work at the hand and the knee, cleaning them, then applying an astringent.

"Where did you come from?" Silverman asked.

"I live a few miles from the school. I'm the campus doctor."

"You're from the outside world. Has the storm lifted?"

"Just barely. We had a lull this afternoon. I was delivered by snowmobile. It was hazardous. However, the forecast says we should be out from under by tomorrow."

"Thank God. I've just got to get out of here."

"Don't get your hopes up yet. The tail end of a big blizzard can be treacherous. In any case, everything is in a mess across the entire midwest. We'll be days digging out." As he bandaged, the doctor asked, "Have you been tested for HIV?"

"Yes, I have. I test as part of my yearly physical. Negative, negative, always negative."

"But you are a sexually active homosexual, I understand."

"I'll answer that because I already volunteered the information in a public lecture four days ago. Yes, I am, but as part of a stable, trustworthy relationship of many years. I hope you'll help me set everybody's fears at rest. This place is a hothouse of stereotypes and prejudices. There was a near riot this afternoon."

"A reasonable concern, don't you think?" A note of clinical iciness surfaced in the doctor's voice.

"It wasn't concern," Silverman corrected. "It was panic, all based on stupid bigotry."

Dr. Sorensen finished patching the wounds. "People in your part of the country may be more relaxed about these matters, whether wisely or not. Here, I think the concern is legitimate, independent of any moral judgment."

Silverman felt his temper rising to the boil. *Ugga-bugga*, he said to himself. *I am talking to the witch-doctor of the tribe. He believes in demons.*

"I was asked to evaluate your case," Dr. Sorensen continued. "I'll recommend that you be restricted to this room until you can be taken to the airport. I've already put in a call for an emergency vehicle, but so far with no response. There's still a great deal of confusion in our public services, so we may have a long wait. Mrs. Bloore has even agreed to hire a private medical helicopter, though that seems extreme. In any case, that may be even harder to locate."

"Please don't discourage her. I'd be so grateful."

"We'll see."

The acidic air outside his room stung his eyes. "I gather they're scrubbing the whole place down."

"At my suggestion. A wise precaution."

"I told you there's no need."

"Even so, one can't be too careful. It will, in any case, give the residents some greater sense of security." He rose to leave. "I've brought your dinner. Your meals will continue to be delivered to your room. There are fresh towels and linens just outside the door. Here's a bell. If you need anything, you are to ring the bell at the door. Someone will be on duty to hear you at all hours. No need to leave your room."

"I suppose when I leave, they'll burn the building down." The doctor showed no sign of appreciating his sarcasm. "Before you go, may I ask what you think of the way I'm being treated? I'm curious."

"I happen to be a deacon of the church," Dr. Sorensen said. "I share the same moral viewpoint about homosexuality as our entire congregation, though I try to keep that quite separate from my medical practice. Since you're a stranger in our community, an admitted homosexual, and have open wounds, I think the restrictions that have been imposed on you are prudent. The school has to place the safety of the students foremost. The two students you bled upon will be tested for HIV to set their minds at rest. I see nothing improper in any of this. The college's reputation is apt to suffer a great deal simply because you were brought here at all.

Had we any idea what Dean Swenson was up to, all this would never have happened. Four families have already served notice that they intend to withdraw their students from Faith. I gather you know two of them. Alex Peterson and Jack Shaw. Perhaps you've done some good in alerting us, however unintentionally, to the spiritual danger the two boys are in."

"Is homosexuality totally unknown in North Fork?"

"Of course not. I currently have two homosexual patients. There have been others in the past. We don't, of course, stage parades, but we are acutely aware of the growing prominence of homoeroticism. I can tell you for certain that the practice is not welcome in North Fork."

"Do you believe AIDS is the judgment of God?"

The doctor never batted an eye. "Yes."

"And you can practice medicine, feeling that way?"

"I think it makes me a better doctor. I have no liberal, politically correct reservations about identifying sodomy as an unnatural practice and recommending that it be cured before it costs the patient's life as well as his soul."

"Cured?"

"There are ways."

"Aversion therapy?"

"If applied promptly, it can work wonders. I've seen it do so."

"Is that how you'd handle students who confessed to being homosexual?"

"That would be left up to their parents to decide. But I'd be likely to recommend the treatment—as an act of redeeming love."

"Doctor, things like that are straight out of the Middle Ages."

For the first time, Dr. Sorensen let some emotional heat enter his voice. "Come now, tell the truth. Don't you wish someone at some point in your life had loved you enough to teach you how to restrain yourself before the habit took root?"

"Resist, repent, and restrain. Isn't that the phrase?"

"Yes. And it can be done—maybe even now, Mr. Silverman."

"Thanks. I'll think about it." The doctor packed up and made ready to leave. "That's the trouble with this place, you know," Silverman said.

"What?"

Silverman pointed to the little red pin the doctor wore on his lapel. "JIW. I don't see the difference between Jesus watching and Big Brother watching. It's hard for people to be human with each other when the authorities are watching."

"And by 'being human' you mean what, I wonder. Avoiding shame, I suppose."

"That's actually a good way to put it. I don't think much good comes of shame."

Dr. Sorensen raised a disapproving eyebrow. "We come from very different worlds, don't we?"

He was at the door when Silverman remembered to add, "Please, have them bring in the medical chopper. I'm ready, I'll be happy to go. It's the safest thing to do. God wants it, I'm sure." Sorensen gave him a final chilly glance, but said nothing.

Alone again, Silverman went at once for the phone. The dial tone was there. He at once tapped in a call to Marty. After several rings, a recorded voice came on the line, but it wasn't Marty. It was that woman, that robot woman the phone company hires to sit there and say the same thing over and over. "I'm sorry. Your call cannot be put through at this time. Please hang up and call back later." *Later.* Sure. After the world ends. After you're dead and buried. Silverman had a mental picture of this woman. She was made of see-through acrylic with all her electronic wires and switches showing. More calls. He must make more calls. But to whom? The school must be doing all it could to get him out. Hanna? Why worry her? Swenson, yes. But now he couldn't find Swenson's phone number. The room had become a complete mess, papers and clothing scattered everywhere. Calm down, he told himself. It can't be long now.

And then all by itself, the phone rang. He reached for it so eagerly that he nearly upset it. He didn't recognize the voice at the other end, a female speaking in hushed tones. "Professor Silverman?"

"Yes?"

"This is Tilly. Are you okay?"

"I'm bleeding a little. That's the apocalyptic news of the day in these parts. 'Fag Bleeds! Run for the Hills.' Otherwise, I'm okay, thanks."

"I heard about what happened. It's nauseating. The Snow Ghosts are the worst, real macho pig homophobes. I dated one of them. He started bugging me as soon as I wouldn't, well, I won't tell you what I *wouldn't*. So when I don't put out on demand, this guy warns me, 'If you keep acting like that, guys're gonna think you're a dyke or somethin'.' When I didn't flinch, he started putting two and two together."

"Do good Christian boys at Faith College act like that?"

Tilly blew out a big sarcastic breath. "Oh, please. The things that go on."

"I thought abstinence was the rule around here."

"Only if you define 'abstinence' to include any penetration of any orifice short of impregnating intercourse." There was a pause. "They found out about Alex and Jack. They have them confined to their rooms. Gloria Dawes must have ratted on us soon's she saw us all together in the library. Actually, people had already started talking about the guys."

"So, what are they planning to do with Alex and Jack?"

"Depends on what their parents want. Alex's parents are very strict. They might want him exorcised. For sure they'll both be expelled."

"Expelled? I wouldn't let my heart bleed. That's like being sent home in disgrace from Buchenwald. How about you?"

"They want me too, but I'm hiding."

"Where is there to hide?"

Her voice fell into a whisper. "I have a place. A haunted attic. When the weather clears, I'm out of here."

"Good for you."

"Only I don't know where to go."

"Don't you have some kindly relatives to run to?"

"My whole family is in the church. I think my Aunt Sue in Bemidji would at least try to understand. I used to hide out with her when I was kid—so I wouldn't get strapped. She's sort of dumb; I don't think she ever even heard of lesbianism. But once I let the cat out of the bag ... "

"Tilly, you're not even sure there's a cat *in* the bag."

"Oh, yes I am. I know what goes on in my own head. And I'm

not the least bit ashamed."

Silverman thought it through. "I don't know the law in these parts. If I told you that you could look me up in San Francisco, I might be—technically—contributing to the delinquency of a minor, if you are a minor, or some other offense. So I'm not going to say that, understand? If you thought that's what I said, I wouldn't tell you that you were right or wrong."

"Yeah, I get it. Thanks."

"Good luck."

"You too."

"Oh, hey, do you know Swenson's phone number?"

"Yeah." She passed the number along to him and hung up.

Silverman dialed the number at once. The ringing went on and on. No answer, nobody home, not even an answering machine.

Better give up for the night. After a healthy big swig of Canadian whisky, he settled down to a shallow sleep. And then found that his eyes were open in the dark, his body tensely alert. He was awake. He had heard something. Or rather nothing. The wind was gone; the storm was over. He rushed to the window and stared out. Yes, the world outside was still and clear under a bright full moon. Don't wait, not another minute. Seize the opportunity. Make a dash for the highway or for Swenson's house. Just get out, get out, get out. He went for his clothes, then discovered he had fallen asleep fully dressed. His shoes were on his feet. He threw on his scarf, his raincoat, grabbed up his suitcase, and slipped out of the room.

The building was silent as a grave. He tiptoed down the stairs to the front door, a sense of exhilaration flowing through him. Beside the door, he found coats and hats. He put on something warmer over his raincoat and stepped into the courtyard. Remarkable! It wasn't even that cold. He headed off toward the road that led to the front gate of the college. He was on his way, he was breaking out.

Halfway across the courtyard, he heard a voice, a moaning voice. He stopped and turned. He saw no one. The voice seemed to come from the ground. He looked down. The snow was moving. Somebody had been covered by the snow. He saw a hand emerge and then another. It was a hunched figure clearing away the snow that covered it. A woman. She stood up and turned to look at him. Her face was as cold and bright as ice. It was Miss Henreid, the biology teacher who was buried in the yard. But how did he know that? He had never met Miss Henreid. She was mumbling something. "There is only one way out. Let me show you." She wanted to take his hand. Run! He turned, he stumbled. And then he was awake on the floor of his room. And the wind outside was as fierce as ever.

24

Arm Us, O Lord, Against the Enemy

Quarantine. That meant this room and only this room, with nothing in it but a bum television set, a Bible, and a copy of *Pilgrim's Progress* he had already read twice. The next morning he rang his bell, but not for food. His brain was starving. Two brawny young men responded to his call, neither willing to come within more than three feet of the door. He noticed that they were wearing latex gloves. They looked like members of the Snow Ghosts, lending a distinctly paramilitary aura to his confinement. These were not kindly helpers; they were guards.

"There's a copy of the *Encyclopedia Britannica* in the library downstairs," Silverman said. "Will you please bring me the first five volumes?" They stared at him stupidly. "I need something to read, anything."

"There's a Bible in your room, isn't there?" One of the men said.

"I already know the Bible by heart," Silverman answered. "In Jewish. I need some new material. Please bring the books or I'll begin to bleed profusely from terminal boredom."

An hour later, he had finished an article on Peter Abelard and was just beginning another on the great Tantric philosopher Abhinavagupta, whom he had never heard of. Well, it wasn't the worst way to spend his time. Afghanistan, Africa, and then just as he was starting Agathocles, he heard a quiet shuffle and clatter in the hall. He had reached the dinner hour. Peeking out the door, he discovered his prisoner's tray left on the floor by the good elves. It was the usual meager fare, little more than emergency rations. He made the modest meal last as long as he could, but soon found himself as hungry as before.

He was about to toe on the television when he heard voices somewhere in the building. Many voices, a low rumble. It sounded like a chorus chanting. He put his ear to the door and listened. He could just make out the words "Satan," "evil," "Jesus." It was a sing-song prayer.

He unlocked the door, opened it a crack and looked out. Gundersen Hall was dark. The lights hadn't been turned on. The praying voices welled up from the downstairs lobby. He could see flickering candlelight on all the walls. He slipped out of his room and took a peek over the railing. At that moment, he felt like one of Custer's scouts peering over the rise and seeing a hundred thousand Indians. The lobby below was crowded to capacity with people, many of them still dressed in heavy coats and parkas. All were on their knees, each holding a candle. In front of the kneeling throng stood Oxenstern, wearing a long black robe. The others were repeating after him. Silverman could pick up the words now.

"Lord Jesus, defend us from the adversary. Be our fortress in this hour of peril. Arm us with thy saving grace. Get thee behind me, Satan. Blessed is he who endureth temptation, for when he is tried, he shall receive the crown of life."

Someone in the crowd saw Silverman looking over the banister, and in a moment all eyes were on him. The voices rose. Silverman spotted Reverend Apfel, with Mrs. Bloore beside him, leaning on her walker. The pastor presented a particularly menacing image. The man seemed to be balancing on the edge of religious hysteria. He was rocking to and fro like a huge dark column that might teeter over and collapse at any moment. His hair stuck out from his head as if he had been tearing at it and his eyes were goggling with wild emotion. At the back were all the Snow Ghosts kneeling in a line. And at the end of the line was Axel Hask, his face glowing with fury.

"Arm us, O Lord, against the enemy. Reprove and rebuke for righteousness' sake!"

This is getting way beyond ugga-bugga, Silverman said to himself.

Covered with a cold sweat, he rushed back into his room and locked the door. A lot of good that did. He tried to move the dresser in front of the door, straining his gut in the process. He couldn't budge it. Hastily, he piled whatever he could move against the door. Two chairs, the television set, the five volumes of the *Encyclopedia*. How pathetic. Mrs. Bloore could push her way through a barrier like that. The phone! Did they have 911 in Minnesota? Would it do any good to call for help? He lifted the receiver; there was a dial tone, but when he punched in 911, he got endless ringing. *There should be a 911 to get through to 911*, he thought. After minutes of ringing a stiff, recorded voice said, "We are sorry. All emergency services are now in use in the wake of the storm. Please hang up and call back later." *Sure, if you're still alive.*

The chorused chant was growing louder. Maybe they were coming up the stairs. What was that knocking? It was in another part of the room. He turned to see something moving outside the window opposite him. There was somebody there, on the roof. They were coming for him. Silverman killed the lights, then crept across the room. It was a man at the window; he was wearing a ski mask. Silverman started to bolt toward the door, but realized he had no escape that way. The man at the window had a flashlight; he had pulled up his mask and was holding the light to his face, throwing a ghastly pattern of shadows across his features. It was Swenson.

Silverman threw open the window. From outside, a pair of what looked like tennis rackets came bouncing into the room. They were followed by Swenson, tumbling through the window in a flurry of blown snow. "What the hell is going on?" Silverman cried. "They're doing voodoo rites downstairs." He slammed the window shut against the cold.

Swenson lay on the floor gasping for air. "I tried to get the four-wheel drive over here," he puffed. "Thought I could get you away without anybody knowing. I'm not welcome here. Road's hopeless. Eight-foot drifts. Went over the shoulder. Stuck in a snow bank. Had to make it on foot. The interstate is blocked anyway."

"Well, damn it! You've got to get me out of here. They're getting ready to lynch me."

Swenson sat up and listened. "No, it's just an exorcism. Maybe it's good. It might get it out of their system."

"Oh, really? I'm sure hanging me from the steeple would be even more cathartic. How far away is the van?"

"Four miles maybe. Out at the junction. Lucky I had the snow-shoes. No way to get over those drifts."

"Take me with you back to the van."

"Do you have snowshoes?" Swenson asked, pointing to the pair he had lobbed through the window.

"Of course not. Just get me out!"

"Can't. Not without snowshoes. You could suffocate in drifts like this. I'm sure you're safe here."

"The hell I am. The Snow Goons are down there. So is Adolf Eichmann Hask. All this is doing is working them up. What I ought to do is open a vein and threaten to bleed all over them."

"The forecast says—"

"Fuck the forecast! You go back for the van. Be there when the wind eases off. Soon as you can get moving, come. Tonight."

"I'm so tired. Maybe I can talk to them. Maybe I can calm them."

But as he spoke the words, the chant, which had been keeping to an orderly, prayerful rhythm, began to give way to a new variation. High wailing voices emerged, moans, groans, and eruptions of babbling.

"Oh my," Swenson said. "That's unusual."

"What?"

"Somebody's becoming charismatic. That's not part of a normal exorcism."

"A *normal* exorcism? So exorcism is *normal* and now something *abnormal* is happening? What?"

"I could be wrong, but it sounds like the baptism of the holy spirit. Speaking in tongues. It happens on certain special occasions—Pentecost, most obviously—though the Brethren tend not to encourage it. Some people think of it as a second work of grace. Among the evangelicals, there's a more structured. . . ."

Another unsolicited lecture. Meanwhile, whatever this was, more of it was happening. There were now several voices breaking through the chant, wailing and jabbering. "Cut the theological crap!" Silverman cried. "What exactly is happening?"

"Well, they seem to be getting emotional."

"Oh, really? Well, well, I hadn't noticed. And this means what exactly?"

"It's the Christian form of ecstasy. If they find gratification in the descent of the spirit, they may forget about you."

"What you mean is that they're getting hysterical. They're freaking out. You think that's an improvement?"

"As long as it doesn't go too far."

"And who's going to make sure it doesn't?"

"I definitely think I should talk to them."

"Yes, of course, since you enjoy their full confidence. I'm sure they'd love to hear from you, the man who brought the plague to Minnesota."

"I know these people, Professor Silverman. I know how to appeal to them."

"I hope so, because, man, I feel like the missionary among the cannibals, and the natives are getting damned restless. If you want to volunteer to be the first course, be my guest."

"I'll talk to them." Swenson started unbuttoning his coat. "It's the best way. I could never find my way back to the van anyway." By the time he got his boots and parka off, the noises from below had ceased to sound anything like a chant. There was whooping and screaming. In the midst of the hysteria, Silverman was sure he heard his name.

"Maybe we should just barricade ourselves in here," he suggested.

"Nonsense," Swenson said. "I got you into this, I'll get you out."

"Please don't go," Silverman pleaded. "They might hurt you."

Swenson looked at him with blank-faced innocence. "Professor Silverman, these are my people. I have no reason to be afraid of them." He stepped to the door and slipped into the hall. A moment later, a collective whoop of rage went up. "Judas," voices were shouting. "Apostate," cried others. "In league with the devil," shouted others. Swenson put out his hands calling for silence, then quickly ducked as an object shot by his head. It struck the wall and fell to the floor. A boot. Hardly a promising beginning.

"Come back," Silverman called.

Swenson turned to wave him off. "Please," he said. "Leave this to me."

At a loss, Silverman struggled again to slide the dresser against the door and this time, with the strength of desperation, succeeded.

With his back against the barricade, he closed his eyes and whispered *ugga-bugga, ugga-bugga*. No good. The savages were getting ready to eat the anthropologist. Opening his eyes he saw Swenson's discarded parka and boots. Here was another possibility. Warm clothes. Escape. He moved at once to put on Swenson's gear, all of which seemed several sizes too large for him. What about the snowshoes? He had no idea how to use them; he couldn't imagine getting down from the roof with them on. But if Swenson could find his way to the campus, why couldn't he find his way back to the junction? And then? He had no idea. But from the hall below he was hearing nothing but a rising tide of righteous fury, voices raised in condemnation and sheer hatred. "You brought him here," a great, growling voice was crying—obviously Axel. "You brought the plague." Gambling that Swenson could spread oil on the troubled waters didn't seem smart, not at all. Of course, it was risky, leaving in the dark. He might try waiting a bit longer.

And then, before he registered what he was doing, he was on the roof, scrambling toward a fire escape at the far end of the building. He made his way down, dropping the last several feet into a soft snow bank. He dug his way free and made a quick decision. He would duck into the first building he came upon if it was open and conceal himself for the night. And in the morning? In the morning he would make up a new plan. Now there was quick thinking for you. By the morning, there was at least some chance the mass hysteria at Gundersen Hall would have blown over. Maybe Dr. Sorensen would succeed in bringing in the helicopter, or maybe Swenson could find his way back to the stalled van. In any case, the very fact that he was taking action exhilarated him.

Through the darkness and the falling snow he made out a building and headed for it. He spotted a short flight of stairs leading to a basement door. The door was unlocked. He slipped into a large, warm basement room. At its center was a big roaring furnace; overhead, a maze of pipes and ducts. Down one dimly lit corridor, he found a darkened alcove lined with shelves and cupboards, a storeroom of some kind. He slipped under a work bench and spent several minutes listening. No voices, only the sound of the furnace and of water surging in the pipes. He allowed himself to take a deep breath. At last he felt safe. And having nothing better to do, he soon dozed off.

· · · · ·

He slept, not soundly, but in fits and starts. His cramped position kept waking him up every few hours to listen for pursuers. And he dreamt. He dreamt of Grandpa Zvi. Zeyde had some lesson he wanted desperately to teach him. Silverman could see the old man's mouth laboring away, but he couldn't understand the words. Was he speaking Hebrew? Whatever the language, Silverman knew that the tirade was all about "the Great God One," who, fittingly enough, turned out to be a gigantic number one standing tall as a high-rise building, and as menacing as the towering erection Marty had once imagined his phallocentric psychiatrist to be. Grandpa Zvi implored his erring grandchild to appreciate Big Number One; it was, after all, his heritage. "We, the despised, the persecuted, lowest of the low, *we* invented Big One." Yes, that much got across and stuck in his mind. How it all went together: macho God, macho One, macho power of the upstanding prick. But it wasn't a good dream. Silverman decided he would delete it.

When he saw traces of dirty morning light in the tiny basement windows, he pulled himself out from under the table to discover he was stiff in every joint. His watch said just after seven in the morning.

He found his way back to the door he had used to enter last night and looked out. There was a fine-grained snowfall, dry and crisp, but the wind had hushed. When he opened the door he could tell at once that the weather was turning. The hard chill was gone. Just inside the door he noticed some grounds-keeping tools. He paused to pick out a shovel and a bucket. He might look less conspicuous carrying them. Also, the shovel might double as a weapon.

He had only one thought: to get away. That left him no choice but to try the lake again. This time, with warm clothes and better weather, he could surely make it across. As he moved among the buildings, he became aware of a droning sound overhead above the low clouds. It was a circling aircraft, a helicopter to judge by the staccato chatter of the engine. Had Dr. Sorensen succeeded in summoning a medical chopper? Another good reason to get out on the lake. If the clouds lifted, he could be seen there in the open, away from the trees. He could stand and jump and wave his arms.

The farther he moved from the building where he had spent the night, the more aware he became of a certain brittle tension in the air around him. There was a sense of ambient activity. Now here, now there, he could hear voices, groups of people somewhere out of sight to one side or the other. Though he couldn't pick up words, the hubbub had an urgency to it. He caught sight of a group of heavily muffled figures jogging rapidly across the grounds. Then he heard louder shouts. "We checked the chapel," somebody was saying. "Go back through the main building. Check again." They were searching, no doubt, for him. Another heavy, commanding voice called out, "Round up everyone in the women's dorm. Hold them in the lobby for questioning." Then he picked up the name "Swenson," something about "did you find Swenson?" Everything he heard sounded tense, like people working against time.

He began to scurry, staying close to walls and behind trees as he headed back past the courtyard. Another group of men came rapidly trotting by, all wearing ski masks. He couldn't be sure, but they seemed to be carrying guns, very ominous rat-a-tat-tat guns. More voices, heavy with command and anxiety: "Don't let anybody through at that end." From another direction, he heard approaching vehicles: snowmobiles, a group of them—four, five, six Snow Ghosts shooting across the grounds between the buildings. Voices were shouting, angry tones. "Stop the bikers!" somebody cried. "Swenson, they got Swenson." Silverman began to sweat with anxiety under his heavy, oversized parka. He could feel something ominous building all around him. And overhead, the chopper droned on, growing louder, then more distant, then returning. Helicopters always meant trouble, didn't they? Their chatter was the signature sound of foreboding, like a dark angel hovering in the sky.

But now he could see the lake between the last two buildings on the west side of the school. In another moment, he could make a dash and be on his way. He would also then be visible until he got far enough out to move toward the trees. That was the big risk he was taking, but it was the only way out. *Only way*—he remembered the words. He paused and put down the shovel and bucket as he tried to summon up the nerve he needed for his last dash.

Just as he was edging cautiously away from the last building, the bell in the steeple began ringing, an erratic bong, bong, bonging. Then a voice he had no trouble recognizing boomed across the campus. It was Axel Hask in a towering rage. "Smite them!" he was shouting. *Smite?* Was he really saying *smite?* "Smite them, Lord!" Yes, he was. And then there was a shot, a loud shot. A chorus of alarmed voices went up from every direction. "Shooter on the roof," somebody called out. Other voices urged people to take cover. But not Silverman. If anything could move him out, it was the thought of Axel Hask with a gun. He stepped out, he ran. And then, nearly tumbling down the slope of the shore, he was on the lake, traveling at a surprisingly good clip for an amateur aerobic runner, even though the boots he had borrowed from Swenson were a lot heavier than the jogging shoes he was accustomed to. He knew he couldn't maintain this pace for long, but he was determined to keep going until he just wore out. He was vaguely heading toward a line of trees that jutted out into the lake to his right; he might manage to stay out of sight there. Looking ahead, he could see the far shore. He could see the Swenson house.

A good start, but it didn't last. He heard a voice from the shore behind him, and then another, "There he is, that's him." He turned, running backwards for several paces. People were gathered on the edge of the lake. They were waving and pointing after him. He was sure they were carrying guns. Some were already on the lake. Behind them, he saw four of the Snow Ghosts guiding their vehicles onto the ice and revving up. Two masked figures, out in front of the others, were running toward him full tilt. He could never outdistance them, but damned if he wasn't going to try. He turned and did his best to speed away, but he was already gasping for air. *Faster, faster,* he was shouting to himself inside his head. *Are you watching, Jesus? If you are, call 911!*

"Silverman! Stop!" a voice was shouting. His pursuer was gaining on him rapidly. He was about to try running backwards again, but two snowmobiles rocketed by him to his left, then circled to come back. He bore right, heading for the trees he now knew he couldn't reach. Then, something odd happened. He slipped once, then again, almost taking a spill. His boots were sloshing under him. He was running in water. Looking out over the lake in front of him, he could see a huge half circle of water, a puddle spread over the ice, and he was heading into it. One of the snowmobilers was shouting to him, "Not that way! Stay away from the channel!" He corrected, bearing left to get to dry ice, but before he had changed direction, the surface he was running on became springy. Inside, his stomach spasmed with a sick feeling. Before he could turn back, there was a sharp crackling sound. As if an invisible hand had drawn it on the ice, a straight black line emerged from between his feet and raced on ahead of him. The line grew thicker and split open. He took one more step and found no resistance underfoot. What he felt instead was water sinking away as he leaned his weight into the stride.

And then he was in the water. It was closing over his head, filling his mouth and throat. He was a mediocre swimmer at best; but even an Olympic champion would have had trouble paddling against the weight of the heavy boots he was wearing. The air trapped under his parka served to lift him once to the surface, as if he had bounced in the water. For a moment, his face broke the surface; he thought he saw people standing some paces off gesturing at him. A memory broke through: a voice saying, "Him! The Sodomite, let him drown. Who would care?" Then he sank again, deep enough to feel the lake bottom under his feet. He gave as much of a kick as he could and put everything he had into beating his way back up and at last, just as his breath gave out, he managed to fight his way into the light, but this time his head knocked against an obstacle. He was under the ice sucking for air that wasn't there. At that point, he grew so tired he stopped struggling. Well, you poor *schlimazel*, he said to himself, amazed at his calm, this means you're going to drown. Get ready for it. Are you ready for it? Okay, let's see. Gazing upward at the gray sky as he slipped ever deeper below the ice, he found he had only one thought in mind: Silverman's final words. *Shit! I won't be able to use that first class ticket home.*

Click! went his writer's memory, quickly capturing the moment of truth that was flying by. *But when am I ever going to stick that in a novel?* he wondered.

And when that thought was gone, nothing replaced it.

25

World to Come

"Baby, oh baby, come back to me."

I know that voice, Silverman said to himself inside the dark and muffled chamber of his head. *That's Marty's voice. Dear old Marty! He used to be my friend when I was alive.*

"Baby, please . . . hear me."

Well, actually he was a lot more than a friend. He was my . . . he was my . . . And he began to choke up. *Now that's interesting,* Silverman observed with the objectivity of a practiced novelist as he listened to himself snuffling. *After you die, you still have these feelings. I would have thought. . . .*

"Baby, I'm not gonna make it without you, you hear?"

And he choked up still more. *Oh yes, you will,* Silverman answered silently. *A big, strong guy like you. Still, it's nice of you to say so. I just wish I could see you.*

But of course he understood that was impossible. Where he was, on the far side of the River of Death, even the Light is Darkness. That's how Bunyan described it. And he was certainly right. Silverman couldn't see a thing. Well, that's really for the best, he decided. Because, as he recalled, this was where the Hob-Goblins and the Evil Spirits lurked—just beyond Doubting Castle, not far from the Plain of Ease. He would just as soon not have to deal with any Hob-Goblins. Remarkable how vividly the geography of the book was coming back to him. There was a place called Bye Path Meadow somewhere over there. But you weren't supposed to stray that way. You had to stick to the straight and narrow. Dark as it was, he decided it wouldn't be so bad as long as he could at least take Marty's voice with him. Come to think of it, now that he was in Bunyanland, he needed a good name for Marty. Great-heart, perhaps. Or how about Delectable Friend? He liked that. And what was Delectable Friend saying now?

"I'm praying all the prayers I got left for you, baby. I'm telling my mother's own God to hear me. Give me a sign."

But Silverman was becoming preoccupied with other things. He was trying to remember the way that led to the World to Come. He didn't want to make a wrong turn. How did it go? First, there's the Gate of Pearls and Precious Stones. Head for that. Then there's the Valley of the Shadow. That's where you remove your Mortal Garments. Or maybe he had done that already. He couldn't remember. He searched around for sensation. Legs, arms, shoulders—no, he wasn't feeling anything. Probably he was a pure spook ready to enter the Celestial City.

"Are you hearing me, Danny? Are you hearing me, baby?"

Hold on! That didn't make any sense. The Celestial City was for Christians. No Jews or queers allowed. In fact, the Celestial City wasn't even for all Christians. Only the right kind, though he had no idea how they sorted that out. Take the Evangelical Brethren back there in North Fork. Probably nobody who was "in Christ" was going to share Heaven with anybody who was "of Christ" or "by Christ" or "for Christ." If there was one thing he had learned, it was that those prepositions made all the difference. Prepositionism, that's what Christians believed in. Most likely the Celestial City was divided into exclusive neighborhoods, one for every church, and all of them pretending they were the only ones in town. Fat chance they were going to let any humanistic homosexual Jews through the gate. Hell—that's where a queer's quest winds up. Hell—by way of the Road of Carnal Policy. Wasn't that right, Professor Oxenstern? Well, Silverman didn't care. He was sick of hanging out with Christians. Who wanted to live in their Celestial City anyway? There probably wasn't a decent bookstore or restaurant in the whole place. And he was sure they liked it that way. In his mind now he was seeing a swirling form: two carousals going around in opposite directions. On one he saw all the people he had met at Faith College, and on the other he saw Bunyan's cast of characters. They were traveling past each other at break-neck speed, so fast it made him dizzy. But what an intriguing idea. Imagine having two overlapping stories, one told forwards, chapters one, two, three, the other told backwards, chapters thirty, twenty-nine, twenty-eight. He must work that out. And find a good agent. Were there agents in Hell, he wondered. Of course there were. Where else would they be?

"I'm sticking by you, baby," he heard Marty's voice saying. "I'm gonna be right here. Just gimme a whisper, gimme a twitch."

Sorry, old pal. Can't give a twitch without some Mortal Garments. You know, fingers, toes, eyelids. Well, Silverman decided, he didn't mind going to Hell, not really, not as long as Marty showed up there sooner or later. And the rest of the gang from the Annex. With that, the tears began. But then he thought: *Queer's Quest. You know, that's not a bad title. A sort of upside down, inside out riff on Bunyan.* Not bad. Jaspers would be Intolerant, and Reverend Apfel would be Giant Slay-Good, and Mrs. Bloore would be Madam Rancor. Wait a minute. He had to get this down.

"Has anybody got a pen?" Silverman said out loud, though not very clearly. Actually, the words came out sounding more like *haw-wah-bah-bahdy-ga-ga-pm-pm-pm.* "I want to make some notes," he added. *I-wah-wah-takka-s-s-nuts.*

Silence on all sides. And then a gasp. His hand, reaching out for the pen, was suddenly locked in the grip of another, holding him fast, trembling. "Baby, baby, baby," Marty's voice was saying from someplace close overhead. Something like a veil was being drawn away, a bandage that stuck for a moment at his temples and then came loose. The World to Come was flooded with light. If this was Hell, it looked remarkably hygienic.

• • • • •

Left to his own battered powers of recollection, Silverman would never have known how his sojourn in North Fork ended. His last vivid memory was that of being pursued by a lynch mob out to slay him for the greater glory of God. Not until Marty told him did he know that, besides the Snow Ghost snowmobile squad, his pursuers on the lake included several state and local law enforcement officers who got to him in time to pluck him off the bottom of Beaver Lake and blow the breath of life down his throat.

But where had all these people come from in the nick of time?

"We'll get to that," Marty promised. "First, let's take some time here to count our blessings. We saved your life, baby."

True enough, and Silverman did want to appreciate that rather significant fact. And yet, whatever the truth of the matter, he would never forget what it felt like to be running for his life. Because that was the conviction that drove him into the blizzard. That was the snapshot his literary memory would always hold, a blind and raging terror that allied him to hounded thousands, to every fugitive and refugee that ever fled from certain death. If he stood back and thought about it honestly, that lent a remarkable logic to his adventures in North Fork, a sort of existential arc that curved from ignorance to experience. He had gotten into trouble at Faith College trying to win a modicum of sympathy for Aunt Naomi from a scorning audience. Nobody in that audience could have guessed how painfully presumptuous he felt associating himself with his aunt's suffering, which was no part of his pampered life. And yet, before his sojourn ended, he had learned what it was like to flee from a persecuting pack. What else in all the world could make him flesh of her flesh?

So this clean, well-lighted place he was in wasn't the World to Come. It was the intensive care unit at Minneapolis Metropolitan Hospital. And this wasn't eternity, but the ongoing saga of Daniel Silverman seventy-three hours and thirty-seven minutes since he had been pulled from the River of Death. "And thirty-two hours and fifteen minutes since you stopped being blue," Marty added, squinting at the clock on the wall.

By now the room was filled with people in white. Nurses who were drilling needles into his veins, doctors who were shining lights into his eyes, listening to his chest, pinching him here and there. "Feel that? Feel that?" the doctors kept asking. And sometimes he felt it and sometimes he didn't, especially from the waist down. When the doctors were finished, an intern stepped forward with a little paper cup. "This will help you get some rest," she said as she offered to finger a couple of pills into his mouth.

"Resht?" Silverman said, his tongue still not quite trimming the rough edges off the words. "Why I need resht? I been in coma for sevy-sixy hoursh."

One of the doctors looked up to enforce the order, but Silverman turned his head away looking for Marty. He spotted him lingering at the door. "Him! Marty! Tell me. I wan-to know," he pleaded.

"Okay," the doctor said with a resigned smile. He beckoned to Marty. "But make it quick."

Marty stepped to the bedside and looked down at Silverman. But he wasn't alone. There was somebody with him, a tall, thin, neatly bearded man with glasses and a balding head.

"Honey," Marty said, "this is Jerry. Remember Jerry?"

"Jerry Simon," the thin man said. "Hi. We met on the phone, remember?"

"Most of what you want to know," Marty said, "Jerry can tell you better than me. I just got here seven hours . . ."—again he checked the clock on the wall—"and forty-five minutes ago. First plane to land in the snowbound hell of Minneapolis in four days."

"Jerry," Silverman said, his voice throbbing as he gazed into Jerry Simon's face. His eyes flooded with tears as if we were greeting a long-lost brother. Why all this emotion? He was feeling too woozy to work it out. He simply knew he loved this man whose voice had once been like a life-preserver for him. But what was good old Jerry Simon doing here?

Jerry bent to say what he had to say close to Silverman's ear. "When I lost you on the phone that first day, I felt really worried. Because the way you described your situation, I felt certain you were in big trouble. I mean coming out in front of a red-neck crowd like that. That wasn't smart. Anyway, I did my best to get through to Marty; there was just no way. So I started in on law enforcement. But as long as all I had to go on was some story about you being an unhappy visiting lecturer, they didn't have any time for me, not in the middle of a roaring blizzard, for God's sake. Of course I didn't dare say anything about you being, you know." His voice dropped to a whisper. "Gay-bashing isn't too high on the middle-American list of legal priorities. So really, I didn't know what to do. But then I got through to Marty. That was Thursday evening."

"And what I told him," Marty said, "was to stop farting around and think up something super-911-urgent. Myself, I was convinced you were already crucified."

"So Marty and I, we pulled out all the stops and made up this story about me getting a call from a family in North Fork that was being held prisoner at Faith College by religious terrorists. 'It's got something to do with abortion rights.' That's what I told the highway patrol. Also the local TV news. I said there were little kids involved and that one of them had already been killed. You know, it's really a lot of fun, making up things like that. And, believe me, I put all I've got into it. Even so, I don't think they would have done much if the weather hadn't lifted by the next morning."

"And guess what," Marty added. 'You know how they got there so fast? They got a chopper patrol. Swooped right in that next morning, soon's they got a clearing."

"Of course they didn't find any prisoners," Jerry continued, "which truly pissed them off. But they got there just as you took off across the lake with the whole school after you. Now that looked serious. And then, luckily, you fell through the ice."

"Luck-ly?" Silverman asked more with his eyes than his croaking voice.

"Well, after the story I told them, I'd be up shit creek for sure if they didn't find something more or less murderous going on when they got there. I guess they figured you were one of the prisoners making a run for it. The reports say somebody started shooting and screaming about smiting the Anti-Christ. And then some of the students began trying to keep the cops from searching the campus. Oh, there was a big ruckus. The cops arrested a whole bunch of people, couple professors, and the lady who runs the school. They've been on the news telling everybody that their campus was invaded by the forces of the Zionist, Sodomite conspiracy or some such."

Silverman, tickled pink, wanted to burst out laughing, but it hurt too much. "Who s-s-ssaved? . . ."

"Who saved you?" Jerry said. "Well, we're not too clear about that just yet. It was one of the cops pulled you out. They say he had to dive a couple times to find you, but I haven't heard any names. All we know for sure is that you got air-lifted out of there *pronto*. Even so, you were more dead than alive when I got here."

Silverman, medicated to the eyeballs and at the limit of his stamina, had been sliding in and out of consciousness through most of Jerry's story. Besides there was something else weighing heavily on his mind, something he wanted to jot down. Where was his pen? He groped around the bed. No pen. "Pweass cany huva p-pin?" he muttered, but nobody understood. Well, he would just have to do his best to remember the words through the night.

And so, Goodhearted Queer woke from his fearful dream. . . .

Yes, that might work, if he could get the tone exactly right, neither quaint nor satirical, but a sort of respectful pastiche, something like what Joyce had done with *The Odyssey*. Well, not that ambitious—he had never actually read the whole of *Ulysses* himself (who ever had?) but something along those lines. Or maybe more like those Jewish folk tales that Isaac Singer managed to salvage so entertainingly.

And so, Goodhearted Queer woke from his fearful dream to see the face of his dear Delectable Friend hovering over him. This must be an hallucination, said Queer to himself, for had he not passed over the River of Death? But before he could doubt his salvation one moment longer, lips whose loving warmth was certainly no illusion were pressed against his own. Thus he learned, like so many pilgrims before him, that there was a way to Heaven even from the gates of Hell.

His eyes flickered open to see Marty, leaning over him. Who needed an airplane? Who needed California? Even in the intensive care unit of a Minneapolis hospital, he was at home. Backing off to the door of Silverman's room, Jerry Simon found himself standing along side the ICU nurse who was waiting to bed her patient down for the night. As she watched Marty plant a long, achingly sweet kiss on Silverman's lips, her brow furrowed more with confusion than disapproval. She turned to give Jerry a quizzical look.

"It's okay," Jerry explained with a wink. "They're from San Francisco."

26

"Brilliant—*The New York Times*"

Silverman tacked the review to the wall above his desk. Some day he would frame this long, skinny piece of paper. But for now, he was content simply to sit gazing at it like a man who had come over a sand dune and discovered an oasis after forty days in the desert. Ah, the excellent *New York Times*. Where in all the world was there a publication of such good taste and sound judgment? More than a newspaper, it was a cultural beacon summoning its readers to ever higher intellectual standards. Especially so its unsurpassed *Book Review*. Here, let us read this exemplary piece of criticism again.

> Daniel Silverman has made his career as a literary hitch-hiker. Freud, Flaubert, Hugo, Melville, and Zola are among those who have given him a lift along the way. His forte is to insinuate his way into somebody else's book by artfully reconfiguring the tale from a contrasting perspective, a marginally innovative technique that runs the risk of losing its edge after the second chapter. It is a device that served him well enough in his early works, especially his highly-regarded first novel, *Analyzing Anna*, written from the viewpoint of Anna O., the famous hysteric who served as Freud's first case history. *I, Emma*, his retelling of *Madame Bovary* from the heroine's vantage point, was similarly well-executed, though with rather too much sentimentality where one expected wit.
>
> Subsequent efforts to recycle the classics began to

read like a parody of the author's intention. *Deep Eye* (*Moby Dick* retold from the whale's viewpoint) or *Parliament of Monsters* (*The Hunchback of Notre Dame* presented through the all-seeing eye of a gargoyle atop Notre Dame) teeter on the edge of the ludicrous. Of all the vehicles on which Mr. Silverman might have chosen to thumb a ride, none might seem less promising than *Pilgrim's Progress*. But in *Queer's Quest*, he has achieved what few authors would have dared, a deliciously mordant pastiche that updates the old Puritan classic into a timely plea for tolerance, compassion, and *joie de vivre*.

As self-appointed booster for the pleasures of Vanity Fair, Mr. Silverman ingeniously turns the tables on the Moral Majoritarians as he enters an appeal for sinners of every stripe. Those who believe the allegory has become a cultural relic have a delightful surprise in store for them. Mr. Silverman may have single-handedly revitalized the genre. Never less than richly layered and at times brilliant, *Queer's Quest* is apt to stand as a landmark of humanistic Judaism as well as. . . .

And there Silverman stopped reading. Like most novelists, he read until he found the selling quote, then quit while he was ahead. "Brilliant—*The New York Times*" would do. It would do very nicely. Who was this perceptive critic who seemed to have read all his books? Natalie Kleindienst, Assistant Professor of American Lit. at Brandeis, author of *Saul Bellow and the Burden of Jewish Humanism*. A junior academic who could cite you as further support for her graduate dissertation. The ideal reviewer.

Silverman's reluctant visit to the bottom of Beaver Lake had cost him the top joint of his left little toe; it had laid him up for six months of physical therapy. But if the reading public was still gullible enough to believe every book on the stands somehow managed to be at the top of *The New York Times* list, in return for his pains Daniel Silverman once again had a shot at becoming a number one bestseller. And he was right. Two Sundays later, *Queer's Quest* was number seven on the list, there to stay for another four weeks. It didn't rise to six; nor did it gradually subside to eight, nine, ten. Like an obedient quantum particle, it simply assumed its allotted position in the literary universe and then vanished. But a month on the list was good enough to draw calls from agents—including Tommy Sutton, whose message was left unanswered—and to pin down a decent paperback deal.

When Silverman and Marty got home from Minneapolis, they had found their answering machine clogged with messages, more than it could handle. Four of them were from Alex, Jack, and Tilly anxious to send their best wishes. Each call ended with the hope that someday they would meet again, but since they left no number, Silverman had to wait for them to call back. When they didn't, he assumed he had seen the last of them. The only call that came through from Minnesota was from Jerry Simon, who had been left with a standing invitation to come visiting. Jerry showed up a few months later, spent a week prowling the Castro as the West Coast Emissary of Brother Jerome (the Church of the New Testicle believed in the priesthood of all believers) and decided to relocate. In the wake of Silverman's departure, the cops and the phone company back home had been giving him too much trouble. His report about the religious terrorists was looking more and more exaggerated all the time. One of his superiors had been muttering about "malicious mischief." "Time to move on," Jerry decided. "I'm really sick and tired of freezing my buns in the great American heartland."

"You know," Marty commented to Silverman one morning, "you may have gone to North Fork intending to get in and get out fast, but that little junket of yours may have changed more lives than you'll ever know."

"Like for example?"

"Well, Jerry, for example."

"Come on. Jerry was on the edge and ready to jump."

"Yeah, but somebody had to give him a little push, didn't they? You got responsibilities, man. Responsibilities."

Silverman was sure that Marty was exaggerating until one day—it was about a week after *Queer's Quest* made *The New York*

Times list—three more refugees showed up at the front door: two males and one female. The males were Alex and Jack. They came properly costumed for their new life: tight tee-shirts and tighter jeans, buzz-cut hair and neat goatees, a pair of golden earrings shared between them. They had clearly mastered the stereotype, but (Silverman wondered from the moment he saw them) could they outgrow it?

As for the female who was with them, Silverman might have guessed it would be Tilly, but it wasn't.

Before he could yip with surprise, the guys were all over him with love and kisses. He was so flabbergasted, he collapsed into the nearest chair. "Marty!" he called. "Look who's here!"

Silverman didn't have to ask; their story came spilling out. After Silverman was sent home, the boys had bolted Faith College before the campus sex patrol could get its hands on them. Jack's family, knowing when it was licked, agreed to accept his sexuality, though not without sincere anguish. Alex's parents, on the other hand, were stolidly unforgiving. They threatened to send him back to Faith for psychological reconstruction. He threatened them in return: he would run off to live with Jack. And that's how things finally worked out. The boys took off for two months of traveling, mainly camping out for the summer. Finally, Alex's family relented and took him back, but with strict rules of conduct while he stayed under their roof. In their respective, still God-fearing homes, Alex and Jack managed to put up with a half year of strained relations while they pursued something like a higher education at a nearby community college. But as soon as they spotted a review for *Queer's Quest*, they were off and running—straight to Silverman. They brought some money from home, but not enough to rent better than a Tenderloin hotel. What choice did Silverman have but to let the boys use the back room of the apartment until they worked up some traction? Meanwhile, it was more fun than Silverman could have imagined treating them to a Cook's tour of the city. They came, they saw, they were conquered by everything they wanted to find in Shangri-la by the Bay. In spite of himself, Silverman got a rise out of sharing their naïveté and bright expectations.

Not so Marty. Marty was worried from day one. "Danny," he

confessed after the boys had been with them for only a week, "in case you're wondering: I'm putting a lock on the bathroom door. This morning Jack walked in on me in the shower, not really by accident. And once he was in, his environmental consciousness made him ask if maybe we should share the water. Fair warning, that boy is a chaser. If he keeps hitting on me like that, locks and chains won't make any difference. The temptation is gonna be overwhelming."

Silverman tried to laugh off his concern. "Resist, repent, and restrain, brother," he advised. But he realized Marty had a point. Four guys in close quarters with one bathroom. But he needn't have worried. Maybe out of respect for Silverman, Jack was soon looking for greener pastures. Before another week was up, he was out of the house and Alex was suffering through his first busted love affair. Silverman and Marty offered all the worldly-wise consolation they had on hand, but time and Prozac proved more effective. Anyway, Alex was a lot easier to have around the house; so Marty agreed to rent him a room until he found better. From time to time, Silverman came across Jack, who quickly became a star of the local gay scene—or rather a shooting star. Discoveries like Jack turn up regularly in the Castro, three or four a year, actors or athletes usually. They sweep through the community making their round of the clubs and burn out fast. Not many survive the acclaim. Staying safe under that kind of pressure isn't easy.

Alex and Jack had arrived on Silverman's doorstep with a female, one of the last people Silverman expected to see again in his life. It was Syl, who had also uprooted herself. Baby Jessica was with her, now old enough to toddle. Though Syl was as smiley-faced as ever, her story was a sad one. It had to do with Swenson.

The last Silverman had seen of Swenson was the night he tumbled out of the blizzard and into the Founder's Suite at the college. He had gone to reason with the headhunters. Silverman had always been curious to know how that confrontation had gone, but Swenson never wrote to tell him. That was left to Syl.

"I guess facing the whole school that night was too much for him. A lot of the teachers were people he had known since childhood. The only way he could think of asking their forgiveness was to break down and tell the truth. So he came out, right there in front of them. And once the words were spoken, he melted with guilt. By the time they were finished working on him, he was so thoroughly mortified that he agreed to undergo the whole works: shaming, exorcism, aversion therapy. It was just so cruel. I mean they made him confess all the things we did, as well as what we didn't do. Sleeping with a Sodomite. I felt embarrassed for my whole life.

"They—Professor Jaspers and Oxenstern and the rest—probably thought they were going to send Richard back to me all bright and shiny new, a real man at last. Well, it didn't work like that. I can't say Richard and I had ever been on the warmest terms, but I really liked the person he was, sex or no sex. He was sincere about opening up the church. That gave him a goal in life we could both share. Now that he was straightened, he wasn't the man I knew. He became prissy and narrow-minded. Goofiest thing was: there wasn't any more sex going on between us than before. Less, in fact. Instead, we spent whole nights praying. And then he started in on wifely submissiveness.

"Alex and Jack and Tilly were the only people I could talk to. I must have cried an ocean of tears on their shoulders. Finally, when the boys said they were leaving, I asked them please to let me come along. I don't know what I'm going to do with myself, I really don't. My whole family has ostracized me. I can't go back."

She looked at Silverman with a sad-faced smile that made him love her all the more.

Silverman and Marty found her a place to stay with Sally Weeks, but when it came to thinking beyond that, they drew blanks. Syl had never been to college; she had no career in sight. Her future looked pretty problematical. Silverman would have been willing to go broke helping her out, but that wasn't what she wanted. She wanted a life of her own, a chance to be her own woman. And then, one afternoon, the problem solved itself. Sally came knocking at the door carrying a big covered bowl in her hands. "I am about to announce a miracle, gentlemen," she declared, with mock fanfare. She uncovered the bowl and spilled a few dozen chocolate-chip cookies on a plate. "Take. Eat," she commanded. They took, they ate. And the sensory memory flowed back into Silverman's metabolism. The best cookies in the universe. Marty, savoring one and then another and another, sat stunned. "Well, if I was ever going to eat saturated fats again, I'm glad it was saturated fat at its finest."

Sally asked: "Is there any reason why Maurice's Finest Madeleines can't distribute Minnesota Syl's Finest Chocolate Chippers? Unless, of course, Maurice is afraid of the competition."

Maurice wasn't. He knew a good thing when he saw it—or tasted it. Nor was he afraid to add Minnesota Syl's Finest Biscuits and Muffins to his line of merchandise—with home-brewed sarsaparilla yet to come. "Syl," Marty admitted freely, "you are a down-home gold mine." Within a year, the team of Marty and Syl, with more orders on their collective hands than they could fill, decided to move out of their cramped kitchen quarters and rent a fully equipped bakery with staff. Marty could sometimes be heard complaining that he was spending more time with shortening than with Shakespeare, but nobody thought he really cared.

Silverman had invested a good deal of time feeling guilty about the way he abandoned Swenson on that final, hair-raising night. Now that Swenson had been "turned," as they put it in spy novels, he was more angry than ashamed. He regarded Swenson as a defeat for the cause. One more reconstructed gay chalked up to the opposition. He could see Professor Jaspers offering prayers of thanksgiving for scoring a win over the Sodomites. Ah, but that loss was soon to be balanced out, thanks to Tilly Schurz.

After Jack and Alex and Syl left North Fork, they lost track of Tilly. They had called to say good-bye. "I'll meet you in San Francisco," she announced. But months later she still hadn't shown up. Phone calls to her home produced nothing but angry threats from her parents, who claimed to have no idea where their reprobate daughter was. "Something's gone wrong," Alex concluded. "If we don't hear from her in another few weeks, I'm going to go back and start looking."

But he didn't have to. Tilly found her way to the underground railway. And she came with a friend. The day Silverman answered the door he had no trouble recognizing Tilly. But who was this with her? He had to X-ray his way through lipstick, eyeliner, and blusher to find his way to Gloria Dawes. There she stood in Silverman's living room, the woman he had last seen glaring at him as he did his best to wipe his own blood off the floor of Gunderson Hall. Dressed to the nines, high-heeled, short-skirted, and stunningly coifed, Gloria was exactly what Bunyan had in mind when he thought up Madame Wanton the Temptress. All very overdone, of course: the heels too high, the skirt too short, the make-up too garish. But Silverman could understand. Gloria had climbed the wall, tasted the forbidden fruit, and decided to let herself gorge. For, yes, she and Tilly were an item.

"At the university, I had heard gays tell their stories," Gloria explained over dinner that evening. "I was fascinated, but I wouldn't let myself believe them. I could never accept that anybody could have been born that way. I certainly couldn't imagine I was hiding feelings like that myself. True, I wasn't dating. In fact, I was getting so stand-offish, guys started calling me the Snow Queen. But I told myself that was because I was protecting my virginity, waiting for the right Christian mate to come along. And if the right man never seemed to come along, well, that was because I had very high standards. If I did sometimes have shameful dreams about other women, that was temptation. All the more reason to get off that secular campus and take refuge in the bosom of my family where Satan could do me no harm.

"Then, on that night when we decided to exorcise you, things got too weird. There were people babbling in tongues all around me. And what I heard them saying made my blood curdle. I heard one of the Snow Ghosts say they should drag you across the lake and drown you. They were convinced you were a homo-terrorist who was putting HIV in the water and poisoning our food. You'd ceased to be a human being in their eyes. You were nothing but a walking virus.

"The day after you were gone, they started in on Richard. And we all had to participate, the entire faculty. It was the most sickening thing I've ever experienced. But it backfired in my case. Richard started confessing his homoeroticism, and as I listened, I recognized it all—the dreams, the fantasies, the sex films and magazines he wanted to look at. It was the story of my secret life told from a male viewpoint. That's when the light broke through. I couldn't bring myself to heap shame on Richard, even if he was asking for it. I was out of there the next day. I didn't even leave a note. I was running with no destination. I took a bus to Minneapolis, checked into a hotel and started trying to connect with Tilly. I felt so ashamed of what I had done to her. I was the one who snitched on Alex and Jack and her. I said I saw all of you exchanging secrets in the library, and that I knew you were all Sodomites. I was pretty sure of that about Tilly already. I mean, I could recognize it; she was *me*. I was hounding her because I wanted to confirm my own fears. I never expected her to forgive me."

Tilly filled in the rest. "*Forgive you*? My God, I had a crush on you that was driving me up the total wall. I don't know if it was ESP or pheromones, but somehow I knew that the one woman on campus who was persecuting me the most was the most like me. I was having the wildest fantasies about you, at the same time I was cursing you to high heaven. Well, when Gloria finally found out where I was—with my Aunt Sue in Bemidji—and phoned to ask if we could meet, it was like a dream come true. I got off the phone trembling. Part of it was just the excitement, the two of us on the run. But there was more, like some secret language we'd been speaking since we first met. When we got together at this little coffee shop in her hotel, we never said a word. She just took my hand and burst into tears. We never even ordered coffee. We went straight to her room."

"You know," Gloria said, "I can't remember talking at all. What was the first thing we said?"

Tilly remembered. "About four hours later, I said, 'I didn't bring a toothbrush.'" And they both broke out laughing.

Silverman was curious to know how Gloria's father took the news of her transformation. "Well, after he picked himself up off the floor, his first concern was to keep this strictly within the family. He was willing to pay to do that, so—I feel really ashamed to say this—I held him up to a pretty stiff ransom. He agreed to bankroll my graduate work and the rest of Tilly's higher education, provided we stayed well out of sight for the next few years. As to where we might go, well, that was the subject of considerable negotiation.

I'm sure he would have liked us to leave for Tierra del Fuego, but we couldn't find a decent graduate program there. He actually did suggest Perth. We finally compromised on the University of Hawaii, where I'll be using my mother's maiden name—a small, temporary cover-up. I'm sure I could make Dad's political future pretty rocky if I advertised the fact that Senator Jake Dawes was footing the bill for his daughter's gay marriage. Somebody in the media is going to find that out eventually, but that's his problem. If he suffers any damage, that's the price you pay for being a high-profile moral authority."

Silverman hears regularly from Gloria and Tilly since they set up housekeeping in Hawaii. Tilly currently thinks she wants to become a photographer, her third career choice to date. Gloria has a clearer target in her sights. She intends to become a psychotherapist whose special frame of reference will be normal lesbianism.

· · · · ·

One evening at about the time *Queer's Quest* was approaching its final revision, Silverman came upon a book in an upstairs alcove of the Midnight Bookshop, a favorite neighborhood haunt. The price—forty-five cents—suggested the volume must have been collecting dust there for years. It was titled *Highlights from the Talmud: Five Thousand Years of Jewish Wit and Wisdom*." There was no date, but the book, foxed and yellowing, was certainly more than fifty years old. The publisher was Kaddush Press of Brooklyn, surely no longer in existence. At once Silverman was reminded of Grandpa Zvi's vain attempt to make a good Jew of him one Hebrew letter at a time. He had used the Talmud to play their alphabet game. Silverman never got beyond the letter *teth*, but here was his chance to learn something about the book his grandfather loved so dearly—and at a reasonable price. He bought the book, and then let it sit beside his bed for several weeks before he gave it any attention. Then, one night, as he flipped through its brittle pages, he came upon this story.

In the time of the prophet Ezra, after the children

of Israel had returned from their cruel captivity in Babylon, the elders decided to rebuild the temple. And when the temple was ready for dedication, they vowed to drive away the Evil Impulse once and for all so that all the Lord's people might live without temptation. No sooner had all the wisest and holiest men in Israel gathered for the ceremony that would place the Lord's commandments beyond violation, than a great bestial form rose in a cloud of smoke and sulphur through the floor of the temple. No one present could fail to recognize that Evil itself in all its hideousness stood before the assembled congregation. In the battle that ensued, it was by no means certain that the elders and the priests would prevail; but at last the Evil Impulse began to weaken and it became possible to confine the dread being in a vast metal vessel that had been prepared for its everlasting imprisonment. In this way Evil was removed from the world and great was the celebration that followed.

But when the congregation emerged into the world on the first day after the final triumph over Evil, they noticed at once that the leaves and fruit had disappeared from the trees and that the song birds had ceased singing. And later, in the spring of the year, they were horrified to see that the crops did not grow and the flowers did not blossom. The kine and the oxen, the lamb and the chicken failed to procreate, and so too in their own homes, men and women found one another so unpleasing that the marriage bed grew cold, and in that year not a single child was begotten.

"We have done a great wrong," the high priest at last proclaimed. "Quickly, let us free the Evil Impulse from its confinement." And so they did with all possible haste. At once the monster fled into the nearest woods, snarling and blaspheming. At that very moment, the birds woke and sang, the trees put out their leaves, the crops stood high in the fields, and men and women felt love blossom between them.

And the high priest rose and spoke. "And so we have learned the teaching of the prophet Isaiah: 'I am Yahweh unrivaled. Apart from me, all is nothing. I form the light and create the dark. I make peace and create evil. I the Lord do all these things.'"

Silverman wondered if Grandpa Zvi had ever given much thought to Isaiah's teaching. Certainly the intolerant saints of North Fork never had. For that matter, how many people could grasp the meaning of a God who encompasses the whole show? Here was Silverman with his eyes on North Fork, seeing evil, evil, evil. And back in North Fork Mrs. Bloore and the whole evangelical gang had their eyes on San Francisco, seeing evil, evil, evil. But what if God is all the eyes looking in all the directions? And wherever He looks, He sees a piece of Himself acting out. Wouldn't that amount to saying that Vanity Fair is the mind of God?

There was probably some subtle theological formulation for all that—but right here and now, it was Silverman's idea. No, he had no idea how it would account for Axel Hask or Adolf Hitler, but then he wasn't a theologian—thank God!

The Author

Theodore Roszak is Professor of History at California State University, Hayward. He holds a B.A. degree from the University of California at Los Angeles, and a Ph.D. in History from Princeton University. He has taught at Stanford University, the University of British Columbia, San Francisco State University, and Schumacher College in the U.K.

His books include *Longevity Revolution: As Boomers Become Elders*, a comprehensive study of the cultural and political implications of our society's lengthening life expectancy, and the widely acclaimed *The Making of a Counter Culture*, a much discussed, best selling interpretation of the turbulent sixties, now available in a new edition from the University of California Press. He has also written *The Voice of the Earth* (Touchstone Books), *The Cult of Information*, (University of California Press) a study of the use and abuse of computers in all walks of life, and *The Gendered Atom: Reflections on the Sexual Psychology of Science*, a study of gender-bias in the theory and practice of science, with a preface by Jane Goodall. His books *The Voice of the Earth* and *Ecopsychology: Healing the Mind, Restoring the Earth* are the founding texts of the ecopsychology movement. With his wife Betty, he is co-editor of the anthology *Masculine/Feminine: Essays on Sexual Mythology and the Liberation of Women*.

His fiction includes *Flicker*, (Simon and Schuster and Bantam Books) and the award-winning *The Memoirs of Elizabeth Frankenstein*, (Random House and Bantam Books), both of which are under option for major feature films. Theordore Roszak has been a Guggenheim Fellow and was twice nominated for The National Book Award. He makes his home in Berkeley, California.

About the Type

This book was typeset in Caslon, originally released by William Caslon in 1722. Because of their incredible practicality, his designs met with instant success. Caslon's types became popular throughout Europe and the American colonies; printer Benjamin Franklin used hardly any other typeface. The first printings of the American Declaration of Independence and the Constitution were set in Caslon.

Book interior design and typesetting by JTC Imagineering.